BEYOND
THE CODE

KELSEY RAE BARTHEL

Published by Inkshares, Inc., San Francisco, California
www.inkshares.com

Edited and by Carlisa Cramer and Chersti Nieveen
www.writertherapy.com

Cover design by CoverKitchen | Interior design by Kevin G. Summers

ISBN: 9781947848092
e-ISBN: 9781947848108
LCCN: 2017956963

First edition

Printed in the United States of America

To Carol, my warm and supportive mother. I wish you could've been here to hold this book in your hands.

PROLOGUE

SOMEONE ONCE TOLD me that the true enemy of truth is time. And after what I've seen, I'm inclined to agree with him.

Time is the unstoppable force that will eventually overrun the great civilizations of man. Time can take a proud history of an entire people and turn it to nothing more than fanciful legends. Mere stories that are far from the mind's ability to believe. Or it will leave the truth to be forgotten entirely. Some try to fight against this enemy by recording their history in books or recalling the grand tales of their heroes, but their efforts always fall to time's relentless march. Those in the present are at the mercy of those who tell the tale.

No concrete evidence exists on the origins of our Knighthood or the Order of which we were bound to. We only have the stories we were told by the ones we shouldn't have trusted.

It is said that long ago, before the world's borders were drawn and cities were built to reach the sky, people with extraordinary abilities roamed the land, searching for purpose and belonging. Those gifted individuals could call lightning from the sky, move mountains with a thought, and even heal the sick or wounded with a touch. Despite their almost godlike powers, their hearts and minds were still very much human. Thus, they had the potential for great good or profound evil. Some would journey the lands, bringing miracles to those in need while others would use their powers for their own selfish gain.

Despite the varying intentions of these gifted people, tales of the immense power they could wield spread far and wide. Kingdoms waged horrible wars to try and gain that power for glory and conquest. This deep impact to the lands and its people followed the gifted ones wherever they laid their feet. They became the harbingers of misfortune by mere birthright.

With their very existence poisoned by fear and their people scattered to the winds, the gifted ones needed something to bring them together and keep them safe. Their hopes and prayers were answered when a brave warrior appeared with powers that rivaled every one of the gifted. He traveled the world and gathered the gifted ones under his leadership, providing safety for the tormented and order for the ones driven wild by their greed. He gave them all the purpose and belonging they always knew they needed, and for that, the gifted ones made him their king.

For the good of his people and the mundane world, the king decided to hide them away from the rest of the people in the land. With the help of some trusted and influential lords and ladies, the king was able to cover the existence of the gifted ones in a shroud of secrecy. Over time, the knowledge of the gifted ones fell into obscurity and, eventually, became nothing but an unbelievable legend.

But the king was too wise to know they couldn't completely cut themselves off from humanity forever. To help build a bridge between the gifted ones and the mundane humans, the king pledged some of the strongest of his people to the lords and ladies who helped hide them from the world. They served these people from the shadows as their Knights under the strict laws laid down by their king. This structure became the unquestionable Order all the gifted ones followed.

This Code is something I can never forget. As a Knight, these rules are engraved into our minds. This is a necessity, for the consequences of breaking the Code are severe, and all Knights are fearful of the punishment.

The first law of the Code forbids the Masters from knowing the true names of their Knights, who must live two separate lives that can never touch to protect their families from the enemies of their Master.

All Knights and Masters of the Order must engage each other with the utmost respect and honor. Petty acts of dishonor and treachery would cause a rift between the members and could fracture the stability of the Order.

The word of the king would supersede any Master's orders. A knight's pledge to a Master is only at the king's sufferance. The king is the Knights' ruler, and his word is law.

Above all else, the veil of secrecy between the Order and the mundane world must never be broken. Any member of the Order, be it Knight or Master, that breaks this law was considered an enemy of our people and was punished as such.

Loyalty, honor, and secrecy. Those were the three pillars of the Code that kept our people safe. Upon his passing, the king entrusted a collective of three of his trusted advisors to safeguard the Order and enforce the laws of the Code. They became the ones who guided the powerful and were known as the Hand Council.

The Order the king created kept the peace throughout generation after generation of Knights and Masters until the present day. We foolishly thought that peace would last forever. But reality is often far from the dream and nothing lasts forever.

CHAPTER 1

THE SILVER LIGHT of the full moon bathed the capital city of Lorne with its glow. At this late hour, all was silent from the commercial warehouses to the massive corporate towers. Not a whisper to disturb the darkness. Everyone had long since retired to their homes to rest.

The sound of colliding metal echoed in the darkness, cutting through the silent night like a sharp knife. Again and again, the repeated clash of steel sang with a steady rhythm from a vein of back alleys that ran behind a strip of trendy stores.

A tall woman appeared from an alleyway, and the warm glow of the streetlights stretched her shadow across the concrete road. Her long raven-black hair flowed gracefully down the center of her back from a high ponytail. Her narrow, pale jade eyes showed the keen focus of a trained warrior. Her formfitting black clothes concealed her ivory skin from sight, camouflaging her in the darkness. They were tailor-made for stealth and flexibility. She held a masterly crafted curved blade with practiced ease, and the folded steel glinted beautifully in the moonlight. A pistol with the word "falcon" etched onto the barrel sat nestled in the holster strapped to her left leg.

She jumped against one wall and propelled herself up toward the opposite, and ricocheted between the narrow walls of the alley with the strength and agility unseen in a normal human. With a final leap, she landed on the rooftop in a readied battle stance. She stood still as a statue, her body prepared, and her eyes scanned the smooth concrete slab of the roof. She searched the stillness for signs of her opponent's approach.

Her attention was instantly caught by the whisper of muffled footsteps. The female warrior took a slight step to avoid her opponent's blade as it plummeted down toward her back. She twirled in place, and the weapon and her arm moved as one to strike her attacker in a wide arc. The silver buckles on his black jacket gleamed in the moonlight as he arched backward, and her razor-sharp blade cut clean through a stray lock of his long golden hair. He snapped upright like a spring and swiped her sword away to clear his short retreat, his intense blue eyes still tracking her moves. The lock of hair floated smoothly to the ground, its color shimmered with its golden hue and turned to jet-black. The attacker gathered himself into a proud stance.

The woman sprung forward, her sword dead set on her enemy. He stepped back and deflected her steel with a flick of his blade. The woman recovered in a heartbeat and unleashed a flurry of swift attacks. The swords' clash rippled through the still night air. Their battle flowed from strike to block like an elaborate dance, every movement connected to the next in a show of each warrior's skill.

Her opponent raised his sword high and forced it down on her. The woman threw herself backward, narrowly avoiding the hefty sword, and landed flat on her back with a rough thud. He seized the opportunity of her vulnerability and struck down at his fallen enemy. The woman rolled across the coarse concrete as the sword dug into the floor beside her. Tossing her legs up, she bounded into a backward somersault and landed in a low battle stance.

He thrust his blade down at the woman as if he were trying to skewer a small animal. She swiftly scurried across the pavement like a spider, his strikes flaring sparks from the stone roof. Her luck ran out as she felt the edge of the rooftop at her heel. She cursed under her breath at her misfortune.

"Caught ya," the man proclaimed confidently as he swiped his large blade down at the woman. She leaped to her feet and braced her sword to receive her opponent's blade as it barrelled down on her. She met his smug satisfaction with stern defiance to mask her weakness. The superior strength of his athletic build with the addition of gravity gave her attacker a clear advantage. He pushed his sword down, trying to force her arms to buckle under the pressure. The woman's teeth gritted and her knuckles whitened as she held him at bay, but she was painfully aware she couldn't keep up this struggle. She could feel the strength in her arms wavering and her knees starting to wobble. He was fighting smart and playing to his strengths. His seemingly frantic strikes had been meant to lead her to a corner. She would have been more in a mood to commend him for his tactic if it hadn't worked so well. She had to find a way to turn the tables.

With a quick little motion, she tilted her blade downward and redirected the momentum of her opponent sending him into a stagger. The steel of his weapon screeched viciously as it slid down the length of her sword. She spun like a top, sweeping his legs out from under him with a smooth motion. He fell flat on his back, the surprise hitting harder than the roof. She leaped to her feet and thrust her blade down at her fallen enemy. Her sword skipped off the roof as the male fighter rolled away to safety.

As a show of respect, she held her advance as he scrambled to his feet, keeping her keen jade eyes on him. She charged him with an intense ferocity. He recoiled as the woman's blade whistled just inches from his chest, and he sprung back to counter. With only a few efficient movements the female sidestepped and drove her blade down on his, pinning it to the ground. The man heaved up against her sword in a show of strength the woman strained to match, her arms burned with fatigue. With a heavy grunt she pushed him back and landed a solid kick to his exposed chest. He staggered backward, breathing heavily as he struggled to recover. He settled, catching his breath, and formed a defensive stance.

The warriors were wrapped in a focused standoff. Their eyes fixated on each other, studying the slightest movement, keeping their swords readied. The moonlight illuminated the intricate carvings on each fighter's weapon. The pattern of swirls etched on the woman's sword ran along the blade like rising streams of smoke. The man's steel was decorated with symbols from a foreign and ancient culture.

Suddenly a wide grin crept over the woman's lips and evolved into a soft chuckle, her stance remaining steady. "I have to commend you on your cleverness, Claymore. Luring me into a corner like that."

Claymore returned her grin with a toothy smile, his body still ready for battle. "That advantage did not last long, unfortunately. You turned the tide swiftly. I knew you would. The stories about you speak well of your prowess, Luna."

Luna's wide grin turned into a sweet, but forcefully innocent smile. "I wasn't aware my abilities had earned such a reputation. I'm flattered. You're not so bad yourself, Claymore."

He let out a soft chuckle. "Coming from you, that is a real compliment."

Luna's sweet smile then shifted back into a stern, focused stare. "You are a formidable opponent, and this fight has been enjoyable but only one of us can come out victorious. We must hurry; daylight will come soon."

Claymore nodded. "You're absolutely right." His expression changed to a hardened gaze. "Let's stop playing around and get this over with."

Without another word, they charged each other, leaving fear and hesitation behind. His blade whistled like a bird of prey, cutting through the air at Luna's midsection. Predicting his attack, Luna leaped over the sword and planted her boot into Claymore's face. She pushed off and twisted into an acrobatic flip, landing gracefully on her feet as he tumbled to the ground.

He jumped to his feet, staggering to recapture his stance. The struggle didn't go unseen by his opponent. Luna could see his labored breathing and shaking arm behind the armor of his warrior's will.

Claymore charged forward, belting out an intense battle cry, and struck out at Luna with wild abandon. He heightened his strength and aggression, thinking Luna may lose her footing. He was playing a dangerous game of chicken, hoping she would budge before she realized his weakening state.

However, the sudden show of unhinged ferocity was nothing more than a thin layer of deception to Luna's sharp observation. Luna kept calm like still water in deep contrast to her opponent. She could read his dulling attacks like a street sign. She knew victory would come with endurance.

Claymore swung his blade for Luna's head. Luna arched her body into a backward crab, the blade passing just inches over her. She sprung her legs up and cartwheeled back, landing a firm kick to Claymore's jaw. He stumbled back as Luna landed gracefully on her feet and rushed for him, unleashing a series of short swings. The sound of clashing steel echoed through the night as Claymore struggled to block Luna's assault.

Luna focused her attack on the hole in Claymore's defense created by weakening arms wielding a large weapon. The blow fell true as her cold steel bit into the flesh of his arm. He stepped backward, retreating to a safe distance.

Keeping his eyes targeted on his opponent, he freed one hand to examine his arm. A sharp sting shot through his arm as his fingers touched the gash. His eyes quickly darted back and forth from Luna to his fingers painted scarlet with his blood. Luckily, the blood was light and the cut not too deep . . . this time. She could see the hint of panic in his eyes as he scanned the battlefield. He was taking an assessment of his options, searching for openings and weaknesses, but Luna gave him nothing. She was in ideal form and kept her expression calm as a spring breeze. His eyes were then drawn to the pistol holstered to her leg; she hadn't touched it the entire battle. It was only a backup; she always concentrated her strategy around her sword. Claymore retreated, leaping to the rooftop of the neighboring building.

Luna sighed and shot Claymore an irritated frown. "Are you going to continue this rooftop chase until dawn, or are you going to try and defeat me?"

"In due time, but first, could you answer a question for me? Why do you use a sword?" Claymore asked. "We live in an age of modern conveniences. We have cars, vast cities, computers, and weapons that make duals like this a breeze. You don't use your weapon to augment your powers, or I would have seen it by now. So why do you use a sword as your main weapon?"

Luna eyes shifted to her sword as she contemplated the inquiry. "Tradition. My grandfather taught my father to fight with a sword, and he taught me. To my family, it is the ultimate show of skill and strength. But it's not that reason alone. When you're in close combat with a sword, you get a sense of your enemy that more convenient weaponry can't give you. To me, duels are about bettering myself and giving my opponent the respect of an honest test of skill. It's not simply about winning."

Claymore nodded. "I can relate to your morality. In a perfect world, all warriors would share your view. But this is far from a perfect world, and I have an entirely different reason for using a sword."

He raised his left hand and placed the palm on the flat of his blade. Suddenly, his sharp blue eyes morphed into brilliant silver, as if they were filled with molten metal. A grayish glow emanated from his hand and transferred into his sword.

His blade began to move and come alive. Twisting and extending longer and longer, rising into the air like a steel snake. Luna immediately recognized the danger and sprinted for Claymore to close the distance between them. A feat of that caliber required concentration. She had to pull the battle back to close combat; he wouldn't be able to keep focus while fending her off.

Claymore's blade struck down at Luna, forcing her backward and halting her advance. She deflected the attack with a swift swipe of her sword, but it just recoiled back into the air. The steel snake swayed with a smooth flow, patiently waiting for her next move. It was as if Claymore could see through the senses of his creation.

Luna cursed under her breath. Claymore wasn't going to let her anywhere near him. She stared at the sword trying to work out a plan. She could fight Claymore's creation, but that would get her nowhere—she couldn't wound a sword. Claymore was weakening; maybe if she waited him out he would falter and lose control of his ability. The more she rolled the plan around in her thoughts, the more she didn't like it; it ran on too many maybes.

The blade shot out at Luna with the speed of a bullet. She gasped in surprise and jumped out of its path as it sped past her. She recovered and sprung into a low defensive stance. *The second strike was faster then the first. He's gaining more control over the metal the longer he works with it. This is bad. If he keeps this speed and control, I won't have a chance to get within striking distance. Unfortunately, closing the distance is out of the question. But maybe . . .* Her mind shifted to her gun. That would certainly break his concentration, but under the circumstances, she couldn't guarantee a clean shot. She could miss or even kill him. *No. Claymore is just a Knight doing his duty for his Master. There has to be a better way.*

The blade turned midair to double back and strike again. Luna sidestepped and swiped at the blade, knocking it off its path. It recoiled up above her and began to rain down rapid attacks, like a cobra hunting a swift mouse.

The steel construct shot like a bullet on a deadly trajectory for Luna. With an instinctive gesture, she blocked the weapon with hers, struggling to push it away, but her strength was quickly faltering. Sparks flared and faded in the night as the weapons clashed. A faint groan of pain escaped her lips as the metal beast's sharpened edge bit into her upper arm. Blood trickled slowly down her skin as she continued to push against the metal snake.

"You think this makes us even, Claymore?" She spat between clenched teeth as she rolled onto her back and used her sword to fling Claymore's weapon away from her. The steel snake clanged on the rock then slithered back to its readied form as Luna rolled gracefully to her feet.

The sword lunged for her chest too quickly to block. She threw herself backward, falling hard on the solid concrete. A pained wheeze escaped her as she struggled to catch her breath. Luna forced her body into mobility in time to see the blade careening down toward her. She rolled across the rough pavement, narrowly avoiding the weapon as it bit deeply into the roof. Much like a trapped animal, the steel snake twisted and struggled to free itself from the concrete's grip.

Luna had to act at that very second or else she would lose her chance at victory. She had only one opportunity to end this fight without unnecessary bloodshed. She reached out her hand and laid her palm on the flat of the blade. "Now it's time for you to see my ability, Claymore," she whispered as her eyes flared into a radiant azure blue dancing with sparks of electricity around her irises. A surge of lightning formed from her hand and on to Claymore's steel snake, traveling rapidly to its wielder.

Claymore screamed as the electrical charge burned into his hand, forcing him to drop his weapon. The blade withdrew, and the menacing steel snake morphed back into a long sword embedded in the roof. Claymore fell to his knees, clutching his charred hand as the silver in his eyes morphed back to a sharp blue.

Claymore froze at the cold touch of steel lightly pressed against his neck. He slowly turned his gaze behind him to see Luna at his back, his sword in her hand. Her expression was as stern as the steel she wielded. His heart leaped into beats of panic. The woman with whom he had fought furiously now held his very life at the tip of her sword.

"Concede, Knight," she said coldly. "Concede defeat."

Claymore closed his eyes and hung his head low. There was nothing he could do. She was right; this battle was over. The shame he felt in his heart was as painful as the burns on his hand. "Luna, I admit my defeat. You have won this duel tonight."

Luna withdrew her sword and sheathed it before offering a friendly hand to aid Claymore to his feet and handing him back his sword. Luna's pleasant smile was unwavering as Claymore took his sword in hand. The tension and high emotions of the battle had disappeared like the moon fading to the dawn. They faced each other now as equal Knights, no longer opponents.

"Now I believe you owe me something as per the conditions of victory," Luna said, her tone all business.

Claymore nodded his head solemnly. "Of course." He sheathed his long sword while keeping his burnt hand close to his body and then pulled out a small data drive from his jacket pocket. He tossed the device to Luna with a casual flick, and she snatched it from the air. Luna gave the data drive a critical gaze as she examined it. "Satisfied?" he asked.

Luna's eyes turned back to meet Claymore's gaze. "You would stake your honor on the authenticity of this data?"

Claymore humbly bowed his head to Luna. "It's exactly the same data our Masters confirmed earlier. You have my word. We both fought a close duel, and I have lost. This was a fair wager between our Masters, and it would disgrace me to disrespect that. The device contains the information and evidence we have gathered on our common enemy and their wrongdoings, exactly as was discussed."

The smile disappeared from Luna's face, and her eyes filled with sympathy. "My apologies, Claymore. My intent was not to call into question your honor, but to cover my bases. We are playing a dangerous game, and one can't be too careful."

"It's of no consequence," he said, waving away the apology with a careless gesture. "I understand your suspicions, but I assure you they are unfounded. My honor is a treasure that I hope to keep with me until my dying day."

The smile returned to Luna's lips. "You are an admirable man, Claymore. Not many put value into treasures they cannot see or touch, but I believe them to be the most precious of them all." Luna's gaze met Claymore's steely blue eyes, and her train of thought suddenly halted. She could've sworn she saw something hiding behind his friendly face. She saw guilt in his eyes, and she didn't know why. She brushed the uneasy feeling from her mind, reasoning that the guilt was most likely due to his loss.

She shook her head. "It's a pity our Masters couldn't work together in this matter. I feel the likes of our common enemy can't be taken down by one knight alone." She then looked at the data drive she had won. "But with this, my Master and I may have a chance." She placed the device in her pocket and gave Claymore a courteous bow. "Goodbye, Claymore," she said, bidding him farewell before she vanished into the night.

As she leaped away from rooftop to rooftop, she tried to shake the odd feeling of dread that was weighing heavily on her mind. She'd hoped that there wasn't more behind the shame she saw in Claymore's eyes.

CHAPTER 2

LATER THAT NIGHT across the vast City of Lorne, a young man remained awake in spite of the city's slumber. He sat on an ornately carved, high-back chair with his fingers tapping a relentless beat. He ran his fingers through his golden curls and rubbed his eyes to stave off the weariness of the sleepless night. His piercing blue eyes stared deep into the crackling flame nestled in a large stone fireplace. The white shirt and black trousers he wore were ragged and untidy. The need for rest beckoned to him like a siren's call, but he could not answer, not while Luna was still out there.

He could feel the heat from the smoldering fire brush against his skin as his eyes watched the light play with the shadows of the elegant willow leaves carved into the mantel. The warm glow of the burning embers lit the large room showing the tall cherrywood shelves that lined the walls. Each shelf was full of old books and beautiful trinkets, a collection that fostered much pride in its collector. To the back of the library were two adjacent staircases that led to a second level of bookcases that parted for a large doorway leading to the rest of the house. The beam of moonlight through the glass balcony doors added a white contrast to the orange glow of the fire.

The young man retreated from the fireplace to the balcony. He threw open the doors and took in a deep breath as he felt the brisk night breeze against his face. His gaze drawn to the starry sky, he hoped that the sparkling spectacle would distract him from the anxiety weighing heavily on his mind. The helpless feeling of being able to do nothing but wait for her return, he hated that more than anything. As a Master that was all he could do; he could never fight with her no matter how strong he was. The battle of Knights was a clash between beings that were more than human. It was no place for a normal man. This was a fact in his mind, but not his heart.

He stared at the ring on his hand with a deep sense of longing. It was a simple band of silver decorated by black-and-white pictures of each phase of the moon. He spun the ring around his finger as he looked back to the night sky.

Suddenly, the ring began to shimmer with a familiar silver light. His eyes lit up, and his lips curled into a happy but wry smile. "Decided to take your time, Luna? I was starting to worry," he welcomed.

Luna stepped out from the shadows of the second level and greeted Cole with a smile and a respectful nod. "Forgive me, Master."

He turned back to his Knight, a charming smile painted his expression. "Luna, we've known each other for a long time. It's silly to continue this Master-Servant business. Call me by my name," he reasoned.

"If that is what my Master wishes," Luna said as she descended the staircase with a graceful step and bowed to her Master. "Cole."

Cole smiled. "Thank you, Luna. Did the duel end in our favor?"

Luna reached into her pocket and pulled out the small data drive, her prize from the hard-fought duel, and handed it to

Cole. "This has the information Morgan Clouse and Claymore promised. Now we have the evidence linking Damon Lexus to the murder of the Lou Tian family and their Knight. This will bring us much closer to stopping this insanity."

Cole examined the device momentarily before his eyes turned back to Luna, charming and wanting at the same time. "That's good news. You have been a great ally to me, and I am grateful."

Luna kept her gaze to the floor to avoid Cole's intense stare. "I was merely fulfilling your will to the best of my abilities. That is my duty as your Knight," Luna asserted.

Cole placed his gentle hands on Luna's shoulders. Her stern demeanor softened as she looked up at Cole's pleasant smile. Her cheeks flushed when her eyes met his. "You have never been just a weapon to me." His hands began to travel down her arms. "I mean it when I say you are my best ally. Together we can do anything."

"Cole," she whispered, but her voice cut off and her arm gave a sharp jerk. Cole removed his hands and saw the crimson blood smeared over his fingers.

Cole carefully moved aside the fabric of Luna's sleeve and examined the bloody gash on her arm. His face hardened with worry. "You're hurt," he fretted.

Luna glanced at the wound with indifferent eyes, as if she had forgotten about it. "It's nothing, a mere flesh wound. I am fortunate it is only that," she assured Cole, but her words failed to erase the anxiety in his eyes. "You shouldn't fret over me. I am a Knight. We are at home in battle and wounds like this are a regular occurrence. I will take care of it at my first opportunity," she promised.

"Wait here for a moment. I'll be right back," Cole instructed before venturing out into the house and retrieving a well-stocked first-aid kit.

"What are you doing?" Luna asked.

Cole opened the case and sorted through the contents to find the supplies he needed for dressing a wound. "I may not be able to do much but I am capable of dressing a cut. It should hold up until you can get it properly looked after." Cole led Luna to take a seat on a plush sofa. "Could you take off your jacket, please?" he asked.

"Cole, I'm fine. You don't need to do this," Luna protested, moving to step away from the seat.

Cole grasped her hand before she could go far. Luna turned sharply to Cole to pull her hand back but froze in place when she saw the look of helplessness and frustration behind his eyes. "Please, let me do . . . something for you," he pleaded.

Luna found she was unable to stand against his request and accepted his aid with a soft smile. She took her seat once more and removed her jacket, revealing the gash on her arm surrounded by dried blood. Devoting his attention to the task at hand, Cole carefully cleaned the wound and began to dress it in starch white bandages with the little skill he had.

"I hope you didn't beat down Morgan's Knight too badly. He may be uncooperative now, but maybe this defeat will bring him to his senses on the issue at hand. He would be a good ally, wouldn't you agree?" Cole asked, turning the atmosphere between them back to business.

"Indeed, Claymore gave a good fight. He has an interesting ability that he has perfected. He and I would make a formidable duo."

"I'm glad you think that way. Sooner or later, Morgan will realize that he cannot fight this war alone. You'll see," Cole preached confidently and finished wrapping the bandage around her arm. "How's that?" Luna didn't answer. Her eyes grew distant and Cole could see the worry behind them. "Luna?"

Luna's expression hardened. "Later may be too late."

Cole had known Luna long enough to see through her outward stoicism to the base of her thoughts. He saw the worry behind her stern eyes and knew she was planning for the worst. Cole slipped his gentle hand in hers and locked eyes with his Knight, shattering her proper demeanor.

"Don't be like that, Luna. Things are working out for us, at least for now. Try and enjoy it. And don't worry. If Morgan doesn't see reason, others will. Damon Lexus is using her resources to integrate other Knights into her command and killing whoever resists." Cole's calm demeanor tensed as the anger inside radiated from him. "We can't allow her to continue what she's doing, nor should anyone else. The path she is treading puts everyone, Master and Knight alike, in danger." Cole bit back his frustration and regained his composure, forming his kind smile once again.

His words failed to produce the desired effect. Luna looked back at him with a sweet smile, but he knew her calm assuredness was only skin-deep. She would never let him see a more vulnerable side of her. She always felt she needed to be the pillar of strength. She worried that Cole might lose faith in her even though he'd had made it clear that would be impossible. He only wished he knew whether her forced mask of strength was because of a stubborn sense of duty or a lack of trust.

"You have no need to worry, Master. I will not fail you, no matter what." Luna pulled her hand back and built up a wall of formality with a slight bow.

Cole nodded. "Of course."

"Cole, I've been meaning to talk to you about this woman you've been seeing," Luna said to change the subject.

Cole raised an eyebrow, confused by Luna's choice in topic. "You mean Aurora? What about her?" His stare of bafflement suddenly switched to a sly grin. "Is it that you object to me seeing her? You're not jealous, are you?"

Luna crossed her arms and let out an irritated sigh. "Of course not; quit being childish. I need to know what you've told her about us."

Cole's grin turned all the more mischievous, and he stepped closer to Luna. "What about us?"

Luna's face hardened at Cole's off-collar behavior. "About the Knights and the war we are in."

Cole turned away from Luna, avoiding eye contact and sauntered slowly to the fireplace. He didn't want to face Luna with the answers she asked for. He felt her eyes fixed on him unwavering in her demands. "Yes, I've told her about you, the order of Knight's, the war, everything," he confessed, bracing for Luna's judgment of his actions.

"You told her everything? Why? Are you in love with this woman?" Luna inquired.

"It's not what you think, Luna. I didn't tell her the truth because I was feeling guilty for lying to her. I told her about the war because she is from a very powerful family. The Fallons are one of the most influential people in the country, and Aurora is the daughter of the head of the family. I knew she had feelings for me, so I had to act. Now she is more than willing to aid us in our struggle," Cole explained.

Luna shot him a sharp scowl, radiating her disapproval. "So you intend to use her, is that it?" she snapped.

Cole flinched in surprise at Luna's harsh words and darted to her side to attempt to explain. "Luna, don't think harshly of this action. This is an uphill battle no matter which way we look at it; you know that more than anyone. We need all the help we can get, and Aurora has a lot at her disposal that we can use."

Cole could see Luna harden to his charms. "Do you love her?"

Cole gawked at Luna, utterly baffled by her behavior. Luna had usually kept her composure very professional. He always was the one to try and loosen things between them; she had never been this forward with him. "What's gotten into you? We may never get another chance like this, Luna!" he insisted, his calm and collected disposition withdrew into nervous stammering as he struggled to avoid the question.

"You're stalling, Master," she barked.

Cole paced to the fireplace with exasperated breaths before turning back to Luna, his expression twisted in conflict. "This is silly. It doesn't matter, so why are you being like this?" he shouted.

"Why can't you just answer me? You say we're more than just Master and Knight, but you refuse to answer my question," Luna berated him.

"I don't know," he finally admitted. The words spilled out like water from a cracked glass. He turned away from Luna and stared deeply into the crackling flames in the fireplace. "I really don't know how I feel about her. She's smart, funny, and beautiful, but I just don't know yet."

Cole felt her gentle hand on his shoulder. "The heart is a fragile thing, Master. It's not something that should be carelessly played with. Take your time to figure out how you feel. If her feelings for you are strong, she'll wait for you."

The soft touch of Luna's hand pulled away from Cole. He turned toward her but it was too late. He faced an empty room with the curtain fluttering in the breeze.

CHAPTER 3

THE STENCH OF age emanated from every dust-filled crevice of the abandoned sewer tunnel. The tunnel was wide but barely tall enough for a person to stand in. Each side was molded into a narrow walkway that dipped sharply in the middle forming a channel where the city's water used to flow. All that remained of its once bountiful flow were small, shallow puddles of stagnant filth. The walls had several copper pipes bolted to the walls and ladders that led to sealed exits. The only life in the old sewer was a couple of rats that had made this pitch-black, forgotten hole their home.

Among the hushed drips of water and chatter of rodents rang casual footsteps. The rats scurried back into their holes as a bright glow broke through the darkness. Luna stepped from around the corner holding a glowing rod out in front to light her way. Her eyes were sunken, and her movements were weary after a long night. A tired yawn escaped her lips as she lazily continued to stroll down the dank tunnel.

After a short while walking, she came across a spot of familiarity. Slowing her pace, she pointed her light source down, her eyes scanning the bare floor. She halted when she spotted a white X drawn at her feet. On the wall to her right was a collection of ten copper pipes on the wall. She pressed her ear to the pipes and started to knock on the metal, listening carefully. Each pipe sounded with a hollow, metal echo until the sixth pipe resonated with a short, shallow knock. She wrapped her hand around the bolt at its center and twisted it ninety degrees to the right, thirty degrees to the left, fifty degrees to the right, and back to the starting point. A loud mechanical click from behind the wall reverberated through the tunnel followed by multiple turning gears.

A small chunk of the wall opened, revealing a number keypad behind the brick. Luna entered in a six-digit code causing the wall to jerk and pop open into a small room no bigger than a closet. The closet-like room had chrome metal walls and a ladder at the back. Luna entered and pressed a green button on the wall, closing the door behind her, to reset the security system.

She climbed up the ladder to an overhanging hatch and pushed it open. The hatchway opened into a larger room in the same fashion as the entrance. The narrow room was lined with several chrome drawers and cupboards. A metal bench sat at the room's center and another exit at the back. Sterile fluorescent light illuminated the area with a flaccid white hue. It was a room meant for functionality, not comfort. Despite that, the sight of it gave Luna a great sense of ease. She was finally home.

Suddenly, the door swung open, and an older gentleman stepped into the room. His usually well-groomed silver hair was in a scuffled mess, and his stern gray eyes were sunken. His professional white dress shirt and vest were worn loosely with his black slacks and dress shoes. The night appeared to have been rough on him as well.

Luna regarded the man with a familiar smile. "Oh lord, Zander! You look terrible. You didn't wait up all night worrying, did you?"

"It's my job to worry about you, Aurora, and this is cutting it a little too close. The sun is rising and you're just getting back now," the man lectured.

"It's all right, Zander," she reassured him. "The battle has been over for some time now. I just went to see Master Cole to give him the prize that I won off Claymore. You didn't have to wait up for me."

She reached back to undo the clasp of her necklace and removed it from her slender neck. She held the silver crescent up to her lips and whispered a short, but intricate incantation. The pendant and her body shimmered as if her appearance were a mirage. The black-haired warrior with milky jade eyes shifted out of sight revealing someone radically different. In her place was a tall brunette with hair that fell in chocolate waves and brilliant azure blue eyes that sparkled like almond-shaped sapphires. Her complexion blossomed from a marble white to a sweet honey. She stood once again as Aurora Fallon, her other self.

Zander's eyes focused on the tear in Aurora's jacket and the blood-soaked bandage underneath. He rushed to her side to closely examine the wound, shaking his head in disapproval. "Apparently, I did. Should I call in Dr. Hewitt?"

Aurora shook her head. "No, it's just a nick; you could stitch it up easily. I would rather not call Dr. Hewitt unless it's absolutely necessary. She'll think of any excuse to run one test or another for her research. I don't have the time to be her guinea pig tonight," she assured as she pulled off her sword and sat on the bench. She drew the blade from its sheath and began to examine the steel.

"You should be thankful, Aurora. Her fascination with your physiology is probably the only reason she stays quiet about your situation. Plus, she's a brilliant doctor, someone you need considering the trouble you get yourself into," Zander lectured, reaching a waiting hand out to her.

Aurora's eyes spotted Zander's hand. She placed her sword aside for a moment to remove her tool pouch and gun and handed them to Zander. She immediately turned her attention back to her sword. "I do what Master Cole needs while keeping my honor. It's that simple."

"You're becoming more reckless in battle because of that simplicity, Aurora. Your fear of disappointing Cole overwhelms your caution," Zander analyzed.

Aurora's bright blue eyes turned stern at Zander. "Of course I don't want to disappoint him. I am his Knight and he is my Master. I will always strive to give him victory."

"Victory isn't worth your life. I'm sure he would rather see you return home safely then have his victory."

"I can give him both," Aurora stated as if she were reciting a known fact.

Aurora gave Zander a quick glance as he turned his back to her. She could hear the clinking of her tools and weapons as Zander stepped into his routine of putting away her equipment. She couldn't see his face, but the many years of Zander's company gave her a sense for his disapproval. The sound of the metal slide rang in the silence between them as Zander removed the magazine from Aurora's gun. She could clearly hear the gruff sigh of irritation that Zander did little to hide. "You didn't use the Falcon."

"Didn't have to," she replied, turning her gaze back to her sword. She finished her thorough inspection and sheathed the blade. "That's what I thought. It needs to be sharpened," she concluded before she placed her sword on its rack with a respectful gesture.

"How close was the battle?" Zander asked.

"It was a good fight. Claymore has a very interesting ability." She removed her jacket, stuck her finger through the hole from the cut, and frowned before tossing the jacket into a small bin in the corner. "The manipulation of metal, he used it to make his sword move like a snake at great speeds. I've never seen anything like it."

"Is that how you got that injury?" Zander asked. His harsh tone, accompanied by an abrupt slam of the drawer, stole Aurora's attention from her task. He pulled out a small medical kit from a cupboard and retrieved a needle, stitching thread, and a bottle of rubbing alcohol. He sterilized the needle with a precise and practiced hand and sat down on the bench beside Aurora.

Aurora extended her injured arm to Zander. "Yes, he was a little too quick on that side, and I wasn't able to block the brunt of the attack," she explained.

Zander removed the blood-soaked bandage of Cole's amateur first aid and began carefully cleaning the wound. "That could have taken your arm off," Zander said in a low, irate tenor.

"I'll be faster next time," Aurora assured him.

Zander slammed his hand hard on the bench, his gray eyes deadly serious. "Maybe you should be smarter next time."

Aurora raised an eyebrow. "Are you saying there is something wrong with my strategy?" she asked.

He answered her with an unrelenting rigidity in his gaze. "I'm saying you have a major flaw. Your commitment to your Master doesn't allow you to lose, and your honor makes you always fight the hard way." Zander drew the needle through Aurora's flesh, making her flinch from the sudden sting. "The dangerous way. Don't you understand? It's not about being faster or stronger. It's about the risks you take. You have to be more cautious. You might not be so lucky next time."

"I am a Knight, Zander, a warrior. I am not afraid of injury; it's a common occurrence in battle," Aurora preached, her voice unyielding and proud.

"I know that, Aurora, but just because you don't fear injury doesn't mean it can't cripple you. It certainly doesn't mean it can't kill you," Zander spat back.

"What would you have me do, Zander?" Aurora asked, frustration starting to boil up in her voice.

"I'd have you use your gun!" Zander shouted.

Aurora gave an exasperated sigh and turned her gaze away. *Not this again*, she thought to herself. "I told you, Zander. I didn't need it."

"This time, maybe, but you have to realize something. Even though your sense of honor is a trait that I wouldn't trade for the world, not all Knights share those ideals. While you're just working toward a harmless victory, your opponent may be going for the kill. You need to know that if it comes down to that, you have to be prepared to do whatever it takes to make it out alive," Zander pleaded.

Aurora's lips pinched into a thin line, and her brow crinkled as she bit back her disgust. "Are you saying I should kill them?" She forced the words out through clenched teeth.

Zander sighed and laid a gentle hand on Aurora's shoulder. "If you had to. You may think I'm selfish for this, but my first interest is that you come home safely."

Aurora swatted his hand away; her anger blazed off her like a smoldering flame. "What about them? What about the Masters, family, and friends they'll be leaving behind?" she barked.

"If they are prepared to kill, they should be prepared to be killed. They bring it upon themselves. You can't blame yourself for wanting to live," Zander reasoned.

Aurora's hand balled into a fist as she slammed it on the bench. "Knights don't try and kill each other!" she shouted. That was a rule she strongly believed in. It was part of the Knight's code of honor that Aurora lived by. The thought of other Knights throwing that away without consequence seemed unimaginable to her. It was equally as unimaginable that she would go down to their level.

"Don't be so naive, Aurora! You're not a child anymore. This is a fact your father, your grandfather, and every other Knight born into your family all came to terms with."

Aurora shook her head. "No, not this time. Cole and I are working toward something different, something better," she said, trying to make Zander see what was so clear to her.

"Do you think your enemies won't try and stop you two? They aren't just going to lie down and let you both succeed. These people have tasted power, and they'll stop at nothing to keep it. That's how it is in the real world, Aurora." The bitter anger that had painted Zander's expression was replaced with subtle anguish.

"Just try and imagine what you would've felt like if your father went on a mission and never came back," Zander said. Aurora turned to face Zander with fire in her eyes, but that flame diminished as Zander's sad eyes focused on her wound. "Or how Cole would feel if you never came back? When you lose someone you care about tragically, it's like a piece of you dies with them, and you're never the same. If you throw your life away, it's the people you leave behind that suffer. You may not be afraid to die, but we are afraid to lose you. I'm not asking you to throw away your honor; I just want you to keep us in mind next time you go out there." Zander finished the stitching and neatly wrapped the wound with fresh white bandages. "I hope you won't think ill of me for this, but you're like a daughter to me, and I worry about you."

Aurora's anger and irritation melted away. It sometimes slipped her mind just how long Zander had been her caretaker. He had served Aurora's family since her father was young. He had always been there. Aurora realized that he was just looking out for her. "I know, I'm sorry, Zander," she whispered.

"Think nothing of it and excuse my meddling. I sometimes still see you as the little girl I cared for. I apologize if it's an annoyance," Zander said.

"No, it's not. I guess I just take advantage of how much you care for me. It's a real blessing and one I couldn't live without." Her lips curled into a sweet smile.

With her grateful words, the worry and sadness in Zander's eyes seemed to vanish. Aurora was happy to see that all was well again between them; she loved Zander and never meant to upset him.

"You're all patched up for now. You should get some rest. You have the meeting with the university tomorrow at one o'clock so sleeping the day away is not an option," Zander reminded her.

Aurora's shoulders fell, and she let out an aggravated groan. "I forgot all about that."

"Just because Luna stayed out all night doesn't mean Aurora Fallon can dodge her appointments," Zander said with a self-satisfied grin painted on his face.

Aurora nodded. "Of course not."

CHAPTER 4

THE RHYTHMIC SOUND of pacing footsteps echoed off the hallowed walls of an abandoned warehouse. Claymore kept his gaze to the dreary concrete floor. He only gave the barren room subtle glances in the brimming dawn light to ensure their privacy. Despite the hot summer weather, the cement floor kept its overnight cool, chilling his legs as he knelt in submission to his pacing Master. He kept one readied hand touching his sword that lay on the floor beside him and his injured hand tucked close to his body. Staring through the stray strands of his golden hair that draped freely over her shoulders, Claymore finally braved enough to turn his gaze up to face his Master's ire.

The man before Claymore was of small stature and presence. He continued to pace in a jagged line, ringing his bony hands. Beads of sweat rolled down the stark features of his dread-filled face. His sunken blue eyes shifted at a frantic speed around the warehouse as if the solution to his problems could be found in the bare room. His chest heaved with a panicked breath as he loosened the dark blue tie of his black suit in a vain attempt to capture more air.

The frantic man finally ceased his pacing and faced Claymore. His judgmental gaze barreled down on his Knight like a tidal wave. "Claymore, this is inexcusable," he berated.

"I know," Claymore whispered, his voice brimming with shame and regret. "I apologize for my failure, Master Morgan."

Morgan's face twisted with rage as his hands balled into clenched fists. "You apologize! We had a plan, Claymore! I arranged this duel so Iver would show us what he had on Damon Lexus. All you had to do was beat Luna and win the evidence so we could bury it. That was the only way we could form an alliance with Lexus."

Claymore remained unwaveringly still as his Master's furious voice echoed off the walls of the barren warehouse. "It was a hard battle, but in the end, she came out victorious. There's nothing that could've been done about it."

Morgan leaned down and met Claymore's eyes with an intense glare. "Was there really nothing you could've done?"

Tightening the grip on his sword, Claymore stared up into the eyes of the shell of a man that used to be the Master he respected. *Amazing how fear can completely transform a man,* Claymore thought. He struggled to keep his gaze blank to hide his utter disappointment. "What are you trying to say, Master?" Claymore spat.

"With the powers you have perfected, you could have easily . . ."

Claymore knew exactly where his Master was leading, and he couldn't hide behind the mask of stone any longer. "I could've easily done what, Master?" Claymore's voice snapped like a tightly strung trap.

Morgan leaned back from his Knight, caught in the surprise of his servant's frightening passion. He quickly reasserted his authoritative stance as a Master as he faced his Knight with the weight of his title. "With your abilities, you could have easily killed Luna and got what we needed."

Claymore shook his head and exhaled a surly breath, not trying in the slightest to hide his disappointment. "What happened to you? You used to think that the unnecessary death of a Knight in a duel was a waste. You thought it was a tragedy. You felt shame for Masters who thought the way you're thinking right now!"

"You need more than just honor to survive in our world now. You need to make the right connections. This alliance . . ."

Claymore jumped to his feet and met Morgan with an intense stare. "Don't be a fool, Master! This isn't an alliance. Lexus is just using you as a pawn, and she'll throw you away just as easily."

Despite Claymore's domineering stature towering over him, Morgan stood his ground. "Claymore! Don't you realize that the moment Iver and Luna find out you gave them a fake drive, they will see us as an enemy. We need Lexus now for protection."

"I can deal with Luna and Iver. They follow the Code and have a sense of honor. I can't protect you if you partner with Lexus," Claymore protested.

Morgan took a passive stance to bite back his anger and frustration. "Claymore, I know you aren't the happiest with me right now. I don't think you'll ever agree with me on this, but if you ever had any faith in me, please trust that I'm doing what's best for the both of us," Morgan pleaded to his Knight, trying desperately to draw on the trust they once had between them.

Claymore listened to his Master's plight and felt a sense of pity for him. He had believed in Morgan once. He believed in what they would accomplish together and the hope they had for the future. That feeling was all but gone, but the memory remained. It replaced his bitter discontent with a deep sadness over the decisions Claymore made, even if they were for the best. "It won't turn out the way you want, Master."

"Morgan!" a demanding but feminine voice hollered from the entrance of the warehouse. With a practiced motion, Claymore drew his sword and fell into a readied stance between his Master and the intruder. Despite the throbbing in his hand and the fatigue taxing his body, he stood strong as a shield for his Master. No matter what Claymore currently thought of him, it was still his duty.

From out of the shadows across the warehouse stepped a tall woman with a domineering stride, three figures following closely behind. Her long, raven-black hair fell seductively over her shoulders. Together with her rich complexion, she cut a striking silhouette. Her dark eyes locked with them in a glare laced with hate. The heels of her leather boots made a threatening click with every step as she marched toward them.

Claymore's studied the two men and a woman at her flanks. All three of the woman's entourage carried themselves as if ready for battle with hands. Claymore's warrior instincts beckoned him to take a closer analysis of their unwelcome guests.

One of the men was fair-skinned with thin black hair tied in a low ponytail. His facial features were as sharp as the pair of vicious daggers at his hips. His intense black eyes locked on Claymore as his lips curled into a malicious grin. His sleek, dark outfit contrasted with his pale skin, showcasing the matching wings tattooed on each bicep.

Beside him marched a man with spiked, ghostly white hair, calm copper eyes, and a bronze skin tone. His baggy clothes and faded gray trench coat just added to his ghostly facade. Claymore could easily recognize the trained step and form of a fighter but could see no weapons on his person.

The woman stood a foot shorter than the men, but the brutal maliciousness that radiated from her assured her place among the rest. Her deep olive eyes stared ahead with cruel intentions and her fiery red hair dangled down the center of her back from a high ponytail. Her pale skin was covered from the neck down with black leather that hugged tightly to her curves. With an impatient eagerness, her hands hovered over the two pistols strapped to her legs.

The sight of the intruders put Claymore's temperament on a permanent edge. "It's Damon and her goons," Claymore warned. "How did they find us?"

"I called her here to make a deal," Morgan informed him.

"You did *what?*" Claymore's eyes bulged with surprise, his face twisted with a mix of frustration and panic.

Morgan's face didn't show the same anxious fear as Claymore's. Instead, Morgan showed an air of nervous optimism. As if the dealings with Damon were a simple business deal. "We can offer something else and make a deal. We can still make this work."

Claymore felt an overwhelming sense of dread in the pit of his stomach. He swallowed hard as the consequences of his actions marched toward him. "You don't know what you've done."

Morgan moved past Claymore to meet Damon at the center of the room with an open welcome but was met with a hard slap from her across his cheek.

"Where is it?" Damon demanded with a sharp bite to her voice.

Claymore leaped to his Master's aid, shoving Morgan behind him and pointing his sword at Damon.

Drawn into action by Claymore's aggressive stance, Damon's Knights' followed suit and drew their weapons against him. The standoff wound the tension tight like razor wire.

Damon raised her slender hand to halt her Knights' action. "Stand down. We need them alive for now." Her Knights relaxed their stances but kept their weapons in hand. "Where is it, Morgan?"

"Where is what? What are you talking about?" Morgan cried out in confusion, desperate for an answer.

"The data drive! Where did you stash it? Do you plan to betray my trust and use it against me?"

"No, of course not! We only used the drive to convince Iver it was worth the duel. Claymore gave it back to your Knight," Morgan explained.

"The drive you gave to us was empty. Your servant must have switched them," Damon asserted. "Did he give Iver the real one when he lost the duel?"

"That's absurd!" Morgan's demeanor began to crack with the accusations Damon was throwing at him. "We have dealt in good faith with this arrangement. Claymore, assure Damon that you gave them the right drive." Morgan moved to face Claymore, but the innocent optimism in his composure vanished at the sight of Claymore's face. "Claymore?"

Claymore's battle-hardened eyes continued to drift between Damon and her Knights, preparing for the worst. "You should get out of here," Claymore instructed with a disposition like granite, not giving Morgan a moment of his gaze.

"Claymore, what is going on?" Morgan asked.

"It looks like your dog was working without his Master," Damon theorized with a snide smirk painted across her lips. She turned her attention to the man with the answers she wanted. "Where's the drive, puppet?"

"You'll never find it," Claymore declared, a strong sense of spite emanating from him.

Morgan put himself in between Claymore and Damon with his hands up in a passive motion to calm the situation. "Wait, hold on! There's no need for this to get out of hand." He turned a desperate gaze to his Knight. "Please, Claymore.

If you give them the drive, we can still make this work. I'm begging you! Just give them what they want."

"I can't do that."

"Why?"

"Because this needs to stop!" Claymore bellowed. "Her brutal climb to power has to stop, and my actions may ensure that."

"Listen to your Master, Claymore. It's in your best interest to give us the drive voluntarily. You don't want us to drag it out of you," Morgan warned, a promised threat lacing her words.

Damon's threat was met only with a steady glare of defiance from Claymore's blue eyes. "That drive is in the right hands to bury you."

A thick layer of betrayal washed over Morgan's expression like a waterfall. It was a look Claymore couldn't ignore. "Why didn't you tell me?" Morgan asked.

"You're not the man you once were, Master! If I told you what was really going on, you would've sold me out to Lexus just to save your own hide! Because that's the man you are now, the kind of man that will sell anything and anyone just to keep breathing." The words spilled from Claymore like an open faucet, releasing everything he held inside about his Master.

Morgan flinched back from the lashing of Claymore's judgment. His face twisted with an inner torment. "I was only thinking of our safety."

"I know," Claymore replied with a soft sense of understanding. Pushing down the tension and heartache he felt, Claymore gathered his focus into his unique ability. The molten silver of his eyes began to manifest, striking fear into Morgan's heart. "But I have to think of the safety of everyone."

A radiant shimmer flowed down to the tip of Claymore's blade, commanding the steel to his will. The solid weapon snapped into motion and struck down at Damon like a metal snake pouncing on prey.

The fiery-haired women at Damon's side leaped into action. With her eyes ablaze with brilliant golden light, she reached out her hand and manifested a shining bubble of energy around her and her Master. The metal construct bounced harmlessly off the bright shield, and a intense flash emanated from the point of impact.

"Get out of here, Master! I'll cover you," Claymore demanded. Pushing his rage and desperation into his weapon, he had the blade split into several razor-sharp tendrils. The construct immediately waged a relentless attack on the force field as Morgan bolted for the door as fast as his terrified legs could carry him.

"Keep the shield up, Solaris," Damon ordered her female Knight. She turned her commanding gaze to the Knight at her back with the bone-white hair. "Spector, go after Morgan!"

At the command of his Master, Spector pursued Morgan with an unearthly glide. A sharp tendril from Claymore's weapon lashed down at Spector to block his retreat, but the deadly blade past through Spector's ghostly form, not even slowing his exit from the warehouse.

"Hermes, stop Claymore but keep him breathing. We need that drive, and dead men can't spill secrets." Damon's commanding voice echoed from behind Solaris's shield. Before Claymore could react, the black-haired Knight zipped through his defenses at an inhuman speed and thrust his knee into Claymore's stomach. As a pained wheeze escaped him, Claymore lurched forward, struggling to catch his breath.

Latching a firm grip around Claymore's arm, Hermes leaned into his momentum and tossed Claymore to the ground. With a sharp frame of mind, forged by diligent training and battle, Claymore fought against the pain to keep his sword in hand as he landed flat on his back. His force of will kept his metal construct moving and commanded the blades to lash down at Hermes like giant claws. The attack forced Hermes into a short retreat long enough for Claymore to scramble to his feet.

He knew that his metal creation couldn't match Hermes's supernatural speed, so a direct attack was out of the question. Claymore had to try and cover his retreat. Claymore pulled his focus together and willed the tendrils to sweep in wide arches to cover as much ground as possible while he took careful steps back to the door.

Hermes swerved and weaved through the series of attacks with a dizzying finesse to close the distance between him and his enemy. He then snatched Claymore's hand at the wrist, swept it to his back, and pushed hard against Claymore's shoulder, forcing him to release his sword. The steel construct recoiled back and fell to the floor in its original form.

Claymore moved with the grapple and spun to face his attacker, landing a solid punch to his face. Hermes staggered back, clutching his nose as blood started to trickle down his face. Taking advantage of the stagger, Claymore kicked Hermes square in the stomach. The impact swept Hermes's feet out from under him, and he landed with a painful thud.

In an efficient motion, Claymore seized his sword from the ground and leaped toward Hermes to strike down at his prone form. Unfortunately for Claymore, the speedster recovered faster than he could act. Hermes rolled away from Claymore's blade, and it hit the floor with a harmless clang.

Hermes smoothly rolled to his feet, launching himself toward his enemy the moment his boots touched the ground. Using the momentum of his speed, Hermes landed a harsh kick to Claymore's ribs. The force of the attack sent Claymore tumbling across the cold floor. When he finally came to a stop, his head swam with the immense pain of two freshly cracked ribs, as he struggled with all his being to gather his wits and climb to his feet.

Before Claymore could drive the fog from his mind, Hermes continued his relentless assault with a firm boot to Claymore's face. A wash of panic washed over him as he lay prone. Claymore reached down and pulled a small but deadly knife from his boot and attempted to scramble to his feet once again.

But Claymore's battered body couldn't keep up with Hermes's speed, and he was on top of Claymore before he could sit up, pinning down Claymore's arms with his powerful legs.

Their eyes locked in an intense gaze as Claymore struggled against Hermes's grapple. "You're not going to win this, Claymore. Just give it up and give us what we want."

"You won't break me!" Claymore asserted through clenched teeth. A shimmer of silver light flowed from his hand into the knife and transformed it into a long spear, impaling Hermes through the shoulder. Hermes screamed in agony as he frantically clutched at the blade imbedded in his flesh, releasing his grip on Claymore.

With a fierce battle cry, Claymore heaved Hermes off him and turned the tides of the grapple. With Hermes under his weight, Claymore clocked Hermes on the side of the head, knocking him out cold. Hermes's body fell limp to the ground.

The silver shimmer dissipated from Claymore's boot knife as it pulled out from Hermes's shoulder and reverted back to its original form. The adrenaline of Claymore's survival instinct drove his broken body forward to retrieve his sword, not willing to give in to his enemy.

Mere steps from his weapon, a muffled pop echoed in Claymore's ears, and his leg buckled under his weight. His calf pulsated with a white-hot pain as blood oozed from the bullet hole. He searched for the source and found Solaris with the smoking gun.

Claymore gripped his sword firmly, trying with all his being to push through the agony and focus his powers into his blade, but his efforts were in vain. Despite how hard he concentrated, his sword kept its shape. His abilities wouldn't answer his calls. With his leg crippled and his power drained, he could only stare as Solaris and Damon marched toward him, fury twisting Damon's feminine face.

From within the depths of Claymore's hopeless fate came a small ray of hope in a form Claymore thought he'd never see. Sprinting toward them with reckless abandon was Claymore's cowardly Master, Morgan, a gun in his one hand and a strange canister in the other.

"Claymore, *duck!*" he cried. Without breaking his stride, Morgan pulled the pin from the canister with his teeth and tossed it at Damon.

Solaris quickly throw up her golden shield at the sight of the projectile, but her defenses failed to prepare them for the blinding light and deafening roar that exploded from the flash bang grenade.

As Solaris and Damon stumbled in a fog of temporary blindness, Morgan rushed to Claymore's aid. His tear-filled eyes couldn't help but focus on his Knight's wounded leg. "We have to go. Can you stand?" Morgan asked.

Claymore shook his head. "You shouldn't have come back. I can't protect you now," he protested through strained breaths.

Morgan grabbed Claymore's arm and stretched it over his shoulder, struggling to pull him to his feet. The moment Claymore put weight on his leg, thick blood began to ooze from the gunshot at an alarming rate. He cried out in pain as Morgan lowered him down again and attempted to slow the bleeding with his hands. "I'm going to protect you now,

Claymore. This is my fault. I should've listened to you. I'm so sorry." Morgan's apology broke with a flood of tears that fell onto his hands, mixing with Claymore's blood.

"You won't be able to get us both out of here. You need to leave me behind."

Morgan shook his head in a frantic refusal. "No! I never planned on doing this without you! I can't do this without you!" Morgan pulled off his coat and tied it around Claymore's leg as a makeshift tourniquet.

Seeing such a show of bravery from the man Claymore believed to have been overtaken with fear manifested a feeling of pride and respect for his Master that he hadn't felt in a long time. That emotion was closely followed by a deep sense of shame. "I'm sorry I didn't tell you about the drive. This is as much my fault as it is yours."

"We can both apologize till we are blue in the face later. Now we need to move," Morgan insisted, a forced smile pushing through his grief.

They worked together to stand up, but time was not on their side. Appearing at Morgan's back like a foreboding shadow was Spector's ghostly form.

"Master!" Claymore warned.

Morgan turned to face the looming danger but couldn't react quick enough to stop Spector's hand as it plunged deep into his chest. The color drained from Morgan's face, and he gasped for air that would not come as Spector's hand strangled him from the inside.

In defense of his Master, Claymore raised his heavy sword and swiped down at his assailant only to have the steel pass harmlessly through Spector's vaporous form. Spector retaliated against Claymore's resistance with a solid kick to Claymore's wounded leg. A bolt of excruciating pain tore through

Claymore, causing his leg to buckle under him and his battered body to collapse onto the cold ground.

The white-hot agony of Claymore's broken body was a drop in the well of pain he felt as he witnessed Morgan's strangled cries go silent and his body go limp. With a careless motion, Spector released Morgan's body, allowing it to fall like a ragdoll into Claymore's arms. Claymore desperately called out Morgan's name, hoping beyond hope that the dreaded reality before him wasn't real. His forlorn delusion was in vain as his Master would not answer his calls. Morgan was gone.

Spector's unfeeling eyes looked down on Claymore and his misery. "It didn't need to happen this way, Claymore. We could've made a deal. All you had to do was surrender the drive. We would've shown you mercy," Spector said, his tone steady but frigidly cold.

An inner fire of rage and disgust could be seen through Claymore's defiant eyes as he faced his enemy. "You speak of mercy with my Master's blood on your hands. How brainwashed are you?"

"Remember, Claymore. You started this when you dealt in bad faith. But you could make it right. Just tell us where you sent the drive, and we'll spare you," Spector persisted, keeping the goal of the mission in the forefront on his mind.

Claymore wished with all his being that he could strike back at the enemy who had beaten him. He wished he could continue the fight, but he had nothing left to fight with. His powers and strength were drained, and his Master was dead. He had nothing left but the knowledge of the data drive and its location. He wouldn't let Damon and her thugs take that along with everything else they already tore from his hands.

A bleak answer to his grim defiance came to him when he felt the smooth handle of Morgan's pistol at his fingertips. "Soon, Spector. Soon you'll all have to answer for what you've done, and you won't be able to hide behind your Master as a convenient excuse. I only regret that I won't live to see it."

Before Spector could intervene, Claymore pressed to gun to his temple and pulled the trigger, taking his secrets down with him.

CHAPTER 5

STANDING WITH A pensive bearing, Damon Lexus stared at the sun as it crept over the horizon. Her manicured fingers tapped impatiently on her hip while her other hand held a cell phone in a tight grip. The sleek black pencil skirt and dark blue blouse she wore hugged her curves to form an attractive shadow that stretched over the polished floors with the encroaching sunlight.

The expensive artwork that decorated the walls of her home failed to grab her attention away from her anxious vigil. The trendy, but comfortable furniture, picked by professional eyes, was unable to pull her off her feet. Not even the heavenly soft silk sheets upon her plush bed could lure her to sleep. Damon stood stagnate and stubborn, awaiting word from her agents. She needed to know where her pieces landed to plan her next move.

Her cell phone suddenly came alive with an insistent ring tone. She calmly flipped the phone open with her thumb and placed it to her ear. "Yes," she spat in a short, irritated tone.

"Master, it's Alias," a voice that sang like a sweet bell answered.

Damon's face lit up with a wide smile at the sound of her Knight. "I suppose your report is better late than never. Did you keep your cover?"

"Of course, even your Knights think you were there with them. I play the part perfectly," Alias assured.

"Excellent. It's important that they see me down in the trenches with them. Did the extraction go as planed?" Damon asked. The question hung in the air without response for a long, silent moment. "Alias?"

"There was a complication."

Damon's wide smile instantly vanished and surrendered to an irritated scowl. "What kind of complication?"

"Claymore was planning on leaving his Master and working against us. He was going to take the evidence in the drive and use it to bury you," Alias reported.

The restless tapping of her fingers continued at a speedy pace as the weight of her Knight's words set in. "I knew Morgan didn't have the backbone to keep Claymore in line. What happened with the drive?"

"Claymore sent it to someone, kept saying it was in the right hands. I don't know who he meant."

"Then make him give you a name!" Damon commanded; her voice snapped like a sharp whip. All Damon could hear in response to her order was a string of nervous mumbles that set her temper blazing like a wild fire. "What?"

"Claymore's dead. A battle broke out when Claymore refused to hand over the drive."

"How could you *idiots* kill him without bleeding the location from him?" Damon interrupted with another lash of her spiteful tongue.

"It wasn't us. Morgan tried to save Claymore but was killed by Spector in the struggle. Claymore must have gotten ahold of his gun and took the last shot to his own temple. He wanted to take what he knew with him." Alias concluded her grim report.

Damon took a measured breath to compose her disposition, forming a stern inner wall to hold back a sea of fury. "Dammit," she muttered between clenched teeth.

"What are your orders, Master?" Alias asked, Damon's anger sending a tremor through her voice.

As the sun's light blossomed over the city skyline and its warm rays illuminated Damon's home, her path became clear. She knew what needed to be done. "Claymore must have given the drive to Iver in hopes of creating an alliance without his Master. He must have thrown the duel in order to hand it off without showing his hand to his Master. Fall back to your position inside Iver's home. Find out where he's keeping it," Damon ordered.

"There are only so many places I can get to and still maintain my cover. What if it's hidden well?"

With a confident and commanding stance, she mentally prepared her demeanor to bring down a serious and grim plan. "We can't risk the possibility that Iver has already seen what is on the drive. In order for our goal to be reached, we need to stop his meddling once and for all. I'll have Venom take care of that part of the mission."

Alias let out a soft chuckle. "About time."

"You have your orders, Alias. Report back when they are complete," Damon instructed before closing the phone. Her eyes were once again drawn to the radiance of the rising sun as her mind drifted in thought.

As if a frigid chill tugged at her subconscious, the hairs on the back of her neck suddenly stood at attention. She wasn't alone. She turned her gaze away from her penthouse view to the deep shadows at the back of the room.

At home in the darkness, a statuesque man stood tall, completely clad in a pitch-black robe. His eyes were two bright blue orbs shining in the dim corner of the room.

"Morpheus, what gives you the idea that you can simply appear in my home like this?" Damon snapped, the bitter scowl adding a vicious bite to her stern words.

"My Master's orders gave me that idea," Morpheus answered, his eerie voice carrying an unnatural cold with it.

Damon rolled her eyes in a noticeable show of disgust. "And what does Irving want?"

"You lost the drive, didn't you?" Morpheus asked.

"Are you spying on me?" Damon asked, shooting Morpheus a frightening glare.

"We're just trying to keep you honest. How did you lose it?"

"There were complications. I'm moving my Knights against Cole Iver to retrieve it as we speak," Damon assured.

"Are you certain Iver has it?"

"It's the best option he had. He had the perfect opportunity to hand it over without anyone knowing and no one else is openly moving against us. He's probably been planning this for a while," Damon reasoned.

"That data drive contains evidence that connects you to a murder. If we didn't clean up after you and your inexperienced Knights, you never would have climbed as high as you have. You owe your success to my Master." Morpheus drove home his point with a frigid snap to his tone.

"And we wouldn't be in this situation if your Master didn't keep that file to lord over me. I owe her nothing," Damon barked back.

"My Master thinks you'll try and take her down with you."

"I'll get it back, puppet!" Damon asserted as she stared straight into the inhuman lanterns of Morpheus's eyes. "I'll solve this problem and get rid of Cole Iver, and do you know why? It's the reason that I've made it this far, and it has nothing to do with what she covered up. It's because I get the job done, no matter what. Don't let her forget that."

CHAPTER 6

THE WARM SUMMER breeze caressed Aurora's face as she gazed out the back-seat car window into the busy streets of the city. As she fought to keep her weary eyes open, she grew envious of the citizens she saw, full of lively energy as they casually strolled the streets' many small shops.

She pulled her free-flowing hair behind her ears and took a moment to inspect her appearance in a small compact mirror. Her makeup was tidy, and the delicate silver earrings that hung gracefully from her ears formed a smooth line to her elegant blue blouse and formfitting black pencil skirt.

Every piece of clothing, brush of makeup, and stylish accessory was a carefully planned tool much like her tools of battle. They were all strategically selected to paint the lovely picture of a pampered heiress. It was a perfect mask to hide her true self.

"How are you holding up, Miss Fallon?" Zander asked, his gray eyes quickly catching a glance at the tired Aurora in the rearview mirror.

Aurora directed her attention onto Zander in the front driver's seat. She often wondered how he could seem so poised in a full three-piece gray and black suit in the hottest part of summer. "I've been better. I only wish I hadn't let my appointments get away from me."

Zander let out a soft chuckle. "Cheer up, Miss Fallon. You've been looking forward to the tour of the university's greenhouse for a while now. It should be fascinating, and I'm sure you'll enjoy it."

"Life is full of trials. It is the warrior's way to grin and bear it. Whether it be a near-fatal wound or lack of sleep," she replied, pushing though her fatigue to strengthen her practiced demeanor. In the midst of her involuntary dozing, a story being read on the car's radio grabbed her attention like a coiled snake.

"Turn up the radio!" Aurora commanded, listening intently.

The words rang through the car speakers. "Business and family man, Morgan Clouse, was found dead in his home early this morning. Authorities suspect heart failure, but an autopsy has yet to be performed."

"My god," Zander said in a sad, hollow whisper.

Aurora felt a sick feeling in the pit of her stomach as she continued to listen for something she hoped wouldn't come. After some other unrelated stories, her fears were confirmed.

"The body of an unidentified male between the age of twenty-five to thirty was found in a dumpster off 108th Avenue downtown. True cause of death is still unknown, but the police say the victim suffered severe stab and gunshot wounds. Police also commented on a strange burn on the victim's hand. The authorities ask that if you have any information regarding the crime or the victim's identity to please contact them immediately." The radio news anchor finished the bone-chilling story.

"They killed them, Zander," Aurora said between clenched teeth, her expression locked in a state of stunned shock. It was the calm before the storm of rage that was brewing just below the surface.

"Who killed them?" Zander asked.

"Lexus. She must have found out what we were doing and went after him," Aurora spat.

"How are you sure it was them?"

"I left that burn on Claymore's hand myself. That must be him," Aurora insisted.

"Aurora, don't get carried away. It could be a coincidence," Zander reasoned.

Aurora shook her head. "It's entirely too much of a coincidence. The body had the same burns in the same place as Claymore, and I doubt if anyone looked into it they would find any history of heart problems with Morgan. They killed Claymore in battle, and they staged Morgan's death to look normal. Then they just threw Claymore out like trash." Aurora slammed her fist against the car door, and the polished paneling cracked under her hand. "Claymore was a strong and honorable Knight. He deserved better than that."

Without warning, Zander swerved the car through traffic to the shoulder and came to an abrupt stop. He turned around to face Aurora with a deathly serious gaze. Aurora stared back at him, eyes wide and mouth agape in shock. "Zander! What do you think you're doing?"

"Bringing you to your senses!" Zander spat back. "Aurora, I know what happened to Morgan and Claymore was unforgivable, but you can't deal with that right now. You're not Luna right now. You are not part of this battle, and you don't know them. Right now, you're Aurora Fallon and you have a meeting to attend, so you need to calm down. Do you understand?"

"How do I do that, Zander? How do I just push this aside and forget about it?" Aurora asked, her face pleading for an answer.

"I'm not saying you forget about this, but you do need to harden yourself to it. There will be a time to fix this wrong, but that time isn't now."

Aurora lowered her eyes, her mind and heart interlocked in conflict. She knew he was right. Even though every fiber of her being drove her to seek justice that very second, her sudden disappearance would raise unwanted questions. This was just one more reason that Cole and Luna had to take down Lexus, but she could only act as Luna. Justice for Morgan and Claymore would come then and only then. Aurora nodded, taking in a deep breath to regain her composure. "You're right, Zander. I have to move past this for the time being, at least. It won't be easy."

"I know, but you can pull it off. You are one of the best," he reassured. Zander faced forward and fired up the car, starting again toward their final destination.

They made their way at a brisk pace and arrived quickly, a grandiose sign reading "King Bradford University" marked their arrival. As they drove through the cobblestone roads on the grounds of the university, Aurora couldn't help, but stare at the rich visual splendor of the massive property. The majestic, historically inspired buildings were wonderfully accented by the lush green lawns and beautiful oak trees sprinkled over the grounds. The car came to a smooth stop before an ornate iron gate, veins of ivy intertwining through the bars.

Aurora spotted two men in humble business suits waiting at the gate, their eyes trained on the car. One man was tall but lanky in his stance, sporting noticeable thinning brown hair and baggy blue eyes. Despite those qualities, he stood with a strong sense of authority, arms crossed over his chest. The man at his side may have stood tall in his youth, but time had worn his back to a hunch as he held his balance with a wooden cane. His hair was full but snowy-white, and his eyes were overshadowed by the wrinkles in his skin. It was a face Aurora was familiar with. The old man smiled warmly as he prepared to welcome their new benefactor.

Zander politely opened the car door, and Aurora glided from the car like a summer breeze. She smiled sweetly through her grief, masking her emotions with a disguise of contentment she had worked her whole life to perfect. "Hello, gentlemen."

The younger man took Aurora's hand in a hearty handshake. "Good afternoon, Miss Fallon. It's such a pleasure having you here today. I'm Benjamin Belfred. I head up the Financial Administration department for the university and this is . . ." Benjamin gestured his hand to the older man.

"Lyle Traze, the dean," Aurora cut in as she shook Lyle's hand politely. "We've met before."

Lyle's face came alive in a wide, joyous smile. "Yes, I met you and your family when your brother graduated our university. How is Adonis? I remember him as one of our finest students."

"He's now running our family's business endeavors and is doing fine. Thank you for asking," Aurora answered.

"It's a shame we never had the privilege of welcoming you as one of our students," Lyle noted.

"I agree; Adonis told me many good things about this place. You're running a fine institution," Aurora praised.

"The praise doesn't only lie with me. There are dozens of people that aid to the functionality of this school. What school did you attend?" Lyle asked out of curiosity.

Aurora fell silent for a moment, her mind running rapidly for an answer. "I sought more physical training before focusing on charitable endeavors with my part of the family's wealth," she answered, carefully wording her response. "Now, we don't want to burn the day away out in the entrance. Let's get to business, shall we?"

Lyle nodded. "Of course, let's get this underway. We'll meet your tour guide inside."

CHAPTER 7

HIS ONLY COMPANION in the small, cluttered office was the continual creaking of the desk chair as the office's owner leaned back and forth. His sharp, dark eyes were focused on reading the paper in his hand, occasionally marking the writing with a red pen. He removed his wire-framed glasses and rubbed his work-worn eyes, trying to train his attention back to the task at hand. He glanced over to the stack of other papers piled on his small desk beside his computer; they drew only a disgruntled sigh from him.

How did I get so backlogged? he asked himself.

To lift his spirits, he looked past his pile of work and past the shelves full of books and trinkets that covered the walls of the office to a deep blue potted orchid on the only windowsill in the room. That beautiful piece of growth in the chaos always managed to drag a smile out of him. He ran a hand through his short black hair and undid the top button of his shirt for the small relief from the heat it provided and turned back to his work.

Suddenly, Benjamin barged through the door with a quick step and shut it with a harsh slam to call the attention of the man at the desk. The man slowly raised his head, giving

Benjamin an indifferent gaze. "Hello, Benjamin," he greeted flatly while setting the paper he was reading back atop the pile.

"Hello, yourself, Ethan!" Benjamin spat as he scurried to the desk. "What are you doing here? I told you to be at the gate at noon for the meeting with Miss Fallon."

"Yes, I remember," Ethan answered calmly.

Benjamin's lips formed a flat line and his brow crinkled in an irritated scowl. "Then what are you doing here?" he repeated.

"As I told you when you first asked me to play tour guide, I can't spare the time," Ethan retorted.

"Can't spare the time?" Benjamin ranted. "What is so important that you're refusing the request of one of our best benefactors?"

Ethan raised an eyebrow at the frantic Benjamin. "My job," Ethan answered, gesturing to the pile of papers on his desk.

"Oh, that can wait. Listen, Ethan. Do you know exactly who that person you stood up is?" Benjamin asked, his eyes twitching with aggravation.

"Aurora Fallon," Ethan answered, his apathetic tone unwavering.

"Exactly. She is one of our biggest benefactors and part of a very influential family. She's giving loads of money to this school, and all she asked for is a tour of the greenhouse. We are going to give her precisely what she wants, and considering I know little to nothing about the subject, when I say we, I mean you," he insisted.

"Why does she want a tour of the greenhouse?" Ethan asked.

"I don't know why! It's doesn't matter why. Just do it!" Benjamin commanded.

"Look, Benjamin. You know that I take this day off every year, and the only reason I'm here now is because I'm backlogged with all these papers. No offense to this Aurora Fallon, but I really can't deal with this today," Ethan explained.

"I am well aware of your situation. You make it perfectly clear every year, but this is extremely important and I wouldn't be asking you if it wasn't."

Ethan groaned, his well-mannered shield showing cracks of frustration. "I can't. I have way too much work to do to indulge in some rich girl's stunt to soften her public image. Or maybe it's community service. Whatever it is, you may have time to waste kissing her feet, but I don't, especially today."

"You don't have to kiss her feet. All you have to do is show her around the greenhouse. Please, Ethan," Benjamin pleaded.

Ethan's civil demeanor morphed into an irritated scowl. "What do you even know about her, anyway? Until now, I never knew the Fallons had a daughter, and I taught her brother. Now she shows up primarily out of nowhere. She's probably a party girl trying to earn her inheritance."

"That's not true," Benjamin argued. Ethan stared straight-faced at Benjamin and raised an eyebrow, forcing Benjamin to rethink his assessment. "I don't think, but Lyle seems to like her and he's a great judge of character."

"Benjamin, the only reason I'm here at all is . . ."

Benjamin cut Ethan off midsentence. "Yes, yes, yes, I know the only reason you're here is to catch up on work and you don't want to be here and I put too much work on you. Yeah, yeah, yeah, I'm sorry. But this is extremely important, and, if you do this I promise I won't ask anything of you ever again," Benjamin begged, making an active effort to look as pitiful and desperate as possible.

Ethan's stoic demeanor couldn't hold up to the onslaught of Benjamin's guilt trip. "If I say yes, would you stop staring at me like that?" Ethan asked. "It's extremely creepy."

Benjamin nodded like a child.

"All right, I'll show her around the greenhouse." Ethan rose from his chair and walked to the door.

"Thank you, Ethan. You won't regret this," Benjamin said. Before Ethan could open the door, Benjamin called out in protest, "Wait. Would it be possible for you to . . . straighten yourself up a bit?"

"Don't push it," Ethan retorted before exiting his office. He was welcomed with the sight of a lovely woman with chocolate-brown hair in the hallway admiring the interior of the school.

As they both exited the office, Benjamin caught the woman's attention and gestured to Ethan. "Miss Fallon, this is Ethan Chang. He knows the greenhouse like the back of his hand and has agreed to show you around. He actually spends much of his time in there and should be able to give you an interesting tour."

Aurora flashed a sweet smile and gave Ethan a hardy handshake. "Nice to meet you, Mr. Chang."

Ethan smiled awkwardly. "Hello. Nice to meet you, as well. You can call me Ethan. To tell you the truth, no one really calls me Mr. Chang."

"All right then. It's refreshing to be on a first-name basis with someone. Call me Aurora," she replied as her eyes scanned Ethan up and down, studying his relaxed appearance.

The possibility that Aurora was judging him on his sloppy appearance suddenly crept into Ethan's mind and he jumped to his own defense. "Please excuse me. So long in this country and I'm still not used to the summers here."

Aurora waved her hand. "Oh no, it's fine. You set a very relaxing atmosphere, Ethan."

Ethan nodded. "Sounds good."

Benjamin slowly started to slink away. "Well, then I'll let you two get to it. I would join, but I have a formidable mountain of paperwork to get to."

Ethan shot Benjamin a sharp glare. "Don't we all?"

Benjamin rubbed the back of his neck as a nervous laughter erupted from him. "Yes, well, it was a pleasure meeting you, Miss Fallon. I hope to see you in the future and all that. Have a splendid evening." He gave a slight bow then scurried down the hallway before Aurora could reply.

She stared after him for a moment with a perplexed expression and said, "What a strange man."

Ethan chuckled. "That's one way to describe him. Well, let's get this underway. The greenhouse is this way." He gestured down the hallway to guide Aurora to the greenhouse.

"How did you get into teaching, Ethan?" Aurora asked.

Ethan fell silent, surprised that a millionaire heiress would even care why he got into teaching. *Maybe she's just making small talk,* Ethan thought. He quickly snapped back into reality. "Oh . . . umm well, when I immigrated to Ebony from the Daiyu Empire, I worked odd jobs to make a living. One of them was at the university. I met Lyle Traze, and he taught me a lot about the history of this country so I decided study it in university. I was able to scrap together tuition and get my doctorate while I worked here. After that Lyle hired me to teach history here," Ethan explained. His gaze trailed over to Aurora, who was hanging on to his every word, genuinely interested.

"Why did you leave the Empire?" she asked. Ethan paused a moment on the question. "Oh, I'm sorry. Am I getting too personal?"

Ethan shook his head. "No, no, it's perfectly fine. I guess you could say my family's . . . business brought me here," he answered, carefully wording his response.

"What did your family do?" Aurora continued her inquiry.

"Medicine . . . but I chose to give it up shortly after I came here." Ethan's thoughts flashed back to painful memories. He swallowed hard to regain his composure. "My heart just wasn't in it anymore."

"It's good that you followed your heart; not many people feel they have that choice."

"That's good insight." Ethan turned his gaze to Aurora, but she did not return it. Her eyes suddenly became forlorn and distant, showing what Ethan swore was heartache. It was a familiar sight to him.

Aurora snapped back to attention, and the sadness was once again buried. "Thank you. I'm sorry I'm asking you so many personal questions. This might sound a bit odd, but I've never met someone from Daiyu before and I'm a little curious."

Ethan wondered for a moment if he had imagined the extent of Aurora's inner grief that had seemingly disappeared. "It's fine. I actually get that a lot. The people in Daiyu are extremely elitist about their country and heritage; they hardly ever think of living anywhere else. I could count the number of Daiyians I've seen in this whole city on one hand."

"What do you think of your former country?" Aurora asked.

"Most of what foreigners hear is a romanticized version. The real Daiyu leaves something to be desired. It rains entirely too much, but I guess it's not really bad. I chose not to limit myself away from the rest of the world."

Aurora smiled. "It's a good thing you didn't."

Aurora and Ethan continued their friendly chat as they walked out into the courtyard to a great dome-shaped building with walls made of glass and iron. Surrounding it were four identical but smaller domes attached to the main building through short enclosed walkways. "Here we are," Ethan announced while opening the greenhouse gate.

Immediately upon their entrance into the dome, they were welcomed by many visual delights that firmly captured Aurora's attention. The lovely, natural paradise incased in glass was diverse with lush oak trees that reached to the ceiling. Every sense was stimulated by the collection of beautifully colorful flowers, fragrant herbs, and strange plants. The picturesque environment's only disturbance was a stone walkway that split into three paths. The stone swerved and crisscrossed throughout the man-made habitat.

"It's gorgeous," Aurora said, gasping in astonishment.

Ethan couldn't help but smile as he observed her delight. It was a new take on a sight that had grown mundane to him. Her enjoyment breathed new life into the garden, made him see it through her eyes. "It sure is. Let me show you around."

Ethan led Aurora down the center path into the trees. "This is the main center of the greenhouse. It holds all of our more resilient specimens that don't need a specific growing climate, so we can easily raise them together."

Aurora gazed at the forest around her, mesmerized by her surroundings. "It's like you made an entire little world in here."

"We try and keep the greenhouse as much of an enclosed environment as we can. We have to simulate things like rain and temperature control, but other than that, this place pretty much stands on its own," he explained.

"How long has the university had this?" Aurora asked.

"It's been here ever since the castle became a school. Apparently one of the queens loved gardens so the king had it built for her. They decided to keep it when the university was established."

"Now I see the benefit of having a history professor give me this tour."

Ethan chuckled. "I'm glad I could be a passable substitute. This country has an interesting form of government. You have a blood monarchy system in power, but there are several failsafe systems so the king can't abuse his power. It's very clever; you keep rule to one entity to avoid power struggles, but there are ways to peacefully overthrow the ruling body if they ignore their people."

"That's right. This country was lucky to have been founded by very innovative thinkers who made our system of government. They were smart enough to know that absolute power corrupts absolutely."

"That concept is simple, but at the same time, difficult for some to understand," he agreed. Out of the corner of his eye, Ethan spotted a flutter of golden wings from behind Aurora. "Turn around slowly," Ethan requested as he laid a gentle hand on her shoulder, kindly maneuvering her to face the opposite direction. He pointed over her shoulder.

Aurora's face lit up at the sight of the tiny butterfly. The intricate pattern on its wings shimmered in the rays of the sun with red, yellow, and orange shades like a blazing flame. "A Solaris butterfly. It's beautiful."

Ethan smirked. "You really are a sharp one, aren't you? Do you know where this little guy's from?"

"The eastern shoreline of Ebony. I never thought I'd be able to see one," Aurora said.

"It is a rare treat. They usually are very shy. It must've wanted to see you." Ethan glanced at Aurora with a charming smile that disappeared once he saw the same sad eyes from before. *I guess I didn't imagine it,* he thought to himself.

Ethan thought carefully about trying to comfort her. Their relationship was a professional courtesy at best. Did he really have any right to go poking around in her private life? *On the other hand,* he thought, *what kind of a man would I be if I did nothing?*

Ethan swallowed hard. "Since you have been asking so many questions about me, can I ask something about you?" he asked with a slight stammer.

Aurora snapped to attention and turned back to Ethan, regarding him with forced happiness. "Yes, of course. What would you like to know?"

"Are you all right?" he asked, his eyes showing concern.

Aurora smiled and tried to laugh it off. "Yes, I'm fine. Why do you ask?"

"I ask because you look a bit sad. You're trying to hide it, but I recognized that look of grief," Ethan explained.

Aurora let out a deep sigh as she surrendered the pretense of the young woman with no problem. Ethan was relieved to see Aurora face him with a grateful smile instead of an irritated scowl. "You're right. On my way here I got some bad news about someone I worked with. I'm just having a harder time getting through it than I thought," Aurora confessed.

Ethan looked into Aurora's eyes with nothing but genuine sympathy. "I'm sorry."

"Thank you," she said, regarding Ethan's compassion with a kind smile.

"We could reschedule the tour. It wouldn't be a problem," Ethan suggested.

Aurora shook her head. "No, it's fine. I was taught that the world doesn't stop when someone is lost. They wouldn't want your life to be held up because of them. I know that is what I would want if I passed."

Ethan frowned slightly. "You sound like you've seen a lot of death."

"No, I have been fortunate in that manner, but I was taught by someone who was formally part of the military. He said if you stop for the dead, you will soon join them. Mourn them in your heart and mind, but don't hold your life back because theirs is over."

"That may work when you look at death objectively. When you lose someone important, your life stops even if the world doesn't," Ethan mused, his eyes distant.

"Do you know from experience?" Aurora asked.

Ethan stepped away from her and gestured down a stone walkway, swiftly shifting his demeanor. "We should move on to something less depressing. Let's continue with the tour. I'd like to at least try and take your mind off your worries, even it's only for a while?" Ethan asked, his invitation shifting the topic abruptly.

Aurora's brow furrowed as she met Ethan with a long stare. Ethan held her gaze, hoping she wouldn't pursue her inquiry. He was released when her painted lips formed a sweet smile of surrender. "I'd love to," she answered before following him further into the man-made forest.

They continued to sample the wonders the main dome provided before venturing into the smaller subsections of the greenhouse. From the tropical island paradise that made the heat outside seem refreshing in the desert climate, the greenhouse hosted a living picture of far-off lands Aurora had never seen. They strolled at a leisurely pace from climate to climate, talking about the greenhouse, their likes and dislikes, and their ideas and dreams. They even tasted the much sought-after fruit of the Bohlou tree, a sweet fruit that could only grow from a specific tree in the Island Republic. In this lighthearted outing, Ethan was successful in his goal. Even if it was only for a small time, he believed he had taken her mind off her troubles.

Aurora suddenly halted in place and peered deeply into the trees.

Ethan followed the trail of her gaze, trying to see what had caught her fascination. "What is it?"

Aurora stepped off the path, heading straight for what she had seen. Ethan followed closely behind her as they hiked into the center of the forest before stopping at the base of a large oak tree. A lovely smile crept over Aurora's lips as she stared down at a cluster of wild roses with petals of a vibrant blue hue.

"The Lynnaya rose. I can't believe you have these here." Aurora crouched low to sniff the rich aroma wafting from the stunning flower. "This brings back memories."

"You like this flower?" Ethan inquired.

Aurora nodded. "This flower grows deep in the forest around my family's main house. Back when I still lived there, my father would hike into the forest at the break of dawn on my birthday and set one by my bed. I woke up to that smell every year until I was ten," Aurora mused.

"That's a beautiful sentiment. That's quite a hike to undertake so early in the morning. Your father's a good man to do something so special for his daughter."

Aurora's smile suddenly faded. "My responsibilities have kept me away from home for quite some time. I haven't seen him in years. It's times like this that make me remember how much I miss him."

There was a long silence in between them before Ethan spoke. "I also haven't seen my parents in many years," he admitted, his words dredging up memories and feelings long since buried.

"It's amusing how even as adults we still miss our parents like children," Aurora joked, trying to lighten the mood between them.

"Yeah, it is pretty funny once you think about it," Ethan said through a humored chuckle as the sadness drained away. Ethan glanced at Aurora with a kind smile that gave an unspoken air of gratitude toward her. "I've got a great way to finish off this tour. There's this café on campus that uses the lemons the students grow to make iced tea and lemonade. I often go there on hot days like this. Would you care to join me?" Ethan offered.

Aurora's lips curled into a charming little grin. "I'd love to."

CHAPTER 8

AURORA AND ETHAN sat on the patio of a small café nestled on the edge of the campus's courtyard. The café's walls were every bit a visual splendor, collaged with several different paintings of various diverse scenes and mediums. The floor was a stunning tiled mosaic picturing the sun and the moon in a wonderful display of artistry. There were several petite tables with an assortment of metal chairs, stools, and soft sofas spread throughout the room surrounding the server's counter at the back. A wide canopy provided the patio with much-needed shade from the harsh sun as a refreshing breeze wafted past them. They sat comfortably, enjoying the tall glasses of iced tea as well as each other's company. They chatted about their mutual likes, dislikes, views and opinions until Ethan fell silent.

"Is something wrong?" Aurora asked.

"I must apologize to you, Aurora," he admitted. "I made a judgment about you before I even met you. It's just, when I heard that an heiress who was donating money to the school wanted a tour of the greenhouse, I didn't know what to think. I just jumped to the conclusion that this was just a publicity stunt to brighten your image."

Aurora cocked her head to the side with a sly grin. "Do you usually make rash judgments about people, or am I a special case?"

"No, no, it's just . . ." Ethan paused, trying to find the words to defend his character. "Today is a hard day for me. I wouldn't even be here if I didn't need to catch up on work. I guess I was running on a short fuse to begin with. I know there's really no excuse for that kind of thinking, but I hope you'll accept my apology. You're smart and fascinating, and I couldn't have been more wrong."

Aurora grinned. "It's all right. There's a certain amount of gratification knowing I proved the professor wrong."

"In this case, I don't mind being wrong," Ethan retorted with a charming smirk. Aurora shot Ethan a strange glance as if she were pondering the answer to a puzzling question. Ethan's smile quickly shifted to a look of confusion. "What?" he asked.

A sly grin crept over Aurora lips. "You're flirting with me," she accused.

Ethan's cheeks flushed as he erupted into an awkward chuckle. "You are sharp. I was trying to be subtle," he confessed.

"You're very charming, but I'm afraid the point is moot. I'm actually seeing someone," Aurora said, trying her best to shoot Ethan down gently.

Ethan nodded. "I'm surprised that with someone from such an influential background that isn't public knowledge. You guard yourself well from the media. To tell you the truth, until today, I didn't even know the Fallon family had a daughter."

"That's understandable. I had a condition growing up that kept me indoors for the majority of my childhood. My father thought it would be best to keep me out of the media's eye. They centered their focus on my brother, and the media hardly knew I existed," Aurora explained.

Ethan stared at Aurora, his eyes filled with concern. "Are you okay? Have you been cured since then?"

"It's not something you can cure, but I do have it under control now. I'm trying to see and do as much as I can now that I am able. I spent a lot of my time when I was young reading about the world, and now I'm trying to be part of it."

"I'm happy for you," Ethan praised.

"I'm curious, Ethan. Are you like this with all the women you meet?"

Ethan chuckled. "Believe it or not, there aren't many intelligent heiresses coming around the greenhouse. You really can't blame me for trying. I hope I didn't give you the wrong impression of me."

"Not at all. You may be a bit of an opportunist on some level, but all in all, I had a great time. You're a good man, Ethan, and it shows," Aurora said as she reached out a tender hand to Ethan's forearm. As she moved, the delicate fabric of her blouse's sleeve slid up, exposing the stark white bandages around her upper arm.

Ethan's eyes darted to the dressed wound, his relaxed demeanor fading to worry. "What happened to your arm?"

Aurora swiftly pulled her arm back and covered the bandage with her sleeve. She shot a hurried smile to ease Ethan's worry, subtly stalling for time. "Oh that, it's nothing really. I was merely careless in the kitchen, that's all."

Ethan's eyes slowly worked their way back up to lock a strangely intense gaze with Aurora. "It looks pretty bad. Are you okay?"

"Of course. It looks worse than it is, I assure you," Aurora insisted, focused on naturalizing her forced smile.

"You should be more careful," Ethan replied with a stoic calmness that seemed uncharacteristic of what she'd learned of him.

Aurora met Ethan's acute gaze and felt unnerved. She had a faint but persistent feeling that Ethan wasn't buying her story. It was almost as if the eyes staring back at her were not of the charming professor she had spent the last few hours with. These eyes were of a hunter.

Her rational mind took hold, forcing her to realize how ridiculous and paranoid she was being. He wasn't a predator or an enemy; he was simply a professor. Even though there was a possibility that he could be a Knight, there would be no quarrel here. *There's nothing to worry about. Just keep acting naturally,* Aurora repeated in her mind. With a disarming smile, she said, "Thank you for your concern. I'll be sure to be more careful in the future."

A catchy melody sang from Aurora's small purse, cutting the tension like a finely sharpened sword. Aurora shuffled through her purse and pulled out a small cell phone. Its small display showed the name Zander on the caller ID. "Excuse me," Aurora said politely before stepping away from the table and answering the call. "Hello?"

"Miss Fallon, I hope I'm not interrupting your tour, but we really should be on our way if you wish to make your other appointments for the day," Zander's voice spoke through the phone.

"Is it that late already?" Aurora quickly glanced to her small wristwatch, her eyes bulging at the reality of just how much time had flown by. "Oh dear, it's good to see one of us is keeping track."

"It's what I do, Miss Fallon. I'll bring the car around to the gate in a moment."

"Thank you, Zander, I'll be right there." Aurora finished her call and placed the phone back in her purse. She gracefully pivoted to face Ethan with a lovely smile and an offered hand.

"Looks like my time is up. Thank you very much for the tour, Ethan. It was a pleasure meeting you."

Ethan stood up and took Aurora's welcoming hand wholeheartedly. "Pleasure was all mine, Aurora. I hope we can meet again."

"I hope so, too."

CHAPTER 9

COLE LEANED AGAINST the opened doorframe of the patio, the cool summer breeze brushing across his face. The bright evening sun bathed the library in its warm light, forging a dance of shadow and light gliding across the wooden floor. Before him was a lovely view outside the patio. The grounds were outlined by several lush, tall oak trees and decorated by several hedges, plants, and small flower gardens. Many stone walkways spread through the property like blood vessels, all surrounding a circular water fountain ornately carved by marble.

Despite the marvelous vision before him, Cole's mind was miles away, unable to enjoy the beautiful day. He set a contemplative gaze upon a dazzling diamond that was set delicately on a gold band shaped like vines of ivy and cushioned in a red velvet box.

His troubled expression was a window into a mind tangled with questions and possibilities. He thought about the real meaning behind the ring in his hand, what it meant for him, his mission, and his future. Was he doing the right thing, and if so, was it for the right reasons? Every answer he thought he had just gave him more questions, and every action he tried to plan out only awakened more doubt. He had never felt this conflicted.

Then the true irony of his situation came to light, and he couldn't help but chuckle at it. "This is a strange feeling. I've always been so sure of my actions and decisions, but now, all I have are questions and doubts over something as insignificant as this tiny ring." His smile slowly diminished into a disgruntled frown. "It's like a bad joke."

Cole was suddenly snapped out of his pensive daze by a soft rapping at the door. He quickly closed the velvet box and hid it away in his pocket. "Come in," he called.

The door opened slowly to reveal a small-statured maid with honey-colored hair and large brown eyes. She stepped into the room with a shy bow, her hands folded neatly at her front. "Miss Fallon is here to see you, Mr. Iver," the maid announced in a voice that rang like a soft bell.

"Thank you. Send her in," Cole replied politely.

The maid nodded, stepping to the side to allow Aurora to enter. Aurora stepped into the room with a confident stride, her long brown hair cascading freely over her shoulders as the bright sunlight accented its color. The sheer fabric of her light green dress draped attractively over her body's curves, showing off the shapeliness of her calves. Her face lit up with delight when she set her sights on Cole.

Cole returned her smile with a hearty greeting. "Aurora, I was just thinking about you."

"Well, you know what they say, *speak of the devil*," she joked.

"And she shall appear. But in this case it's more like an angel that answered my call," Cole said softly as he gently took Aurora's hand and raised it to his lips to kiss her soft skin. Her cheeks flushed to a rosy hue.

"Would you like some tea for you and your guest, Mr. Iver?" the maid asked.

"We're fine, thank you. You can go," Cole answered. The maid bowed cordially and left the room, closing the door behind her.

Aurora and Cole stood in silence listening to the maid's footsteps fading into the distance before they spoke. "Is it safe to talk here?" Aurora asked.

Cole nodded. "It's safe. This room is checked for bugs every day. Why do you think we always meet in here? It would draw too much attention and take too much time to sweep the entire property, so I just settle for making one room perfectly secure."

Aurora let out a small sigh of relief. "That's good. I don't want my helping to put you in danger."

Cole caressed Aurora's cheek with a gentle hand, his deep blue eyes meeting hers. "My dear Aurora, I know I can trust you, and so I have no worry about our partnership. So don't worry yourself."

"A little worry is necessary to keep safe," Aurora retorted.

Memories of Luna telling him almost that exact same thing the night before flashed through his thoughts.

"Cole," Aurora called.

Cole snapped to attention. "Sorry, dear, I was just thinking how I'm hearing that from more and more people lately."

Aurora shot a critical glare at Cole. "Have you ever thought that there might be some truth to it?"

Cole flashed a wicked smirk. "The way I see it, worrying is a waste of time. I'm sure of my decisions, and I accept the good with the bad, so why bother worrying about it? It won't change anything."

Aurora rolled her eyes at her foolish beloved. "Worry forces you to see danger and stops you from making foolish decisions. It's necessary to be cautious to stay safe."

"When you're too careful, you get nothing done," Cole retorted. His sly smirk swiftly faded when he saw the anger swelling in Aurora's eyes. The last thing he wanted was to spend their time together arguing. He threw up his hands in surrender. "I'm sorry, Aurora. Let's talk about something else."

Aurora nodded. "How was the mission? Did you get the data?" she asked.

"It went well. We won the duel and retrieved our prize without loss on either side," Cole summarized.

"And was the data useful?"

Cole shrugged. "Don't know yet. It's encrypted, and very well, I might add. But I have the means to deal with that speed bump. It should be cleaned up by tomorrow," Cole assured confidently.

"The disc was encrypted!" she blurted in surprise. "Why do you think they did that? Why would Claymore and Morgan put the information up if they didn't want us to have it? Why encrypt it so well?"

"It may just be a precaution to buy time in case our enemy got ahold of it," Cole reasoned.

Aurora let out an uncertain breath as she crossed her arms over her chest. Cole recognized the anxious look in her stance. She wouldn't openly question the actions of a potential ally, but he could tell she wasn't entirely convinced. "That makes sense," she half-heartedly agreed.

"Don't worry. Even if Morgan didn't trust us completely, we have it now, and come tomorrow, we will know what he knows. Besides, it's probably a good sign that it's encrypted so well," Cole mused.

"Why's that?"

"Morgan had a fairly sophisticated encryption to protect the information and also insisted on challenging my Knight for it in spite of her reputation. You don't protect something like that unless it's very valuable," Cole reasoned with a confident smirk, his eyes showing the excitement of his breakthrough.

"Reputation?" Aurora asked.

Cole nodded. "Luna has a bit of a reputation among the other Knights. Many have heard of her prowess in battle and the power of her abilities. Yet Morgan still challenged us."

Aurora's expression lit up with what Cole thought was pride. He concluded that she was merely glad he was in the right hands. "So what you're saying is that he wouldn't risk gambling his Knight against a superior opponent and encrypting the data if the information wasn't worth it."

"Precisely, if I'm right, this may be just what we need to close the book on Lexus. We might be celebrating very soon."

Aurora laid her index finger gently on Cole's lips and locked her gaze on his. "Don't get ahead of yourself, Cole. Things are hardly ever as easy as you think. If Lexus is as threatening as you say, she won't go down without a fight." Her fingers glided tenderly to Cole's neck as he noticed an unspoken weariness and grief in her forlorn eyes. "Did you hear about Morgan's death?" she asked.

Cole's expression drew grave as he broke from Aurora's stare. "Yes, I heard about it and sent his family my condolences. We did some business together a while back so it shouldn't seem suspicious. But it wouldn't change anything if it did raise questions. He was a good man, and I feel for his family."

Aurora slipped her fingers between his tenderly, trying to ease his pain. "You don't think it was just a heart attack, do you?"

Cole shook his head. "Would've been nice if he had just died peacefully in his sleep, but I doubt that's the case. From all the amazing things I've seen a Knight do, it's not that unlikely that they could disguise murder as a simple heart attack. We can only hope that Lexus is still playing by the rules."

"I'm sorry."

Cole turned his gaze back to Aurora with a somber complexity she'd hardly seen from him. "Aurora, do you regret me bringing you into all this?"

"Of course not," Aurora answered instantly.

"Honestly?"

"Cole, when you told me what was really going on in your life and the dangers you had to face, I was afraid for you. The whole idea of a war fought by people with extraordinary powers under everyone's noses seemed so unreal. But my fear lessened when you asked me to help you. It actually made me very happy. The fact that you were able to trust me enough to let me into your life, it made me realize how much being able to help you has meant to me. I've decided that I'd do anything I could to get you through this," Aurora proclaimed lovingly.

"Why do you want to help me?" Cole whispered as he moved his body closer to hers.

Her breath felt shallow, and her cheeks flushed with a rosy hue as Cole locked his piercing blue eyes with hers. "Because I love you."

The raw intensity of Cole's stare suddenly diminished into surprise at her answer. That reaction stretched into a long silence. "I'm sorry," Aurora stammered, stepping away in embarrassment. "I apologize. It just slipped out," she continued, her words spilling out in a panicked stammer.

Without another word, Cole wrapped his arms tightly around her, sweeping her into a deep kiss. He could feel her body surrender to his embrace, letting out a muffled moan of pleasure beneath her lips.

Cole slowly parted from her lips while gently caressing her soft cheek. "Marry me," Cole whispered.

Aurora's blissful smile dropped and her eyes bulged. All she could muster in response was a simple, "What?"

"Marry me, Aurora," Cole repeated.

Aurora abruptly stepped back and turned away from Cole's wanting stare. She swallowed hard to regain her composure. "Do you know what you are asking? Have you thought carefully about this?"

Cole sauntered to Aurora, tracing his hand from her neck to the small of her back. "Is that a no?" he asked.

"No, that's not it!" Aurora protested as she immediately spun to face him again. Aurora's words fell short when she was met with Cole's awaiting gaze. Her eyes shifted frantically from side to side, as if searching for what to say. "Cole, it's not that I don't want to marry you. Far from it actually. It's just that I need to be sure that you know fully what you are asking. I need to know that you won't be regretting this later."

The uncomfortable tension was hastily broken when Cole broke out in joyous laughter. Aurora raised an eyebrow at her beloved's odd behavior. "Did I miss something?" she snapped.

"No, no, it's nothing. I was just thinking about how you've got to be the most caring individual I have ever known." His laughter soon extinguished as he regained his composure. He reached into his pocket and took a knee, his hand holding hers in a tender embrace. A tiny gasp came out of Aurora as Cole presented her with the dazzling diamond ring. "You see, Aurora, I've actually given this quite a bit of thought over the last while. I know what I want, and I want this. So what do you say? Will you, Aurora Fallon, marry me?" Cole asked once again.

Cole could see behind Aurora's sapphire eyes her mind was going in circles, thinking of every aspect and possible outcome of the situation. He'd come to know that contemplative gaze all too well. As long as he'd known Aurora, she would always take the prudent amount of time to fully think through a problem before acting. His recent question was no exception.

The room lit up for Cole when Aurora's thoughtful stare turned into a bright smile that rivaled the radiance of the diamond. "Yes, yes, of course I'll marry you."

CHAPTER 10

DAMON LEXUS SAT with a tense posture in the high-backed, leather chair in her office. The room was dark, only illuminated by the golden rays of the setting sun. The anxious tapping of her index finger on the glass top of her desk reflected an inner impatience and an air of deep thought. In her other hand, she gripped a vicious curved dagger that emanated a sickly green glow. The restless atmosphere she had created for herself cultivated an intense mood Damon liked to have when dealing with her Knights.

The gentle caress of a summer breeze shook Damon from her trance. She swung her chair to the source and saw an open window. "My time is extremely valuable. I strongly suggest that in the future, you remember that when I summon you," Damon belittled as she stepped across the room to shut the window.

Out from the shadows crept a domineering but feminine form clad in black leather from her tall boots to the dark hood that shrouded her face in mystery. "I apologize, Master," the woman said in a smooth but chilling voice. In a practiced and respectful motion, she pulled her hood down to address her superior. The dismissal of darkness revealed the woman's unnaturally green eyes and dark mosslike hair that fell untamed to her shoulders. The tar black of her thin lips were a vibrant contrast to her sickly pale skin, adding depths to her serious demeanor when addressing her Master. Her features carried a strange personification of death and decay.

Damon moved at a slow saunter to settle back down in her chair, her intense eyes acknowledging her Knight with a strong sense of their standing. "Actions speak louder than words, Venom. I have a mission for you."

"What are your orders, Master?" Venom asked in a respectful tone with a slight bow of her head.

"Due to Claymore's betrayal, the evidence we used as bait has fallen into Iver's hands. Alias is using her position in his household to find it, but if she is unable to, I want you to force the location from him. I trust you can do this for me."

Venom let Damon's orders sink in, and she thought out the plan and its implications. "Attacking a Master outside of the Order is a violation of the Code. Even if Alias were able to find the drive, Iver would be wise enough to know we were behind its disappearance, and he may go to the Hand Council. How do we plan on accomplishing this mission without bringing on the Council's judgment?" Venom asked.

Damon flashed her Knight a knowing smirk, assuring her servant with a glance that she was certain of her plan of attack. "At this point, we don't know if Cole Iver has read through the evidence yet or not. He poses a continued threat to our mission with or without the evidence. He must be dealt with if we hope to continue."

A look of realization struck Venom's deep green eyes. "I imagine that is why I was called for this mission?"

"All of my Knights are capable of killing, but you alone have what I need for this mission. You have the ability to make it look natural. If you do your job right, his passing will just be a tragic tale of greatness cut short, and all Luna will do is mourn him," Damon explained.

"What if he calls for Luna's aid?"

"Steps are being taken to make sure Iver's attack dog won't interfere."

With a steady stance and a somber bow, Venom took on the weight of her Master's grim orders. "I understand and will fulfill your orders, Master."

Damon rose from her chair and faced her servant, locking her severe glare with Venom's. "Understand this, Venom! It is an absolute necessity that this mission not be connected to me in any way. If you are at all connected to Cole Iver's death, I will dissolve our alliance and you'll be on your own. Is that clear?"

"Yes, Master."

CHAPTER 11

THE COOL BREEZE of the waning summer day carried with it the refreshing smell of the trees around Aurora's home, but the wonderful scene before Aurora failed to catch her attention. She sat on the wide railing of the large balcony lost in thought with her eyes fixated on the lovely jewel on her finger.

The memory of Cole's eyes when he asked her to marry him kept haunting her. She thought she had seen hesitation in the man she always knew to be so sure of himself. Why did he make such a serious decision if he wasn't sure about it? Or was she just imagining the whole thing?

She wished he would look at her the way he looked at Luna. The way he talked with her, looked at her, interacted with her, there was desire in all of it. Although she wasn't sure if his yearning was for Luna or the power she possessed. Was that the source of his hesitation? Did he have real feelings for Luna? The aggravating situation was doing nothing but tie a knot in Aurora's stomach.

A light tap on her shoulder sprung Aurora from her trance. She turned to see a young man with wavy brown hair and sapphire-blue eyes. "Penny for your thoughts?" he asked to catch her attention.

Aurora met the young man with a familiar eye and a wide smile as she hopped off the railing into his arms. "Adonis!" she called happily as she hugged her twin brother. "When did you get in?"

"This morning. I took an overnight flight. Tiring, but it gets the job done," Adonis explained.

"How was the Island Republic?"

"Hot, and unfortunately, my business isn't quite done yet. I have to go back the day after tomorrow," Adonis replied with an aggravated groan. "I could've stayed there, but this is the only free time I've had in longer then I care to imagine, and this is how I want to spend it."

Aurora smiled ear to ear. "I'm so happy to see you. It's been so long. I've hardly seen you since you fully took over the family estate."

Adonis sighed. "I know, but that's my duty to the family. I am the heir to the name and you are the heir to the sword. I have to keep our family's high status to the rest of the world. You're lucky your responsibilities keep you in one place. Traveling constantly is exhausting," Adonis complained, leaning heavily against the railing.

Aurora stood beside her weary brother. "At least you can experience it. Sometimes it feels as if I'm merely in the world and not a part of it."

Adonis's eyes turned down from Aurora's gaze, a trace of shame lining his expression. He wrapped a comforting arm around his sister's shoulder and replied with a pensive nod. "You're right. I'm sorry."

"It's all right. I'll get my chance," Aurora promised with a confident smile.

"By the way, I got you something from the Republic," he said before reaching into his bag and pulling out a familiar red fruit. "I hope you like it. The fruit only grows on a small island in the Republic on a tree called—"

"The Bohlou tree," Aurora interrupted, remembering the kind professor who gave her the same precious fruit.

"You've heard of it?" Adonis asked.

Aurora nodded. "I must be extremely lucky. Such a rare treat, and I will have had the privilege of tasting it twice."

"Oh right, you're donating to the university, aren't you?" Adonis determined. "Did you like the greenhouse?"

"It's beautiful. I can understand why you spent so much time there."

"It's one of the only quiet rooms on campus. Mostly because students weren't allowed to loiter, but I was always good at hiding. They're also really touchy about the Bohlou fruit. They must really appreciate your donation."

"I guess you could say I had an inside man. One of the professors at the school, Ethan Chang, gave me a tour of the greenhouse. He was very accommodating, showed me all the greenhouse had to offer."

"Ethan Chang. That's a name I haven't heard in a while. I almost forgot that along with being the history professor he helps run the greenhouse. How is he?" Adonis asked.

"He's doing well as far as I could tell," Aurora answered. The memories of the kind professor bubbled to the surface of her mind, regrettably accompanied by the image of his intense stare when he set his eyes on her wound. "Adonis, did you ever notice anything out of the ordinary about him?" she asked, struggling to gather the words to describe the strange feeling she had gotten from him in that moment.

Adonis raised an eyebrow at her unusual question. "What do you mean?"

"The feeling that he's more than who he says he is."

They sat in a short silence as Adonis pondered the question. He shrugged and then faced Aurora with a questioning look. "Not really. Why do you ask?"

Aurora debated continuing with her concerns, but she just couldn't shake that strange feeling from her mind. "It's probably nothing, but when he and I were talking he saw a wound I had received in battle and asked about it."

"He was just concerned. To a normal person, the everyday wounds a Knight receives would seem very serious," Adonis reasoned.

"That's not the part I'm worried about. When I lied and told him I cut myself in the kitchen, it was like he saw right through it," Aurora explained.

"Are you sure you didn't let your guard down for a moment?" Adonis asked.

Aurora shot him an irritated glare. "I've had years to perfect this persona. I would never let it down, especially in front of someone I'd just met," she snapped. Adonis threw up his hands in surrender. "It was as if he had more of a trained eye than a simple professor. For that moment, his eyes were like those of a trained soldier."

Adonis's brow furrowed, and he stroked his chin. "I think I might know what you're talking about. When I would hide in the greenhouse no one ever saw me . . . I think."

"What does that have to do with Ethan Chang?" Aurora asked.

"A couple times when he would pass me, he would look straight at where I was hiding as if he could see me when no one else could. But then he would just look away and continue walking. I'm not sure if he actually saw me or if he was just looking in that direction." The two siblings stood in consideration about their common acquaintance. "Don't worry, Aurora. I doubt he is what you think he is."

"How can you be sure?" Aurora asked.

"In the time I've known him, there were no signs of erratic behavior, and he was almost always at work. I hardly ever saw him go home or have a life outside the university. As far as I know, he only took one day off a year," Adonis explained.

"Only one day. What was it for?"

Adonis shrugged his shoulders. "As far as I know, he never told any of the students. Something about family matters, I think."

Aurora felt more at ease as she reasoned out the facts. "It would be almost impossible to keep up a busy career life while being a Knight. I suppose you're right. I'm making too much of this."

"Glad I could put you at ease." Adonis then grabbed Aurora's hand and looked down at the diamond ring on her finger. "Now, on to a much bigger issue. Is this what I think it is?" Adonis asked with a wry smirk painted across his face.

Aurora quickly broke eye contact. "That all depends on what you think it is."

Adonis's wry smirk stretched into a wide smile. "It's an engagement ring, isn't it? I didn't even know you were seeing someone. What's his name?"

Aurora took in a deep breath as she built up the courage to tell Adonis the truth. She knew she couldn't hide it from her family for long but all the same, she wasn't looking forward to the backlash that would ensue. "Cole Iver," she answered in a tiny voice.

There was a long uncomfortable silence between them, and Adonis's bright smile vanished. "Cole Iver? Master Iver? Our Master?" Adonis asked, hoping there was some other Cole Iver out there. His distant hope was dashed at a quick nod from Aurora. "Aurora, what were you thinking?" he shouted in a harsh tone.

"I'm sorry, I didn't at all see this coming and I got . . . caught up in the moment." Aurora explained trying desperately to defend her actions.

"Caught up in the moment! Aurora, this is serious! How does he even know you as Aurora?"

"We met at a charity event, and it just continued from there," she explained.

"Why did you continue to see him?" Adonis berated.

Aurora fell silent, looking at her brother with eyes as serious as death. "You know why, Adonis."

Adonis's face softened with sympathy at her situation, but was simultaneously weighed down by his family's duty. "Aurora, I can't imagine how lonely you must have been back then. You must have been terrified of that power flowing through you, and the way father cut you off from us . . . it wasn't right of him to do that to you. I regret so much that I wasn't there for you. For that I am deeply sorry."

The gentle touch of Aurora's hand steadied Adonis demeanor as she tried to take away the guilt in his heart. "It's all right, Adonis. Father was right in the end. Without control, I was a danger to everyone around me. But it's different now. I have the control I need. I won't be alone anymore."

"I wish it were that simple, Aurora, but it's not. You know the Code backward and forward. It's engraved into who you were raised to be. The two worlds can't touch, and the Master is part of that world," Adonis reasoned. "If the Hand Council finds out . . ."

"If they do find out, I will accept their punishment," Aurora answered quietly, her head held low.

"What if they go after Cole?" Adonis asked.

"Cole doesn't know I'm Luna. He shouldn't be blamed for my actions." Aurora jumped to Cole's defense, her eyes blazing with defiance.

"You have to stop this, Aurora," Adonis demanded.

"I won't," she snapped, her quiet shame morphing into an angry stubbornness. "I have given so much of myself to the Code, to my title, and to my training. He's the only thing I have ever wanted. You can't ask me to give that away as well."

Adonis sighed. "Aurora, be reasonable. The punishment from the Hand Council won't be just a slap on the wrist. They could brand you a Rogue and have you hunted. Why is this so important that you would risk that?"

Tears started to form in Aurora's eyes at the thought of having to give up her love for Cole. She desperately searched for the words to make Adonis understand. "When I first met him as his Knight, he told me a story about a Knight and her Master from long ago. Instead of simple obeying her Master's orders, she worked together with her Master as equal partners to help change things for the better."

"Cole then told me that was what he wanted, a partnership, not a servant. He told me his dreams and plans for a bright future, and I could see it so clearly. His words gave me strength to let go of my fears and become the Knight he deserved. I saw a future for the first time since my powers had manifested. When I met him as Aurora, he captivated me with those same dreams, and I was happy when he asked for my aid. I couldn't stop seeing him, and I never want to stop. I love him, Adonis," she confessed.

Adonis's anger and frustration parted like the clouds after a storm leaving only pity for his sister's lonely heart. Adonis smiled weakly and gently wrapped his arms around her. "Then why did you look so sad?"

"I'm not sure Cole really wants this," Aurora admitted.

"What do you mean?"

"I think he may be in love with Luna."

Adonis stared at Aurora with a confused expression. "But you're Luna."

Aurora shook her head. "Not to him. As a Knight, you don't just have to play the part of two different people; you have to be two different people. There can be no crossing over. Personal traits from one persona cannot exist in the other even though they both make one person. Cole may care for Aurora, but the look he gives Luna is unmistakable. It's a look of passion and desire that he never showed Aurora. Even though the traits he loves in Luna are part of the whole, he can't see that in Aurora. Cole is intelligent and perceptive. If I were to be myself around him, he would see what I really am."

"Would it really be that bad if he found out?" Adonis queried.

Aurora's eye bulged with surprise at how Adonis could even suggest something like that. "What are you saying?"

"Why don't you tell him the truth?"

"I couldn't. The Master cannot know the identity of the Knight," Aurora quoted.

"I think it's a little late to be strict about the Code in this matter, Aurora. The way I see it, you only have three options," Adonis said, laying out his plan. "You could leave Cole and stay being his Knight. You could marry him, but live a lie, hiding what you really are from your own husband. Or you could tell him what you really are and hope for the best." He gave her a steady hand and reassuring smile.

Aurora thought carefully about her brother's argument. She always had it set in her mind that Cole could never know she was his Knight. Listening to a logical thinker like Adonis break that problem down in such a way made her see through the barriers. The once unthinkable act seemed to be a viable option. Her lips curled into a joyous smile as she looked to the darkening sky with new hope. "Do you really think it could work if I told him?" Aurora asked.

"I won't lie to you, Aurora. There are a lot of risks in this. The Hand Council could find out, or Cole could not take the news as well as you hope. He may not forgive you for deceiving him, but you love him and you shouldn't have to live a lie or in misery. You put your life on hold because of what you are; you deserve to follow your heart for once."

"What am I going to say to Father?" Aurora asked, a sense a dread apparent in her voice.

"I'll talk to him. You just worry about how you're going to break the truth to Cole."

Aurora felt an inner delight that she hadn't felt in some time. What she was doing was risky and unheard of, but it could lead to something she had only dreamed about. To be with Cole, not as Aurora or Luna, but as herself. It was more than she could've hoped for. "Thank you, Adonis."

CHAPTER 12

THE DEEP RUMBLING of thunder echoed against the thick, blackened clouds that blanketed the sky. The few droplets that fell to the earth were only a precursor to a heavy downpour as a bright flash of lightening darted across the sky. Cole stared into the raging storm through the rain-soaked window of his sitting room, absentmindedly fastening his silver cufflink.

Cole watched the progression of the weather with a sinking feeling in the pit of his stomach. *The storm's moving faster than I thought. I hope Aurora makes it to the restaurant safely,* Cole fretted.

Cole's mind rolled with turbulence like the thunderstorm, but he was unsure of its source. Was he truly worried about Aurora's safety or was he uneasy about the potential change in his future? This engagement was going to alter his life as a civilian and as a Master. It could vary the entire way he'd fight this battle. There was great change on the horizon, but was it for the better?

Cole's train of thought was abruptly derailed by a soft knocking at the door. "Come in," he answered, turning to the entrance.

The door opened to reveal Cole's honey-haired maid. "Hello, sir," she greeted sweetly.

"Hello, Laura. I'll be stepping out for the night," Cole expressed. "My plans tonight are too important to be held up by the weather."

Laura smiled warmly as she stepped into the room. "I've heard. Congratulations, sir, on your happy engagement. The rest of the staff and I are very happy to see that you're settling down with a nice woman. She is a delightful girl. Will you be meeting her at the restaurant?"

Cole glanced over to the wall clock. "The reservation is in about an hour, and that's if she's not held up by the weather," Cole congratulated.

Laura grasped Cole's hands in hers. "I really meant it, sir. I am glad that you have found happiness. I hope the best for you both," Laura praised.

"Thank you, Laura. I appreciate your enthusiasm," Cole said, returning her caring smile with his own.

Laura released his hands and gave a small curtsy. "Well then, I'll leave you to your night. Have a pleasant evening," she said before exiting the room as quietly as a church mouse.

Cole turned his attention back to his cufflink for only a moment before his peaceful preparation was shattered by a frightened scream from the hall.

His heart leaped in his chest as he dashed toward the doorway to the source of the terrified wail. Waiting for him in the sitting room was a sinister figure shrouded in black clothes. As the intruder slowly stepped from the shadows, the dim light of twilight glinted off the multitude of blades strapped to a feminine but domineering form. She held the terrified Laura with a tight grip and a vicious blade pressed against her neck.

Cole's hands balled into fists as he fought hard to suppress the raw panic that threatened to surface. He had to stay calm, for Laura's sake. "Who are you?" Cole asked, his tone as flat as he could manage.

"My name is none of your concern," the intruder snapped in a womanly but eerie voice. "And don't even think about trying to call your Knight. If I see a flicker come from that ring, I will kill her."

"What do you want?"

"Where's the drive?"

"What drive are you talking about?" Cole bluffed, using every possible muscle to keep his expression composed. With a violent jerk of her blade toward Laura's vulnerable throat, Cole's calm facade was shattered and the terror he felt inside was dragged to the surface. But the intruder's sudden movement and show of power let a lock of moss-green hair fall over her face and into Cole's line of sight. The strange hair color summoned from his memory a piece of information he had studied on his enemies' Knights. His eyes followed the theory to the assailant's left hand. The fingers were misshapen, as if they were more like talons tips with ink-blank claws. Cole swallowed hard as the gravity of the situation weighed down on him.

"Don't play games with me, Cole Iver," she threatened.

Cole's frantic eyes sped between the knife and the deformed hand, not knowing which of them posed more of a threat. His heart raced and his mind searched for a plan among the spiral of panicked emotions. His gaze suddenly settled on Laura's tearstained eyes and a wash of guilt fell over him. She was just an innocent girl, in a dangerous situation because of him and his mission. No matter what he would lose that night, he had to get her to safety.

"It's going to be okay, Laura. I'll get you out of this," Cole reassured.

The intruder tightened her grip. "Not if you don't give me what I came here for."

"Help me," Laura begged between frightened sobs.

"I don't have all night! Where is the drive?" the intruder demanded in a harsh tone. She increased the pressure of the blade against Laura's sun-kissed skin as a small droplet of blood painted the knife's tip.

Laura erupted into terrified screams that shook Cole to his core, dragging him over the line of indecision and forcing him to act. "Wait! Stop!" Cole pleaded.

The intruder loosened the pressure of her weapon and gave Cole her attention. "Are you going to give me what I want?"

"You're one of Damon's Knights. Venom, right?" Cole asked.

"Why do you say that?"

"You're hair color and your hand. I took it upon myself to learn as much as I could about Damon's Knights. I could recognize all her minions by sight."

"Are you trying to stall for time?"

Cole raised his empty hands in a passive gesture. "I just want to reason with you. What you're doing is a grave violation of the Hand Council's laws. Even if you were ordered to do this by your Master, Damon might get a slap on the wrist, but they'll be out for your head. The death of a civilian will just add to the charges. It's not worth it."

"If I leave now then my betrayal of the Code will be for nothing."

"No one has to know what happened here. If you walk away now, that is where it will end. I will take no action against you, and no one needs to know."

"I won't abandon my mission!" Venom spat with a stubborn finality.

"Then let Laura go. She has nothing to do with this. Please," Cole begged.

"Tell me where the drive is, and I'll let her go, but if you keep stalling . . ." Venom's threatening words were underlined by a promised threat as she slowly started to move her deadly talons for Laura's neck.

Cole knew the dangerous power Venom held in that crooked hand, and that fact caused his heart to pound faster and faster with every inch she moved toward Laura's body. He was out of time and options. He had no hope in taking on Venom by himself, and if he moved to summon Luna, Venom would kill Laura on the spot. The importance of the information they had recovered was immeasurable. Cole had seen a portion of the contents, and he was certain of its gravity. He had risked his Knight to obtain it and wouldn't hesitate to put his own life on the line to protect it. But no matter what impact the intelligence on the drive may have on his mission and their potential future, it wasn't worth the life of an innocent girl. He had to push away the possibilities of his mission and concentrate on the reality before him.

"Stop!" Cole announced his surrender. His shoulders drooped with the heavy weight of his actions. "In the downstairs game room there is a large clock on the wall. If you turn the hour hand right to five o'clock, the door to the panic room will open. The drive is plugged into the computer in that room. It should be done decrypting the data by now. Please, just take it and go."

"Good choice," Venom spat as she released her grip on Laura and shoved her toward Cole.

Laura stumbled forward into her employers waiting arms, her breath rushing from her in frightened gasps.

But the moment she fell into Cole's caring embrace, the facade of the terrified housemaid faded like a mirage disappearing into the desert. In a swift action that took Cole completely by surprise, Laura snatched his hand at the wrist and swept it to his back, jamming his arm up with a painful jerk. Before Cole could even think of retaliation, she grabbed his other arm and held it firmly in place.

"Hold him still," Venom instructed, swiftly closing the distance between them. She took a firm hold of his golden locks of hair and yanked his head forward, exposing the back of his neck.

"What is this? Let go of me!" Cole protested, struggling against the hands that held him captive. A short yelp of pain erupted from him as he felt a sharp sting at the back of his neck.

With everything inside him, he concentrated on calling Luna to his aid with the mental link every Master shared with his Knight, but his calls went unanswered. He felt a strange distance from the connection that was always close at hand. He flailed and fought to break free until his vision started to blur and a powerful fatigue washed over him, leaving his body as malleable and weak as a newborn kitten. His head swam in a torrent of dizziness as he was carefully lowered into a soft chair. His body slumped back into his seat helplessly, and he could only stare, watching the horrible events unfold. He tried calling for Luna once more but was only met with the same dreadful result.

"What is happening?" he asked himself. In a search for answers, his eyes wandered to his right hand and discovered his naked ring finger. The silver ring he wore, the beacon that tethered the mental link to him, was missing. His eyes were drawn to a glint of metal in Laura's hand. The truth of her betrayal was brought to light as the familiar image of his sweet, honey-haired employee faded away before his very eyes. The golden shine of her hair receded to a snowy white and the soft hazel in her eyes morphed to an inhuman lavender. The hue of her sun-kissed complexion bled from her body to a porcelain pigment.

Few knew the woman before him by her appearance, but Cole knew her by her unique abilities. "Alias."

Alias's lips stretched into a satisfied smirk as she flaunted the silver ring she had stolen. "I thought this piece was a bit feminine for a man, so I took it off your hands . . . literally," Alias confessed; her voice sang like a soft bell. "We wouldn't want your attack dog to interrupt us."

"Where's Laura?" Cole demanded with all the authority he could present in his weakened state.

"She's been unavailable for the last few weeks. I was kind enough to fill in for her. No one ever realized she was gone," Alias revealed. A sadistic pride in her performance was clearly painted over her expression.

A burning anger erupted from deep in the core of Cole's being, but his body would not respond to his fury. He could only grit his teeth and meet his enemy with eyes filled to the brim with contempt. "You're a monster!" Cole spat. "She had nothing to do with this!"

"She was a way in. You should've thought about that before you challenged us." Alias responded to Cole's defiant eyes and verbal lashing with smug, self-righteous reasoning.

With a keen eye on their mission and a steady hand on Alias's shoulder, Venom pulled her back to the task. "Alias, stop playing with him. We need to complete our mission without being discovered. Time is of the essence."

Alias rolled her eyes at her comrade. "Don't worry. He said he was meeting his girlfriend at the restaurant. It will be hours before she comes looking for him. We have time to savor this."

"We shouldn't put the mission in jeopardy because you want to play with your food. Even you revealing your real face was an unnecessary risk. You just wanted the dramatic reveal."

"Why can't you just enjoy our victory?" Alias asked.

"We can celebrate when victory is assured, not before," Venom lectured. "Now, can you please just go get the data drive? We can't risk him having an unannounced visitor."

"Very well. I'll let you know when I get it, and we can get rid of him," Alias conceded with a heavy sigh before exiting the room.

A stale silence hung in the air as Cole faced his attacker with a steady calm but, unfortunately for him, nothing else. "You're going to kill me, aren't you?"

Venom met Cole's question with an unwavering stare from under her dark hood. "It's can't be helped. You know who we are and who our Master is. We can't have this linked back to us."

"The Hand Council will find out what happened here, and when that happens, Lexus will throw you away to save herself."

Cole could see the tension rise in Venom's hands as they balled into tight fists. He wondered if she was biting back anger or fighting back the fear that he had a point. "You don't know that."

"I know you wouldn't risk me dying before you got what you came for," Cole deduced. "You drugged me to make me more pliable, but you haven't used the venom from your hand on me yet."

"It would've been foolish to risk losing the information you have. You could've been lying earlier."

"I meant what I said earlier. You could just walk away from this. Are your Master's goals worth your life? You won't be able to cover this up." Cole formed his words as calmly as he could manage to formulate his last plea of reason to Venom. They weren't dangerous, but his words were the only weapon at his disposal now. As long as he was still breathing, he had to try and survive.

Venom turned her gaze down, as if she were considering his proposal. That brief moment of indecision summoned a small twinge of hope for Cole's dark situation. Without a word, Venom stepped up to Cole and knelt to be face-to-face with him. She reached up with a slow motion and pulled back her heavy hood, revealing a face that sent chills down his spine. With eyes like pools of green toxins, lips as black as tar, and a sickly gray skin framed with a untamed mane of mossy-green hair, her appearance embodied the essence of death and decay.

"I will tell you this once and only once. I will never betray my Master. I believe in what she is doing, and I will sacrifice anything and anyone to see her plans realized. As for the Hand Council, my venom will make your death look natural, and Alias and I are the best at covering our tracks. There will be nothing for the Hand Council to find. Your death will be an untimely tragedy, and that's it. Now be quiet!" Venom preached, her voice carried a frigid finality in it that made his mind tremble with terror.

The thick tension that blanketed the room suddenly cut when Alias stepped back through the door, her face twisted with frustration. "We have a problem."

Venom rose and turned to her comrade. "What is it?"

"The drive is empty. It's a decoy," Alias informed her partner.

"He lied!" Venom shot a cold glare at Cole.

"No, the encryption on the drive was the same as the other fake drive Claymore gave me. He double-crossed both of us."

Those words dragged Cole's heart down like an anchor, and his face reflected the sting of Claymore's betrayal and the hopelessness it brought with it. Why would Claymore give them a fake? Where was the real drive?

In the shadow of Cole's bleak future, all he could do was hope that Claymore knew what he was doing and that Luna would find the strength to go on without him. He was uncertain what the future would hold for those he believed in and those he held dear, but he was sure of one thing: he would not see tomorrow.

CHAPTER 13

THE RAIN PELTED the windshield of Aurora's car as she idled in the driveway of Cole's home. She sat in the driver's seat, nervously tapping her fingers on the steering wheel. Unfortunately, the wait was doing little to fortify her courage. Aurora shook her head to push the worries and doubt from her mind. She pulled down the vanity mirror and made a quick study of her appearance. Her eyes wandered to the clock, and she knew she couldn't linger. She was supposed to meet him at the restaurant, but with the confession she was going to deliver, it was best to be done in private. Taking slow, deep breaths to calm her stress, she combed her fingers through her hair and smoothed out her deep-blue satin dress.

"This is no matter to get so nervous about, Aurora," she whispered to herself. "This is just like every other evening you've spent with Cole . . . except this time you'll be telling him that you're Luna." She frowned, the full implications of her chosen path coming to full light, and sending her into a spiraling panic. "Yeah, you're going to tell him you've been lying to him the entire time you've known him. That's a great thing to hear from the woman you just proposed to."

Letting out an aggravated grunt, she let her head fall limp against the steering wheel. Thousands of possible outcomes swirled about her mind in a violent vortex. What was she going to say? How would she say it? How would he react? Would he hate her for lying to him and break off the marriage, or would he understand her situation? Every question, concern, and worst possible outcome struggled in her mind for dominance. It was maddening.

Aurora raised her head from the steering wheel and caught a glimpse of the beautiful diamond she wore, remembering Adonis's words of advice. This was her choice, and she knew in her heart that she was making the best one. No matter what would happen, it was better than living a lie. She would just have to find the words and hope for the best.

She grabbed her purse and a small umbrella to shield herself from the pouring rain and then she hurried to the house. She carefully shifted her umbrella and purse to retrieve her key, but at her soft touch, the door swung open effortlessly. Aurora glared at the door with curious eyes. *That's odd. Why is the door open in this weather?* she asked herself.

Aurora entered the house with caution behind every step but was welcomed only by silence and cold darkness. All she could hear was the roaring thunder and pelting rain upon the windows. There was usually at least one or two of the hired help around the house at any time. Why were all the lights off? Why was there no sign of activity? Aurora continued through the entranceway, slipping off her high heels so her steps would fall without a sound. She searched through the hallowed halls, hoping to find anyone going about their business, but it was in vain. The home of her beloved felt still and empty, like a tomb. Aurora's instincts were screaming at her to tread wearily. Everything was out of place, unusual. Something was wrong.

The silence was suddenly shattered by a bone-cracking scream heard clear over the rolling thunder. It was Cole. Aurora dashed forward as fast as her legs could take her toward the source of the scream. The unbearable cries led her to a sitting room on the far side of the mansion.

She halted mere steps away from the room when she heard the smooth voice of a woman under Cole's painful moans. "Don't worry. The pain might be excruciating, but at least it's a relatively quick death," the woman purred maliciously.

Aurora crept along the wall and peeked through the open door to assess the situation. Her heart began to burn with fury when she saw the brutal scene before her. Cole was slumped back in a chair, his body uncontrollable and limp. A tall woman with dark green hair stood over him. The nails on her hand, which more closely resembled talons, pierced through the flesh of Cole's chest.

Aurora had to resist the urge to jump into action at that very moment. She was unarmed and without her glamour, so she couldn't use her abilities by the rule of the Code. Even if she were to ignore that, she couldn't use her power without the potential of hurting Cole. Her heart sunk into her stomach from the sound of Cole's pained groans. She knew he couldn't take much more of the torture.

Aurora carefully reached into her purse and pulled out a small pistol. It was the only instance where she felt grateful that Zander insisted she carried a weapon when she went out. She placed her purse on the floor and shifted herself into a readied stance before she charged into the room.

"Get away from him!" she bellowed.

The green-haired woman turned to Aurora, her face stricken with surprise, and drew a knife from her vest to attack. The threat was answered by Aurora firing two slugs in rapid succession into the intruder's chest. Venom's body fell back, violently hitting the floor in a limp heap.

"Cole!" Aurora called as she rushed to her beloved's aid. She looked him over, trying to figure out what the intruder had done to him. He sat in a daze, unresponsive to her call. Without knowing the extent of his condition, she dared not move him.

The moment those words left her lips, she saw the form of Cole's cruel fate. Five points on his chest, dark and sickly as if they were infected. Veins black as death were visible under the skin at the source of those points and traveling throughout his body. His once rich and healthy skin had faded to pale gray as if the attacker leached his very life essence from him. Aurora was paralyzed with shock and confusion. No normal person could've done this. This woman had spread this black death with her own hand. What was happening?

As the love of her life struggled to gaze upon Aurora with his tired eyes, the sight forced a gasp to pass from his lips. His eyes, once bright and intelligent, had become weary and sunken, and the whites had been polluted with a nauseous yellow. They were devoid of all hope. He slowly parted his darkened lips and tried to speak. "It's all over. There was nothing on the drive. We have nothing to fight with. You need to run or they'll kill you too! Run and forget all this," Cole pleaded.

Aurora shook her head. "No, I can help you. We'll get you help, and you'll make it through this. I promise." She leaped to her feet and scrambled to the phone in the corner of the room, but the receiver only gave a dead tone. At a frantic pace, she scurried to the hallway to retrieve her purse and the cell phone inside it. As if the universe in its entirety was working against them, the cell phone's display showed a heartbreaking lack of service. She deduced the storm and out-of-the-way location of Cole's home must have been interfering with the phone's reception.

"Dammit!" Aurora cursed as she snapped the phone shut, fighting the urge to smash it on the floor in frustration. "I have to get you to a hospital." Wrapping her arms around Cole's limp form, she braced herself to take on his weight and move him to her car.

Before she could get him up, Cole reached out with a weak hand and clutched Aurora's arm with all the strength he could gather to demand her full attention. "It's too late. Aurora, please! You have to cut yourself off from this, or they'll come after you. You can't fight them."

"Just hold on, Cole. It's going to be okay." Large tears swelled up in her eyes as she begged him to hold on to his fading life.

With a gentle caress of her cheek from Cole's frail hand that somehow still carried its familiar tenderness, Aurora froze in place. He turned her head to lock his eyes with her. Those sickly eyes reflected a deep well of sorrow, the sorrow of a man facing his end with regret. "Forget about me." Cole's words flowed from his lips on a tired breath, his last breath.

That truly terrible moment held Aurora captive in her own shock. All she could do was watch the life drain from her Master's body, unwilling or unable to accept the reality before her. She was trapped in a moment of heartache, and silent seconds that felt like hours. The deep thunder rolled in the sky above, but its bellowing seemed worlds away.

The stillness of her reality was suddenly interrupted by a rustling in the room. Aurora turned to the disturbance to see Venom, pulling herself back onto her feet like an old nightmare coming back to haunt Aurora's dreams.

In a terrifying moment of synchronicity, as Aurora watched Venom's threatening rise, her mind was suddenly flooded with a memory that wasn't hers. Through the link of Master and Knight, she could see his last moments through his eyes, feel the excruciating pain of his death, and see his murderer. The death vision overlapped her perception of the present, filling her mind with the dread and fear he had felt and directed those feelings at his killer in a fury of self-preservation.

"You weren't supposed to show tonight. I'm sorry, but we can't have any witnesses. At least you'll be able to die with him," Venom said as she reached her poisonous talon down toward her promised next victim.

In a move of pure instinct, Aurora leaped away from Venom's attack with Cole's gun in hand. The visions from the past that continued to invade her mind mixed in a confusing haze with the real danger before her. That blind need to survive shattered her warrior's steadiness and left only a feral drive to attack.

She aimed her pistol at Venom, but before she could pull the trigger, Venom kicked Aurora's hand, knocking the gun across the floor. Venom's body flowed from one attack to the next, and she struck down at the disarmed Aurora with her deadly hand.

Aurora dove away from danger and snatched the iron fire poker from its rake. Improvised weapon in hand, she sprung to attack, propelled by her rage. She swung the iron rod with a wild ferocity; but her blind charge drained her warrior's prowess, broadcasting her moves. Venom's body swerved and twisted around Aurora's assault before she grabbed the fire poker at the shaft and pushed hard to pin Aurora against the wall.

They both continued to push against each other in a vigorous struggle until Aurora shoved her knee into her enemy's stomach, breaking the grapple. Venom lurched forward as a strained weave fell from her, and her body was forced to stagger backward.

Aurora dove on the opportunity like a hungry lion dives on meat. She barreled ahead with reckless abandon, slamming all her weight against Venom and forcing her to the ground. The fire poker fell out of her hands and bounced against the floor with a loud clang that was shrouded by the violence. With a grip like a vice, Aurora snatched Venom's poisonous talon at the wrist and slammed it hard against the floor. She then jammed her knee into the elbow of Venom's free arm, leaving her prone and vulnerable as she began to punch Venom repeatedly in the face, her pain and anger radiated from each strike.

Venom's hand scurried over the smooth floor in search of anything that would help her escape Aurora's vicious assault. The tips of her wanting fingers found salvation in the form of the fire poker's polished handle. She swung the improvised weapon with all the strength she could muster and struck Aurora a solid blow on the side of her head.

A painful cry erupted from Aurora's lips as she tumbled onto her back. The freshly opened gash in her scalp pulsated with a throbbing ache. The terror and agony of Cole's death vision and the encroaching fog of her head wound sent her mind spiraling into a disoriented mess. She fought through the confusion to drag herself to her feet. Her instincts drove her forward as she saw the distorted blur of Venom moving to close the distance between them. Aurora stumbled into the dark hallway, striving to regain her focus. She could hear the threatening steps of Venom's advance, each one adding a desperate need to Aurora's struggles.

In the midst of her retreat, the terrifying nightmare of Cole's murder hit its agonizing finale, paralyzing her body as she felt her Master and love slip away. Aurora staggered to the nearest wall to brace herself against the shock when Venom landed a firm kick to Aurora's side, sending her tumbling across the smooth hardwood floor.

That feeling of vulnerability was unlike anything Aurora had felt before. She lay on the cold floor, clutching at her aching ribs and gasping for air, her mind completely taxed from the heartbreaking image she was shown. She wondered for the briefest of moments if she could go on. But as the death vision finally faded and her clouded thoughts began to clear, she was confronted with her present reality. Cole had just been murdered. The agonizing pain of his death was still fresh in her mind, and the one responsible was before her, ready to attack.

A deep hate swelled from the very core of her being. It left her with nothing but a burning urge to act, to strike back against the source of her rage.

Venom reached down with her poisonous claws to deal a deadly blow to her victim when Aurora jumped into action and delivered a solid uppercut to her attacker's jaw. Venom staggered back into a fog, defenseless as Aurora grabbed her by the arm, twisted it with a painful jerk, and snapped it at the elbow. The assassin's excruciating screams echoed through the hallow halls of the empty mansion.

But Venom's agonizing cries fell on deaf ears as Aurora continued her assault without hesitation or remorse. With a powerful battle cry, Aurora spun Venom around and heaved her against a glass patio door. The glass shattered on impact as Venom flew through the door and tumbled like a rag doll across the veranda, broken shards of glass littering the ground around her.

The glass crunched under her feet, and the rain poured down on her as Aurora made her steady advance for the broken Venom. The pain of her feet and soaking body failed to catch her attention as she stared down at Venom, who was writhing in pain on the wet ground.

Aurora didn't know if a reason for Cole's death would quell the red-hot rage smoldering inside her heart, but she still needed to know. "Why? Why would you do this?"

Venom didn't answer her demand. She could only struggle to sit up, holding her broken arm close to her body as the rolling thunder and pelting rain drowned out her pained groans.

That silence infuriated Aurora. "Tell me why! You're a Knight! The Code of honor you're sworn to uphold is everything to us, and you . . . you broke into a Master's home and murdered him. You killed an unarmed man, and for what? You're not a Knight! You don't deserve that title. You're nothing but a common criminal and murderer. So tell me why! Why would do this?" Aurora screamed, her face twisted with a choked frustration.

"Because I was ordered to!" Venom confessed with a powerful cry despite her broken body. She gathered herself and stood proud against Aurora's judgment with a stern composure. "You say I've forsaken my honor, but you're wrong. I'm serving my Master, and that is the true and only purpose of the Knights. I feel no shame for what I've done."

Those words hit Aurora like a freight train, sending her into a speechless stammer. "No . . . shame?" Aurora whispered. "No shame! You break the Code, murder a Master, and then you hide behind Lexus's orders and feel no *shame!*"

Under the barrage of Aurora's verbal lashings, Venom still stood tall, head held high. Whether that proud stature was a product of a sadistic satisfaction or pride delusion, Aurora would never know, but that didn't matter. All that existed in the world to her at that moment was her soul-shattering grief and the cause of it.

Her body began to tremble with a fury and anguish so deep and vast she thought she would drown in it, but instead she used it. She used it to call upon every drop of power she could manifest and reached out, further then she had every before, and found a source of immense power coursing through the sky.

With a fierce cry that embodied her pain, she pulled that power down to the earth to strike down the one who wronged her. A bolt of lightning struck Venom with the blinding force of nature. The night sang with the frightening chorus of the rolling thunder, Aurora's battle cry, and Venom's blood-curdling screams until it fell into an eerie silence and Venom's body crumbled to the ground.

Aurora stared in shock at Venom's smoking corpse as her powerful cry faded. She was only left with the steady pace of the downpour and the faint scent of burnt flesh. Her body began to shake and her stomach started to turn, the gravity of her actions weighing down on her like a lead coat.

She fell to her knees as an overwhelming fatigue coursed through her trembling form. Aurora grabbed at her aching stomach and started to hyperventilate, unable to tear her eyes away from her fallen enemy.

"What have I done?" Aurora asked herself.

Despite her weakened body, she still had her battle-hardened discipline that gave her the strength to pry her gaze away from the grisly scene and forced herself to focus on what she had to do next.

Turning her weary gaze to the house, she thought of Cole's body resting limp in his chair. All she wanted to do was go into that house and be with him, even if it was only to say goodbye. But she couldn't. If he had met his demise in any other way, it would have been different. She could be there for him. Even though Cole was gone, she still felt a need to stay by his side until someone came for him. But Cole was assassinated, and Aurora used her powers to kill the Knight responsible.

Aurora Fallon could not be recorded on the murder scene of Luna's Master and Venom. That would lead her enemies or the Hand Council to connect the dots of her real identity. She had a greater responsibility to the Code and the safety of those close to her. She had to walk away.

She turned and began a slow retreat from Cole's home that wrenched at her heart with each step. The pouring rain ran down her face, hiding her tears.

CHAPTER 14

DAMON STOOD IN cold silence as she stared into the storm-pelted city through the window of her dark penthouse suite. A frightening scowl dressed her expression as she held a curved dagger, the symbol of her and Venom's connection, tightly in her right hand. Her eyes darted to the dainty watch around her slender wrist to see the hour. It was late, later then it should've taken for Alias and Venom to finish the job. Her grip on the dagger tightened and her scowl intensified as she continued to wait with an uneasy posture. A bolt of lightning flashed across the night sky, bathing the room in a flare of white light.

Damon's anxious attitude was compounded by the still presence of Morpheus. His statuesque form obscured by the shadows set her nerves on pins and needles. She felt his cold eyes constantly upon her, watching her every move and patiently waiting to report back to his Master.

The unyielding watch of Morpheus's frigid gaze drove Damon's temper over the edge. She spun sharply and shot an angry glare like a bullet at her observer. "Your continuing presence here annoys me to no end! Leave now!" she hissed.

"My Master wishes to be informed on your progress in this matter as soon as possible," Morpheus replied. His tone was flat and bitterly cold, like a marble slab in winter.

"She will receive my progress when I wish to give it to her," Damon snapped.

"My Master is running out of patience with you and wishes to know of your progress on her terms. She believes you have come up short of late and is losing faith in your ability to produce results."

Damon's scowl intensified, her eyes burning with disgust and fury. "Know your place when you speak to a Master!"

Damon words cracked like a whip, but Morpheus stood his ground, keeping his unwavering stare. "These are my Master's words, not mine," he answered calmly.

"I have some words of my own for your Master," Damon hissed. "Tell her that this is my game we are playing, and she is in it at my sufferance. If she would like to go back to her former snail's pace, she is welcome to . . . but I will not wait for her. She'd do well to remember that fact." Damon spun sharply on her heel and strolled back to the window to stare into the roaring storm.

In midstride, Damon's mind was suddenly flooded with terrifying screams of agony. Her body became racked with intense pain as it started to tremble uncontrollably. Images of Venom's body burning to a charred and unrecognizable piece of flesh scrolled across her vision. She could smell the rank odor of sizzling skin and could hear a horrifying crackling sound. Damon screamed as she threw the dagger to the floor and covered her ears, trying in vain to block out the petrifying cries.

As quickly as the nightmare invaded her mind, it was gone, leaving her with a scarred mind and little breath. Damon focused hard on regaining her composure as they both turned their gaze to the dagger to confirm what Damon already knew.

The dagger emanated a scarlet glow that burned brightly in the darkness then immediately diminished like a candle being snuffed out. The gleam of the dagger blade faded as the metal turned a bleak, ashen black.

"Venom has perished," Morpheus proclaimed.

The blinding agony and soul-shaking fear from Venom's death vision left a terrifying imprint on Damon's mind. She struggled to regain her senses and pull herself back to her feet.

"Shit!" Damon cursed. She sprinted to the table and picked up her cell phone, dialing Alias's number as fast as her fingers could move.

The phone rang only once before it was answered by Alias, her voice carrying a nervous quake to it. "M-Master . . . I . . . ."

"What happened?" Damon demanded with an aggressive tone that spoke volumes to her urgency.

"Venom's . . . Venom's dead," Alias informed.

"I know that. My brain was just bombarded by her death vision, so stop wasting my time and yours and tell me what went wrong!"

"We had to force Cole to tell us where he head hid the drive. He had it decrypted but hadn't look at the results. It was another fake. Claymore pulled one over on all of us," Alias reported.

Damon gritted her teeth and clenched her hand into a white-knuckled fist at the sound of her Knight's report. She knew what that loss would mean to her plans. The endless possibilities of where Claymore could have sent that delicate information put her nerves on a wire's edge. "Where would he have sent the drive?"

"I don't know. It could've been anyone."

"What about Cole Iver?" Damon asked.

"He had nothing more for us. We were going to get rid of him as ordered. I left Venom to finish the job and make it look natural with her toxins but . . ." Alias's voice trailed off for a moment.

"What happened to Venom?" Damon probed, snatching her minion back on task.

"Before I left, I heard what sounded like a struggle coming from that room. I went back and saw Venom and someone else facing off outside. I didn't hear what was said between them but then . . . the woman brought lightning down from the sky and killed Venom with it," Alias explained, a frantic shriek lacing her words.

Damon let Alias sit in a tense silence for a long moment before asking one question. "What did you do after?" The sound of Alias's stunned stammering was the only response so Damon asked again. "Alias, what did you do after?" Her words sliced deeply like a freshly sharped knife.

"I ran," Alias confessed in no more than a whisper.

"You ran!" Damon spat the words from her mouth, as if the taste of them on her tongue disgusted her.

"It was Luna. She must have somehow known her Master was in danger. I don't know how. She pulled lightning from the sky! Bent nature to her will. I couldn't stand up to that!" Alias's words fell into a spiraled rant.

"Alias!" Damon screamed to command her attention. "Listen to me! What Luna did must have been a fluke. Something she was able to do in the moment. She is not some unstoppable force. She is a Knight just like any of you. Now, get a hold of yourself!"

"I apologize, Master. Please forgive me."

"Thank your lucky stars that I don't keep you around for your bravery, but remember this, Alias: if your cowardice gets in the way of my orders again, I'll need to reassess your value as my Knight," Damon warned with an icy finality.

Damon snapped the phone shut as the tension built up inside of her like a volcano. The fury within hit a violent boiling point and she slammed the phone hard against the floor, its broken pieces skidding across the polished surface.

"What happened?" Morpheus inquired; his tone was flat like paper.

Damon leaned hard against her desk, taking in a deep breath to regain her lost composure.

The silence in the room stretched over a long moment before Morpheus continued his query. "What happened with the mission? I need to report back to my Master."

The composure she was struggling to maintain fell apart at Morpheus's requests, and she turned to face him with eyes full to the brim with spite. "I will not be interrogated by another Master's servant!"

Morpheus faced Damon's ire with the same indifferent posture, unshaken by her blustering. "You've received Venom's death vision, haven't you? And you are sure who killed her, so the only question is, was her mission a success or was her death in vain?"

Damon stormed away from his stoic gaze, stepped over to the drink tray on her desk, and poured a stiff drink. "The mission was doomed from the start. Claymore kept the drive from both of us. It could be anywhere."

"What of the Master Iver?"

"His death is the only fortunate detail of this mission. At least no one else will be sniffing around for that evidence with Cole Iver gone," she mused, taking a small sip of her drink.

"What about his Knight? How'd she know this was going to happen?" Morpheus asked.

"Pure coincidence, I suppose. Luck was not on our side."

"Will she simply take on another Master to continue the mission?" Morpheus asked.

Damon lifted the glass to her lips for a bigger sip before shaking her head. "No, she wouldn't take another. I've seen them together and they seemed very . . . close. She would never take orders from another Master."

"That's unfortunate for you," Morpheus warned. "There's blood in the water now. If they were as . . . close as you say, then she will throw the mission away and focus strictly on vengeance."

"She got her vengeance. Venom is dead," Damon argued.

Morpheus's head shook slowly under his pitch-black cowl. "She knows it was on your orders. Even if she doesn't know for sure, that's what she'll think, and for someone looking for someone to blame, a hunch is good enough reason for action."

Damon's chest rolled in a soft chuckle. "You sound like you care about me."

"If Iver's Knight comes after you, she will start look deeper into your actions and those connected to them. That may lead her to my Master."

"I can deal with her," Damon answered with a confident sneer.

"Can you? Are any of your Knights strong enough to take her on? They haven't had much success in the past."

"This is different. The stakes are much higher. My Knights can't afford to fail."

"How did Luna kill Venom?" Morpheus asked.

Damon shot an intense glare to Morpheus, her lip curled into an ugly scowl. "You overstep yourself, Knight!"

"Luna has killed your assassin and has your second-in-command trembling with fear. Can you honestly say you can handle her?" Morpheus pushed.

Her temper was nearing an explosive chorus but halted in its advance when her eyes caught the sight of the ashen-black dagger that was once her connection to Venom. A flash of inspiration shot across her mind like a shooting star that brightened her grim demeanor. She picked it up off the floor and smiled at her newfound plan.

"Maybe not, but I can find someone who can," Damon purred. "Morpheus, do you still have the ear of the Hand Council?"

"Yes, I do. Why?"

"I need you take a message to them on my behalf. Tell them I believe Venom went against my orders to kill Cole Iver, and I fear for my safety. I humbly beg the Hand Council for their protection."

"They will need proof."

Damon gestured to the dagger. "I'll give them this."

"What if Venom told Luna that you ordered her Master's death?"

Damon's lips curled into a self-satisfied smirk. "It will be my word against hers, and I am very persuasive. If we play our cards right, the Hand Council will handle this problem for us."

CHAPTER 15

ZANDER SAT COMFORTABLY at the table in the kitchen of the Fallon mansion. The radio on the counter spread the smooth serenade of Suzy Spruce, a famous jazz musician, from wall to wall. Zander tapped his fingers along with the beat against the table's wood finish and sipped his coffee while watching the storm rage outside. He was thoroughly enjoying his night off and was glad he got to listen to his favorite musician.

The song moved into its exciting and expressive finale before the gruff but charming voice of the male host chimed in. "That was wonderful, Suzy, and we can't wait to hear more at your show."

"I feel the same way. This city has always been great for performing. It houses such a wonderful atmosphere," Suzy said in a voice as smooth as silk.

"Thanks for coming on our show."

"Pleasure is all mine."

"And just a reminder to our listeners, Suzy Spruce will be performing this Saturday at the Terrace Club. There are still some tickets available, but they are going fast so hop to it. That's all for tonight, brothers and sisters. We're going to cap things off with the lovely Suzy Spruce and her new single, 'Lost in the Golden Hue.' I'm your host, Larry Shae, and that's all for tonight."

Once again, the kitchen was filled with the easy sway of smooth jazz. The fierce storm outside summoned the usual aches and pains to his leg that harsh weather often brought. Zander rubbed at his knee to soothe his muscles when suddenly the peace of the music was interrupted by a loud clang from the back door.

Zander crept around the corner and peered down the hallway to the back door. Lightning flashed across the dark sky, framing a rough silhouette in the entrance. Zander flipped the light switch to reveal Aurora stumbling into the house. She carried chunks of mud and wet grass on her bare feet, and rainwater fell with a steady drip from her torn dress onto the floor. Her pale skin was painted with smears of blood from her split knuckles and a painful gash on her forehead.

But what drew forth Zander's worry more than her ragged appearance was the deep sorrow he saw in her vacant stare. It was a chilling expression that echoed an intense trauma and hopelessness. Whatever had happened to her, Zander was certain that it had shaken her to her core.

"Aurora!" he called as he leaped to her aid. "What happened?"

"He's gone. He's gone. I couldn't go back for him. I had to leave," Aurora babbled, maintaining her blank stare forward.

Zander couldn't grasp what she was trying to say. She was giving pieces of a story but no context. He frowned at the harsh wound to her head. A concussion may have been to blame for her incomprehensible behavior.

"Let's get you cleaned up and a bandage on that cut. Then we'll talk." Zander wrapped his steady arms around her shoulders and led her to a soft chair and warm fire in the sitting room.

Aurora sat like a rag doll on the chair, gazing longingly into the fire and wrapping herself in an eerie silence. Her present state filled Zander with a sense of dread that hung off him like a heavy coat. He wanted to know what could've possible put her into such a state, but he couldn't push for the answers he wanted. He tore his eyes away from her and set his mind toward doing anything to help her feel normal again, if that was even possible.

He moved through the house with purpose, gathering all the necessary materials to clean and dress Aurora's wounds and a towel before heading back to her side. With the tender and caring hands that had taken care of her throughout childhood, he wrapped the fresh towel around her slumped shoulders and began to clean her injuries.

"He's dead," Aurora spoke in little more than a whisper.

Zander paused in his labors and devoted his full attention to her words. "Who?"

"Cole. A Knight broke into the house and killed him. I wasn't fast enough to stop it. I failed him," Aurora revealed before her voice broke with emotion and tears began to flow down her cheeks.

Zander pulled her close to him to stand as her rock in her time of need. She let the tears fall freely in an act of weakness only shown to those she trusted the most. She could let her sadness rain down in the safety of her home with a trusted shoulder to cry on.

Moments passed until Aurora was able to calm down and compose herself. "Tell me what happened," Zander asked.

Her eyes trailed off, as if looking to the past to recount the painful memory. "I went to Cole's early to talk to him before we went to dinner. When I came to the door, it was open and the security system wasn't set. With the storm outside it seemed strange that he left it open like that. When I entered the house I didn't see anyone around, and all the lights were off. There was no sign of Cole or the staff until I heard a terrible scream. I ran as fast as I could, but I was too late to stop the Knight that attacked him. He died in front of me. I was too late to help him."

"How do you know the attacker was a Knight?" Zander asked.

"I've seen her before. Her code name is Venom; she's one of the Knights recruited into Lexus's ranks. Her hand had talons that secrete a deadly poison. That's what she used to kill Cole."

Zander's chest heaved in a deep sigh as he held Aurora with a sound stability. "I'm so sorry, Aurora. I can't imagine how you must be feeling right now. How did you get away?"

"I . . . I killed Venom," Aurora confessed.

Zander released his embrace and locked eyes with Aurora. "What did you say?"

"I killed Venom. There was a struggle, and Venom was killed in the fight."

Moments passed as Zander struggled with his reaction to Aurora's intense news. "Aurora, I'm . . . I know you did what you thought you had to, but was Venom's death necessary?"

"Zander, you told me that I had to be prepared to do whatever it took if it meant coming home," Aurora argued.

"I know," Zander said, resting his worried head on his palms as he fought to formulate his words. "It's just that you fought me tooth and nail on that opinion. That stubborn need to keep with your honor was part of who you were. I just hate that you may have lost that."

"I felt him die, Zander!" Aurora shouted, the raw emotion in her words echoed against the walls of the large room. "When he died, I got the death vision. I felt every bit of his pain until the end. He was tortured, Zander. It wasn't quick or painless. It was terrible, and Venom did that to him. The agony of his murder was so fresh in my mind, and I was so angry. I demanded an answer of why Venom would go against the Code and the Hand Council. She admitted she was ordered by Lexus to kill Cole. She admitted it! She said she was proud for doing her Master's bidding, and I just . . . I couldn't control what I did. I just reached out with all that rage and . . . and then it was all over. Venom was dead."

Zander's heart sank. To hear that Aurora had lost herself in an act of primal rage shook his impression of her. He remembered how she used to be: the Aurora who refused to take a life, even if it meant losing her own. That part of her was in the past. It died with her first love. "Do you feel any more complete now that you've killed Venom?"

Aurora turned her eyes away from Zander's questioning stare, as if she was searching for the answer around the room. "I don't know wha . . ." Her response trailed off, and her gaze suddenly grew distant.

"Aurora, what is it?" Zander asked, her strange demeanor immediately catching his attention.

"They're calling to me," Aurora mumbled before rushing out of the room at a purposeful pace.

"Aurora, where are you going?" Zander asked. He shot up from his seat and followed closely behind her as Aurora hurried through the hall, into the kitchen, and into the walk-in pantry. With a practiced familiarity, she reached up and pulled the cord to the light fixture three times. That signaled a small rectangular piece of the wall at the back of a shelf to flip around and reveal a number pad. Aurora's fingers darted across the pad as she entered a six-digit code followed by the enter key. The number pad went back into hiding, and a door disguised as the back wall swung open, exposing Aurora's weapons room.

Her eyes were immediately drawn to the necklace that hung from a hook on the wall. The once-silver crescent moon was now ashen black with the death of her Master.

Zander recognized the signs of who was calling to Aurora, and taking in the frightening story she just told him, he feared what that call might mean. "The Hand Council?"

She answered with a weak nod. "It must be a messenger of the Hand. Only they and Cole could summon me through this link."

"What do they want?"

"I don't know. It might not be good, but I need to answer."

Before Zander could utter another word of protest, Aurora took hold of the pendant. The instant she touched the symbol of her connection as a Knight, her eyes glossed over and her expression grew flat. It was as if her mind was far away.

"Aurora," Zander called out to her, but she stayed unresponsive. He approached her with a careful step to examine her physical state. He remembered this strange behavior with Aurora's father when he was the family's Knight. All he could do was stay at her side to anchor her to reality.

Before long, her eyes came back into focus, and she acknowledged Zander's calls. "I'm back, Zander," she said as she placed a reassuring hand on Zander's shoulder and shook the fog from her head.

"What happened?"

"I've been summoned by the Hand Council."

"What do they want?"

"They said they are opening an inquisition into the deaths of Venom and Cole and they want me to come unarmed. It's merely a search for the truth at the moment, but . . . but if I don't attend they will see it as a disregard of the Hand Council's orders, and they will assume the worst of me," Aurora explained.

"Do they believe you were solely responsible for this?" Zander asked, a noticeable sense of worry painted across his face.

"They didn't say that in so many words, but considering the situation, it's most likely one of their theories," Aurora deduced.

"How could they already know that you were involved?"

Aurora ran her thumb down the line of her jaw as she contemplated the query. "The death vision. Lexus would've seen Venom's end and threw herself at the mercy of the Hand Council with her lies." Aurora laid out her theory with a spiteful bite to her words.

"Then you have to go to them and tell the truth. Tell them that Lexus sent Venom to assassinate Cole. You were avenging the murder of your Master, someone you cared for deeply. They can't fault you for that. If you go to them with what you know, they'll see that Lexus broke the Code by using a Knight as an assassin. They will see that she is the criminal, not you," Zander pleaded; the rising fear in his heart swelled into his voice and frightened eyes.

"It's my word against hers. I have no evidence that she ordered Cole's death. If my words are all I have, the council won't act."

"They are the Hand Council. They are meant to keep order and balance within the Knighthood. They will find the truth, no matter what," Zander reassured as he kept a steady hand on her shoulder.

Aurora shook her head. "I'm not so sure. After what happened, I can't be sure of much of anything anymore. Our struggle with Lexus has been going on for some time. With the resources at their disposal, the Hand Council must have known something of this by now. What if they don't plan on doing anything, or worse yet . . . what if they're working with her?"

"That's ridiculous, Aurora. The Hand Council, from what I know, has been around for generations before this ever started. Why would they work for or with Lexus? What would they have to gain?" Zander asked.

"I don't know, but it's clear we can't depend on them. If this is to be set right, I'll have to take matters into my own hands," Aurora vowed, her tone determined and unsettling.

Zander's heart leaped in his chest at the weight of Aurora's declaration. "What are you saying?"

Aurora set her frightening gaze upon the ashen-black pendant, the grim reminder of her Master's demise. A vengeful fire began to burn in her sapphire blue eyes. "I'm saying that either by the Council's rule or by my own hands, Lexus will pay for what she has done."

A stark panic flickered in Zander's eyes as he rushed to defuse the escalating situation. "Aurora, no! Don't do this! Venom is dead; you have your revenge, and now you need to move on."

"They tortured him, Zander!" Aurora screamed, sending Zander into a stunned silence. "I saw it. I felt it. It was torture, and Venom admitted that Lexus ordered her to do it." Aurora took a deep breath to pull back her fury and regain her calm disposition. "His last moments were ones of utter agony, and Damon Lexus is responsible. Venom was just the weapon; I want the wielder. I'm going to end this so no one else has to suffer like he did."

Zander ran his shaking hands through his silver hair, and his heart leaped in sheer panic. "This is insane, Aurora. You plan to kill Lexus in front of the Hand Council and its agents. You'll either be killed in the attempt or executed as a punishment. There's no way you'll survive if you do this," Zander said, laying out the certain peril of her plan to desperately try and talk her off the path of destruction and hatred, but his plea was in vain. Her eyes showed no regret or hesitation, only determination accompanied by painful silence. He was certain that she knew the possible outcomes to her plan and had accepted them. Zander felt his heart breaking. "You don't plan on coming back, do you?"

Aurora turned away from Zander's pleading eyes and fastened the necklace around her neck. "This has to be done, Zander."

"No, it doesn't! You're out of the war now. You don't have to sacrifice yourself for this. You can still escape with your life."

Aurora's anger suddenly flared up like a wildfire. She slammed her fists against the countertop, the loud bang echoing against the walls. "Escape to what? My whole life is . . . was wrapped up in being his Knight. I am the heir to the sword, and that's all I have ever been and all I am. I worked so hard to be stronger for him, and now, because I wasn't there, he's gone. I have no purpose. No reason to move forward now," Aurora ranted before her voice broke with heightened emotion. She held her hands in clenched fists that shook like leaves in the wind. Her face was twisted with a distorted mixture of hatred and sorrow. "Making sure Damon Lexus pays for what she has done is all that matters now. Making sure no one else has to suffer like this again will give me the purpose I have lost . . . even if only for a short time."

Aurora struggled to regain her composure and looked back to Zander, not with anger, but with a weak smile and tears in her eyes. "I may not have much left, but I still have my honor. It will not allow me to stand for this. Someone has to end this cycle of pain, and I am prepared to do so."

I can't reach her, Zander thought. She was too far gone down this road; she could not hear him begging her to stop.

Zander would've given anything for Aurora to forget all about her revenge. However, he knew her well enough to understand she would not change her mind. She was set on righting what she saw as an injustice. Zander silently cursed the world for this misfortune. "Please, don't do this," Zander whispered in one more desperate attempt.

Without another word, Aurora wrapped her arms around Zander in a sweet embrace. Zander remembered how she would do this as her way of thanking him for being there through the hardest times of her life. Cole's death was a pain unlike any she had ever felt, and Zander was there with her like he always had been.

"I'm sorry," Aurora whispered as she slowly raised her hand to Zander's neck and, with a skilled touch, applied pressure to a single point. His body suddenly fell limp in her arms, and she carefully lowered him to the floor.

Zander felt his mind rapidly slipping into a deep sleep. His farewell from the waking world was Aurora's crystal-blue eyes staring back at him. He prayed it wouldn't be for the last time.

CHAPTER 16

THE SHACKLES THAT bound Luna hung heavy on her wrists, but she would not allow the discomfort to show through her warrior's demeanor. The two guards, clad in black combat gear with featureless masks, held her by the arms with trained grips that failed to sway her stoic posture. She stood steady as a marble statue and calm as still water in her combat uniform as if nothing had changed. She was still a proud Knight despite losing her Master, and she would present herself to the Hand Council as such.

The two Hands guards led her into a large windowless room, dimly illuminated by three light fixtures installed in the ceiling. They settled at one of two tables at the back of the room; the bright light centered on them shrouded anyone in the shadows from her sight. But she could see clearly the occupant of the other table, illuminated by a similar light creating a uniform symmetry. Luna's composed conduct became labored at the sight of Damon Lexus, sitting comfortably at the other table in fashionable clothes and two Hands guards at her side. Luna forced her gaze away from Damon to the front of the room, continuing to take stock of her surroundings. At the head of the room were three large monitors mounted to the wall with the three spotlights centered before the screens, which were yet to be occupied.

The Hands guards suddenly jumped to attention as the three monitors came to life, revealing a different figure on each screen, their faces hidden. The figure on the left screen wore a mask that was made of elegant porcelain and flawless, feminine lines that were accented by shades of blue. In deep contrast to the fair lady was the mask to the right. This mask was designed after a monster of nightmares with its jagged edges, vicious teeth, and maddening eyes painted in blood-red and the darkest black. The man at the center of the fair lady and the beast did not wear a mask. He wore a metal helm of extravagant craftsmanship as though it were made for a king. It gleamed brilliantly, yet was stern and frightening in its coldness.

"We are the hand that guides the struggle," the three mysterious figures began to chant in unison. "We are the order in the chaos. We are the voice that governs the powerful. We are the Hand Council, and our word is absolute."

"This inquisition shall commence," the center mask bellowed in a deep, commanding tone. "The parties in question shall present themselves starting with Master Damon Lexus. Appear before the Hand Council."

Damon stood with a courtly flourish, her hair falling freely down the back of her brown trench coat. "I, Master Damon Lexus, thank you Lords of the Hand Council for giving me the opportunity to straighten out these unfortunate events," Damon said in a subservient tone that did not become her.

"This inquisition would have happened with or without your request, Master Lexus. Do well to remember that you are one of the parties in question. You are not out of the woods yet, so to speak," the feminine mask informed Damon coldly in a voice as smooth as velvet.

"My apologies, Lords of the Council." Damon bowed again and took a seat at the table.

"Now the second party, Knight Luna, may present herself," the center mask commanded.

Luna regarded the Hand Council with a respectful, yet solemn bow. "I, Knight Luna, have answered your summons, Lords of the Hand Council. I hope you will see to the truth of this disgrace and right this wrong."

"That is what we hope for, as well. We apologize for the restraints, but with the circumstances the way they are, we had no choice," the center mask explained.

"I understand. I would've done the same," Luna replied flatly.

The Hand Council turned their attention away from Luna and addressed the group. "Now that all the parties have been presented, this inquisition for the truth behind the deaths of Master Cole Iver and Knight Venom shall begin. First, Master Lexus shall stand before us."

Damon rose from her seat and gracefully sauntered to the center of the room to present herself to the Council, the two Hands guards close at her side.

"Young Master, you understand that if any word from your mouth is proven as a falsehood, you will be stricken of your title as Master. Is that clear?" the frightening red mask warned with a sinister hiss.

"Crystal," Damon replied confidently.

"Now, what do you know about the circumstances leading to the deaths of Master Iver and Knight Venom?" the center mask asked.

"Cole and I had been exchanging blows for some time now. He believed I had gained too much power when other Knights decided to accept me as their Master. He wanted to see my kingdom crumble," Damon explained.

"Do you know why he was moving against you?" the woman mask questioned.

"He believed that I was upsetting the balance for my own selfish gain."

The feminine mask cocked her head and met Damon with a quizzical stare. "You believe otherwise?"

Damon showcased a self-satisfied smirk. "I believe his reasons were more basic than that. He felt what any man would feel when outdone by a woman: jealousy. Rest his soul, but the poor boy was probably bitter that he couldn't attract followers like I could. Not everyone can have the natural presence of a leader. He simple wanted what I had. Forgive me for speaking ill of the dead, but that is what I believe," Damon explained, trying to paint over her boastful arrogance with a voice of humility.

The calm summer breeze of Luna's expression started to become clouded. Her outward appearance only showed a slight irritation that was dwarfed by the raging torrent of fury within her heart and mind. The sight of Damon, the snake in woman's clothes, defiling her fallen Master's name with her revolting slander was more than she could bear. She could not allow this. "Lies! You are no leader; you are a thief that stole them from their Masters, and Cole knew it," Luna shouted in her Master's defense.

All eyes turned to Luna in surprise at her sudden outburst. "Knight Luna!" The center mask's voice rumbled through the room like thunder. "You forget your place and the purpose of this inquisition. You'll have your chance to speak your peace in due time, but until then, we will not allow these outbursts. Do you understand?"

Choking back her anger and disgust, she respectfully bowed her head. "Yes, I understand," she answered in no more than a whisper.

The center mask turned his authoritative gaze to Damon. "And you, this is not a smear campaign. Keep to what you know."

"Of course, my Lords, forgive me." Damon lowered her gaze to the floor timidly. "It was later brought to my attention by one of my other Knights that Venom had begun to take the rivalry personally, but I knew Venom and was certain that she wouldn't act without my orders . . . at least, I thought I knew her. Then I received the vision of Venom's horrible death. You have the dagger as proof of her demise." Damon raised her hand to her mouth with a frightened expression on her face. "It was terrifying. I wasn't able to see the killer's face, but I felt her die. She was killed with lightning, turned into a charred sack of flesh. From the vision, I concluded that Venom had gone too far and went to kill Cole, thinking it was my wishes. She must have been caught in the act by Luna."

"How do you know that Venom went after Cole Iver?" the blue mask inquired. "You only have a theory about Venom's killer; you don't know the circumstances behind the event. Venom could've attacked Luna directly or vice versa. Venom could've attacked Luna directly or vice versa."

"Venom isn't the greatest in direct confrontation, but Luna is well-known for being a danger in close combat. Venom wouldn't risk going after her directly and Luna had no way of finding Venom. From Venom's perspective, Cole was the best target. My guess is she didn't plan on Luna being so close," Damon answered.

"So we're supposed to believe that a loyal Knight under your service, moved without orders to assassinate a Master," the fearsome red mask said, snickering sarcastically.

Damon slowly raised her open hands to the Hand Council. "Unfortunately, I have nothing to offer you but my word as a noble Master. I beg of you to believe me when I tell you I did not order Venom to kill Master Cole Iver."

There was a long moment of pensive silence as the Hand Council gazed upon Damon with long, contemplative stares. The silence was suddenly broken by the commanding voice of the center mask. "That will be all then. You may step down now, Master Damon Lexus," he allowed with a haphazard wave of his hand. Damon bowed courtly, spun on her heel, and strolled back to her seat.

"We have heard Master Lexus's side of these events. Now we will hear from the other party. Knight Luna, present yourself before the Hand Council," the center mask instructed.

Led by both arms by the two Hands guards, Luna marched to the center of the room. She stood tall with pride and determination as she addressed the Hand Council. Unlike Damon's painted-on charm, Luna showed no fear or weakness. Much like an animal facing off for territory, Luna stood her ground. In this manner, she earned the council's respect. "Now tell us, Knight Luna, what do you know about the deaths of Knight Venom and your Master, Cole Iver?"

"I went to see my Master that night to discuss some matters at hand, but when I got to his home, I found Venom standing over his dying body. She had poisoned him with her toxin, and I was too late to try and save him. He died before my eyes." Luna's body tensed, and her hands uncontrollably balled up into tight fists. The memory of Cole's life fading from him opened a flood of sorrow and anger that was difficult to keep within. That image would forever strike a chord inside her heart; all she could hope for was to learn to control it. Luna gritted her teeth and forced herself to continue. She had to have the truth known. "I take full responsibility for Venom's death. When I witnessed what she had done, I flew into a rage and wanted nothing more than to avenge my Master's murder."

"The Council recognizes your right to avenge your Master and does not begrudge you for this. From the information we have, it seems assured that Venom did indeed break the laws of the Code. Her fate would have been the same at our judgment. This matter will be left at that," the demonic featured mask ruled.

"Far from it," Luna interrupted. "In the struggle, I demanded to know why Venom would do this, and she admitted that she was following the orders of her Master, Damon Lexus. She is the one truly responsible for this crime," Luna proclaimed.

"Unfortunately, with Venom dead there is no one to back your claims. It's simply your word against Master Lexus's. Do you have any evidence to solidify your story?" the lady mask questioned.

Luna sighed. "I only have my word of honor as a Knight and the knowledge of Venom's personality. She was loyal to a fault and fiercely protective of her Master, but she was a mere follower. I don't believe she would've ever entertained the idea of moving on her own. She was also a Knight, and like all Knights, she would've known the Code and the punishment for breaking it. She wouldn't risk bringing the wrath of the Hand Council down on her beloved Master unless she was ordered to do so. When you look objectively at Lexus and my Master's history along with Venom's known behavior, the story that she went rogue seems entirely too convenient," Luna reasoned to the Council.

Mumbles and murmurs floated through the room as the Council contemplated the plausible nature of Luna's argument. "This may be by your word only, but it makes for a plausible theory. Do you have anything else to say for your side of this story?" the feminine mask inquired.

"Only that I sincerely hope you will see to the truth in this matter."

"If both parties have said their peace, the Hand Council will assess the information gathered and will render any necessary judgment," the center mask instructed.

The Hands guards led Damon and Luna back into the rooms they came from while they waited for the Hand Council's decision. Minutes that to Luna felt like hours passed before another one of the Hands guards signaled everyone to return to the conference room. Luna could feel her heart pounding in her chest as she waited with bated breath for the Council's ruling.

"We, the Hand Council, after hearing both sides of these events have come to what we see as a fair judgment," the center mask spoke, his voice commanding the attention of all who heard it. "In the matter of Knight Venom, the Hand Council recognizes Luna's right to avenge her Master's murder, thus there will be no punishment for it. In the matter of Master Cole Iver's murder, we have concluded that Venom is solely responsible and there is not enough evidence to suggest otherwise."

"You can't be serious!" Luna barked with outrage.

"The Hand Council is sorry for your loss, Knight Luna, but simply a theory is not enough for us to take action. You've taken your revenge, and your Master would be proud. You should leave it at that and live your life peacefully from here on. He would've wanted it that way," the fair lady mask suggested, her voice calm but unsympathetic.

"You know nothing of what my Master would've wanted. He wanted the Knights and our way of life to be kept safe. That's what my Master wanted, and Lexus threatens that. Why can't the Council, with all your wisdom, see that?" Luna protested.

"Hold your tongue, Knight! You're addressing the Hand Council; do not forget that," the monstrous mask hissed. "You've walked away from this with no punishment. So unless you have something more than theories, our decision stands. This inquisition is over!"

The Hands guards at Luna's side roughly turned Luna away from the council and began leading her to the room she came from. Luna stared at Damon as she strolled to the exit with a smirk of self-satisfaction, completely free after all she had done. Luna's heart and mind screamed with injustice. Damon had to be held responsible for Cole's death, and the Council would do nothing. Luna had to right this wrong even if it meant her certain death. But with every pompous step of Damon, Luna was losing her chance. If she were allowed to walk away, Damon would strengthen her defenses or disappear forever. This was the best and possibly only chance Luna would ever get. She had to act quickly; all she needed was a clear shot.

Before anyone even realized what had happened, Luna smashed her heavy shackles into the face of one of the Hands guards holding her. He staggered backward, loosening his grip on Luna's arm as blood began to trickle out the bottom of his mask. His counterpart moved to defend, but not fast enough to stop Luna from landing a swift kick to his knee, a grinding pop echoed in the hollow chamber. Luna grabbed a long dagger from the guard's sheath as he collapsed on the wood-paneled floor.

Clutching the dagger with a trained grip, Luna sprinted for her target as the Hands guards on Damon drew their weapons and moved to intercept. Luna quickened her pace and leaped into the air, firmly planting her boot into the first guard's chest, the momentum forcing him backward. In a talented gymnast flip, she leaped off the guard's body as if it were a springboard and sailed over the head of the second guard, landing gracefully on the ground behind them at a full run. She was in clear sight of Lexus.

Steadfast and determined to see this through to the end, Luna sped for her target, staring into the face of the root of her despair. Lexus did not cower behind the Hands guard or try and flee from her attacker. Instead, she locked her gaze with Luna's with a sinister, almost daring grin stretched across her face. No visible signs of fear or anger. She only showed a confident smirk that taunted Luna to make the first move. Lexus was either incredibly cocky or she had something up her sleeve.

Every survival instinct in Luna's mind told her something wasn't right, that she shouldn't continue, but she couldn't stop. Trap or not, she had taken the leap and there was no stopping the fall.

Luna closed in on Lexus and thrust the dagger forward to pierce Damon's cold heart. Damon's cocky smirk still lingered as she gracefully cartwheeled backward, kicking the blade from Luna's hand. Springing from hands to feet, she skillfully tumbled out of harm's way and landed with the same obnoxious sneer staring back at Luna. Luna was only able to react with a gawk of astonishment.

"That's not possible," Luna muttered to herself as the pieces of the puzzle began to fit together. A strange whistling sound pulled Luna's attention back to the guards to see a bola twirling through the air coming right for her. She started to run before it struck her from behind, the rope wrapping tightly around her body and forcing her to the floor. The Hands guard wasted no time and quickly moved to subdue the threat.

"Bring her forward!" the booming voice of the center mask commanded. The guards dragged Luna across the floor to the center of the room. Luna struggled to her knees and faced the Hand Council once more.

"Knight Luna, how dare you disgrace us like this!" the blue mask snapped. "You acted against a clear ruling of the Hand Council. Do you realize the consequences behind this misguided sense of revenge?"

"I do understand, and I stand by my actions. Venom admitted that Damon Lexus ordered Cole's death, and I still intend to bring her to justice even if you will not. Her cowering is proof of her guilt. She sent a Knight in her place out of fear of facing the Hand Council with her lies," Luna accused, her eyes fixated on the one they thought was Damon Lexus.

The feminine mask turned her gaze to Damon. "What are you saying? This is not the real Lexus?"

Luna shook her head. "It couldn't be her. You all witnessed what happened. If this was really Damon Lexus, my revenge would be complete and she would be dead."

The red mask hissed with displeasure. "You insolent servant! How dare you speak of a Master in such a manner! We could have your head for that!"

The center mask rested his chin in his palm as his gaze grew distant in thought. "Knight Luna did step far out of line. This is true, but she knows the breath and flow of battle better than most. I believe her when she says that Damon should have fallen to her attack." The lead mask's ruling led the attention of the rest of the Hand Council to Damon. "That leaves us with one question. Who might you be? We, the Hand Council, demand you reveal yourself."

Damon's eyes, riddled with disdain, darted to Luna, an uncontrolled reaction to her accusation that swiftly morphed into startled innocence. "This is absurd! I am Master Damon Lexus."

"Do not patronize us, young one! You have been found as an imposter so reveal yourself or you will be held until you do." The center mask's roaring voice rose in intensity, cutting through Damon's defenses.

Damon's expression hardened, and her hands clenched into fists to hide the sudden rush of fear in the pit of her stomach. She pushed it down and out of the way to regain her still composure then shrugged. "Damn, you caught me. I shouldn't have been so careless." She slowly ran her slender fingers through her long dark hair, the color fading from the roots to the tips into a snowy white. The pampered tan of her skin dissolved into a pale ivory and the deep brown of her eyes receded to a rich violet.

"Alias." Luna's voice was sharp with contempt.

Alias turned to Luna with the same snide grin. "You've heard of me?"

"I've heard of you, shape-shifter. You're Lexus's spy," Luna spat.

Alias chuckled softly. "You got a problem with me, Luna?"

"My problem is with your methods. How often have you assisted your Master in her cowardly plans?" Luna shouted.

"This inquisition has ruled that my Master has done nothing wrong and, by that extension, neither have I. I am of use to my Master, and that is all I have to answer for. We all have our part to play." Her tone was as soft as a bell but bit like a viper with hatred. "We can't all be prodigies of war like you."

"Enough!" the monstrous mask screeched. "Why have you taken the place of your Master? She must know the deep disrespect she has shown to deceive the Hand Council like this."

Alias turned to the Council and bowed her head. "She is aware and hopes that she can be forgiven, but the situation called for it. I am proud to be of service to my Master in any way I can."

"Where is Damon?" the blue mask demanded.

"She is safe, and that is all she needs to know." Alias gestured to Luna. "I am merely protecting my Master like any Knight would."

"We guaranteed her safety," the center mask reassured.

Alias chuckled. "And we all saw how far that got you. Luna was right when she said Damon would have been killed if she were in my place. Your guards would have been adequate if she were any normal Knight, but this is the famous attack dog of Cole Iver." Alias turned her gaze back to Luna, disdain flowing from her violet eyes. "She's dangerous. The dog has tragically lost her Master and become rabid. She should be put down before she kills again."

There was a long silence as the Council considered Alias's position. "Her reasoning is sound, but tell your Master that she has not heard the last of this," the blue mask ordered. Alias bowed elegantly to confirm her understanding before the Hand Council turned their attention back to Luna. "Now, the last bit of business to attend to. What to do with her?"

"Yes, how shall we punish the newest Rogue?" the red mask asked with a sadistic snicker.

The other masks fell silent as they waited patiently for word from the last council member. He locked his intense gaze with Luna for what felt to her like an eternity. She felt a strange and powerful presence wash over her as if he were peering into her mind and soul. An immense force engulfed her consciousness. She couldn't move, couldn't speak; she could only stare back at him. She gazed past the mask into the eyes of the man. They were strange eyes, dark as night with white speckles as if she had been staring at starlight.

The force upon Luna then disappeared, lifting an enormous pressure from her. Her breath fell heavy from her lips as she looked up at the center mask, asking without words what had happened. He only answered her with a knowing regard. "Let her go," he ordered.

A simultaneous gasp fell over the room from everyone present. Alias's face twisted with fury. "What?" she screamed. "This is an outrage. She fully intended to murder my Master in your presence and you're just going to let her go?"

"Be still, Alias," the center mask insisted calmly.

"But she won't stop until my Master is dead. She . . ."

"Silence!" he commanded loudly, cutting Alias off midsentence. He gestured to the remaining guards. "Get her out of here!" he bellowed. The guards rushed to Alias and grabbed her firmly by the arms to lead her out of the room, her relentless protests falling on deaf ears as they faded into the distance.

"I'd have to agree with Alias. Why are we turning her loose? She has clearly betrayed our laws," the female mask asked.

"Are you questioning my judgment?" the center mask asked, his deep voice challenging her position.

The red and blue masks' postures shriveled as he set his dominance over them. It was clear they disapproved of his decision, but they would not speak against it. Even under their disguises, their fear was noticeable.

"Guards, you are now ordered to take Knight Luna away from here and turn her loose. She must be alive and unharmed. This is a direct order from the Hand Council and any of you who disobey shall face our judgment. Do you understand?"

The guards bowed in answer and promptly left the room with Luna between them. Luna walked with a dull limp, following at a slow pace to listen to the Hand Council from the other room.

She could hear the familiar voice of the red mask, but only in a timid tone. "Not that I am questioning your decision, Lord, but do you honestly think Luna will stop her attacks on Damon?"

"Of course not," the booming voice of the center mask spoke. "She will surely attack Damon again. It's only a matter of time. I will summon Ranger to make sure that doesn't happen."

"But he ceases to be a Hunter. He will not come," the female mask reminded him.

"He will come when summoned by the Hand Council. He is still obedient. With his abilities and cunning, he should fare well against Luna. Everything is going the way it should. Now farewell, until next we are needed."

CHAPTER 17

THE MIDSUMMER SUN beamed through the tall, narrow windows that surrounded the large classroom. The room was lined with rows of small desks descending in levels leading down to the front of the room. At the base of the room sat a solid but plain table and chair before a rectangular chalkboard that hung on the wall.

There, writing on the board with a dexterous hand, was Ethan Chang. The students of his class sat lazily in their chairs trying to keep their attention on the lesson while the clock, ticking away the last moments of the day, continuously stole their focus away.

Finishing his writing with an efficient flow, Ethan spun to address the class. "All right, I know it's the end of a long day, but you need to know this for the course," Ethan made clear before moving on with his lesson. "In the tenth century of the years before the treaty, the seventeen warring countries of the eastern continent were finally united under one flag to become what we know now as the Daiyu Empire. Their first emperor, Jianguo, was a general in the war for unification. He and his descendants ruled the continent in prosperity and good fortune. Their economy was thriving; their people were well off and happy. They were where every country would want to be, and they stayed that way for around four hundred years. It was then that Emperor Guang got a thirst for conquest and moved his armies west to invade the islands."

Ethan's eyes scanned the room for a quick assessment of the students focused on the lesson. The numbers were dwindling. With a quick jerk, he smacked the chalkboard, making a loud crack that drew the eyes of the students back to him. "At this point in history, the islands were much like the Daiyu Empire when they were scattered and independent of each other. It wasn't until the Daiyu armies had taken almost half of the islands that the remaining tribes banded together and requested the aid of the kingdom of Ebony. With the kingdom's help, they were able to drive the Daiyu armies back to their continent and crippled their advance. Seeing his clear defeat and shame, Guang committed suicide. His son Xifeng became the next emperor and promptly surrendered to the alliance. The politics of the entire world took a different direction after that. The once independent tribes of the islands formed the Island Republic, and with the king of Ebony and the new emperor of Daiyu, they came up with a way to establish a potential peace between the countries. That solution was the Treaty of Laurinburg."

Ethan turned around and began writing on the chalkboard once again. "Now that the many small tribes, colonies, and regions had become three major countries, it was the perfect opportunity to establish common ground between them all. The treaty of Laurinburg marked to the beginning of the United Era and was signed by King Fletcher, Emperor Xifeng, and Representative Naomi Fin of the Island Republic. These are just some of the main points in the treaty," he said, gesturing to the list on the chalkboard. "Border lines, trade agreements, and sharing of information were all agreed upon in the treaty. This would shoulder a strong peace between them that has lasted ever since. They all had enough land, and with the trade agreements, they would all have enough resources for their people. The only land that was not distributed among the three ruling factions was the continent on the most northern tip of the globe. In all the radical changes of the treaty, they decided to leave that land unaffiliated. This action produced the land's popular nickname, 'No Mans Land.' Now, why do you think they made this decision?" Ethan asked, directing the question to the class.

A young girl with bright blue eyes and corn-colored hair raised her hand, and Ethan addressed her for her answer. "The continent is a wasteland. There's nothing up there."

Ethan nodded. "As far as we know, at least. When exploration of this continent first became possible, the explorers, for the most part, found nothing of value. The explorers that attempted to move further inland were met with complications ranging from freak weather to random disappearances until they abandoned the venture. The lands infamous history caused the countries' governments to discourage further exploration into No Man's Land. This brings me to you . . ." Ethan's voice trailed off as he suddenly felt a familiar tug on his consciousness. It was like someone was calling out to his mind, but it was coming in no more than a whisper. He fell silent, staring forward in a daze.

The students stared at him, confused and wondering what the pause was for until the blue-eyed girl spoke up. "Professor Chang?"

The girl's voice quickly snapped Ethan back to reality. He shook his head and focused his attention on the class while the mental beckoning continued to pull at his brain. "Yes, your assignment is to write a paper for or against the campaign each government took to discourage exploration into No Man's Land. That's it for today. Class dismissed."

Confused mumbling rose up in the crowd of students as several of them looked at the clock. Ethan still had close to twenty minutes left in class, but he couldn't stay. Ethan hoped the more observant students who knew he would often drag out his class to the last minute were few and far between. Ethan rushed to shove his papers into a modest messenger bag and darted out the door before anyone else.

He scurried through the hallways at a quick walk, attempting to get out of the building without attracting too much attention. He focused on keeping his pace steady but leisurely.

"Ethan," a voice called from behind him. Ethan stopped dead in his tracks and cursed under his breath. He knew all too well who that voice belonged to. Taking a deep breath to mask his irritation, he turned to his balding and often annoying colleague. "Hello, Benjamin," Ethan greeted as politely as he could muster.

Benjamin approached Ethan with a wide grin plastered over his face. "I wanted to thank you for coming in and doing that tour for Miss Fallon. She really enjoyed herself and has committed to more donations."

The mental calling in Ethan's mind was getting stronger, making it that much more difficult to keep his normal disposition. "That's great. If you could excuse me, I have to go," he urged, trying to rush along the encounter.

Benjamin gave his watch a confused glance. "You don't usually leave this early. Is something wrong?"

Ethan shook his head. "No, no, it's just that I have an appointment to keep, and I'm running late."

"Is it with a doctor? Are you not well?" Benjamin pried.

Ethan's eye twitched as he strained to hold in his impatience. *What part of running late doesn't he understand?* Ethan thought. Ethan forced a feeling of calm to the surface of his mind to bring about rational thought. He knew Benjamin didn't mean any harm by holding him up; he was just nosy. Ethan had to keep his emotions in check; he couldn't show signs that something was out of the norm.

Ethan flew a polite smile and flung up a story that ensured a quick getaway. "No, it's nothing like that. An old friend of mine is in the city, and we set a time to meet. He's only here for a short while before going back home, and he has little time to spare. I just don't want to miss him."

Benjamin nodded, satisfied with the answer. "All right then, I'll see you on Monday, Ethan."

"Have a good weekend, Benjamin." Ethan waved goodbye and casually continued on his way.

Ethan made it to the staff parking lot without any more interruptions and got into his car. It was a small economy car painted in a dull gray. No discernable features to speak of. The kind of car you wouldn't even look once at on the street. It was just how Ethan wanted it. A turn of his key brought the plain car to life, and he started to drive.

Ethan turned off the chattering radio and sharpened his focus toward the road. The tug on his consciousness was becoming louder the closer he came to his home, demanding his attention and making it difficult to drive. He had to concentrate fully on the task at hand or he feared he might crash.

The call in his mind was practically deafening by the time he approached the gray concrete walls of his apartment complex. "Almost there. Just stay calm and don't stand out," he said below his breath as he gently rubbed his temples. It took mountains of self-control not to dash out of his parked car and bolt to his apartment. Instead, he calmly walked into the building, retrieved a few letters from his mailbox, climbed the stairs to the third floor, and stepped into his apartment.

His apartment was much like everything else he owned: ordinary. The door opened to a short hallway with the kitchen and living room on the left side and the bedroom and bathroom on the right. The walls were a plain white and the floor was paneled with wood. The kitchen and living room were open to each other except for a narrow counter between them. The kitchen was clean but showed little signs of use. Stocked with the bare minimum of food, appliances, and dishes, there was no questioning that only one person had used it in a long while. The living room had two stools sitting at the counter for an improvised dining area. By the patio door sat a light-brown love seat with a small wooden coffee table at its front. Along the one side of the living room stood a tall shelf with books of several different genres except for the middle shelf, which held a stereo system and a vintage album collection. Opposite of that was a large, pine china cabinet with several random little knickknacks placed on its shelves.

This unassuming apartment could have belonged to anyone. The modest living area was not a home but merely a place to sleep and to keep his belongings. Nothing about the small abode said anything about Ethan apart from one exception: on a petite table in the corner were two picture frames made of elegant crystal, designed in the form of white lilies embracing the photos. One picture was a family snapshot of two young boys and their parents under a full and lush willow tree. One boy, no older than four, had short black hair and glasses and the other was in his early teens with shoulder-length dark hair, brown eyes, and a soft smile. The mother's long hair was tied in a high ponytail to show a pretty, young face with delicate pale skin. The features of the father showed brightly in the sons he held close, his expression gleaming with pride. The other photo showed the older son a few years down the road standing under the same willow tree smiling the same soft smile.

The moment Ethan set the deadbolt on his door, he dropped everything and dashed to the patio to close the curtains, shielding his actions from prying eyes. He then opened the china cabinet and, with a practiced motion, moved the bottom shelf out only a few inches, exposing a hidden button. He pushed the button, moved the shelf back into place, and closed the door. A series of mechanical clicks echoed through the silent room as the back of the cabinet popped open to a hidden compartment. The contents were an extreme contrast to the common knickknacks that served as its disguise. The secret compartment held an impressive long-range sniper rifle, a couple small pistols, knives, a bulletproof vest, and several other dangerous tools. Nestled with respect on its own shelf was a short, curved blade with a deep-green sheaf and hilt. It was accented with a mythical dragon carved in black entwined along its length. Ethan felt the mental call like a choir in the presence of this ornate weapon.

Ethan steadied his mind and body with a deep breath before clutching the curved blade in his hands. The message flooded over his consciousness like a mighty wave revealing the image of a man wearing a dark cowl, his features hidden in the night. The man stood in front of a large neon sign on top of an old building.

The man's words echoed in Ethan's mind as if it were a stone cavern. "Ranger, the Hand Council is in need of your service once again. Meet me here at one a.m. tonight for the details. Given your experience it is needless to inform you of the consequences for not complying with the Hand Council's summons. I trust you won't disappoint them."

The scene of the darkened rooftop faded back to his small apartment and left Ethan with nothing more than a slight migraine. He shook the fog from his vision and gave his rifle a long glare, his expression grave. "This isn't good."

CHAPTER 18

THE RANDOM CHATTER and lively energy of the late-night bar scene increased the noise in the street to a dull roar. Everyone on the street was focused and preoccupied, trying to get in or back into the most happening clubs. Every person but one.

The one man on the street not looking for a fun time made his way through the crowds at a brisk pace, his gaze periodically looking upward for a particular neon sign. He kept his hands firmly tucked in the pockets of his dark trench coat, keeping it close to his body to hide the pistol strapped under his arm and the knife at his waist. He suddenly halted in place at the sight of a large neon sign shining brightly in the night in a deep red, perched on top of an old brick building. He glanced to a clock in a store window, reading the hour: one o'clock.

Right on time, he thought to himself as he ducked into the alleyway and started a steady march up the fire exit. In the midst of his assent, the reflection from a windowpane caught his eye and forced him to stop. The face of his glamour was one of sharp features, short jet-black hair, and dark, calculating eyes. It was a face he thought he'd never see looking back at him again, a sobering reminder of many things he wanted to forget. He tore his eyes away from the image and continued to the roof.

The roof was a barren concrete slab among the lively energy below, centered within the hustle but simultaneously separate from it. The neon sign bathed the roof in a strong red glow, stretching the ink-black shadows along the stone. At the base of a long shadow stood a figure shrouded in a dark cloak, a silver pocket watch in his hand. The cloaked figure turned to him as he stepped onto the roof.

"Ranger," the hooded figure said, welcoming the Hunter he had summoned. "Nice to see your punctuality hasn't suffered over the years. Let's hope your skills are still as sharp," he added with no small amount of cockiness in his tone.

Despite the fact that the messenger had the words of the Hand Council behind him, Ranger met his authority with nothing but a cold stare of indifference. "Why have I been summoned? The Hand Council released me from my duties as a Hunter," he stated in a voice as icy as his expression.

"The Hand Council has decided to call you back for a particular mission. They believe no other hunter can accomplish it."

"What about Nightmare?" Ranger asked. "I'm sure he's just itching for a target."

"What insolence!" the man barked as he advanced on Ranger to stand face-to-face. Working against his own small stature, he used his authority to puff up his self-importance. "You are a servant of the Hand, and you will do as you are ordered without discussion! Your dismissal came only at their mercy and can be overturned at their leisure. It is not your place to question their will. It is your place to hunt down traitors and Rogues. Am I clear?"

Ranger did not fall back or falter from this hooded man's verbal lashes. He had dealt with Knights like this messenger before. They all thought they carried the Hand Council's authority because they acted as their voice. They threw around power they didn't have, but that mattered little to Ranger. He was merely making sure the Hand Council needed him specifically. No matter how much he disliked the idea of another hunt, he could do nothing but get it over with as quickly and painlessly as possible.

"Who's the target?" he asked casually.

"Cole Iver's Knight, Luna."

Ranger raised an eyebrow. "Luna went Rogue?"

"That's what I said!" the messenger snapped.

Ranger lowered his gaze in contemplation. "That doesn't make much sense. I had heard that both of them, Luna especially, set the bar for loyalty to the Code and honor. Why did she turn Rogue?"

The messenger's lips crinkled into an ugly sneer. "That is none of your concern, Hunter. You just need to know who your prey is and that is all."

Ranger turned away from the messenger and sighed. *This puppet's power trip has quickly gone from irritating to detrimental,* Ranger thought. *This child has no idea what is needed for an operation like this. I need to know why Luna went down the path she did to know where she is going. This moron expects me to just press a kill button and make it all better. If I have any hope of hunting down Luna, I have two choices: I could get what I need on my own, costing valuable time and wasted effort, or I could take a shortcut.*

Ranger stood face-to-face with the messenger, answering his scowl with a perfectly unreadable stare. With small but efficient motions, Ranger pivoted around to the messenger's side and shoved him to the ground, sweeping his feet from under him with his own.

The messenger fell flat on his back with a painful thud as Ranger kept his firm grip on him. The hood fell from his head, revealing a young man with dirty blond hair, gray eyes, and facial features that seemed to have not fully grown into themselves. The messenger's furious eyes quickly turned into pools of fear when Ranger pressed a small but deadly knife firmly against his throat.

The man gulped, noticeably trying to hide the raw fear in his expression. "What do you think you're doing?" he said, struggling to keep his trembling limbs in check. "The Hand Council can have your head for this! You know how this works."

"I know exactly how this works. I've been hunting since before you could use your powers. Considering that your inexperience is so obvious, let me tell you how this works, pup. You give me every scrap of information I ask for, and I make the Hand Council's problem go away. If you don't give me what I need, I will have a problem with my mission and a problem with you. I don't like having problems, so I usually deal with them fairly quickly . . . and quietly. Are we clear?" Ranger threatened with an everyday steadiness of voice that you would see from someone ordering coffee, not someone holding a person's life in their hands.

That steadiness brought the messenger's arrogant back talk to an abrupt halt. Ranger looked the messenger straight in the eyes and could see the overconfidence and bloated ego fall away to a pool of uncertainty and fear.

"I'll tell you what you want to know," he peeped.

Ranger nodded. "Good answer. Now, why did Luna go Rogue?" He asked, keeping the blade pressed lightly to the messenger's skin to avoid any further complications.

"Luna wants Damon Lexus dead. She has already tried once, right in front of the Hand Council," the young man answered in short order.

"Where is her Master in all this?"

"Cole Iver is dead. Damon's Knight Venom went against her orders and assassinated him, but Luna caught her in the act and killed her for it. The Hand Council held an inquisition into the matter and concluded that Venom went against orders, so they didn't punish Luna for killing another Knight."

"So why have I been called to hunt her if the Hand Council didn't pass judgment?"

"Luna doesn't believe that Damon is innocent. She thinks that Damon ordered the death of her Master and has sworn revenge. The Hand Council has given Luna her freedom, but if she continues on this path, the Hand Council has authorized an execution."

Ranger chest rolled in a soft chuckle as he assessed the information given to him and its typical nature. *Nothing ever changes. The Hand Council could have executed her on the spot, but they decided to let her roar free, knowing full well what she would do. They don't want to save anyone. They wanted to seem justified in their actions. They haven't changed in all these years,* Ranger thought. He picked through what he knew of the situation and the target to solidify his next move. "So, all I need to do is watch Damon until Luna chooses to strike," he decided.

The messenger stared at Ranger, baffled by his judgment. "You're just going to wait until she attacks? What if she succeeds in getting her revenge before you take her down?"

Ranger gently moved the blade from the messenger's neck. "That won't happen," he replied flatly as he stood up and extended his hand to assist the young man.

The messenger glared at Ranger and pulled himself to his feet, stubbornly ignoring the gesture. "And how can you be sure that she'll attack Damon? The Hand Council let her go with her life. The smart thing to do would be to disappear."

Ranger shook his head. "Saving herself is the last thing on her mind right now. Her Master was murdered, and she believes Damon is the one to blame. She'll risk anything and everything to get her chance at what she believes is justice because she thinks she has nothing to lose. I can guarantee you she'll strike at Damon the first chance she has, and I'll be waiting."

CHAPTER 19

PERCHED ATOP A tall office building in the west end of the city, Ranger watched the building across the way through the eye of his sniper scope. His eyes were intent and focused like a falcon scanning for prey. He had come to the time of truth as he had in many hunts before. After all the planning, positioning, and predictions, all that was left was to wait and hope the target followed the path laid out.

To most others, setting the scenario for Luna to have a shot at her revenge would seem foolish, practically irresponsible. But Ranger hadn't survived this long in this deadly game by being foolish. He survived by living with one important rule: know your enemy. It was always imperative to gather as much information on the prey as humanly possible before engaging in a hunt. This situation was no exception. His plans and actions were governed by what he knew of Luna. He knew it was impossible for her to know what Hunter would be on her trail, so she would ignore that entirely and focus on her target.

He also knew that even though her thirst for revenge was strong, she still was an honorable Knight. She wouldn't want this path she walked to be stained with unnecessary bloodshed. She only had one target to take down, clean and simple. That was a sniper's job, and the bread and butter of that tactic was a good vantage point. That was provided by the office tower across the street that was under construction.

Ranger peeked through his scope, carefully scanning the empty shell of a building. He could see the interior guts of the undeveloped structure through the open walls and various plastic sheets. The empty floors were dimly illuminated only by the pale moonlight that stretched a short way across the floor. It was the perfect place for a sniper to roost. He just hoped he was right.

Two hours ticked by with Ranger continuing his diligent watch to no avail. His effects finally bore fruit when he caught a faint glimmer of movement at the corner of his vision. He zeroed in and found exactly what he had been waiting for.

Clear as day through his powerful lens, he saw a tall female crouched low to the floor. He could see the moonlight gleam off her long black hair as it hung gracefully from a ponytail down the center of her back. He could see many practical tools and weapons strapped to her formfitting black combat uniform. Ranger focused on the metallic gleam of a long-barreled rifle. His predictions were falling into place.

With a practiced motion not dulled by years of inaction, Ranger took aim at the target but his finger remained off the trigger. The renowned cold expression of Ranger was wrought with uncertainty. He never wanted to do this again; he had decided that a long time ago. Unfortunately, his release was merely a delusion. It was time to awake into the nightmare that was the kill. Where a target was merely prey and no one asked questions. A Hunter could only ask himself why this woman deserved to die or whether the actions that led her were justified. These were the questions Ranger asked himself every time before he pulled the trigger.

Ranger shook his head, forcing his mind clear. He couldn't afford to hesitate; he knew the consequence of failure for a Hunter and who it would affect. He may have felt sorry for Luna, but he didn't know her. He couldn't sacrifice everything for that.

He aimed precisely where the shot would count so she wouldn't feel any pain; she would be gone before she even knew it. That was more mercy than other Hunters would give. He could remember the agonizing cries of other targets from those Hunters he had the displeasure of working with. They thrived in the hunt and delighted in the pain. *Trust me, Luna,* Ranger thought. *You got the nicer part of the deal when they called me in.*

Luna lifted her head slightly upward, stealing Ranger's attention completely. He paused, wondering what had caught her eye. Ranger's heart leaped and eyes bulged when Luna's soft jade eyes stared directly at him.

At that moment, different parts of Ranger's mind were at odds with one another. One part asked quizzically, *Does she see me?* and wondered how that could be. The other side screamed in a panicked fury, *Take the shot!* and *You have to act now!*

Ranger swiftly focused his shot and squeezed the trigger. The sound of the rifle expressed in a muffled echo as the bullet sailed down and punched through the floor as Luna rolled to the side. "She dodged it," he muffled under his breath, hardly believing the words as they left his mouth.

He chambered another round and aimed but saw Luna's roost steadily flooding with thick smoke. "Dammit," Ranger cursed as the depth of her strategy came to light. She cut off his line of sight to force close combat. She was moving the confrontation to her field of expertise.

He stepped back from the building's edge and sprinted forward, flinging himself headlong off the tower. The darkness of his eyes instantly faded to a foggy white as the winds began to shift and move below him. A strong current in the air directed his descent to Luna's perch in a focused stream. He hit the concrete and rolled into a low crouch.

Ranger slowly rose to his feet, his once-again dark eyes skimming the room with careful precision. The bleak shadows from the uniform support beams stretched across the floor in deep contrast with the moon's glow. The thick smoke danced between the two extremes creating a blanket of low visibility.

Expanding his senses, Ranger drove out the meaningless sounds of the city below and listened for any signs of life in his surroundings. He slowly reached into his jacket pocket and pulled out a pair of plain black gloves and slipped them on, his senses still reaching out for his opponent's position. With careful but fluid motions, Ranger reached into his coat and returned with a curved short sword and a sleek pistol. He held the sword with a trained grip, the blade reaching up his arm and his pistol steady in his off hand, ready for anything.

"Leave now!" a feminine but powerful voice commanded. "I have no need to spill your blood. I'm only here for Damon, but I will not hesitate to strike you down if you continue to get in my way."

Ranger cursed inwardly. He could hear the voice as clear as a bell, but the echo of the hollowed walls made it difficult to pinpoint her location. She could have been anywhere around him. He needed a visual.

"You must be Luna. I've heard a lot about you," Ranger replied politely as he holstered his pistol and stretched his free hand out toward the smoke. His eyes clouded to a ghostly white again as he extended his focus, forming wisps of wind around his hand.

"And you must be Ranger. They said they'd send you. They never even waited to make the call. I have been dealt a grave injustice, and the Hand Council would be fools to believe that

I would let it stand like they have. Do you have any idea what that woman has done?" Luna asked.

"Not my business. I'm not here to protect Damon Lexus; I'm only here to kill you before you kill her. That's my assignment, and I have to carry it out," he replied, his razor-sharp focus steady on the task at hand while continuing a dialogue with Luna, although he couldn't help but wonder why she continued to talk back.

"Do you put no value in the truth or are the rumors the same for all Hunters? That you simply kill on command without feeling or thought?"

"What about the rumors about you? You are renowned to be formidable in close combat, but you still haven't made your move. Why not show me what the stories are talking about?" Ranger urged.

"You still have time to back away and let me do what needs to be done. I have no intention of taking you down with her, but I am willing to if you stay," Luna warned, her voice frightening in its intensity.

"Are you sure, Luna? Are you truly willing to leave a trail of bodies to your goal?" Ranger asked.

"You think I won't kill you? You think I'm not willing to take that last step?"

"You may have taken a life before, but you're not a killer. Trust me, we can smell our own. Your sense of honor reaches to the core. Even after all you've been through. You could've attacked the second my feet touched the floor, but you continuously try and force me to leave." His frigidly cold tone softened with sympathy toward a Knight who didn't turn into a rapid animal at a Hunter's presence. It was a rarity, but it changed nothing. He knew what he had to do, and especially what he couldn't do. "Unfortunately, I have my orders, Luna, and if you're going to pull this off, you're running out of time."

"So be it," she stated stubbornly.

The shuffle of swift footsteps echoed from all sides. Ranger jumped into action and swung his hand in a wide semicircle, the strings of concentrated current flowing with it. The air pushed the smoke from the building like a wave revealing Luna on a straight charge.

In the same motion, Ranger gripped his pistol and fired three shots in rapid succession. Luna swerved her upper body to the side as a small metal dart sailed past her to stick deep into an unoffending pillar.

Luna's advance was unfaltering, rapidly closing the distance before swinging her sword wide at Ranger's stomach. With the instinctual reflexes of a soldier, Ranger curved his body backward, narrowly avoiding the blade. He then took a wide step back and countered by firing three more shots with the same swift movements. Luna's first attack smoothly glided into her next as she spun on her heel to avoid the darts and kicked Ranger's hand hard, sending the gun skidding across the floor.

Luna twirled gracefully like a top, her sword coming around again for a blow at Ranger's neck. The clash of metals reverberated against the walls as Luna's weapon struck Ranger's.

They moved in a series of strikes and blocks, each move swirling into the next like notes of a song. Ranger extended little and kept on the defensive, watching Luna's movements with a careful eye to find the first mistake. Luna's style shifted into more and more aggression as the seconds flew by, determined to gain back her window of opportunity. Her growing frustration was clear as day to Ranger.

The small steps of retreat keeping Ranger on the defensive suddenly halted when his back met the hard surface of a pillar. Luna seized the advantage and brought her sword back for a powerful thrust for Ranger's chest. Her blade might have been fast, but Ranger's cunning mind was faster. He waited until the last possible second before making an efficient side step, allowing her sword to dig deep into the structure. Luna cursed as she pulled and struggled to release her blade from the pillar's grip, but it stuck firmly in place. A flicker of moonlight reflected off Ranger's blade, snatching her attention as he swung down at Luna, still clutching at her blade. She was forced to make a choice, give up the sword or lose so much more.

"Dammit!" Luna swore, begrudgingly releasing her grip as she staggered back from his strike range.

Ranger leaped forward and drove his blade down at her, but she skillfully sidestepped and snatched his arm at the wrist. Her thumb dug hard into a pressure point, forcing his fingers apart from his weapon and letting it fall the floor with a clang. At the second his blade dropped, she barreled her hip into his, breaking his center of gravity, and tossed him firmly over her shoulder. Ranger hit the floor flat on his back with a painful thud.

Luna flipped herself over Ranger's head and pinned his body down with hers. Her eyes blazed with intense blue light as small bolts of electricity manifested from her fist that barreled down toward Ranger. In a knee-jerk reaction, Ranger caught her fist on its descent, struggling to hold it in place. Luna cried out a muffled battle cry as she swung her other fist down at him, but it was snatched from its attack as well.

A sign of worry struck Luna's expression. Ranger should have been electrocuted by the power she focused through her fists, but the lightning remained stagnant. Her blazing blue eyes flicked their gaze toward the peculiar gloves he wore.

"That's right; I do my homework," Ranger spat through gritted teeth before jabbing his knee solidly into Luna's stomach. She lurched forward, the air from her lungs flowing past her lips, seeping the strength from her arms. Ranger pushed hard with his legs and flipped her over his head. She fell into a tucked roll to land low on her feet and swiftly pivoted back to face her enemy as he rose.

A brief moment of silence washed over the two as they stood in quiet observation of the other. They were both smart and experienced enough to know that reckless actions with an opponent of their caliber would do nothing but send them six feet under. "Clever move with the rubber gloves, Hunter," Luna commended, keeping her keen eyes trained on Ranger.

"Like I said, I've heard a lot about you. I made a point of it," Ranger retorted.

"But unless you're wearing a full suit, your cleverness is only a speed bump." She sprung for her opponent to unleash a flurry of swift jabs and punches, her fists crackling with electricity. Their hands became a blur of motion as Ranger moved in fluid swirls, deflecting her dangerous strikes with his protected hands.

With every blocked attack, Luna's face contorted with a deep vexation. Ranger knew she was looking for the kink in his strategy, but he imagined she was realizing that he never relied on strength, speed, or agility. Ranger instead relied on pure skill and experience, something that could not be easily overcome by a younger opponent. She was up against a strategy made for her.

She immediately broke off the struggle and retreated to a safe distance with Ranger close behind. Focusing the tide of her abilities into her hands, she clasped them together and formed a bolt of lightning that dwarfed the power he'd seen before. The electricity jumped from hand to hand like a stream of dangerous energy.

Ranger halted dead in his tracks and threw himself out of the path as she fired the destructive projectile. The lightning bolt smashed against a half-built wall behind him, demolishing it. Debris rained down on Ranger as he sprinted away from the danger. If he was going to be a target, he might as well be a moving one.

Luna continued to fire at Ranger, keeping him on the run and unable to attack. The quiet night was shattered as the lightning tore through the interior of the floor, changing it to a scarred battlefield. Ranger kept moving as fast as he could, narrowly avoiding Luna's destructive pathway. Despite the raw power behind Luna's blasts, they were always one step behind Ranger. They bore the sign of mere warning shots rather than attempts on his life. Unfortunately, if he continued to get in her way, that mercy wouldn't last.

A metal gleam on the horizon of his vision gave him the first thread of a plan for his salvation: his dart pistol. He reached down and snatched it off the ground in the midst of his sprint, his momentum unfaltering.

He glanced at the magazine of his pistol and back to Luna, hurling brilliant death his way. He cursed under his breath. He only had a few darts left and he'd require all of them to take her down. Under these conditions, he couldn't risk missing her. He needed a clean shot.

Ranger skidded to a stop when a blast of lightning crashed into the wall in front of him, cutting off his advance. In the span of a mere heartbeat, the heat from the electricity melted a hole in a sheet of plastic that had been covering a piece of missing floor from the upper level. Ranger was suddenly drenched in the rainwater that had gathered there, and his heart skipped with panic.

Fear flooded his mind when his reality truly sunk in. She didn't even have to hit him directly to kill him, just the water. Even a small bolt would be enough to turn him into an unrecognizable sack of burnt flesh. He franticly scanned the room and found a piece of wall that luckily hadn't been destroyed, and he dove for cover. He snapped his eyes shut to quiet the fear in his heart and rushed to make a plan before he noticed a strange sound . . . silence. No explosions, no crackling of lightning, no advancing footsteps, just a cold and confusing silence.

He inched to the edge of the wall and slowly peeked around the corner. His brow raised in a quizzical fashion when he saw Luna standing in place, her hand quivering and an inner torment reflected in her expression. *What is she doing?* Ranger thought. *She literally had me dead in the water, but she hesitated. She seems terrified.*

Ranger's mind rapidly ran through plans of action as he shuffled through his remaining tools. He pulled out a small canister with a pin at the top. His eyes flicked between the canister and the dart pistol. *This may work.*

Ranger peeked over the wall to assess his enemy's composure; she had stopped shaking but still appeared distracted. It was time to move before Luna strengthened her guard. In a split-second motion, Ranger jumped to his feet, pulled the canister pin, and tossed it at Luna.

In a reaction driven by pure reflex, Luna blasted the canister in the air with a bolt of bright lightning. The canister exploded in a flash of blinding white light that spread over the entire level. Luna slammed her eyes shut, blinding her from the coming danger. Suddenly, she felt a sharp pain in her left shoulder and leg. She opened her eyes and saw three metal darts sticking out from her skin. She immediately yanked the darts from her flesh, but it was too late.

He calmly strolled toward Luna, holstering his dart pistol as he walked. She stretched out her hand in warning, but Ranger continued his advance, unfazed by the threat. Luna made the motion to attack with another deadly bolt, but the energy failed to manifest. Her battle-hardened demeanor fell from her expression as she gazed upon her hands with a dumbstruck gawk.

"This is a special tranquilizer that I have picked up over the years. First it dulls the sense of feeling to the extremities making it near impossible for someone like you to use your abilities," Ranger explained as he advanced on her position with a casual march.

"That won't stop me," Luna spat, leaping forward into a charge when her legs suddenly gave out from under her, and she collapsed hard on the floor.

"Next it dampens your motor skills, immobilizing you," Ranger continued, drawing a handgun from its holster. Luna struggled with all her being to get up and fight before losing full control, clawing her way onto her back. Her mind screamed in a frantic panic for her body to respond, staring helplessly up the barrel of Ranger's gun as he stood over her.

She reached a trembling hand to grasp at something hanging from her neck on a silver chain, holding the ring for dear life. As she prepared for her end, she whispered, "I'm sorry, Cole."

Ranger's dark eyes met Luna's gaze as his usual cold demeanor slowly faded. "What did you say?"

"What?"

"What did you say?"

Luna turned away from him. "What does it matter?"

"Tell me . . . please," he insisted.

Luna looked back to him. "I told Cole I was sorry, sorry that I failed him," she spat back her answer the best she could in her weakened state. Tears began to swell in her eyes, summoned by her painful memories.

Ranger's eyes portrayed a strange combination of confusion and sympathy. "Why? Why are you doing all this? Why go so far, to risk your life to avenge a mere Master? Does your life hold nothing else in it that you would leap toward certain death just to avenge a corpse? You could've just walked away from this if you left Damon alone, if you stayed away and forgot all about Luna. What were you thinking?" Ranger probed angrily, his outburst showing the most emotion Luna had seen throughout their whole encounter.

Luna's face twisted with rage at Ranger regarding Cole in that manner. "You wouldn't understand!" she snapped through gritted teeth.

"You're right; I don't understand. I can't seem to wrap my brain around your reasoning, so why don't you help me?" he shouted back.

"What?"

"Help me understand!" he pleaded.

The mask of the cold, calculated Hunter could not hold any longer. Ranger was overtaken with a powerful need to understand Luna's actions. He couldn't just push the nagging feeling raging inside his mind down any longer. He became mentally unable to move forward and be the obedient servant. He needed answers to these questions, even if he was unsure why.

"Cole Iver was more than merely a man that gave me orders. He was a kind and brilliant Master to me as a Knight." She clutched the ring close to her heart. "He was my world, and because of Damon, he's gone and he's never coming back. With a wave of her hand she stole him from me and abused her position as a Master to do it. It's not right, and it's not fair. I don't care if the Council doesn't believe me; I will stop this from happening to anyone else." Her voice began to trail off as the tranquilizer ran its course. "I will . . . stop . . . the . . ." Luna's words halted as she drifted into a heavy sleep.

Ranger's mind stirred with conflict, staring down at the unconscious warrior he was ordered to hunt. He had heard some teary-eyed stories before, but this was different. If he hadn't forced the issue, Luna would have gone into the long night without a word. She didn't preach her crusade in a feeble attempt to save her own skin.

He slowly lowered his gun and knelt down beside her sleeping body. *What was she clinging to?* he asked himself. He gave her a stiff nudge to confirm the drugs full effect and carefully pried her hand open. Nestled in her palm was a beautiful diamond ring that hung off a silver chain around her neck.

Ranger's shoulders slumped down, and he rubbed his weary eyes, feeling the full weight of his final decision. He sighed. "I hope I don't regret this."

CHAPTER 20

MOTIONLESS AND EXHAUSTED, Aurora stared blankly into the seemingly endless darkness that surrounded her. She couldn't mask the dreariness inside her heart; she felt that her whole world had beaten her down to nothing. There was no drive or ambition in the veil of black, only hopeless surrender and a profound sadness. Tears swelled in her sapphire-blue eyes as the burden of her tragic reality weighed down on her like a heavy coat.

"I've lost," she whispered. "It's all over and I've failed." Her emotions rolled into silent weeping as her despair overcame her control. "Cole's gone, and I'm as good as dead. We thought we could change things for the better, but in the end, we were so powerless. Getting rid of us was only a minor undertaking for them. I worked so hard to become strong, to become the best, and I still couldn't stop it," she cried out, furious at the cruel world she couldn't change, but most of all, angry at her own helplessness.

"Avenge me," an eerie voice echoed all around her.

Aurora snapped out of her daze and into a defensive stance, her eyes scanning the veil of pitch black. "Who's there?" she demanded.

"Avenge me," the voiced called again. A frighteningly familiar figure manifested from the shadows to stand before her.

Aurora's face stiffened with resounding shock, and her eyes locked into an unbreakable gape. The sight of the man she watched die standing before her shattered her warrior's will and left only a distraught young woman. Her mind refused to believe the sight before her, but her heart wished it were true. She wanted to run to him, wanted to prove that it wasn't a fevered illusion, but froze when she saw the true nightmare of the image. The man before her was Cole down to the last detail, except his skin had a sickly green tinge and the whites of his eyes were a vile yellow. The undone buttons of his shirt revealed five blackened gashes down his chest, dark discoloration stretching out into diseased veins. He appeared exactly the same as when he had died.

Aurora called out to him desperately, but her cries fell on deaf ears. No matter what she did, Cole would not acknowledge her. He simply stood before her repeatedly asking to be avenged in a calm, ghostly whisper that sent shivers up Aurora's spine.

Aurora fell to her knees and slammed her fist hard on the ground. "I'm sorry, Cole," she pleaded. "I failed to protect you, and I couldn't avenge your death. I'm sorry." Her head hung low in shame as her body started to tremble, Cole's haunting words echoing in her ears.

"I'll avenge you," a woman's voice promised. The voice rang with an eerie familiarity; it was her own voice, but it did not come from her lips. Her breath came in hurried gasps as she slowly tilted her head up and set her eyes upon a truly bizarre sight. She saw . . . herself in her Luna glamour standing beside Cole. She was clad in her battle uniform with sword and pistol in hand. There was a cold steadiness in her voice and a frightening determination in her jade eyes. "I'll avenge you."

From the depths of the black veil appeared a dozen or more Knights prepared for battle with Damon Lexus sitting snug at their back, that usual wicked smile draped over her face. Aurora's double turned from her Master's side to face the enemy, fury burning in her eyes.

She bellowed a ferocious battle cry as she charged into the cluster of well-armed Knights headlong. Her moves were intense, powerful, and always deadly. Aurora's double held back nothing and, without hesitating, went in for the kill. She could only watch in horror at the grotesque scene her double left in her wake. That darkened place quickly became stained with the blood of her enemies. Her face twisted with rage as she slashed through enemy after enemy, leaving only gutted corpses behind, their faces frozen in fear. The sight of herself fighting with the anger and reckless abandon of a vicious beast struck terror into Aurora's heart. It was a fear unlike anything she had ever known.

Aurora cupped her hands over her ears and clenched her eyes shut to block out the panicked screams of the Knights being slaughtered one by one. "No!" she cried. "No, that isn't me! That isn't me!"

"Oh, yes it is, Luna," a smooth voice whispered in her ear. She whipped around and saw the charred body of her fallen enemy, Venom. Empty sockets where her eyes had been burnt out stared back at Aurora. "No one knows that more than me," she hissed as her voice rolled into a hideous cackle that cut right down to Aurora's soul.

She closed her eyes tightly, refusing to gaze upon the laughing product of her rage. "Stop it. This isn't real! This is a dream. It must be. It has to be."

"Of course it's not real. How could it be real? You killed me, Luna. Maybe this is hell where you are confronted by your mistakes and forced to see yourself for the beast you really are," Venom said.

"Stop it!" Aurora shouted.

"You couldn't even imagine the utter terror I felt when I died," Venom continued despite Aurora's pleading.

"Shut up."

"It's a good thing Ranger stopped you or else this horror show you're seeing would be real. You would've never stopped; you would've walked the path of hatred and bitter revenge to the bloody result. Look at it," Venom barked.

Aurora peeled open her eyes to catch a glimpse of the battle, but that was all that was needed to lock her gaze upon it. Her double's face was painted crimson with blood and set with an expression of insane fury. Her silver sword was smeared scarlet as it trailed on the ground, marking her advance on a petrified Damon Lexus. Damon stared with a pure, unending fear as her last warrior crawled desperately toward her before Luna thrust her sword through his skull. Damon let out a shrill scream, and she scrambled into a panicked retreat.

The double then tossed her weapons aside and stretched her hand toward the fleeing Damon. Her eyes sparked into a blaze of electric-blue light and lightning manifested in the palm of her hand. "Die!" she spat with a cold finality to the word. A bolt of brilliant blue energy fired from her hand, smashing square into Damon's back. The force swept Damon off her feet, and her body tumbled to the floor, convulsing from the shock. Luna continued pumping lightning into Damon's fallen body, creating a wide arch of blue electricity between them. Damon's flesh began to sizzle and smoke, and her eyes started to melt in their sockets.

Aurora stared as the frightening vision as her double turned Damon into a gruesomely contorted heap of burnt flesh. "Look familiar, Luna?" Venom asked.

That was the breaking point. Her body trembled violently as her mind flashed to Venom's grisly death. A bone-chilling scream fell from her lips.

Over the screaming, over the sounds of battle and death and over Venom's maddening cackles, a strange whistling noise could be heard. It carried on over the carnage and suddenly, the pitch-black nightmare faded into mere memory.

Luna woke up in a cold sweat, breathing heavily with her nightmare freshly etched into her mind. She shielded her eyes away from morning sun that shined brightly through a window across the room. She blinked to adjust her vision, gathering her bearings and observing her surroundings. The room was plain, without any flare or decoration to its white walls, light blue tiled floor, and one light fixture in the center of the ceiling. Luna had been placed on a soft, caramel-brown couch with a small pillow propped under her head. The only other furniture in the room was a folding chair and a small counter that lined the far wall. The counter had a pale-blue top, a small built-in stove and sink, and white cupboards above it. The whistling of a boiling teakettle sang through the room.

Standing at the stove was Ranger, calmly pouring the boiled water into a white porcelain mug. Luna's heart raced as the memory of staring up the barrel of Ranger's gun flashed through her mind. That was her last conscious memory; Ranger had his finger on the trigger when everything went black. Dozens of questions fluttered through her brain like a flock of birds. *Where was she? Why did he bring her here? What did he plan to do?* And above all else, *Why was she still alive?*

No matter how much these questions ached to be answered, she couldn't afford to stick around to find out his angle. She was alive and that meant she could still fight. She had to escape. Luna locked her eyes toward the door across the room and prepared to run. Before she could even shift her weight, she heard the unmistakable click of a gun's hammer and she froze. Her eyes flicked back to Ranger, and she was once again staring down the barrel of his gun.

Behind the gun she saw Ranger's dark, calculating eyes watching her intently at a side-glance. "I insist you lie down, Luna. We have some matters to discuss."

Several different options fired rapidly through Luna's mind. Should she try and run for freedom in spite of Ranger? Did she even have a chance? No, he had her in his sights and her physical condition was an uncertainty. She didn't know if she would be faster than his trigger finger. It would be foolish to act on a reckless chance. The smart choice was to play along with him until the right opportunity presented itself.

She carefully sat back on the couch, keeping a careful eye on Ranger and the gun pointed at her. "Where am I?" she asked with a tone as flat as she could manage.

Ranger turned to Luna with the steaming cup in one hand and the pistol in the other and sat in the folding chair. His aim did not move from Luna for a moment. His dark eyes were strangely intense, but calm at the same time. They analyzed every detail with a calculated focus and the intensity of a hunter stalking prey. "That's irrelevant."

"Not to me, it isn't," Luna spat back.

"But it is irrelevant to our conversation," Ranger answered coldly.

"Why did you bring me here?" she continued.

"I told you, we have something to discuss."

Aurora scowled at Ranger; he was diverting her questions as if she were a child. It was getting her nowhere. She had to cut to the chase, ask the question that was burning in her mind. "Why didn't you kill me when you had the chance?"

Ranger paused. An air of deep contemplation emanated from him but he never broke his lock on the target. "I don't know yet."

She raised her eyebrow in a quizzical gape. "What do you mean you don't know yet?"

"There are some inconsistencies with the information I have been given. I'd prefer to act after I get the facts straight rather than hastily doing something I can't undo."

Luna watched Ranger's body language and expressions for signs of deception. He was perfectly composed with no visible indications of anxiety. He was either truthful or an extremely good actor. Then again, she knew Ranger was no fool. In battle, he relied on strategy more than strength or power. It was possible he didn't swallow the story Damon force-fed everyone else, but what would he do when he found the truth? "What do you want to know?" Luna asked.

"Why do you want to kill Damon Lexus?" Ranger asked.

"She killed my Master."

"I heard that Venom went Rogue and assassinated Cole Iver of her own will," he replied before taking a small sip of tea, still keeping his pistol on target.

Luna's face involuntarily twitched with anger. "Damon ordered Venom to kill Cole in a disgraceful and dishonorable strategy! That story of Venom going Rogue is nothing but a lie," Aurora barked.

Ranger's composure stood unchanged with Luna's outburst. "Do you have proof?" he asked simply.

"Venom admitted it to me before she died."

"Did anyone witness this confession?"

Luna shakes her head. "But Venom was loyal to her core. She would have never acted on her own," she argued.

"Not even to take the initiative to please her Master?" Ranger theorized.

Luna shook her head. "No, the timing is just too convenient for Damon to be unrelated."

"Why is it convenient for her that Cole Iver was murdered? What is your history with her?" Ranger inquired.

Luna's jade-green eyes grew distant as she began to recall the struggle between Damon and Cole, the core of what Luna was fighting for. "My Master and I started digging for information on how Damon Lexus was acquiring more Knights under her rule a few years back. Each one of their Masters died under suspicious circumstances, and after the Knights would pledge themselves to her family. Cole believed that she was arranging the deaths and strong-arming the Knights to join her."

"Did you ever find proof of that?" Ranger asked.

"We had gathered almost enough information connecting her to these deaths to make a case the Hand Council couldn't ignore. There was another Master, Morgan Clouse, and his Knight Claymore that were also investigating Damon's methods," Luna spat out the words rather than speaking them, as if they made her sick to the core. "But Morgan didn't want to share his findings with us; he held on to it like a precious diamond. So they solved the problem in the manner all Masters do, with their Knights. I fought Claymore in a duel and won the information. Damon must have found that they were working against her. The very next day, Morgan was found dead of a heart attack and a body with the same wounds I gave Claymore was found shot and dumped."

"What happened to Cole Iver?" Ranger asked, his intense gaze never leaving Luna for a moment.

Luna's appearance hardened as she struggled to conceal the despair behind the memory. "I was going to see Cole that night to discuss something of importance, but when I got to his home, it was dark and silent. I was only led to Cole by his screams where I found Venom pumping her poison into him. I was too late; I was only there a few moments before he died."

"Is that when you killed Venom?"

"I did what any Knight would've done. I avenged my Master's murder. She broke into his home and killed a Master without his weapon. She must've known there was a chance of danger," she stated firmly.

Ranger cocked his head to the side and let out a simple, "Huh," as if he'd found something interesting, but he stayed quiet. Luna couldn't help but wonder what he had seen.

"The poison Venom pumped into my Master would have probably looked like a natural passing in an autopsy. That's probably why Damon Lexus picked her. Who knows how many other murders went unnoticed. But they won't be able to hide this one. When the authorities see Venom's body and the signs of struggle, they will question his death."

"You sound very certain of that." Ranger questioned.

"I knew it might expose the rest of the world to the Knights but . . . I couldn't just leave him there like that. When I was retreating back to my home, I used a pay phone and called the police, told them just enough to get them to Cole's house," Aurora confessed, no longer concerning herself with the consequences of that action. "Lexus wouldn't have had enough time to cover it up. They would've found everything."

Ranger's expression turned to a quizzical glower, and he tumbled her story in his mind. "Roughly how long after the fight was that call?"

Luna turned her gaze to the side as she reached for the answer in her memories. "Maybe twenty minutes."

"That time line doesn't match up. I spent some time looking into the case of Cole's death and found the record showing that the police didn't show until four hours later," Ranger informed.

Luna's brow crinkled with discontent as she felt the gravity of those words. "Lexus must have someone with the police who delayed the dispatch, giving them time to . . . clean up."

Ranger's chest heaved in a deep sigh, and his expression was heavy, as if preparing to give bad news. "I'm sorry, but your plan failed. The police found no signs of struggle or forced entry. Due to the high-profile nature of the case, Cole Iver's autopsy was moved up in priority. The medical examiner has ruled it a natural death."

Sitting in a stunned silence, Luna's expression grew weak and distant, the gaze of the utterly defeated. "Then they got what they wanted. The police think it's a natural death, and the Council puts the blame solely on Venom. Lexus gets to go free and ruin more lives, and it's all because the Hand Council can't see past her lies and see how this benefits her. She got Cole out of the way right after we found evidence that would've buried her, and they mark it as a coincidence." The more Luna spoke of the injustice she had witnessed, the more that defeated look in her eyes turned to fire. She faced Ranger with an unrelenting flame that would never completely extinguish. "But I know the truth. Venom admitted she was ordered to kill Cole, and I'm going to prove it. Damon needs to be stopped!"

Her newfound enthusiasm was followed by a long silence. Ranger was unshaken by her reaction and merely kept his eyes upon her, taking in every detail. "I believe you," he said flatly as he slipped his gun back into its holster.

Luna stared at him, baffled. "What is this?"

"Your answers matched your version of the story you told at the inquisition," he stated, his composure steady and unwavering.

Luna gawked at Ranger, speechless as she tried to understand the boggling maze that was this man's intentions. He was impossible to read, and his actions made no sense to her. "If you knew the whole story, why did you ask me those questions?"

Ranger set the cup beside him on the floor and crossed his arms, leaning back into the chair. "I wasn't looking for the answers; I was looking for how you would answer them. I needed to see if you were lying about any of it."

"You knew how to see if I was lying by just watching me?"

"It's something I had to learn along the way as a Hunter. People say a lot more than what they simply speak. It's the things they don't say that often lead to the truth. You told me three things I didn't know before without realizing it. For one, you were romantically involved with your Master," Ranger revealed.

Luna drew in a quick breath in shock.

"Before you passed out, you said that Cole was more to you than just a Master. When you speak of him, there was strong emotion in your words. No other Knight would have reacted the way you did when their Master died because the next-in-line would simply fill the place, but you can't replace someone you love. That's why you went all or nothing for revenge even though the dangers and consequences were staring you in the face. Although that merely shows devotion that could be one-sided, the diamond ring you were clinging to earlier expresses so much more. You held on to it when you were telling him you were sorry for not being able to avenge him. I'm guessing that it's an engagement ring. That fact you gave away easily, but in your defense, you did think you were going to die, so I doubt you really cared."

Luna swallowed hard, trying to keep a steady composure over the growing unease she felt in the pit of her stomach.

Ranger continued his eerily accurate analysis. "You are also a true believer in the Code of Honor a Knight follows. That's why you showed such disgust when you spoke of Damon's methods and how Claymore was thrown away like trash. The fact that other Knights are forsaking that Code and committing these disgraceful acts sends you into a rage. It brings into question all you have believed, and that makes you angry. That's what threw you off the edge with Venom. The fact that a Knight broke into your Master's home and murdered him, giving him no way to defend himself; that drove you into a rage, didn't it?" Ranger probed.

Luna turned away from him, refusing to meet his gaze. She played right into his hands and gave him so much without realizing it.

"Venom was your first kill, wasn't she?" Ranger asked, a tinge of sympathy breaking through the cold stone. Luna looked back at Ranger, her forced calm beginning to fall away faster than she could build it up again. She slammed her mouth shut and refused to speak another word. "I'm right, aren't I? That was the hardest thing to see because you were actively trying to hide it, but not from me. You tried to hide it behind your pride to forget your fear. The real question is, is it the fear of your own mortality or fear of what you're really capable of?"

"Stop it," Luna whispered through clenched teeth.

"When you first take a life, it shocks you to the core, changes you forever. It can make you useless in battle or turn you into a monster. It can make or break a Hunter. I can understand why you would try and hide it."

"Stop it!" Luna shouted, her hands balled up into shaking fists.

Ranger retreated from the inquiry. "I apologize. I stepped over the line." Ranger remained silent but watchful of Luna as she gradually regained her composure. "My point is that I saw no deception in the answers you gave. What you said was right; the circumstances are entirely too much in Damon's favor to be a coincidence."

"You think Damon ordered the killing?" Luna asked.

"From what I heard, Damon is a self-righteous narcissist who thinks of herself as a visionary for a new way. She most likely thinks the Code is outdated and takes it with a grain of salt. I wouldn't put it past her for a moment to use her Knights as personal assassins," Ranger explained.

Luna sat in silence, trying to assess the true nature of this man, but she was continually spun in circles with what she knew. He said that he believed her story and that Damon was guilty, but what exactly did that mean? She had no idea what he was planning to accomplish by not killing her even though he was ordered to. He read her like a book, but then apologized for it. She hated that he took so much from her actions, but she couldn't pull a single thread of insight from him. Whatever he was planning, he had holstered his pistol, and that was an opening she couldn't pass up.

"I need to leave," Luna said as she rose, her legs collapsing from under her on her first step.

Ranger leaped from his chair, bracing Luna in his arms. "Easy, the tranquilizer hasn't worn off yet."

The facade of the fainting woman immediately faded when Luna snatched the gun from Ranger's holster and elbowed him hard in the face. Luna spun like a top and landed a solid kick to Ranger's chest, sending him tumbling backward onto the hard tiled floor. He shook the stars from his eyes and came face-to-face with the barrel of his own pistol in Luna's hand, her feet steady and her aim locked.

Ranger raised a curious eyebrow, not sure what he was seeing. "How are you already standing?"

"That's irrelevant," she spat, throwing the evasive reply back in his face.

"You shouldn't have your balance back yet with the dose you received," Ranger argued.

"I'm a Knight. We're built differently," she retorted.

"Do you think I hunt deer? That composition was made for Knights."

"What does it matter?" Luna barked. "Why are you doing all this? It doesn't make any sense! You don't make any sense! You keep saying you believe my story, but what does that matter to me? You're a Hunter; Hunters only answer to the Hand, so why do you even care if it's true or not? Why didn't you kill me? That's what they wanted, isn't it?"

"I should ask you the same question, Luna," Ranger spat back.

"What are you talking about?"

"You said that all you wanted was revenge for your Master, that you were willing to do anything for it, but I'm not buying it. If that were true, you would've lit me up the second I got drenched by that rainwater. I would've been out of your way, and you would've killed Damon easily. You had the perfect opportunity, but you suddenly froze because you didn't want to kill me. You don't really want to kill Damon either; you just think you do because you want justice for what happened."

"Shut up!" Luna screamed. "Just shut up! I don't know what you hope to gain here, and I don't care anymore. I'm sick of playing this game! What do you want with me?"

"I want to help you," Ranger confessed with his empty hands out in a show of peace and surrender.

Luna blinked in stunned confusion. "What?"

"I want to help you stop this once and for all. This has gone further than just Damon Lexus."

"More Masters are using their Knights as personal assassins?" Luna asked, keeping the gun on Ranger.

"Two others, as far as I know, and they have been doing this longer than her."

Luna shot Ranger a furious scowl. "How long have you known?"

"I confirmed my suspicions a couple years after they started."

"This has been going on that long? Why didn't you take what you knew to the Hand Council?" she demanded, fury beginning to boil inside of her.

"The Hand Council has been corrupted. They couldn't help me then, and they can't help you now, or at least they won't," Ranger said.

Luna shook her head. "No, that's not possible. How do you know this?"

Ranger pulled himself to his feet, avoiding Luna's eyes. "There were other Masters and Knights who tried to make their fight against these people. Soon after they made their stand, they became my assigned targets."

Aurora staggered back a step, her face mirroring her inner conflict. She heard the words but couldn't believe them. She had always known the Hand Council to be the impartial order among the Knights and their Masters. They were supposed to be the ones who kept balance, who made sure Masters didn't take power by dishonorable means. They were supposed to be the Hand that guides the powerful. After what happened, Luna had her suspicions, but to hear it confirmed shook her more than she ever thought it would.

Ranger eyes trailed over her pained expression and stepped toward her, offering a comforting hand. Luna snapped back to attention and reconfirmed her aim with the pistol. "Don't come near me. Why should I believe you?"

"For the same reason I believe you: because it's the truth. And I'm sure you have the resources to find out for yourself," Ranger reasoned.

"If you knew about this, why didn't you do anything?"

Ranger exhaled a harsh sigh, and his eyes became distant. "In a prison, there are two kinds of inmates. There are those who always dream of escape. They value freedom above all. Then there are those who compromise and surrender themselves and do things they are not proud of. They value survival."

"You're not making any sense," Luna barked.

"You are the one who never submits and never sacrifices your beliefs. I'm the one who simply survives," Ranger continued, his gaze avoiding hers.

"You stood back and let this continue just to save your own skin?" Luna snapped.

"If it were only my life at stake, I wouldn't care, but my Master's family's power and influence has diminished over the years. They aren't even involved in the conflict, haven't been for generations. If they could get to someone like Cole Iver so easily, my Master wouldn't stand a chance," Ranger explained, trying to hide the guilt of his inaction behind a mask of reasoning.

Luna's face softened, empathizing with his situation and eagerness to keep his Master safe. She had felt the same when Cole was alive. "What's different now?"

Ranger locked his intense stare with Luna's jade-green eyes. "You. You're what's different. I can't do this alone, and from what I see in you, you're exactly what I need."

"Need for what?" she demanded.

"To take down the prison. That's the only way to break this chain of sorrow and loss."

Aurora paused for a long moment, staring at Ranger with speculation lacing her demeanor. "Are you talking about removing the Hand Council? Is that even possible?"

"The only reason we think it's impossible is because it's never been done, and it's never been done because we all think it's impossible."

"Ranger, we may be strong, but the Hand Council can call on every Knight to go against us if they wished. How do you even plan to pull this off?" Luna asked.

"This has been going on a long time, Luna. There may be others just like you who have lost something precious because of the Hand and those three power hungry tyrants. We can find them, start a resistance. It would be the hardest, most dangerous undertaking either of us has experienced, and it will take time, but it is possible," Ranger explained, his once intense Hunter's glare showed a sense of drive and hope that reminded Luna of Cole.

Luna reflected on the utter pain and anger she felt when Cole was murdered, on how others had suffered much like her. She thought of the unlucky ones who were sent to their deaths. That memory more than anything made her want to take Ranger up on his offer. He was right, this had to stop and if the ones at the top were corrupt, the Order could not be saved. The shining light of a distant hope was shrouded by cold rationality. She knew she had survived through too much to venture blindly into an unknown venture. She needed time to substantiate his claims.

Luna stood in decisive silence, her mind's busy rambling screamed in deep contrast to the still room. It whispered and muttered of a fear to trust anyone, a need to join Ranger and set things right, and a vain attempt to understand his reasoning. Throughout the storm of jumbled thoughts, one voice rang clear as day. A calm inner voice that asked, *Can you afford to throw this chance away?*

She took in a steadying breath and prepared to do something potentially reckless. "There is a restaurant on the corner of 125th Street and 47th Avenue called Lupo. I'll need a couple of days to find out if you're telling the truth. If you are who you say you are, I will meet you there for a nine p.m. reservation in two days. The reservation will be made under the name

Jasmine Lang. If you're serious about this, you'll be there. If you try anything, I assure you, I will be prepared for it. Got it?"

"I won't try anything," Ranger insisted.

Luna slowly backtracked to the door, keeping the gun on Ranger. "I'm keeping the gun, and if you follow me, I'll shoot you in the leg."

"Got it," he answered, but before Luna could leave the room he called out to her. "I'm sorry for your loss."

Luna could hear a tender sympathy in his voice, but from what she had experienced the last few days, she wasn't sure on anything or anyone. She could only hold hope that his benevolent gestures were genuine. "So am I."

CHAPTER 21

WITH A HEAVY heart and tearfilled eyes, Zander picked up the phone and dialed the last option he hoped it would ever come to. He took in deep, calming breaths to regain his composure. The empty ringtone echoed in his ear as his eyes drifted to the morning sun hanging in the sky.

It was the morning of the third day since Aurora had been called to the inquisition, and all his attempts to find or contact her had failed. This was his last duty to perform as her guardian, and it weighed heavier on him then he ever thought it would.

Zander was snapped back into focus by a recognizable click from the other end of the phone line. "Hello, this is the Fallon estate. How may I help you?" a woman with an upbeat charm about her voice answered.

"This is Alexander Garran. I need to speak with Arthur Fallon. It's in regards to his daughter," he insisted, his tone deathly serious.

"Certainly. One moment, please," the woman replied.

Zander sat in silent anticipation before a gentleman with a refined, but masculine voice spoke on the other line. "Zander, what is it?"

Zander decided that the easiest way to explain the situation was to start from the beginning. "Young Master Cole Iver has been killed."

"How?" Arthur asked.

"He was assassinated by a Knight named Venom. Venom's Master says that Venom acted on her own to kill Cole, but Aurora didn't believe her."

"A Master using a Knight as an assassin! This will not stand!" Arthur spat harshly. "Let me talk to Aurora!" he commanded.

Zander froze for a long moment, gathering up the courage to bear the bad news. "She's not here. She caught Venom in the act and flew into a rage. She killed Venom. When she made it home, she was called by the Hand Council to an inquisition. They wanted to know who was responsible for Venom and Cole's deaths. I haven't seen her since."

Zander's news was answered by a long stoic silence. "How long ago was that?" her father asked, his voice shifting down into a sullen tone.

"Almost three days ago. There's something else that you should know. Before Aurora left, she was grief-stricken, wasn't in her right mind. She kept talking about how Venom was just a weapon and the one responsible was the wielder. She was talking about killing Damon Lexus at the inquisition," Zander continued, panic elevating in his speech.

Arthur sighed heavily. "I'll use my resources to try and find out what happened at the inquisition and if the Hunters have been issued any new targets, but that will take some time. If she doesn't contact you in the meanwhile and I don't find anything, we'll have to assume the worst and from the public story," Arthur explained.

The tension inside Zander rose at even the idea of Aurora never coming back and her own father just sweeping it under the rug. The very aspect of what Arthur was suggesting just felt wrong in more ways than he could count. "Sir, with all due respect, maybe if we reported her missing, the police might be able to find something and . . ."

"Out of the question!" Arthur barked. "If we bring the authorities into this, they will start digging into matters that everyone in the Order, including Aurora, doesn't want them digging into. We have a higher responsibility to keep the Knight's Order a secret from the general public. She knows that, I know that, and every generation of Knights before us knew that. Aurora knew of the dangers and knew that she may get hurt or die. She has always known this, and I will not insult her intelligence by thinking otherwise."

"But Arthur . . ." Zander protested.

"Not another word, Zander!" Arthur snapped before quickly lowering his voice to a calm, sullen tone. "If she did indeed try to kill Damon at the inquisition, there are only a few outcomes I can see. She either succeeded and was executed for it or failed and was executed for trying."

"What if she backed out? What if the Hand Council took her side? If there is a slight possibility that she's alive, we should be doing all we can to find her," Zander argued.

"We'll be doing everything we can afford to. Yes, it is possible that the Hand Council took her side, but like you said, she hasn't contacted you for almost three days now. If she were safe, she would've found some way to get word back to you, wouldn't she?" The conversation fell into a dreaded and uncomfortable silence until Arthur spoke up. "Zander, do not think ill of me for my actions. She's my daughter, and my heart breaks thinking of what may have happened to her, but she would want us to stand strong with the Code. That's the way it has always been done, and that is the way it will always be done. Do you understand?"

"Yes, sir," Zander answered in no more than a soft whisper of sad compliance.

"I'll contact you if I find anything. Goodbye, Zander," Arthur said before disconnecting the call. Zander stood frozen, the lifeless dial tone echoing in his ear as he reluctantly hung up the receiver. He leaned against the table, head hung low in sorrow.

"Aurora," he whispered, his words breaking into a mournful sob. "Aurora."

"Zander," spoke a soft voice from the hollowed silence of the empty home. Zander turned to the source, a surprised gasp escaping him as he laid his eyes upon a brown-haired, blue-eyed young woman. His worry slid off him like water, relieved to see her home once again. He began to slowly stagger toward Aurora. "Have I gone insane from grief or just senile?"

Aurora smiled. "Neither. I'm home, Zander." She and Zander met in the middle in a joyous reunion. The reunion of two people who truly thought they would never see each other again. Their mere presence gave each of them a sense of wellness and security they hadn't felt since Cole's death. As if things could be normal again.

Zander fretted over Aurora for the next while, checking her for injuries and rapidly throwing out ideas on how he could help her. They settled on him preparing something to eat. After the adrenaline and heightened emotions had faded, it was frightfully apparent to Aurora how little she'd eaten in the last few days. Zander placed a heaping plate of pasta in front of Aurora and waited patiently for her to finish eating before asking the question that throbbed in his mind. "Where have you been?"

Aurora rested her elbows on the counter and laid her tired head on her palms. Her eyes grew distant as she recalled the rollercoaster of events she had endured. "I went to the Hand

Council's inquisition and told them what happened and that Damon was behind it. They didn't listen; they said there was no evidence to solidly prove that Venom was under orders. I . . . I couldn't stand the idea of her just walking away after all she had done. I couldn't stand the thought of her getting away with Cole's murder. So I took my chance and attacked her before she could leave."

Zander drew in a quick breath. "Aurora, did you . . ." he stammered.

Aurora shook her head. "No, it wasn't the real Damon. It was her shape-shifter in her place. She fended off my attack with speed and agility that the real Damon couldn't match. That's how I knew. Unfortunately, in that moment of confusion, the Hands guards were able to catch and restrain me. I thought they were going to kill me."

"How did you escape?" Zander asked.

"I didn't. It was the strangest thing I had ever witnessed. The Hands guards were ordered to bring me before the Hand Council to be judged for what I had done. Two of the Hand Council kept screaming about my insolence and how I should be punished. The third member just stared, but it was like a force pushing down on me. As if he was staring through me rather than at me. Then he ordered them to let me go."

Zander's eyes widened with surprise. "What? Why?"

"I don't know. The other two members were adamant about their objections, but with one word from him, they were silenced. It was as if he controlled them."

"Maybe he just has more influence than the others, or maybe they're afraid of him," Zander theorized. "But the inquisition was the night after you left. Where have you been since then?"

Aurora turned her eyes from Zander's sympathetic gaze, recalling the actions that gave her neither satisfaction nor pride.

"I was in a dark place, Zander. I wasn't thinking about my own safety or the chance I had been given to move on. All I could think about was striking back at the real Damon. I gathered information on her whereabouts and planned my revenge. The Hand Council must have predicted this because there was a Hunter waiting for me. It was the one they called Ranger."

Zander's eyes trailed off, remembering the name he hadn't heard in several years. "Yes, your father heard of him a while back."

"Everyone's heard of him, and now I know why. He finds out everything about his target and uses the information against them. He fights with pure strategy and skill. He was able to counter me at every turn. I've never been beaten so soundly. He had me heavily sedated and dead to rights when everything went dark."

"Why didn't he kill you? I mean, I am grateful he didn't take the shot, but it doesn't make any sense." Zander rolled potential theories and reasoning in his thoughts, but they just ran him in circles. "Did he just leave you there?"

"No, I woke up later in a small apartment with Ranger. I tried to run, but he pulled a gun on me and wouldn't let me leave until he got to talk to me, so I played along. He asked me about Damon, Cole's death, and the inquisition only to gauge where my true intentions were. He's a master of reading people's reactions. He was able find out facts that I had hardly told anyone by just watching me answer some questions. It was unnerving to say the least."

"Why did he want to know your intentions? What did he want from you?" Zander asked.

Aurora tapped her index finger against the tabletop before answering, timidly releasing a response she wasn't sure of herself. "He said he wanted to help me or, maybe more accurately, he wants my help."

"What did he say?"

A disturbing but very probable theory weighed heavily on her heart and mind. "He believes that the Hand Council has been corrupted. He said he knows of two other Masters who are gathering Knights the same way Damon is, and the Hand Council has done nothing about it. Ranger said they may even be helping these Masters."

Zander's face distorted into a dumbfounded gawk. "That's . . . that's impossible."

"Is it? It seems the more and more I think about it, the more it begins to make sense. That's why he kept me alive. He wants me to help him take down the Hand Council," Aurora explained.

"That's insane, Aurora. You can't do this to me, not again!" Zander shouted, his face flushed with anger.

Aurora's eyes darted to Zander, surprised by the sudden outburst. "Zander, calm down."

"I will not calm down! You tried to throw your life away by trying to kill Damon, but you miraculously survived. Now you're joining with the Hunter that tried to kill you on a suicide mission against the people who control every Knight in the world. That is insane!" he ranted.

"It's not a suicide mission, and I'm not throwing my life away, Zander."

"Really? Because what you described sounds extremely suicidal to me."

"If what he told me is true, there will be others that have suffered like I have, others who will fight with us. It will take time and will be extremely difficult, but it could be possible."

Zander rose from his chair and turned his back to her. He didn't want to face her with anger and frustration bubbling up inside, not after she just returned home.

"I'm sorry for what I did, Zander. Sorry for how much I worried you. I wasn't myself; I was driven by the force of my own grief, and I wasn't in my right mind, but this is different. What's happening to these people needs to stop. It's gone on long enough. I'm not just throwing myself at revenge in a mad fury; I want to make things better. I want to fight so no one else has to die or grieve over loved ones because of these tyrants' greed," she reasoned, her hand unconsciously reaching for her engagement ring.

Zander's chest heaved with a heavy sigh before he turned back to Aurora. "You've thought a lot about this. And I understand why this would be important to you. I just hope you realize the danger you'll be getting into."

"Zander, after what I just went through there is no good reason why I'm still alive. I should have died several times over, but I'm still here. I know now that I can't waste the chance I've been given. If I do this, I want to see this to the end. I want to change things for the better. It's the only way I can make Cole's death mean something. I want to see the peace he envisioned."

As Aurora expressed her newfound goal, Zander saw a glimmer of hope and determination in her that had been absent since Cole's murder. Back when Aurora and the one she had grown to love challenged the strong to make things better for the weak. It was a welcome sight to see that drive once again.

"Aurora, you know I believe in you, but what about this Ranger? Can you trust him just because he didn't kill you when he had the chance?" Zander asked.

"Of course not, I need to get to the truth of the matter. Find out if he can be trusted." Aurora absentmindedly traced circles on the tabletop with her index finger as she contemplated her next move. Suddenly her lips curled into a satisfied grin when her ace in the hole came to mind. "I think I'll meet an old friend for coffee."

CHAPTER 22

THE WARM AIR of the intimate café was thick with the smell of coffee beans and pastries. The olive green walls were decorated with several small paintings and framed pictures. Sets of humble wooden tables and chairs were scattered across the sandy brown floor. A girl with bright cherry-red hair was working behind the counter, serving coffee and other specialty drinks to the few customers she had.

Luna entered the café with a casual air about her, her long black hair cascading over her shoulders. Her milky jade eyes scanned the room through a dainty pair of wire-framed glasses. She hoped the contact she was meeting with would recognize her. She had left her battle garb behind in favor of a black T-shirt, a brown pleated skirt, and tan leather boots. Her appearance put forward the image of a college student rather than a warrior.

At the back of the room, a shaggy young man pulled her attention to him with a waving gesture and a toothy grin. She answered his call with a soft smile of familiarity to her old friend. He also seemed out of his element in a gray paperboy hat over his ratty dirty-blond hair, baggy khakis, and a worn dark green T-shirt. But she could never forget his playful gray eyes and charming smile.

She returned the smile in kind as she made her way to his table. He took his feet off the chair and gestured for her to take a seat. "Hey there, beautiful."

"Hello, Fletcher," she replied before settling into the chair across from him. "I apologize for calling on you to help like this. I know you prefer to stay out of it."

Fletcher shook his head. "Don't apologize. I owe you more than I can repay. You're the reason I'm still here today."

Luna shook her head. "I didn't do anything. Cole set this up, not me."

"You went to him with my case. You believed me when no one else did and saved me from the Hunters. I owe you my life, Luna," Fletcher replied, his heartwarming words were spoken with a feeling of deep gratitude that he wore on his sleeve.

Luna smiled sweetly, taken back by Fletcher's strong words of admiration. She felt his gratitude was gift enough for her actions. "I'm glad you're well, Fletcher."

Fletcher leaned back comfortably in his chair and sipped his coffee. "I've been doing all right. I'm actually surprised you haven't called on me before, considering my talents."

Luna shook her head. "It will be just a one-time occurrence. Considering the nature of the information and the time frame, I had no choice. Were you able to get what I asked for?"

"Yeah, but not all of it. Some of the questions you asked about are very high profile, really hush, hush. No one is talking about it. The good thing is that with the answers I did get, you can pretty much connect the dots," Fletcher explained.

Luna's eyes swiftly scanned the room. "Is this place safe to talk?"

"Course it is. This place isn't that popular, and the only people who come here are regulars from the neighborhood who've been coming here since it opened. I also checked out the little lady behind the counter. She's been working here about seven months while she goes to high school. She's a kitten, and she almost always has those headphones in her ears. She won't hear a thing. I also swept the place this morning, told her I was looking for bugs. She's cute but a little dumb. She doesn't even recognize me at all with the coveralls."

Fletcher sipped his coffee then flagged down the girl behind the counter. She strolled to him with a joyful stride and a bright smile. "Hello, there. How can I help you?"

"Could you get a cup of coffee for my friend here? And I would also like a refill. Would you please, darling?" Fletcher asked, flashing a charismatic smirk.

"No problem, sweetie," she replied before walking to the counter and retrieving a cup and the freshly made pot of coffee. She then happily trotted back, set the cup down in front of Luna, poured the steaming brown brew, and refilled Fletcher's cup.

"Thanks, honey," Fletcher said. The girl nodded and returned to the counter where she promptly put her earbuds back in and continued flipping through a popular fashion magazine.

Luna glanced down at the cup. "I don't need coffee."

Fletcher chuckled. "Do you want to be the only person in a coffee shop without a cup? That's the kind of odd behavior that ordinary people remember." Fletcher drank from the cup, noticeably savoring the strong blend. "So what do you want to hear about first?"

"Is it true that there are more Masters like Damon?" Luna asked in a somber tone.

Fletcher's expression turned grave as he nodded weakly. "Yeah, two others from what I could tell, and these guys are big-buck players. The crazy lady you're fighting is the young one out of them. You don't want to mess with these guys."

A heavy sigh fell from Luna's lips, and her green eyes grew distant. "So there are more like Damon. She's not even the big problem."

"I'll give that bitch her credit where credit's due. She's climbing fast. From what I could gather it's because she takes more chances, goes right for the jewels, if you know what I mean."

"What is the Hand Council doing about this?" Luna asked.

Fletcher leaned in toward Luna, his gray eyes grim. "I don't know how you found that tidbit of information before I did, but you were right. In every incident I found where someone stood against these three, trying to expose them for what they are doing, they all end the same. The Master would die very suddenly, and the fate of the Knight would go only a few ways: they would fall off the grid totally, die suddenly like their Masters, or . . ." Fletcher's voice trailed off as his mouth stiffened to a straight line and his brow crinkled. "Or new evidence would be brought to the Hand Council of them breaking the Code. They would be branded as Rogue then . . . then hunted."

A deep sense of disappointment weighed heavy on Luna. She had hoped that Ranger's news wasn't true, but she trusted Fletcher's abilities. She swirled the bitter taste of this unfortunate fact in her mouth and steadied herself to face the truth. The Hand Council could not be trusted. Ranger was right; this was bigger than she thought.

"Is that what happened with me?" Fletcher asked, panic bubbling to the surface. "My Master and I only sold information about the Order within the Order and the same for the outside. They never crossed over, I swear. And to order my death, the punishment didn't fit the crime. Was their ruling swayed by Damon?"

Luna paused a moment before answering with a somber nod. "It's beginning to look that way."

Fletcher's breathing quickened and his lower lip quivered with a nervous twitch. "This is too much. The Council is in their pocket. We're screwed."

Luna held Fletcher's hand, reassuring him of her stability. She could feel him shaking with a familiar terror. "Fletcher, I need you to calm down. I'm working on a way to keep us all safe, but I need to know what you found. This is very important, so I need you to focus. Can you do that for me?"

Fletcher stared back into Luna's trusting eyes and nodded reluctantly. He wrapped his trembling hands around the cup of coffee and took a drink of the warm brew to calm his nerves. "All right, what else do you want to know?"

"What can you tell me about the Hunter known as Ranger?" she asked.

"He's infamous in the Order, one of the best Hunters around. Very strategic, cunning, and a top pick for dangerous game. He's mostly known for being cold and unfeeling in his hunts. He's a master of efficiency."

"Yeah, I've heard the stories. Do you have anything outside the rumors?"

"Did you hear that he quit?"

Luna raised a quizzical eyebrow. "What do you mean he quit?"

"About ten years ago, Ranger went to the Hand Council and asked them to stop calling on him as a Hunter, and for whatever reason, they said yes. It's like a retirement of sorts. They left him alone until just recently, probably to take down some seriously dangerous prey. Too bad for him."

"Why do you say that?" she asked, blinking with perplexity.

"Haven't you heard? I mean, you're not the greatest at fishing for info, but this news is all over. He never reported back from his last hunt. The unofficial word is that Ranger's taking a dirt nap."

Luna poured her concentration into hiding the evidence of her surprise. Ranger hadn't reported back. Was he trying to get away from them? Keeping Luna alive wasn't a trick by the Hand Council. Ranger was moving outside of their influence. "Really," Luna murmured, her mind trailing off to what this meant for her next move.

"If you ask me, it's good riddance!" Fletcher grunted, his eyebrows furrowed and his lips pinched with discontent.

"Fletcher!" Aurora objected.

"He's a Hunter! If the Hand Council is in the pocket of those bastards, we should just be grateful they don't have a hunter like Ranger to send after us anymore," he snapped back.

Luna sighed. "If there is anything I've learned in the last few days, it's the true weight of death and revenge. You shouldn't take things like that so lightly." Luna rose from her chair and laid a couple bills on the table. "Thank you for your help, Fletcher. Take care of yourself," she said before calmly strolling out of the little café.

Before she could get far, Fletcher sprinted after her to grab her attention. "What's going on? Are they after you, too?" Fletcher asked, panic swelling in his eyes.

Before he could say another word, Luna grabbed his hand and led him into an empty alleyway, leaning close so their words stayed between them. "You don't have to worry about this, Fletcher. I'm dealing with it."

"I can't do this! I can't run forever. They'll catch up with me, and that will be that. This is crazy!" Fletcher ranted.

"Fletcher, calm down. I won't let that happen to you."

"I'm not a warrior like you. I'm just a glorified informant. I can't fight them."

"You won't have to. Just keep your head down and out of the fight like I told you, and you'll be fine," Luna reassured.

"I know what happened to your Master," he stated desperately. Luna fell silent; her body tensed with a sudden mix of surprise and anger that she struggled to chain down. Despite her warrior's discipline, the very mention of the events of that horrible night struck a chord right to her heart. She knew what he meant and what he was going to say. "The police say that it was a natural death. That it was some sudden illness, but that's not true, is it? It's pretty obvious what happened there. If you couldn't protect him, how am I supposed to believe that I stand a chance?" he raved, his lower lip twitching like a frightened rabbit.

"Fletcher!" she shouted, snatching him by the shoulder to lock her eyes on his. "You'll be all right. I won't call on you again after today. Just keep your head down and stay off the grid. They won't be looking for you, I promise. They will be too preoccupied with what I'm planning to even think about you. Trust me," she assured him, weaving her voice to be as calm and soothing as the ocean's melody.

"I wish I could," Fletcher said as he began to step away from Luna. "I really do."

CHAPTER 23

THE SOUNDS OF clanking dishes and vibrant chatter bounced off the walls of the lavish restaurant. The room was warmly lit by decorative light fixtures evenly spaced along the sandalwood-colored walls above each red leather booth. Sprinkled across the polished tile floor were several black and red tables with stylish, high-backed dark leather chairs. Only half of the tables were seated with customers; it was still a week-day, letting the employees work at a leisurely pace.

A tall man of medium build and sharp facial features stepped into the restaurant. His black hair was slicked back tastefully. His dark eyes scanned the room thoroughly before he stepped over to the hostess's desk.

The petite hostess turned to the man, giving him a quick glance before giving her full attention. Her hazel eyes seemed to glitter in the dim light when she set her sights on him. Her long black hair was worn in a tight ponytail that flowed down to her lower back. Her tanned complexion was complimented by her copper eye shadow and her flirtatious smile that shimmered with a rosy lip gloss. She wore neat black slacks and a formfitting dinner vest over a simple white blouse to reflect her slim figure.

"Hello there. How can I help you?" she asked in a breathy, feminine voice. Her expression lit up with an attractive allure to gain his attention. Her eyes were drawn to the striking silhouette he cut in his charcoal-black suit accented with a dark-blue tie. His expression remained still and serious, unresponsive to her hungry eyes.

"I'm here for the reservation under Jasmine Lang," he responded. His tone spoke business and nothing more.

"Your wife?" the hostess asked.

"Potential associate," he corrected.

Her bright smile vanished, realizing the fish was unwilling to take her bait. She grabbed two menus and gestured her hand to the dining area. "Right this way."

The hostess led him to a red booth in the back of the dining room and set the menus on the table. "Your server will be with you shortly." She spun sharply on her heel and returned to her post. The man gave her a quick thank-you and settled into the booth, taking a quick glance at the menu.

The man's eyes subtly shifted from the menu to the room, scanning for anything unusual. The whole scene appeared status quo: waiters balancing trays and customers enjoying conversations over their dinner. Everything looked normal.

His attention was captured by the entrance of a tall, familiar woman. Her jet-black hair was held up with an ornate silver and pearl hairpin. Her facial features were made much sharper with her dark makeup and deep-red lipstick. The stylish black dress that hugged her curves closely showed off her long, sculpted legs that ended with a pair of attractive dark heels. The black of her wardrobe was accented by a silver bracelet on her slender wrist, delicate dangling earrings, and a beautifully crafted black crescent-moon pendant around her neck.

She skimmed the room before her milky jade eyes focused on the man in the booth, advancing on him with a confident stride. Her lips curled into a pleased smirk as she looked him up and down. "You clean up well for a Hunter."

He set his sights on the familiar black moon around her neck and returned the smirk to his potential ally. "Same to you, Jasmine," he replied.

She slid into the booth to Ranger's side, her body's motions as fluid as water. Ranger took in a swift breath of surprise as Luna leaned in close, placing her slender hand on his chest. "Play along, Ranger. We are in a public place," she whispered in his ear, her voice soft as fine velvet. She touched her lips to his cheek gently in a quick kiss.

Ranger swallowed hard to focus his thoughts on the task at hand. "Right," he replied in a short shudder. His heartbeat rose when Luna's hand began to move across his chest, down his stomach toward his waist. He leaned forward, turning to face her. "What are you doing?" he asked in a startled response.

Ranger was immediately shoved back against the booth with Luna's free hand before she met his eyes with an intense glare. "Be quiet," she whispered, the smooth velvet of her tone shifting to granite.

Ranger struggled to keep his eyes forward and his thoughts away from Luna's wandering hand as it traveled up and down his lap. His eyes unwillingly shifted to her when he noticed something peculiar, the tension was only one-sided. Luna's expression was sharp and focused on her task, her eyes keenly following her hand. "You certainly are very direct, Miss Jasmine."

At the base of his knee, Luna finally lifted her hand away, keeping him locked down. She twisted her hand around to reveal a small green light embedded into the back of her silver bracelet. "And you're not bugged," Luna replied flatly releasing his shoulder. She settled into her seat comfortably, placing her elbows on the table and her chin in her palm. Her eyes trained on Ranger with a penetrating stare.

Ranger sat back, arms crossed as he matched her stare. "You don't trust me?"

"No, or at least not yet," she answered.

Ranger shrugged. "I guess I can't blame you given the circumstances we met under. But you are here now, which means you know what I told you is true."

Luna raised an eyebrow. "That's an optimistic observation."

"Why else would you have come here? If you found that I was lying, you would try and stay as far away from me as possible. That's why you set up this meeting. You want to meet on your terms. How am I doing so far?"

Luna's intense glare morphed into an irritated scowl. "Your information has merit, and the more I think about it, the more your theory makes sense."

"So you have considered my offer?"

Luna's eyes strayed, her gaze becoming distant as she absent-mindedly traced her index finger along the rim of an empty glass. "I've thought about it constantly since we last spoke. The information is solid, your theory is quickly becoming a fact, and your plan seems possible. There's only one part of the puzzle that just doesn't fit."

Ranger's eyes narrowed. "What is that?"

Luna gaze shifted back to Ranger with accusing eyes. "You. You are the only part of this scenario that doesn't make any sense. That is why the plan and information is flawed, because you brought it to me."

His confusion showed in his expression like a flashlight in the night. "I'm not following you. How do I not fit in?"

"You don't fit in because I can't figure out why you, an infamous Hunter for the Hand, is doing all this in the first place. When we first met, you appeared to want nothing more than to finish the job and forget all about the war, but when you had the perfect opportunity to do so, you pulled a mental 180. For reasons I can't wrap my brain around, you turned against the ruling power for someone you don't even know and proposed a potentially suicidal mission," Luna argued.

Ranger leaned into Luna and spoke softly. "I told you before; I want this chain of suffering to stop."

"But why? How does it affect you? Embarking on a mission this groundbreaking is not for the faint of heart. You'll need drive to pull you through this, something to gain or lose for yourself, and I don't know what that is for you. You understand perfectly what my motives are, but I know nothing about you. That's why I can't trust you. Unfortunately, if I can't trust you, I can't afford to trust anything you have given me."

Ranger's eyes turned hard, showcasing a disgusted sneer. "Do you think I like what the Hand Council orders me to do? Do you believe that I don't think about those people every day? Just remember what you felt like taking one life and imagine it fifteen times worse. I'm tired of it wearing me down."

"But you were out. The Hand Council granted you freedom from this. Why rock the boat now?" Luna inquired.

Ranger replied with a disgruntled snort as he rolled his eyes, scoffing at her comment. "And we know how that ended. They wouldn't have stopped at you. As long as I played along they would've used me again and again, breaking me down to nothing."

Ranger held little back in his disdain for the Hand Council and what they made him do. It was a gambit he fully committed to in order to win over Luna. He saw the carefully calculated stare she gave him; it was much like his own.

"So you're doing this so you don't have to be a Hunter anymore?" she theorized.

"Is that so hard to believe?"

"Then why did you wait so long? Why not just recruit some-one back then when you decided you had enough of hunting for the Hand? And why, after so many years, you would choose a target for an ally? It doesn't add up," Luna ranted.

Ranger's eyes met Luna's and regarded her with a charming smile. "You underestimate yourself. Do you think that taking on a mission this big would require just anyone? Back when my eyes were opened to what was really going on, there was no one I knew that was strong enough. No one I could trust to stand up against the powerful and not falter. You have a courage that I haven't seen in a long time and a strong sense of honor. You are what I need to make this mission possible and, funny enough, the Hand Council led me right to you." A still silence filled the air around them before his eyes zeroed in on Luna. "Do you believe in fate?"

Luna thought about it. "I have given the ideology some thought in the past."

"Have you ever thought that maybe we were supposed to meet and change things for the better?"

Luna chest rolled in a soft chuckle. "That's a lot to base off faith, Ranger."

"Several different events led up to this meeting. If things didn't work out the way they did, everything would be differ-ent. How the Hand Council didn't execute you on the spot for trying to kill Damon. How they decided to summon me, the only Hunter sympathetic to your situation, to kill you. How we both had perfect opportunities to kill one another but, for one reason or another, decided not to. Those are some pretty extraordinary coincidences, wouldn't you say?"

"Fate," Luna spoke, mulling over the word and its mean-ing. She turned back to Ranger. "I never thought a Hunter like you would believe in such a thing."

"I didn't until you came along. When I found out what you had gone through and how you really were, I almost couldn't believe it. I was drowning in a sea of what-ifs and far-off dreams, and then you came along, a warrior tailor-made to change things for the better," Ranger mused.

Luna chuckled, shaking her head in bemusement. "You expect me to forget every survival instinct I have over your philosophical theory of fate? I don't know what world you're living in Ranger, but this one doesn't work like that. I found that out the hard way."

"That's how the Order used to work," Ranger insisted.

Luna's eyes hardened in bitterness and regret, turning that sneer to Ranger. "Well, those are the magic words, aren't they? Used to."

This is going to be harder than I thought, Ranger thought, realizing the gravity of Luna's trauma and how it had distorted her view of their world. Ranger could vibrantly see the harsh anger in her eyes, the tense nature when he moved close to her. She was on a permanent edge, unable to trust anyone. Without trust between them, they would be unable to work as a unit. He had to try harder to get through to her, do whatever he could to earn that trust. Unfortunately, the answer of what he could possibly do to earn that treasure escaped him.

Ranger carefully placed his hand over hers. Her hand reacted in a slight flinch and she turned to meet his eyes. "Luna, I know what you . . ." Ranger's words trailed off when two large men in business suits standing outside the building caught his eye. His heart leaped in his chest when his keen sight caught the metallic gleam of the automatic machine guns they held. "Get down!" he shouted, grabbing Luna by the shoulders and diving under the table.

Dozens of bullets tore through the building; the eardrum-splitting chaos of repeated gunfire rattled the night.

The deafening screams and clambering footsteps were accented by shattering glass and falling debris. The petrifying rhythm of automatic gunfire was only interrupted in short bursts by a burly voice yelling, "Eddie, you prick traitor! This is what you get for your betrayal to the Buritas! A bullet and a body bag!"

"What's going on?" Luna shouted over the racket.

Raw irritation echoed from Ranger's expression as he pieced together the truth of the chaotic situation. "Really? I think it's a mob hit. Just perfect; we've got to get out of here before the police show," Ranger yelled back.

Luna nodded, her eyes darting to the back of the room. "We can go out the back through the kitchen. It leads to an empty alley. I know a way out from there."

They both kept their keen eyes on the back exit, readying to spring their escape. They sat, calm among the madness until their ears were welcomed by a pause in the gunfire. Immediately, they both leaped to their feet, sprinting across the tile floor littered with broken dishes and shrapnel, hoping they were faster than the reloading of a clip. They slipped through the kitchen door and tucked themselves against each side, listening for the next volley. The painful moans hanging in the air were all they heard.

Luna's eyes fluttered with confusion. "They halted fire."

"This was probably just a quick hit job, two men, two guns, one magazine each," Ranger speculated. "That's still enough to do plenty of damage. This was probably part of a mob war. This place is rumored to be linked to some big players."

Luna shot Ranger a piercing stare as sharp as a blade. "Is that what this was? A coincidence?" Luna spat.

"Do you think I had something to do with this? I was sitting right here with you! Why would I set this up if it put me in that much danger?" Ranger argued, his expression twisted in bewilderment at her accusation.

"That doesn't mean that . . ." Suddenly, a painful groan drifted over the sound of Luna's forceful words to grab both their attention firmly. Luna spun to the source to see the dark-haired hostess lying on the floor. Her blood-soaked hand was pressed tightly against a bullet hole in her thigh.

Luna shuffled over the smooth floor to the poor woman's side, her eyes darting between the hostess and the wound. Ranger moved to follow, but froze in position, instructed by an assertive gesture of Luna's hand. "Stop! We don't know for sure if those gunmen are done. They could still just be reloading. Throw me your jacket and tie and go to the alley like I said," she commanded.

Ranger's eyes hardened with reluctance as he quickly removed and tossed Luna the requested clothing. "I'm not leaving you here alone. I can help you."

"I can handle this on my own, and there is no point in us both getting stuck in here if the shooting starts again. I just need to put pressure on the wound to slow the bleeding. I need to do something now or she'll bleed out long before help comes," Luna explained, placing the jacket in a bulge on the wound and tying it in place. The young woman let out a sharp yelp as Luna applied pressure, tears and mascara ran down the girl's face while she fell into sad sobs.

"Luna, you can't just . . ."

"I'll be right behind you. Go and clear the alleyway. We need to get away without detection," Luna pleaded. Ranger didn't reply; he only stared, torn between the logic of her words and what he thought was right. "Ranger, you said you needed me to trust you, but that runs both ways. You have to trust that I know what I'm doing,"

Ranger's chest heaved in a heavy sigh as his head bobbed in a disinclined nod. "All right, I'll go clear the alley. Be careful." Keeping a low posture, he dashed through the kitchen to the back exit, his eyes watchful of his surroundings. He knelt behind a counter just before the door and pulled a small pistol from a holster strapped to his ankle.

Gun at the ready, he slowly pushed the door open and made cautious steps into the alley. The darkened road's only light was the cast-off illumination from the tall street lamps of the main drag. The area was hardly a roadway for traffic, but instead a dumping ground for the businesses around it. There were two large dumpsters on either side piled high with a variety of different bags, boxes, and assorted other throwaways.

Ranger scanned the alley, his eyes struggling to pierce the veil of black that surrounded him when a callous, feminine voice spoke. "We've been waiting for you, Ranger."

CHAPTER 24

LUNA TOOK A careful step into the dark alley, her movements guarded as her sharp eyes scanned her surroundings. Something wasn't right. Trash and broken items were scattered all along the concrete ground in a chaotic manner. A flash of light from a passing car revealed a gleam of scarlet smeared over the wall. She pressed her index finger against it and examined the red liquid that stained her skin.

"Fresh," she whispered. She carefully eased her hand under the slit of her black dress, pulling out a small, sleek pistol hidden on her thigh. She stood ready, a sinking feeling sitting heavy in the pit of her stomach.

Suddenly, a mechanical click echoed in the eerie stillness of the alley. Luna immediately pivoted and aimed her pistol for the source. She found herself staring at a fiery redhead draped in tight black leather and holding two handguns equipped with silencers at the ready.

"Looking sharp, Luna, but I got you outgunned, so I suggest you lower your little toy," the woman said with a wicked smirk.

"Solaris, I thought this smelled like a trap," Luna spat, recognizing her attacker from past battles.

"You both fell into it like lambs to the slaughter," Solaris retorted.

"I doubt that you'd be able to pull this off yourself. So where are your co-conspirators hiding?" she asked.

The two warriors locked themselves in an intense standoff, guns steady and on target, assessing each other as the thunder rolled in the clouded sky above. Solaris chuckled softly. "You always have to be a know-it-all, don't you? At least this works in my favor." She tilted her head and gave a slight nod, signaling her comrades.

Beckoned by her gesture, two men stepped into sight. The one man was like a dark shadow in all black. The only contrast to his black clothes, black hair tied back in a tight knot, and narrow dark eyes was his ivory-white skin. Two long daggers hung from his hips and a sadistic smile painted his expression. His partner stood slightly taller with bone-white hair that fell in wild wisps over his tanned skin. His long stark-white coat fluttered in the wind like a ghostly veil.

Luna's eyes darted between the two men and Solaris, studying them with the same recognition. "Hermes," she said to the dark-haired man before shifting her gaze to his comrade. "And Spector. It's nice to know that Lexus is consistent in her betrayal of the Code, sending all of you after me. She knows by now that none of you could best me on your own." Luna's voice trailed off, catching the sight of Ranger's beaten form gripped roughly by the scruff of his shirt in Spector's hand. Dark blood slowly trickled from a large gash on his forehead.

Solaris cackled cruelly. "I see by your reaction that you noticed our guest. We gave him a warm welcome to this little gathering. Now, if you don't mind, I suggest you lower your weapon."

"I'd rather not, if it's all the same to you," Luna refused.

"Let me put it another way." Solaris slowly moved to Ranger's still form and aimed one pistol at his head, keeping the other centered on Luna at all times. "You put down your pistol or Ranger gets a gift from me to him," Solaris ordered with a vicious snap in her tone.

Luna cocked her head slightly, quickly glancing to Ranger and back to Solaris. "How do I know he's even still alive?"

"Hermes, give her proof," Solaris commanded. Hermes grabbed Ranger by the hair and yanked his head up hard, showing Luna the pained but defiant expression on Ranger's bloodied face. He was beaten, but still alive. Solaris turned back to Luna with a confident smirk. "Now, we could continue this face-off . . . Tell me why should I care and I'll say because you're working with him, but I'm not going through that. I have the luxury of knowing you well enough to skip that bullshit. I know you care; even if he meant nothing to you, you would still care. You see, behind this tough act you're putting up, you're still a good girl. I'm not. I have no problem with killing this asshole and feeding him to stray cats. So I'll just plainly tell you how this is going to go down. I'm going to count to three, and you're going to put down your gun like a good girl, or I'll paint this alley with the Hunter's brain. One." She knelt down and pressed the barrel against Ranger's temple. "Two." She continued to count in a bitterly aggressive tone.

Luna's muscles tensed, and she cursed under her breath. She had been put into a corner with very little options. Even though she didn't trust Ranger, even though he may be working against her, she couldn't just let him die, not when she could do something about it. She could call Solaris's bluff, but from what she knew of the vicious redhead, she had every intention of pulling the trigger. Luna could gamble with her own life as long as the fates would allow, but she couldn't gamble with the life of another, no matter whose it was.

"Three."

"Stop!" Luna shouted, halting Solaris's trigger finger. She quickly tossed her pistol along the ground and raised her hands in surrender.

Solaris's lips formed into a satisfied grin before moving her gun from Ranger's head. She rose to her feet; a flash of lightning showed the cruel intentions in her eyes. "There's the good girl I know."

Specter negligently tossed Ranger on the cold concrete in front of them. They could hear his weary groans as he struggled to his feet. Before Luna could move to his aid, Solaris turned one gun back to him and fired two bullets in rapid succession into his back. The muffled bark of the silenced shots barely echoed over the rumbling of thunder. Luna's eyes were locked upon Ranger's motionless form as a hard rain began to fall.

Luna found herself beginning to move to Ranger, but she froze in place when Solaris trained both guns on her. "Now, now, don't you move, kitten."

Luna's eyes burned with anger. "Why did you kill him?" she demanded between clenched teeth.

"The Hand Council would've ordered his death anyway when they discovered his all-out treachery. This way, we'll gain some favor with them while taking out an enemy. You, on the other hand, our Master wants you alive for a bit longer. She's taken offense to your attempts on her life and wants retribution, slow and painful retribution."

Luna's face twisted into a disgusted scowl, and her angry eyes zeroed in on Solaris. "You can thank Lexus for the invitation, but I'm going to have to decline. I'm a very busy person," she spat, slowly reaching her hands to her head.

"You punk! I don't care who you are; there are three of us and one of you. You're coming with us whether you like it or not!" she yelled, spite radiating from her expression like heat from a fire.

"Lackeys like you have no idea who you're messing with," Luna said as rain began to fall in a steady downpour, the heavens adding a dramatic punch to her warning.

Solaris let out a detestable snarl that soon turned into a menacing laugh. "You know, I'm sure our Master won't mind if you come to her a little damaged."

In mere moments, the tides began to turn in their standoff. Solaris aimed her one gun for Luna's leg and pulled the trigger while Luna simultaneously snatched the silver pin from her hair and threw it like a dart directly down the barrel. The gun violently backfired in an eruption of fire and light. Solaris screamed in surprise and agony as she dropped to her knees, clutching her mangled hand. Her flesh was painted a deep scarlet as her blood oozed down onto the rain-soaked pavement.

Spector immediately rushed to Solaris's side, his face wrenched with worry and his eyes locked on her contorted limb.

Sporting an ugly scowl for his wounded comrade, Hermes turned to his enemy with fury burning in his sharp eyes. "You *bitch!*" He charged Luna with a tranquilizer dart in each hand.

Luna raised her hand like a gun to fire the dangerous energy she controlled but was met with an unusual sense of pause. With the relentless rain pouring down and that familiar charge of her powers, she felt as if she were back at the site of Cole's death, staring down at the contorted form of the Knight she killed. Her body froze and her heart pounded as she was wrenched back into the trauma of that memory.

But time continued its harsh advance and Luna's moment of hesitation was answered with a swift tackle from Hermes, knocking her down onto the hard pavement. Luna's body instinctively flowed into a backward somersault, landing in a low crouch. The moment her feet touched ground, she pounced like a jungle cat, moving under Hermes's arm as he struck down at her. She fell into a fluid spin as she turned to face him, the cold brick wall guarding her back. Hermes rebounded with the speed he was known for, unleashing a serious of quick jabs and strikes to bring down his target.

With her conscious mind unable to follow Hermes's swift assault, the practiced intuition that was engraved into every muscle from years of battle took over. That reflex moved her limbs without cognizant thought with only one priority above all else: stay alive. She knew what the darts he held were; she knew that if she got struck with one it would be over for her. She couldn't let that happen. She had to stay alive. For the people she cared for and her newfound mission.

She fought against Hermes's strikes with everything she had until luck smiled upon her. One instinctual block granted her the opportunity to snatch Hermes's hand at the wrist when he moved to hit her side. Luna glided to his back and jammed Hermes's arm behind him with a painful yank. She held her ground with a vice grip, twisted his arm to wrestle the dart from his grasp, and stabbed it into his back.

Hermes let out an angry bark, contorting his body aggressively to wriggle his hand free and bounced into a bitter retaliation over the dart. Luna swept to his side and countered with a solid kick to his hip, causing his feet to slip out from under him.

The steady rain that the raging storm brought presented an unforeseen advantage in Luna's favor. Luna could clearly see that the heavy rain and encroaching work of the tranquilizer was dramatically reducing his speed. With this new revelation, Luna's mind worked rapidly to form an attack plan. Luna grabbed a broken piece of wood from a dumpster and faced

Hermes as he scrambled to his feet and charged for her, his face twisted with frustration.

Luna sidestepped Hermes's advance and hit his hand with the improvised weapon, knocking the dart onto the ground. But in the shadow of the overt attack, Hermes didn't see Luna's hand grab hold of the handle of his dagger and free it from its sheath.

But as his anger was the enemy of his perception, his speed became the enemy of his control. As he sped past Luna, he struggled to make a full stop as his feet skidded over the water.

The rage he felt was painted over his face like dark makeup as he let out a furious cry. "I'm not playing around anymore. Screw what the Master says. Let's see how cocky you are when I cut you to ribbons." His eyes promised violent intentions as he reached for his daggers and found one missing. His gaze shifted to his weapon, which was now gripped in Luna's hand.

"I thought it wasn't fair that you had all the toys," Luna mused, her words playful, but her eyes still kept their stern focus.

Angry breaths slipped through Hermes's gritted teeth as he tried to choke down his fury. "You'd better be prepared to use that," he spat as he sprinted forward faster than before to meet Luna's challenge.

The instant Hermes's boots started to pound the pavement, Luna but her plan in motion. She took efficient and fluid movements to meet her enemy's charge and tossed the piece of wood at his feet, forcing him to move to avoid the obstruction. In the same movement, she crouched to the side and swiped at his legs with his own dagger. The cold steel bit deep into his thigh, causing his legs to buckle under his weight. He rolled into a brutal tumble across the alleyway and crashed into a pile of garbage bags. Hermes pulled himself up to his knees, putting pressure on the deep gash on his leg. Dark blood oozed through his fingers with every labored movement.

"Don't move," Luna commanded. "That cut isn't fatal if you stay still, but if you continue struggling you'll bleed out."

"Go to hell, Rogue!" Hermes screamed, furiously trying to power though the blood loss and tranquilizer. His blood pooled into the rainwater, forming a scarlet river.

"Fool!" Luna cursed under her breath as she dashed across the rainsoaked ground, snatched the last tranquilizer dart, and plunged it into Hermes's shoulder.

His hands flew up, and he wrapped his fingers around Luna's neck with a weak grip. Luna wrenched his hand from her throat effortlessly and held him still until the drug fully tool hold and his body slumped over into unconsciousness.

The alarming wail of sirens echoed over the pelting rainfall causing Luna's heart to flutter with panic. She couldn't be here when the authorities arrived. They would have too many questions that she couldn't answer. She had to get out of that alley.

Suddenly the hairs on the back of her neck stood to attention in a cold, instinctual feeling of danger that she had learned to heed. She shifted into a swift barrel roll to the side as Spector's transparent hand reached down for her. She recovered and launched her fist in a quick uppercut to Spector's jaw. His eyes shifted to an eerie bone-white as her hand passed directly through his ghostly form. Luna drifted off-balance until Spector planted his foot squarely into Luna's midsection and launched her across the alley.

Spector turned his gaze to his unconscious and battered comrades. "I'll handle this," he assured, frost lining his tone before charging for his target. Luna leaped to her feet and met his charge, dagger in hand. She held off until the last second before ducking low, swinging the razor-sharp blade at his legs. The steel passed through Spector as if he were nothing but smoke. He pivoted skillfully on one foot and kicked Luna's back, forcing her to the ground. He was on top of her in seconds, pinning her to the ground with his weight as he reached a ghost-like hand into her back.

A panicked gasp fell from her lips as she struggled to breathe against a force blocking her airway. Luna pushed against his weight, but she could feel her strength leaving as her body pleaded for air. Her mind frantically searched for a course of action. She wouldn't go quietly to death or to Lexus.

Her eyes slowly changed into a bright azure-blue, but her power wouldn't manifest outside her body. All that she summoned were a few harmless sparks. Her hands began to tremble as fear of her own demise touched her thoughts. She needed to seize the upper hand once again before it was too late.

Inspiration struck in her oxygen-deprived mind like a bolt of lightning, and it sparked a slight ember of hope for survival. She closed her eyes, pulling all her focus and whatever energy she could muster to form electricity inside her body at the point of the air blockage: Spector's solid hand.

He breathed heavily through clenched teeth, struggling to hold his ground before he could take no more. He ripped his ghostly limb from Luna's body with a painful grunt, his body returning to its solid form.

Using the distraction of pain, Luna whipped her body around and gave Spector a solid kick to his face. Spector rolled over the gathering puddles of rain, grasping his jaw, as Luna scurried to her feet. Her chest heaved with choked coughs as she searched desperately for something she could use. Among the ripples of falling water, the glint of metal caught her attention. It was a small pistol.

Luna sprung forward and snatched the gun off the ground to face Spector, keeping the gun steady while struggling to catch her breath. The screaming wail of approaching sirens and clash of thunder sang to them as Spector drew himself to his feet and set his stoic eyes on Luna.

He cocked his head to the side and raised a perplexed eyebrow. "What are you planning to do, Luna? You'd only be wasting your bullets on me."

"Maybe on you," Luna mused in a tone as cold as winter. Keeping her hardened gaze on him, she turned her gun's aim to the injured Solaris. "But not with her. She's as solid as the rest of us and can't use her powers with that injured hand. She's defenseless."

Spector halted for a brief moment before his worry shifted to skepticism. "You wouldn't. You're an honorable Knight and would never gun down a defenseless opponent." He continued to advance, challenging Luna's plan.

"Are you certain of that, Spector? Are you confident enough in your assessment of my character that you're willing to bet her life?" she questioned as she chambered the next bullet. Spector froze in place, her eyes darting between Solaris and Luna. "You lackeys seem to be underestimating the severity of what your Master has done to me," she shouted, a burning fire of rage smoldered behind every word.

An inner dread had begun to form cracks in Spector's stern demeanor. "You . . . you wouldn't."

"You're not so sure now, are you? I can see it plain as day. Solaris gunned down Ranger when he was battered and beaten; it's almost poetic justice that she suffers the same fate. But I doubt you're just going to attack me when it means her certain death. You rushed to her aid without a second thought. You care about her, don't you?" Luna theorized.

"Take her down, Spector! Don't listen to her!" Solaris urged between clenched teeth.

"Yes, by all means, Spector, don't listen to me. If I kill her, that's just one fewer of Lexus's minions I have to deal with later.

I should show her that actions have consequence and show you what it's like to lose someone you care about." Luna met Spector's eyes with an intense glare as she laid her finger on the trigger and began to squeeze.

Out of pure panicked instinct, Spector dashed forward and placed himself between Luna and Solaris. "Run!" he pleaded. Luna wound up and struck Spector across the head with the side of her gun. He hit the concrete hard and quickly drifted out of consciousness, the steady rain pelting his still form. Luna shifted her gaze to Solaris but only found the red patch of blood she had left behind.

A deep sigh of relief escaped her, glad that Spector didn't call her bluff. The situation could've turned down a dangerous path if he had. His initial assessment of Luna was correct, but so was her assessment of him. Luna was just more confident in hers.

She turned to retreat through the old sewer system access, but her attention was drawn to Ranger's fallen body. A powerful sense of sympathy and longing crawled to the surface, so strong she couldn't take her eyes away. Whether or not his intentions were noble, the far-off dream he spoke of seemed all but impossible at that moment. This crushing reality fell harder on her shoulders then she ever thought it would. She couldn't stop herself from wondering what could have been. With a solemn show of respect, she knelt down to flip his body onto his back. She didn't want to leave him facedown in the street.

Her heart leaped in her chest when a tired moan slipped from the man she thought was dead. She placed two fingers lightly on his neck to confirm what she heard and was welcomed by a faint pulse. "You're alive."

Her first instinct was to take him to safety to try and save his life, but the uncertainty of his intentions halted her in hesitation. She couldn't just leave him in the alley, but if she took him, it would mean exposing a possible enemy to her base. Could she afford to risk that? Could she afford to pass up what he was offering?

The steady flash of blue and red snapped her back into reality. The sight of two police squad cars zipping past forced her into the obvious decision. She couldn't let Ranger die if there was even a chance of his innocence. All she had stood for would be meaningless if she did.

CHAPTER 25

A THROBBING HEAD and aching body welcomed Ranger on his return to the waking world. He peeled his eyes open to a pair of bright fluorescent lights that stung with their intensity. Ranger moved his arm to shield his pained eyes but was met with resistance. It felt like cloth cuffs were around his wrists binding his hands to his side. He groaned, raising his head to shake away the fog and study his surroundings.

The white walls, sterilized cleanliness, and the narrow bed he was restrained to suggested that he was in a hospital. The stark white bandages across his bare chest added to the theory. Ranger listened carefully, but he couldn't hear any voices or footsteps. Hospitals were almost always as busy as could be, always a bundle of activity, but he couldn't hear a sound in the room.

The hospital theory was thrown directly out the window when his weary eyes set on Luna sitting across the room with a pistol pointed at him. "Are you aware of the expression, 'what goes around, comes around'?" Luna asked frankly.

"I'm beginning to see the reality of it," Ranger replied.

"I had my physician take a look at you when you were unconscious. You were beaten rather badly, cracked a rib from taking two bullets in the back. Lucky enough, you came to dinner in what looks like a military-grade Kevlar vest. You're going to be fine," Luna informed him professionally, as if reading an uneventful report.

"Where are we?"

"It's a safe place, and that's all you need to know for now," Luna barked.

"You were able to get away from them. How?" Ranger asked.

"I had the advantage. They were ordered to bring me in alive, so they were holding back. I doubt that will be the case next time we meet." Luna shot a malicious glare at Ranger. "At least next time I won't have you leading them to me."

Ranger's dark eyes hardened. "I didn't set you up. You have to believe me."

Luna practically leaped from her chair and marched to Ranger. She shoved him against the bed, pressing the gun against his cheek. "You were the only one who knew where we were going to meet, and they were waiting for me. How is that not proof of your treachery?"

"They tried to kill me, too! Why would I set it up if it meant my death?" Ranger argued, standing stern in his claim despite the gun in his face.

"A backstabber got backstabbed. That's the way of life in a valley of snakes," Luna snapped, her bitter anger emanating from her like heat from desert sands. "I understand you now, Ranger. You were a plant. Lexus wanted me alive because I tried to kill her at the trial. She didn't want a quick death by a Hunter's bullet. She wants to enjoy in my suffering. That's why you didn't kill me when you had the chance. You were wrapping me up as a gift for that monster!"

Ranger shook his head. "You've got it all wrong, Luna! I want to help you."

"You're not working for the Hand anymore; you're working for Lexus. Is that why you asked the Hand Council to stop calling on you?"

"How did you know about that?" Ranger asked, a rigged tension rising in his voice.

Luna ignored his question and continued her verbal barrage. "You just didn't expect that they would betray you to the Hand. How else would they have known you were alive? Everyone assumed you died when you didn't report back after your last hunt."

"I don't know how they found out, probably the same way they found out where we were meeting," Ranger insisted.

"Have you been helping these people steal Knights from their Masters? Is that how you knew of it so thoroughly?"

Ranger cried out in fury and lunged for Luna, struggling against the restraints. "You've gone too far!" he screamed. "How dare you accuse me of this? Why I left had nothing to do with this! You know nothing about what happened to me! About who I had to kill!"

"Who? Who did you they make you kill?" she asked, leaving her harsh demeanor behind.

The rage in Ranger's expression immediately shifted to surprise at what he'd let himself say. He lay back in the bed and turned his gaze away, taking deep breaths to calm himself. "No one you should concern yourself about. That's all I'm going to say."

A long stretch of silence hung in the air between them, layering the tension like a thick blanket. Ranger refused to meet Luna's eyes. She exhaled a deep sigh and used her free hand to undo the restraints, keeping her gun targeted on Ranger.

Ranger turned sharply to Luna, eyes blinking with bafflement. "What are you doing?"

"I'm letting you go. Even though things are the way they are, I am still a Knight and I still have my honor. I won't keep you locked up like a prisoner. Now get out of here. Follow the tunnel till you reach a surface entrance," Luna instructed before turning away from him.

Ranger carefully slid off the narrow bed, grimacing with pain from his cracked rib. His eyes shifted slowly from the way to freedom back to Luna. Refusing to give up on what he started, he stepped over to her. "Luna, when you went to the Hand Council, you didn't have any proof. All you had was the truth as you witnessed it. I may not have any proof that I'm not working with Lexus, but it is the truth. I honestly just want to help you stop all this."

Ranger reached out his hand and gently rested it on Luna's shoulder. Luna flinched at the touch and spun to meet Ranger's stare with eyes rich with sadness and exhaustion. They were the eyes of one that had seen their fair share of heartache. He remembered them well; they were eyes that he would never forget.

"I can't," she murmured under choked breath. "I can't just believe you like that, not now. Maybe back when the Code meant something to all the Knights, back when things made sense to me, but not now. That kind of blind faith could get me killed. It did get Cole killed," she protested while clutching the diamond ring on her necklace.

"You've lost faith in something you believed in so strongly. You're disheartened, I know, but now you're stuck in indecision. You're unable to forget what happened so you can't go back. You're also unable to trust anyone to help you. You can't get justice so you can't move forward. You're stuck. I know that trap all too well, but I promise I will jump through any hoops, do any test to gain your trust so we can both move forward together," Ranger pleaded.

She stood staring up at Ranger, frozen in the moment. Her eyes kept looking for some sign of deceit, some tell that he was tricking her, but she would find nothing. Ranger could only hope that she would see his true intentions in his genuine character. It was a drop in his defenses he hadn't shown anyone in years.

Through her fear and doubt, she formed a weak smile as she placed a tender hand on Ranger's neck. Without warning, Luna skillfully struck a few pressure points on his neck, and his world went black.

ცა

He regained consciousness in a darkened room on a soft bed and scanned his surroundings with the small amount of light that beamed in through the curtains. The dwelling he found himself in was furnished with the bed, a small bedside table, and a small desk. He pulled himself off the bed and flicked on the light. He was fully clothed again, and his only companion was the sharp pain in his ribs.

He placed his hand on his wound and felt something unfamiliar in his jacket pocket. He reached in and pulled out a small cell phone and a typed note. The note read, "I don't trust you, but I will accept your help only under my rules. If you didn't set me up, then help me find out who did. This phone was paid for with cash and under a false name so it will be untraceable. There is one number in the contact list. You can contact me through that number and that number only. You must keep it on you at all times. We'll work from there."

CHAPTER 26

THE MEMORY OF their failure hung in the air between the three comrades, creating a thick blanket of tension that soured the atmosphere of the sterile, white hospital room. Solaris sat cross-legged on the narrow bed, her expression fixed into a permanent scowl. Her green eyes burned with fury as she stared at her hand wrapped from wrist to fingertips with stark white cloth. Hermes sat in a chair beside the bed with the same look of inpatient rage as he fiddled with a plain metal cane for hospital use. The fabric of his one pant leg was clumsily cut off to expose the thick bandages wrapped tightly around his thigh. As always, Spector was a contrast to his comrades. His demeanor was calm and stoic like it usually was; the only alteration was the deep purple bruise upon his brow.

"I'll make that bitch pay," Hermes mumbled between clenched teeth.

"We messed up. That kind of talk won't help make up for that," Spector answered with a frank tone.

Hermes zeroed in on Spector with a spiteful sneer. "Huh, easy for you to say," he spat under his breath.

Spector cocked his head to one side, returning Hermes's stare. "What was that?"

"I said easy for you to say, Spector. Look at you. You came away with just being coldcocked and look at me! I'm hopping around like some cripple," Hermes protested.

"Don't be so dramatic, Hermes. You heal faster than anyone I know. You've almost completely healed from when Claymore impaled you," Spector retorted.

"These are my legs we're talking about! My speed will be cut in half until I heal completely. Plus, look at Solaris; we don't even know how bad her hand is! So you're damn right I'm going to make Luna pay, and you're damn right I'm going to talk about it," Hermes snapped.

"He's right, Spector," Solaris agreed, turning her intense glare toward him. "I can't play this cat and mouse game after this. I don't want to follow the plan. I want to get even."

Spector took a domineering step toward the other two, asserting his presence. "It's that kind of behavior that cost us the mission in the first place. You two let your reckless attitudes jeopardize our goals."

"Don't give me that crap, Spector," Solaris hissed before she slid off the bed and moved to face Spector, like a small but vicious animal fighting for territory. "We all know what really cost us that mission, and it had nothing to do with our reckless behavior. So let's get the full report of our failure, Spector. Tell me why you came to help me instead of going after Luna when you had the chance!"

Solaris's sudden probing caused his stone-sculpted demeanor to crack. His defense fell from his mouth in useless stammers as his eyes were locked with Solaris. He slowly turned away from her in surrender. She regarded him with nothing but disgust. "I don't need to be defended like some weakling, and I never asked for your help. The next time you do something that idiotic, I'll kill you myself!" she warned, contempt dripping from her words.

Spector turned back to his fiery comrade and gestured a stiff nod in response, the hardened composure of his expression reformed.

The click of the opening door snapped the three into silence before a modest-looking young woman in teal hospital scrubs and a tidy lab coat stepped into the room. She closed the door quietly behind her and turned to regard Solaris with a slight smile, a pen and simple clipboard in hand.

"How are you feeling, miss?" the doctor asked politely.

Solaris's lips curled into a contestable sneer. "Fan-fucking-tastic. What do you think?"

The doctor brushed off Solaris's verbal abuse with nothing more than a pitied glance and turned her attention to the paperwork on the clipboard. "Fortunately for you, the damage to your hand looks worse than it is. There are a number of abrasions, but there doesn't seem to be any serious or permanent damage. It will be good as new before you know it."

Solaris kept a detestable scorn painted over her expression, but she couldn't hide the heavy heave of relief deep in her chest. "Swell."

The doctor glanced at her angry patient and tucked her clipboard under her arm. "I can understand your frustration toward your present situation, especially after such a humiliating and pathetic defeat." The placid frankness of the doctor's tone suddenly shifted to pure condescension, grabbing their attention instantly.

Before their very eyes, the plain female doctor faded feature by feature into the Knight they knew as the eyes and ears of their master: Alias. The three stared with deep-seated worry at Alias's sudden appearance. Alias viewed her subordinates with a presence that spoke volumes of her influence over them. She towered over them not in stature but in dominance. It was in the pure fact that within their collective, her word was only second to their Master. Alias knew this and drove that fact into her underlings to assure complete control.

"You three really screwed this up," she spoke, her voice soft like a bell, but simultaneously hard like granite. The lovely shape of her face and long snowy-white hair began to shrivel and morph until the form of a scrawny, middle-aged man with thinning blond hair and sunken eyes stood in her place. "I set them up perfectly and you screwups couldn't even finish the job," she barked, the harsh rasp of the masculine form morphing back to her feminine chime midsentence as did her womanly form. "Master Lexus will be very put out with you."

Hermes's face twisted with rage as he threw his cane against the slick linoleum floor with a loud clatter. "This wouldn't have happened if we didn't have to fight with kid gloves. We should've been able to take her to the Master dead!"

Alias's deep-violet eyes locked on Hermes with a penetrating intensity that forced him to slink back in his chair. "You think you know our Master's wishes better than Master Lexus herself."

"Of course not," Hermes murmured, forcefully tearing his eyes away from Alias's stare.

Alias turned to address the rest of her underlings. "Master Lexus was adamant that she wanted Luna alive, and that's what we're going to give her. No questions and definitely no more excuses. Are we clear on our orders, or do I need to address your inability to comprehend with Master Lexus herself?"

Solaris, Spector, and Hermes answered with stiff but meek acknowledgment, like schoolchildren being scolded by a teacher. Solaris sat back in the narrow bed, and her lips curled into a smirk of snide satisfaction. "At least when we hit her the next time, she won't have Ranger to help her."

Alias cocked up one eyebrow. "What makes you say that?"

Solaris chuckled softly. "Two slugs in Ranger's back make me say that."

Alias rolled her eyes and gave an irritated sigh. "The only bodies they recovered from that alley were you three useless sacks. Your failure was full-fold."

Solaris sat straight up in a flash, her expression locked in an angry snarl. "I shot him point-blank and he went down hard, I'm sure of it. Luna must have taken his body with her when she got away."

"Luna was on the run and would have to travel as lightly as possible. She would be an idiot to risk her escape over a corpse, and she is no idiot. Ranger is still alive, or at least he was when she took him," Alias informed.

Solaris turned her furious gaze to her mangled hand. "Fine. If I can't take out Luna for doing this, I'll take my frustrations out on Ranger by putting two slugs in his skull next time," she vowed.

"There may not be a next time now. We had the perfect opportunity when the ball was in our court, but you three botched it. Your ignorance is what cost us that chance. Now that she knows we're after her, she will play it safe and won't be drawn out so easily. Plus, we mustn't forget the fact that if Ranger is alive, they are no doubt working together. Luna is a force to be reckoned with in close combat, and Ranger is one of the best Hunters. Together they equal trouble for us. We need a plan that revolves around more than just brute strength. We need to take them down on our terms," Alias said, her slender index finger tracing the line of her chin as she drifted in thought.

"How are we going to lure them out?" Hermes asked.

"Well, that's the million-dollar question, now, isn't it?" Alias snapped.

Spector shifted his stance to regard Alias. "What about the Scout?" he asked.

Alias shook her head. "He sold us that intelligence for his freedom. It was a one-time deal."

"But we still have him, right? I'll sure a beating will make him more cooperative," Hermes spat.

"The unfortunate fact of the Scout's powers is that we do not see what he sees. If he believes we won't let him go, he may feed us false information or lead us into a trap. Unless we have his loyalty, his information can't be trusted," Alias reasoned.

"I'm not saying we use his powers. I'm saying we use him," Spector said.

Alias shot Spector a curious little smirk. "Go on."

"We could use the Scout as bait to lure Luna out and over-run them. Luna may be powerful and Ranger may be cunning, but we have superior numbers on our side, and this time, we won't be made fools of," Spector explained.

Alias's eyes grew distant as she stirred Spector's plan in her mind. "It's a good idea, but if Luna has already discovered that the Scout is the source of the leak, she may not bother. Why would she risk her skin for a traitor?"

Lowering his gaze in a slight show of shame, Spector exhaled a heavy sigh to prepare himself for his confession. "I admit that our failure to complete our mission was, on a wider scale than the others, my fault. I should've stuck to my theory of Luna's true nature. She manipulated me into doubting it, and I acted to save one of my own instead of completing the mission. I won't let that happen again. The Scout said that Luna saved him and kept him out of danger all this time. If that's true, then she'll come and save him again, no matter what he's done."

The stiff line of her mouth and hard look in her eyes suddenly shifted into a mischievous grin as her disapproval in his failure turned to esteem. "There's hope for you yet, Spector. I like the way you're thinking. I'll work out the details and brief you three when things are in place. In the meantime, rest here and recover. We'll expect a better performance this time," she concluded as she morphed back into the humble female doctor and turned to exit the room. She then gave a short pause at the door. "Oh, and Spector, don't ever let your misguiding feelings of camaraderie get in the way again. The wishes of our Master mean more than any of you. You would do well to remember that."

CHAPTER 27

A THICK LAYER of light gray clouds blanketed the city, coating it in a dull palate even at high noon. Ranger sat on a wooden bench in the middle of a lush, mid-city park. His weary eyes scanned the area gingerly through a pair of narrow, framed sunglasses for the counterpart to his meeting. His shoulders slouched with fatigue under a gray T-shirt and black overcoat, and his hands were stuffed into the pockets of his tan pants. He presented an appearance of a man who blended into the scenery, a man no one looked twice at. A strong feeling of exhaustion tugged at his senses, causing his body to reach into a long stretch as he exhaled an extended yawn.

"You look terrible," a smooth feminine voice told him in midstretch.

Ranger immediately sat up straight to address the woman. Her jade-green eyes regarded him with irritation from under a stylish black hat. Ranger had to take a moment to recognize his potential comrade. The deep-red T-shirt, tight blue jeans, and dark-brown leather boots were in deep contrast from the sultry black dress she had worn the last time he saw her. "I've had some late nights," he replied.

"Really?" Luna replied as she sat down on the park bench beside him. "How many late nights?"

Ranger sighed, rubbing his tired eyes. "All of them."

"Have they turned any results?" Luna asked.

Ranger shook his head regrettably. "Every lead I've traced has come to a dead end. I can see why you were so quick to think it was me. No other theory I've come up with has panned out. Have you found anything that might end my suffering?"

Luna shook her head. "I tried to trace back where that information could've been leaked, but it all seems airtight. The reservation was made under a false name and credit card held by a clean identity. I swept the safe house for listening devices before you woke up, and I told no one else where we were meeting. I don't see any way it could have slipped through the cracks."

A gruff sigh fell from Ranger's weary body. "This is maddening. There's nothing but dead ends."

"Now you see my dilemma. We can't make a move if there is a chance our plans are being leaked, and I definitely can't move on with you if there's a possibility that you are the leak."

Ranger cocked his head and shot Luna a long side-glance. "Not to seem patronizing, but would I continue to meet with you under your terms if I were working with the enemy?"

"Keep your friends close and your enemies closer," Luna replied, her expression unaltered from Ranger's intense glare.

Rolling his eyes in aggravation, Ranger turned from Luna and leaned back on the hard park bench. "You are a hard woman to please."

"I'm impressed by results, not constant pleading," Luna snapped.

Ranger's gaze shot back to Luna. "I'm not pleading. I'm trying to reason with you."

"And you present no proof, making your reasoning unreasonable."

They turned away from each other in frustration. They stared straight ahead into the freshly groomed grounds and fed the awkward moment with a long, tense silence. "You are absolutely sure that there's no one you know that could've found out where we were going?" Ranger asked.

"Of course not, I made the reservation in secret and paid with cash under an assumed identity. This isn't the first time I've done this. What about you? Do you have anyone you trust with your secrets?"

"Not in enough years to make it relevant," Ranger answered.

Luna leaned forward and rested her elbows on her legs, hanging her head low. "Then we're at yet another dead end."

"We can't stay in this stalemate forever. The enemy is only recovering for now, but that won't hold them back for much longer. Sooner or later, they'll make another move. We can't just wait for them to attack."

Luna's brow crinkled and her lips formed a vexed sneer. "And what exactly would we accomplish, Ranger? If we don't know how they got that information, it's possible they have access to any plans we have made and will make. Any move we make now may be leading us straight into their hands. So regardless of whether you like it or not, we won't move until we find the leak!" Luna half shouted.

She stood and took a couple of solitary paces, turning her back to Ranger while she regained her composure. Ranger exhaled a surly groan but left only the sounds of birds and far-off traffic between them.

The quiet tension was suddenly broken by the muffled melody of a digital ringtone. Luna reached into her pocket and pulled out a small cell phone singing its mechanical song and flipped it open with her thumb. Ranger watched

Luna carefully as she focused on what he assumed was a text message.

Even though Ranger could not see the message, he kept his keen eyes on Luna. It was small and she hid it well, but he sensed distress and panic in her subtle expressions. Ranger sat up from his seat and stepped toward her, helpful concern on his face. "What's wrong?"

Luna slammed the phone shut, and her eyes suddenly blazed with azure-blue light. The cell fizzled and popped in her hand as a thin line of smoke rose from the fried circuits. She held out an empty and impatient hand to Ranger. "Give me the phone I gave you!" she commanded. Ranger scrambled to retrieve the phone from his pocket and placed it in Luna's waiting hand.

Luna's electric-blue eyes met Ranger's, the smell of burnt plastic filling the air around them. "This meeting is over for now. There's something I have to deal with, and I don't have the luxury of time to waste."

Ranger immediately reached out for Luna's hand before she could walk away from him. His actions were rewarded by a deep scowl, but Luna's contestable aura did not shake him. "You're going to make a move even though we haven't found the leak? Even though you may be running headlong into a trap?" Ranger asked, and Luna replied with an angered nod. "Why?"

"It's because I can't afford not to! I need to fix this now!" she shouted.

"Fix what? Luna, whatever it is, I was right here when you got that message, so how could I be involved? If you're willing to run into a trap, you'll need help," Ranger protested.

The tension between them laced the atmosphere like thick smog as Luna's stern eyes met his. He could see the noticeable struggle she was facing. He could imagine that for someone so powerful and proud, it must've been hard to admit when she needed help. "Why do you want to help me?" she asked in a small voice that seemed foreign to her, not even turning to face him.

"Seems only fair considering I'm asking for your help," Ranger answered.

Luna shook her head and turned to him. "I don't know how much I'll be able to help you from here or if you'll want to help me. The enemy has set a trap I can't stay away from. The odds are not favorable."

Ranger grinned. "But it's a trap we know we're walking into, so we can plan around it. That happens to be my specialty. So what are we walking into?"

Luna gave Ranger a flat but confused look. "We? How do you know I'll want your help?"

"Let's not play around if you don't have time for it. You've probably already weighed your options and know that you're doomed if you do and doomed if you don't. At this point, you have nothing to lose by letting me help you. So fill me in and we'll start planning," Ranger reasoned.

Luna's face hardened with both surrender and disdain. She hated when he could read right through her, but she knew he was right. "They have Fletcher," she confessed.

"Who's Fletcher?"

"He's a Knight I helped hide from Lexus a while ago. The message says that they have him as a hostage and they'll kill him if I don't meet them at the east shipping yard tonight."

"What proof did they give that they have him?" Ranger asked.

"The message came from the phone I gave him to contact me. They must have found him after we last met."

Ranger's eyes grew distant as the facts rolled into place to reveal the truth. "Was it Fletcher who gave you the information about me?" Ranger asked.

Luna yanked her hand away from him. "I can't tell you that!" she protested.

"You don't have to tell me anything. Just ask yourself this: Is there any possible way he could have been gathering information about you without you knowing? Anyway at all?" Ranger asked, his intense dark eyes locked with hers. Luna turned her gaze down, reluctantly mulling the possibility in her mind. "There is a way, isn't there?" Ranger continued.

Her mouth formed into a thin line and her eyes narrowed. "His ability doesn't allow for an extreme distance, but it's still far enough to go unnoticed by his target. The possibility that he was spying on me without my knowledge is there. So what you're saying is that Fletcher sold me out to Lexus. Why would he do that?"

"I'm not saying he did it out of malice. He was probably just scared. He was just looking for a way out. This Fletcher is an information broker, isn't he? He's not a fighter. He's probably been living in fear ever since you put him into hiding," Ranger reasoned. "Your Fletcher sounds a lot like a Knight named Scout who was branded a Rogue for selling information on the Order to the outside. I'll bet the Hunter never confirmed a kill," Ranger said. Luna raised an eyebrow at her knowing companion. "I've kept up over the years."

"So if Fletcher was working for Lexus, why would they hold him hostage?"

"Because they failed in their first shot at us and now they're desperate. They want a way to flush us out."

Luna sighed as she ran her fingers through her jet-black hair; her expression spoke volumes on her frustration. "And it worked perfectly. I got Fletcher into this, and I can't leave him to die no matter what he did. I have to go get him out of danger."

Ranger's eyes lit up, and his lips formed a charming grin. "We're going to have to pull out all the stops to survive this one."

"There's a good chance we won't survive. You don't have to get involved in my problems," Luna insisted.

"You can't do this alone, Luna. You're smart enough to know that."

"And you'll be willing to risk life and limb to save Fletcher even though you think he sold me out. Why?" Luna asked.

The wide grin across Ranger's lips faded into a thin line and his eyes grew distant; his presence suddenly had an air of a heavy burden. "Luna, when I wasn't a Hunter, I chose to hide away while people like Fletcher were killed. Those days are over, and I'm through doing nothing."

CHAPTER 28

THE THICK LAYER of overcast that dragged the city into a dense, bleak darkness mirrored the situation Luna was venturing into. The late hour carried with it an unseasonable chill that set her already tense muscles on edge. She had come to the massive shipping yard as instructed by her enemy, but despite the appearance of a fully functional and operational business, Luna had not seen a soul on duty. The emptiness welcomed an unnerving silence that hung in the air, stretching the tension like a tightwire. Luna's hands hung steady at her hips, her fingers reaching out for her weapons at every turn as she walked through the vast grid of metal shipping containers.

The uniform light posts that illuminated the way through the steel maze did little to soothe her demeanor. Luna peered into every shadow, her head on a constant swivel as she prepared for the worst. It was crystal clear what Damon and her solders were capable of and what depths they would sink to. A deep-seated worry burrowed into her every thought. The uncertainty of her friend's fate in the hands of her enemy sent her emotions into a torrent of panic and dread.

"Lexus's troops are around the next corner to your right. Prepare yourself." Ranger's steady voice spoke in Luna's ear through a sophisticated communication device.

"What are they up to?" Luna asked.

"They seem to be just waiting for you, but stay on guard. We don't know what tricks the may have up their sleeves," Ranger warned. "Wait."

Luna halted her march. "What is it?"

"The count is off," Ranger informed. "I can't see Alias or Spector. They aren't with the group."

Choking down her imagination of what their absence meant to her situation, she exhaled a calming breath focused her mind of the mission. "Do you see Fletcher?"

"I believe so. There is someone being held by Solaris that matches the description you gave me."

"Then I have to go in, no matter what they're planning," Luna vowed.

"I know, just keep your wits about you and concentrate on getting Fletcher back. I'll keep you safe. I give you my word," Ranger promised.

Luna could hear a determined finality to Ranger's pledge, and she knew what that could mean. She struggled with hesitation before deciding to ask something potentially foolish of her comrade. "Ranger, this may sound naive, but I don't want you to kill any of Lexus's agents."

"Even if it's a choice between you or them?"

"As far as we know at this time, they are only following Damon's orders. I killed Venom for following her orders, and maybe that was a mistake. I don't know, but, like you said before, I don't want to do something we can't undo. Please." Luna pled her case for something she didn't entirely understand but felt very strongly about. She just hoped Ranger would see it her way.

"Don't worry," Ranger answered with a reassuring steadiness that Luna could hear over the communication device. "There are several stalling techniques I can employ from here. No one's going to die tonight."

"Thank you, Ranger."

Despite the brief and very complicated history between them, hearing Ranger's voice in her ear and knowing his watchful eyes were upon her gave her the strong sense of courage she needed more than she would admit. She didn't quite comprehend it, but she didn't reject it either. She simply let it fill her with the resolve that was necessary to move forward.

After mere moments that seemed like hours to Luna, she came face-to-face with to the opposing party of this hostage negotiation. Luna took a careful inventory of her enemies, keeping a vigilant distance between them. Staring back at her with a mix of wickedness and hatred in her emerald eyes was the fiery-haired Solaris, clad neck to toe in tight-fitted black and red leather. Her bandaged hand pressed her pistol against the skull of the terrified Fletcher, keeping a tight grip on her captive with the other hand.

Standing loose at her side, ready to leap at the slightest provocation, was Hermes. He scowled at Luna with a dormant rage reflected in his black eyes, the muscles of his bare arms tensing with every moment of inaction. It was as if his empty hands called out to the daggers at his hips.

"So nice of you to show. I'm sure the gutless Scout appreciates it," Hermes said, mocking their captive. The satisfied smirk painted across his lips suddenly morphed into a distrustful scowl. "Where's Ranger?"

"He's not in the picture," Luna answered as flat as she was able.

"If you have him hidden somewhere, we may have to take it out on the Scout," Solaris threatened.

"I don't have that help to fall back on." Luna met Solaris with a glare as sharp as her sword. "Thanks to you."

Hermes answered with an amused chuckle. "Drop the act, Luna. We know you took Ranger with you. You wouldn't have risked your escape for his dead body."

Luna's brow crinkled into an ugly stare that reflected a white-hot hatred. "Shut your mouth!" she barked through chocked rage.

"Or maybe Ranger abandoned you and ran back into hiding," Hermes continued his verbal assault.

"Shut your damn mouth!" Luna shouted. "Ranger didn't make it long after I dragged him from that alley. Are you *happy*? You killed Ranger for the Council, and now you have me right where you want me. You've won. Now, please, just get on with it."

The gleeful smirks on Solaris's and Hermes's faces quickly faded, leaving behind expressions as serious as an early death.

"Fine," Solaris spat. "It's like we said in the message: hand yourself over without a fuss, and the gutless Scout can go free."

"I don't want any civilians caught up in our affairs. Where are all the employees of this shipping yard?" Luna asked.

"Relax, the place has been locked down for fumigation, and if you play your cards right," Solaris said, pressing her gun's barrel against her captive's head, "we won't have to get rid of this pest."

Fletcher flinched with the pressure of metal against his skin, his soft gray eyes wide with fear. A shallow whimper escaped him as he stared helplessly at his rescuer. "P-Please don't kill me. I've done what you wanted," Fletcher pleaded to his captors' sense of honor.

"Shut that hole in your face before I give you another one," Solaris spat. Fletcher's body began to tremble like a leaf in a harsh wind as he held his eyes shut tight and awaited the end.

Despite Solaris's physical and verbal abuse toward someone Luna would always strive to protect, Luna remained as calm as still water and was unsure why. She witnessed this act, but didn't feel the need to step to his defense. It was as if the danger wasn't real to her. Something was missing from his reaction, something she had seen so often before, but she was uncertain of her initial instinct. Unfortunately, uncertainty in a hostage situation was unacceptable. She had to be sure before she could act.

"Whether you live or die is up to Luna now," Solaris stated, turning her malicious eyes back to Luna. "So what's it going to be, Luna? Lucky for the Scout, he isn't worth the bullet. We'll let the little rat scurry away as soon as we've got you in the bag."

"Don't worry. Just get Fletcher out of there, and I'll get you out," Ranger instructed in Luna's ear.

"No," Luna spoke up.

"No?" everyone asked in a stunned synchronicity.

Luna faced Fletcher with a stern, penetrating gaze that cut into him like a sharpened blade. It was the gaze she reserved for enemies in combat, not a victim in need of defending. In a flicker of movement, she drew her pistol and shifted to a readied stance, the barrel aimed at Fletcher's head.

At the first sign of Luna's aggression, Hermes drew his daggers and moved to close the distance. His advance was immediately halted by a series of bullets shot into the ground at his feet. Hermes searched for the hidden gunmen at the source of the shots but could not pierce the shroud of night.

"It's Ranger!" Solaris screamed. "He survived."

"I wouldn't make any sudden moves," Luna warned. "Just one of those bullets could rip you apart, and Ranger is a pretty good shot."

Solaris tightened her grip on her captive and placed her finger on the trigger to represent her threat more clearly. "This doesn't change anything! Call off Ranger and put down your gun or it's bye-bye Scout!"

"Give him to me, Solaris, and I'll show him how traitors should be dealt with," Luna snapped, her tone surprisingly frightening in its stern fury.

"What are you playing at, Luna?" Hermes demanded.

"Luna, what are you doing?" Ranger asked in her ear, a hint of worry in his tone.

"You betrayed me, Scout," Luna declared. She fixed her intense stare on Fletcher, ignoring the questions and demands of the others as she marched forward.

"Luna, don't do this. I'm sorry," Fletcher begged.

"Sorry!" she howled. "I risked my life to save and protect you, and you sold me out to the people who would've had you hunted like a dog if it weren't for me. A quick death is more then you deserve for what you've done."

A faint layer of worry entered Solaris's expression as she witnessed Luna's menacing approach. She took her gun from Fletcher's head and pointed it at her looming enemy.

Luna's demeanor didn't even acknowledge the danger. She knew what she had to do and could not be detoured.

"Luna, be careful! I can't get a shot on Solaris through Scout," Ranger cautioned, but Luna kept her advance strong and confident.

"Please, Luna; I was afraid and so tired of running. I'm sorry," Fletcher continued to plead, dread and panic seeping from trembling movement, but it still was somehow a betrayal to Luna's memories of him.

"Dammit, you bitch! Come any closer and I will end you!" Solaris screamed her blustering threat, trying to stop Luna's advance.

"If you're going to shoot, then do it! I'm sure Lexus won't mind the flagrant disregard of her orders," Luna snapped back.

Out of the corner of her eye, Luna saw Hermes creeping toward her, his daggers at the ready. Before she could react to his action, she heard the familiar sound of a sniper's bullet sailing through the air. The bullet grazed Hermes's leg and struck the dagger in his hand, shattering it to pieces upon impact. Hermes grabbed at the freshly opened wound, choking back a cry of pain.

"That was your second warning, Hermes. You won't get another." Luna laid down the law of the battlefield, expressing her complete control over the situation.

"He can't watch me forever," Hermes spat between clenched teeth.

"Not forever. Just long enough for me to give this traitor what he deserves."

"This plan's going south in a hurry, Luna. I hope you know what you're doing," Ranger said.

"I hope what you traded my life for was worth it because now you're going to die for it!" Luna vowed, stopping her march mere feet from her target. "Unless you want to die with him, Solaris, I suggest you move."

"You . . . you won't. You can't," Solaris stammered, not sure of her words. Her eyes widened with panic as she stared down the barrel of Luna's pistol.

"Please, Luna. Don't kill me," Fletcher begged, his lower lip motionless through his terror. Luna had her answer.

Luna lifted her finger to the trigger and squeezed, assured in her theory and ready to act. Solaris jumped to the left and pushed Fletcher in the opposite direction. The bullet flew through the air between them and punched a deep hole in a metal shipping container. In the confusion, Luna leaped forward and gripped Fletcher's right arm, twisted it with a quick jerk into his back, and jammed her pistol against his temple.

"Strike two, Alias," Luna whispered as she sent a painful shock through her tight grip into the young man's arm, forcing Alias to drop her disguise. As her body contorted with agony, the rat's nest of dirty-blonde hair shifted into a cascade of snowy-white locks. The gray in her eyes receded to a deep violet, and the pasty skin tone bled into an ivory complexion.

Solaris spun and faced her attacker with her gun at the ready but froze at the sight of her commander in the line of fire.

"What gave me away?" Alias inquired, her voice as soft as a slender bell.

"Tell me where Scout it *now!*" Luna demanded.

"I'm not afraid of you. You'll never make it out of here alive," Alias hissed, a statistic glee in her promise.

Luna's eyes blazed with an azure-blue glow as she shot another agonizing jolt into her captive. Alias's body twisted in anguish, but her cries of pain soon shifted into shrill laughter that send a chill up Luna's spine. "Where is he?" she asked again.

"You think you can outsmart me. I am their commander, and you are nothing but an attack dog off its leash. You can't run for long," Alias threatened, her words dripping with spiteful venom.

"Luna, disengage *now!*" Ranger ordered. "I'll cover your escape."

Luna tightened her grip on Alias, ignoring Ranger's commands. "Tell me where he is or I'll . . ."

"Or you'll what? Fry me to a crisp like Venom?"

"Don't tempt me."

"Go ahead. You may feel high and mighty when you preach about your honor, but I've seen what's underneath. You're nothing but a dangerous monster with a pointless pipe dream. So do it! Let out that truly terrifying rage and show yourself for the beast of destruction you really are," Alias ranted.

"Luna, don't listen to her. She's not going to tell you anything. Disengage *now*!" Ranger shouted in her ear.

Luna could see her options disappearing with every passing second, but she had to keep looking for some flicker of hope to salvage the situation. Her mind worked rapidly to form a plan, to take back the advantage and find Fletcher, but even that small drop of faith that she could prevail was fading away. Recovering from this setback to save Fletcher seemed almost impossible.

"Go on and show how much of a threat you really are so the Hand Council will put a priority on your execution," Alias continued, her lips stretched wide into a deranged grin.

The hellish standoff was suddenly broken as the light above them shattered in a flashy spray of sparks that diminished as quickly as they appeared, shrouding the party in a thick darkness.

"Run!" Ranger ordered. "I'll cover you."

Luna finally surrendered to Ranger's instructions, pushing Alias hard to the ground and bolting away at a full sprint. All she heard was calamity and confusion at her back as she made her retreat. Luna prayed she wasn't leaving behind her only chance to save a friend.

CHAPTER 29

THE INTERSECTION OF row four and column fifteen was far away from the center of the metal maze, not too close to the wall so they could avoid being spotted by passing civilians. It was the spot Luna and Ranger designated beforehand as a regroup point in case the mission didn't go as planned. To say the mission didn't go as planned would've been an understatement.

So Ranger waited with his back against the cold container, his senses searching for signs of his comrade's approach. He soon found the sounds of hurried footsteps and labored breathing. With purposeful movements, Ranger peered down the pathway and saw Luna sprinting toward the regroup point.

He waited till she was at the intersection and he grabbed her by the hand and pulled her into the pathway, holding his fingers to his lips to signal for her silence. They both listened carefully for signs of approaching danger. Ranger peeked from the corner, inspecting Luna's path for pursuers.

"We lost them," Ranger informed.

"Them and our chance to get Fletcher back. I knew Alias would try to sneak something by us." Luna cursed under her breath.

"At least you caught on before they could spring their trap. How could you tell that wasn't him?" Ranger asked.

"As long as I've known Fletcher, he's had a nervous twitch of his lip. That's why I did what I did, to push the tension to a boiling point. You can't get rid of something like that in a few days," Luna explained. Her stern eyes suddenly softened. "We don't even know if they kept Fletcher alive."

Ranger turned back to Luna. "Don't worry. Alias isn't stupid; she would've left every avenue open to her. She knows getting him back is the only thing keeping you here."

Luna met his eyes with uncertainty. "How can you be sure?" she whispered.

"It's a principle that has kept me alive as a Hunter: know your enemy. Alias is conniving by nature. She'll try and plan for every possibility and will never attack head-on. Lexus probably uses Alias to keep her more reckless Knights in line," Ranger theorized.

"So what now? How do we get Fletcher back?"

Their conversation was cut short when a familiar voice spoke through the crackling intercom system. "Ranger. I know you're still here, Ranger."

"That's Alias. What is she doing?" Luna asked.

Alias's voice continued to speak from the intercom. "We have a lot in common, Ranger. We don't take this war as personally as Luna or the underlings. We know this is just business, so let's talk. All around this place are telephones that connect to the main guardhouse. Use one of those and give me a ring. I'm looking forward to hearing from you." She exited with a mechanical click.

Ranger's eyes darted left to right until he found a simple green telephone connected to a tall wooden pole at the corner of a shipping container and began to step toward it.

"What are you doing?" Luna spoke up.

"Following a hunch," Ranger replied without the slightest glance back to her. The telephone was an older model modified to have only one button to dial the main guardhouse instead of the usual number pad. Ranger lifted the receiver to his ear, pressed the button, and listened to the systematic ring as he waited for an answer.

"Ranger, I presume?" Alias's voice purred.

"What do you want, Alias?" Ranger snapped, his tone pure business and his expression stern.

"I'm merely doing the smart thing. I want to make you an offer, Ranger."

"Can I expect more of your tricks with your offer, changeling?" Ranger retorted with a sarcastic tint.

"Well, I don't think you're thick enough to fall for that one again. The only other way to finalize this confrontation is to fight. We will win, Ranger. That is a certainty, but at what cost? You and I both know the results will be less than desirable for both sides." Alias's words felt like fine silk in Ranger's ear, even over the old receiver.

"And I suppose you have a better idea."

"My Master gives no care to what happens to you or the Scout. Her only and fondest desire of late is Iver's attack dog. She has taken a personal offense to the attempt on her life at the trial. I'm willing to let you and the Scout leave unharmed if you hand over Luna," Alias offered.

Ranger's chest rolled with a soft chuckle. "I have two bullets that said more honestly how much I can trust you. Besides, I doubt you're that generous."

"At the time, we thought we could gain some favor with the Hand Council. It was a plan of convenience before, but now the situation has changed. We can both make this turn out better for everyone . . . except Luna," Alias continued, trying to persuade him.

They both sat in a tense quiet before the smooth velvet of Alias's words spoke once more. "I know you never wanted to come back to this war. You asked for peace, but the Hand just beckoned you back at their whim and you were helpless to obey. But now they think you're dead and we haven't informed them otherwise. If you give Luna to us and simply walk away from this fight, you can disappear and live the rest of your life with the peace you deserve. No more having to kill out of duty and no more looking over your shoulder. You'll be free. You can't say this isn't appealing to you."

He released a gruff exhale through his nose, the implications and opportunities of Alias's offer weaving through his mind. His intense eyes shifted to Luna. "I can't say that."

A satisfied and almost sensual little hum sounded over the receiver. "The others and I will be at the center of the yard in fifteen minutes. If you want to make it out of this alive, I suggest you meet us there."

CHAPTER 30

FROM YEARS OF experience as a Hunter, Ranger knew the key to tense standoffs was to hold your ground. The Knights of the Order may have had their chivalrous demeanor and honorable decorum, but in the world of a Hunter, things were much more animalistic. His sharp eyes locked onto Alias and her underlings as he marched toward them, Luna's still form slumped over his shoulder.

He could see the look of smug satisfaction plastered over Alias's face as her clever plan came to fruition. Her comrades noticeably failed to share in her glee.

"Let's take him out now. We don't need to play this stupid game," Hermes suggested, his whole body shifting with anticipation. Ranger took notice of a slight hitch in Hermes's stance, favoring the one side, and the tear in his pant leg. The black fabric may have hidden the blood, but Ranger was sure his bullet's graze did more damage than Hermes put on.

His eager hunger for battle was halted by a raise of Alias's slender arm. "No, Ranger wouldn't have come unprepared. It's better to play this out and see if he takes the deal, but watch him carefully," Alias instructed.

Ranger halted his advance a measured distance from his enemies that was well out of immediate striking range but close enough for words to travel between them. His dark eyes scanned the group, taking mental attendance to assure no tricks were at hand. Just as Alias had promised, her Knight trio and the frightened Scout were before him. Satisfied with the count, he heaved Luna's body off his shoulder and negligently tossed her onto the ground between them. Her body tumbled and rolled across the dirt ground like a rag doll. Alias's eyes intently focused on Luna, looking for any movement to read as consciousness. The lamplight glinted off a metal dart protruding from her hip.

A familiar mechanical click echoed through the still quiet that drew all attention to Ranger, holding his rifle at the ready. Alias's laughter was like soft bells as she looked upon Ranger with nothing but amusement. "What are you going to do, Ranger? Fight all of us without Luna to help you? Not what I expected of you at all."

Her delighted smile instantly faded as the rifle's aim shifted to point at Luna's still form. "Actually, Alias, this is my insurance. I know your Master wants her alive and will accept nothing less, so here's the rule. You all will do exactly what I tell you to do, or I'll kill Luna." His eyes shifted to Solaris. "And unlike your lackeys, I don't leave jobs half done."

"You son of a . . ." Solaris barked.

Solaris's curses were frozen in mid-form as Alias's eyes focused on her with a piercing glare. Alias turned back to Ranger, anger tracing the lines of her face. "You don't trust me to keep up my end of our bargain?"

"Not even a little," Ranger answered without skipping a beat.

Alias sneered. "I trust she's still alive."

"She's just unconscious. Should be for another couple hours with the tranquilizer I gave her. "

"How did you do it? Luna's not one to drop her guard. So how did you pull that off?" Alias continued to probe, trying to find deception in his answers.

"Simple. She trusted me," Ranger answered, the words as calm as still water.

Alias cocked her head to the side with a curious gaze. "And you're willing to kill her so easily just to save yourself."

Ranger shot Alias a sly grin. "Have you forgotten what I am? She wouldn't be the first Knight I've killed, but if I play this right, she will be the last. Right now, I just want my life back . . . at any cost."

Fletcher cringed at Ranger's words as the true terror of the situation sunk in deep. He turned to Alias. "Please, you can keep me in your charge. I'll do whatever you want; just let her go. She doesn't deserve to die!" Fletcher pleaded.

"Keep him quiet!" Alias commanded sharply.

"They don't want you, Scout. They only want Luna, and their Master won't hesitate to throw them away if they fail. There's nothing we can do for her. She chose this and knew the danger. You're lucky you and I have a chance to get out of this. So shut up and do what you're told!" Ranger snapped.

Alias's lips formed a small smirk that only partially masked the fury behind it. "Well played, Ranger. What are the rules?"

"You're going to be my helper and bring the Scout to the middle point between us," Ranger instructed flatly.

She slowly stepped over to Spector and, with a mere glance, gave the approval to release their captive to her. She wrapped her fingers around his skinny forearm and the back of his neck, as she moved him forward with a harsh jerk.

Fletcher's tearfilled eyes were fixated on Luna's body, lying limp like a doll on the cold dirt ground. The guilt he felt was vibrantly painted across his face. Alias pushed him to the center of the field.

"Now what?" Alias demanded.

"Send the Scout over to me, and only after he is with me will I put away my gun," Ranger explained.

"Whatever you say, Ranger," Alias purred before shoving Fletcher forward, releasing him from her painful grasp. Fletcher stumbled a few steps, almost falling to his knees. He stood still, his gaze chained to his former savior's still form.

"Scout, get behind me *now!*" Ranger commanded sternly, but Fletcher didn't move. He couldn't tear himself away. His hands clenched into fists and his gray eyes blurred with tears. "Scout!" Ranger shouted.

"I'm sorry," Fletcher whimpered, locking his eyes shut and ripping himself away to run to Ranger's side, choosing his own safety above all else once again.

"Satisfied?" Alias asked.

"Very," Ranger answered as he slung his rifle over his shoulder. In the same motion, he reached into a small pocket at the collar of his trench coat and retrieved three small metal spheres. "Now!" he screamed as he tossed them into the air above Alias.

With that signal, Luna jumped to life instantly, her eyes and hands crackling with blue light as she skillfully shot the balls in the air with a precise arch of electricity. The spheres exploded into a large cloud of thick gray smoke that quickly filled the area.

Ranger pulled Fletcher close to him and sprung into a speedy retreat in the confusion with Luna close at his back. They sprinted as fast as their legs could carry them toward the main gate of the shipping yard. It was a show of good fortune that Fletcher could run as fast with terror as his fuel than Ranger and Luna could with adrenaline.

They came upon a chain-link fence gate large enough for a couple of semitrucks. At the gate's side stood a small guardhouse that, if Ranger's research was correct, housed the entrance controls. It was time to implement his plans.

He reached into one of the many pockets of his trench coat and pulled out a small device with a singular button on it. He quickly tossed the mechanism to Luna. "Go open the gate far enough for us to get through, leave that on the control panel, and press the bottom. Then set the gate to close and follow us through. This will cover our escape," Ranger instructed.

Luna acknowledged his commands with a slight nod and darted to the guardhouse. Once the gate opened, Ranger led Fletcher through but halted his retreat for a moment to crouch down to the base of the fence. He pulled another device from his trench coat and attached it to the chain link. As soon as Luna stepped through the gate, Ranger pushed the bottom to activate the mechanism and continued their retreat.

"What was that thing I left behind?" Luna asked. As if on cue, the time-delayed grenade Luna left in the guardhouse exploded, dark smoke billowing up from the blast. "Okay, then what was the other thing you set up?"

Immediately after Luna posted her inquiry in the heat of their escape, a deafening bang could be heard clear through the night, followed by a pained cry from a male voice. "That was a proximity flash bang. In case they tried to climb the gate. Sounds like one of them fell for it," Ranger informed with a mischievous chuckle in his tone. "They won't be following us anytime soon."

CHAPTER 31

THE LARGE AIRPORT waiting room was bathed in the golden light of the setting sun that streamed in through the wall of windows overlooking departing airplanes. The long shadows of equally spaced rows of cushioned chairs stretched across the polished tile floor.

Luna stepped out into the room, presenting herself with a lazy saunter. She casually ran her slender fingers through her long jet-black hair that hung loose down her back. In her right hand, she held a fashionable red bag that swayed back and forth with each step. She had her other hand nonchalantly tucked into the pocket of a caramel-colored coat she wore over a deep-red blouse and black slacks. Her milky jade eyes scanned the room through a pair of stylish sunglasses until she found who she was looking for.

He sat near the end of one of the many rows of chairs reading a section of the city's newspaper. Even though he was now clean-shaven with shorter hair of a darker brown, Luna still recognized the Scout by his bad posture and weary gray eyes. The click of Luna's black heeled shoes echoed on the tile floor as she made her way to sit behind him.

"Did you really have to make sure I left in person?" Fletcher asked, the lighthearted playfulness of his former tone lost to a new heaviness seeping from his demeanor.

"This is more for your safety than mine, Fletcher," Luna answered flatly, not looking back at him for an instant.

"You don't need to worry. After what happened, I plan to put this place in my rear view as fast as possible," Fletcher assured.

"I'm not here to merely make sure you leave. I'm here to make sure you get far enough," Luna said as she reached her hand into her bag and pulled out a plain brown envelope. She then subtly shifted it in her hands to drop it in between the seats onto the floor. Then she stretched her arms in the air and her feet under the chair, faking an extended yawn to push the envelope under Fletcher's seat with her feet. "Drop something and pick up the envelope under your chair," she instructed quietly.

Luna turned to the monitors on the wall showing the flight schedule to sneak a glance at Fletcher. She saw him fumble with the newspaper in his hand to carefully retrieve the envelope. Keeping the envelope hidden behind the paper, he studied the contents inside.

Luna had prepared a passport booklet with the seal of the Island Republic on the dark-green cover, a photo ID registered from Madori Island with his picture but a different name on it, a couple stacks of Republic currency, and a one-way plane ticket. "What is this?" Fletcher asked, his voice staggering with bafflement.

"Their influence is too large in Ebony. If you stay here, they're bound to catch you eventually, if only to cover up their mistake. You'll be safer in the Island Republic. You should have enough money to last you until you can find work. Just stay there and out of trouble and you should be fine. I have ways of keeping tabs on you to make sure you're okay."

"No, I mean, why are you doing this? After what I've done, you're trying to help me. Why?" Fletcher asked.

Luna leaned forward, her elbows resting heavily on her knees and her expression grave. "I'm not going to sugarcoat this, Fletcher. I respect you too much for that. You always knew before that every bit of information you gave would have an impact. That's why you always came to people like me and my Master, the ones with intentions you could trust. This time you gave information only to help yourself, and as a result innocent people were hurt, drawn into our war. Do you understand?"

"Was anyone killed from the attack?" he inquired in a meek voice.

"Three people as far as I know were killed that night, two civilians and one gunman. Two people just deciding to go out for a night found their end and one died fighting for a lie. I want you to think about that, Fletcher, and always remember what happens when you give power to someone like Lexus. Nothing is sacred to her, and the families of those people will never know the true reason behind those deaths. The responsibility to use our talents wisely is not only for when it suits us best. It is a constant challenge that we must always uphold, and we must carry the consequences if we don't," Luna preached, not able or willing to hide the disappointment in her voice, but carrying the same lesson deep inside for herself. The heavy burden of her past mistakes erupted to the surface of her thoughts.

"After all I've done, the pain I've caused, I get to walk away and start over? It doesn't seem right. You should've just left me to them or killed me yourself. It's all I really deserve," he confessed through choked sobs.

"Some would say you do deserve to die, and the fact that you said it shows that you have remorse. It shows that you realize that what you did was a mistake. So there is still hope for you."

"What did you say?" Fletcher asked.

"It's not my place to decide your fate. I'm not your judge, jury, or executioner. I'm just trying to save everyone I can and make things better," Luna answered.

"I . . . I can't leave you here with this burden. I have to at least try and help. I want to help to atone for what I've done," Fletcher pleaded.

Luna sighed and her gaze grew hard and distant. "It's not that simple, Fletcher. I know that you feel awful for what happened, and I'll do my best to make sure you're safe and taken care of, but I simply can't trust you. If you stay here, you'll be a liability."

Fletcher took in a heavy breath to regain himself as her words sunk in. "I understand why you think that. I'm sorry I let you down."

"You said it yourself: you're not a fighter like me. The best thing you can do right now is clear the field. Let the soldiers fight the war." Her words were followed by a tense silence that seemed to last forever before it was broken by a monotone voice over the intercom announcing a nonstop flight to Madori Island. "That's your flight. You better get going," Luna insisted.

Fletcher nodded as he dried his eyes and gathered his belongings to make his way to the gate. Before he was out of earshot, he stopped. "I may not be able to fight with you, but I can at least help someone who wants to. I know you don't trust him."

Luna raised a quizzical eyebrow at Fletcher's inquiry. "Who?"

"Ranger. With the circumstances the way they are, I can understand why, but if you never believe another word out of my mouth, at least believe this: Ranger was never working with

Lexus and what they said about the Hand thinking he's dead is true as well. Whatever he's doing, he's doing on his own. Heaven knows for what reason," Fletcher said.

The sunglasses hid the gleam of surprise in Luna's eyes as a small smile crept along her lips. It was a glimmer of hope that she had almost forgotten. "Thank you."

"You're amazing, and if anyone can pull off a plan this crazy, it's you. Good luck," he encouraged before walking away from his old ways toward a new life.

CHAPTER 32

THE STALE SCENT of dust and stagnation filled the abandoned sewer way, making Luna's nose crinkle with every passing moment. She had only ever used the abandoned sewer system as a quick and discreet way of travel, but she was quickly regretting making it an impromptu meeting place. The thick layer of dirt that covered every inch of the tunnel clung to her skin and the black fabric of her clothes without any real effort. The true extent of it was unseen as her only light source was the pale-green glow rod she held in her hand.

She sat in the still silence of the forgotten tunnel, the soft sound of her steady breath her only companion. Her wait was ended by the sound of approaching footsteps echoing in the chamber. Her right hand shifted to rest on her pistol in the chance that the company she was about to entertain wasn't who she expected.

Ranger stepped calmly into the pale-green glow. The dark shade of his short hair blended with the pitch black of the tunnel, and his brown eyes seemed like deep voids in the dim light. His hands were comfortably set in the pockets of the usual trench coat he wore over a simple wardrobe of jeans and a T-shirt. Luna took her hand off her pistol and let it rest at her side, regarding the man with a familiar glance. Ranger returned the glance with a welcoming nod as he stepped fully into the light of the glow rod.

Before any words could escape him, Luna reached into her pocket and tossed him a small cell phone. He skillfully snatched it out of the air, examined it, and said, "It's to replace the compromised one. It was bought the same way as the other one, but under a different identity. Unless we have yet another mole in our midst, it will be safe to contact me on it."

"Sorry you had to get another one. It can't be cheap to keep burning through them like this," Ranger observed.

Luna shot Ranger a blank stare, baffled by his apology. "I can afford it."

"Thank you," he said as he placed the phone in his pocket. "I trust that the Scout is taken care of?"

"I saw him get on the plane myself. He'll be safe and starting a new life in a place well out of Lexus's influence," Luna informed.

Ranger's penetrating but calm eyes locked with Luna's. "You put him back into hiding?"

"Yes, of course. If he stayed here, Lexus would come after him, if only to cover up her failings. He's out of the war now and away from this danger."

"After what he did, you let him go, set him up with a brand new life? What if he comes back and betrays you all over again?" Ranger asked without the slightest hint of accusation in his manner. It merely presented itself as inquiry.

"He won't," Luna assured confidently.

"Are you so sure of that?"

"I talked with him before he left. I shared the true results of his actions and what happens when you throw yourself in with the likes of Lexus. He feels remorse; it's almost dripping off of him. He knows that what he did was a mistake."

"You're that confident in your assessment of him. You realize that if he does come back and betrays you again, we may not be so lucky," Ranger persisted. His voice stayed only inquisitive, not apprehensive.

"I realize that," Luna replied, half shouting.

"And you still let him live? You left that loose end untied and that's okay with you?"

"He made a mistake, but I'm not going to kill him over it!"

"You're that forgiving?"

"It's has nothing to do with forgiveness!" Luna shouted, her voice carrying through the tunnel in a loud echo. Luna turned away from Ranger and took in a deep breath to regain herself. "I can't be the one who decides who lives and who dies. You told me to take care of it and I did. He's well out of the war, out of Lexus's reach, and he's not coming back," Luna assured, a slight catch in her throat clutching at her words. "I told him how many people died because of what he did, and it hit him like a train. He's not a warrior; he isn't hardened to the reality of death. He wanted to stay and help me atone for what happened, but I sent him away. I told him point-blank that even though I still wanted to keep him safe . . . I couldn't trust him anymore. If you were there, you would be as sure as I am that he's not coming back. He's just another person I trusted that's gone now," Luna explained, a note of bitter sadness embedded in the words.

"I'm sorry. I'm glad to see my faith in you has not been misplaced. You did the right thing," Ranger said, placing a gentle hand on Luna's shoulder.

Luna shifted her gaze to him and saw nothing but the compassion he had toward her. She couldn't help but soften toward it. "Fletcher told me something about you before he left. He said that you aren't working for Lexus and that the Hand Council really thinks you're dead."

Ranger smirked. "Well, finally somebody's on my side. What do you think? Do you believe him?"

Luna eyes grew distant, mulling over her answer in her mind. "Yes, I do. If you were working for Lexus, you would've just taken me down and handed me to her instead of tricking Alias. If you were working for the Hand Council, you would've killed me when we first met, but . . ." Luna tried to continue but was unable to find the words to truly express her hesitation.

"But you still can't be sure, can you?" Ranger filled in.

Luna sighed, pacing and wringing her hands with an anxious air about her. "I'm sorry. I know you've been bending over backward to help me when you really didn't have to, and I'm so tired of feeling alone in the war. I want . . . I need an ally to pull this off, I know that, but it's . . . it's hard to explain."

"No, I understand where you're coming from. You trusted the honor of others and that cost you dearly. You can't stand the thought of being that vulnerable again. You need security, a safety net. You need assurances that I won't be able to turn against you," Ranger mused, tracing the line of his chin with his thumb, his dark eyes deep in contemplation. "You need a trade."

Luna gawked at him, her expression perplexed. "A trade?"

Ranger's lips widened to a happy grin and his eyes gleamed with a sudden spark of inspiration. "Yes, you need something to lock my allegiance to you, something to hold over me that you can use against me if I betray you." Ranger pulled up the sleeve of his coat, exposing a leather wristband with a Daiyu imperial coin embedded in it.

"What are you doing?" Luna asked.

"Something probably extremely stupid, but if I'm right, it will be well worth it. I'll give you what Knights hold more precious than their honor: my real identity." Ranger raised the coin to his lips and whispered a small incantation in a language

Luna didn't recognize. The stern man she came to know as Ranger suddenly faded before her eyes. In his place was a slightly older gentleman with flat black hair and the same sharp facial features as Ranger but of a more modest proportion. A pair of softer dark eyes looked back at her, and even though they lacked the wire-framed glasses, Luna knew them as the eyes of the kind professor she had met.

"Let me reintroduce myself. My name is . . ."

"Ethan Chang!" Luna blurted, her words moving faster than her thoughts.

He cocked his head slightly, his eyed narrowed in perplexity. "You know me?"

Her eyes darted away from her gaze as she realized her blunder. "No, no, I don't."

"It's all right. You haven't exposed anything of yourself. I know plenty of people in my life and plenty of people know me. You could be anyone," Ethan assured.

"Are you insane?" Luna demanded, her hands balled into fists and her cheeks flushed with frantic anger.

"More like desperate."

"Do you realize what you've done?" Luna scolded.

"Of course. Now you can rest easy knowing that if I betray you, you can find me," Ethan reasoned.

"Why would you do something that reckless?"

Ethan smiled kindly at his comrade. "It's not reckless because I have no intentions of betraying you, and I believe you won't use my identity to betray me. So if you look at it logically, there really is no risk."

"No risk?" Luna shouted. "How can you think that?"

"Because it's true. I trust you and what you stand for. I also have little choice in the matter. We have to work together perfectly to pull this off, and we can't afford to hold back. If this is what I have to do to prove myself, then it's a small price. If you knew me, knew what my life was like, you'd know that I have little to lose and everything to gain. You may not understand my intentions, Luna. Just realize that with what I gave you, I can't afford to betray you," Ethan reasoned.

Luna's pale jade eyes stared long at the man she thought she had known and saw him for the first time with clarity. "Let's get to work."

CHAPTER 33

THE RAYS OF warm sunshine glistened off the crystal-clear water flowing from a beautiful stone fountain that stood as a sparkling jewel in the center of a lush city park. The park was alive with activity on the bright summer day. In almost every direction there was a family having a picnic on the vibrant green grass or joggers making their way down winding network of trails.

Ranger's keen eyes scanned the bustle of the park through his wire-framed sunglasses. He was happy with the day's turn-out. High-population areas were perfect for improvised assurances in his line of work. Plenty of people meant plenty of witnesses if his enemies decided to play dirty.

His search caught sight of a gruff, towering man of solid stature and a face full of untamed brown hair standing by the fountain. The dark tan of his complexion was contrasted by the vibrant red T-shirt and light blue jeans. His stern gaze searched the area much like Ranger's.

He shoved his hands in the pockets of his plain brown slacks as Ranger fell into a casual stroll, making his way to the fountain. He could feel the weight of the pistol strapped to his body under his dull-gray coat, well hidden from the many civilians around him.

Ranger stopped beside the sizable man and stared forward in the sparkling splendor of the flowing water to keep an inconspicuous manner. He only broke the stare with a quick glance to the man at his side. The last puzzle piece of his identity fell into place with the sight of a tribal wolf tattoo painted over the man's rather large bicep. "I hear you need my help," Ranger stated calmly, his gaze never leaving the water.

The tattooed man shifted his dark, humorless eyes to Ranger. "I suppose you're Ranger," he said, his voice emanated with a deep rumble.

"And you're Alexei's wolf, I presume," Ranger answered, keeping a careful but subtle eye on him.

"You got it. They call me Volk." He looked Ranger up and down with a calculating glower. "I thought the infamous Ranger would be bigger."

Ranger rolled his eyes behind his dark sunglasses. "It's resources and skill that's going to help you now, not brute strength."

Volk crossed his arms over his chest and faced Ranger, his stance set in a defensive posture. "About that, I'm sorry for bringing you here."

Ranger shifted to study Volk with a long side-glance. He could see the fear behind Volk's firm demeanor; he had the readied posture of a wild animal feeling the approach of danger. Strangely enough, the wolf's gaze wasn't searching for danger in the crowd; they were strictly centered on Ranger. The cut-and-dry situation of Volk's plea for aid was falling apart with irregularities and suspicion. "Don't worry. They won't be able to try anything in such a public place. No Knight would dare expose themselves to this many civilians," Ranger assured, keeping his suspicions below the surface.

"I'm counting on that, Ranger," a smaller, male voice spoke from Ranger's left.

Ranger turned sharply and saw the source of his suspicion stepping with a confident stride toward him. His muscles tensed and his expression turned to granite when he saw the dirty-blond messenger standing before him, too close for his own comfort. Ranger vividly recalled his cocky smirk from their last meeting on the darkened rooftop when the messenger set down Luna's death sentence. This day, the messenger had traded in his pitch-black robe for a smart light gray suit, accented by a white dress shirt and canary-yellow tie. "You're looking well, Ranger, considering all you've been through since we last met, or have the stories been exaggerated?" the messenger taunted.

Volk moved around Ranger in an apprehensive shuffle to place himself at the messenger's back, his eyes locked on Ranger the whole time. "All right, I got him to show, now can I leave?" Volk pleaded.

"That's depends. Does anyone but you know about this get-together?" the messenger inquired.

"Not a soul. My Master and I make a large effort to keep our noses clean with the Hand Council. We don't want to make an enemy of Ranger, either."

"Good. The less people who know we were here, the better. You may leave." The messenger dismissed Volk with a slight flourish of his hand. "Just remember, Volk. You were never here. If you feel the need to tell otherwise, I will give you a real reason to seek Ranger's protection. Are we clear?" Volk answered with a stiff nod before stepping out of sight at a hurried pace.

The messenger turned his cunning gray eyes back to the stoic Ranger, noticing his arms now folded over his chest in an unmistakable fashion. "Now don't get any ideas, Ranger," the messenger said, his lips curling into a satisfied grin. "All these people are having such a nice day; let's not ruin it with my untimely death. Shooting me in the head with that pistol under your arm will attract more attention then you're willing. Just relax. This meeting place was chosen equally for both our protection."

Ranger exhaled a heavy breath through his nose as his somber eyes glared at the dirty-blond trickster. In a reluctant show of surrender from action, Ranger let his arms fall casually to his side. He stewed in his frustration over his inability to act, but took some solace in the fact that the enemy's hands were equally as tied. They would both walk out of this alive, but what was to be gained? "What do you want?" Ranger demanded, his tone frigidly sharp.

"To talk," the messenger said simply, as if the notion was an everyday occurrence.

A harsh and almost sickened chuckle erupted from Ranger's chest. "The last time I checked, the Hand Council's position on me was, 'Done talking.'"

"That's certainly true. The Hand Council knows that the news of your demise has been greatly exaggerated, and they know you're working against them with the Knight you were supposed to kill."

Ranger met the messenger with an amused smirk. "And they sent you? Are they giving me fair warning or are they extremely hard-pressed for Hunters these days?"

"Bite me, Ranger!" the messenger spat. "Now that the Hand Council knows of your all-out treachery, your execution is only a matter of time. Luckily for you, this meeting is, in a manner of speaking, off the clock."

"This isn't a social call, is it?"

The messenger's mouth fell from his arrogant grin to a thin line, and his eyes stiffened with frustration. "You shouldn't be so quick to blow me off, Ranger. I'll bet everything that what I have to say will pique your interest."

"Then say it! I don't have time for your pandering," Ranger snapped.

The messenger shifted to face the fountain, his solemn gray eyes set on the light dancing on the water's surface. "Two days ago, the Hand Council sent a Hunter to execute a Rogue known as Titan for disobeying a direct command from the Council and actively working against the Order."

"Was Titan actually guilty or was he just an inconvenience?" Ranger spat, his words like a swift whip.

"The mission was a failure and the Hunter is dead. The Hand has taken this killing as a personal affront to the structure they have made and are planning brutal retaliation to send a harsh message."

"The Hand doesn't like to be challenged in the least. As long as they have fear and domination on their side, they have control. You've been in this long enough to know that."

The messenger's hands tightened into fists as he gave Ranger an intense glare. "You don't understand how far this has gone. The Hand has discovered Titan's real identity and plans to use it against him."

A spark of surprise shot through Ranger's mind, the chilling possibilities of the situation sweeping over him like a winter storm. "How did they get ahold of that?"

"I don't know, maybe Titan slipped up somewhere. The specifics on that aren't being shared, even among the Hand's attendants and Hunters. As far as I can tell, the information came from the Hand Council themselves." The messenger's shoulders stiffened, and he held himself with a heaviness Ranger had never seen in him. "This guy has a wife and two kids, a thirteen-year-old boy and a fourteen-year-old girl. The Hand wants them all dead." The messenger let the words sink into Ranger's mind before continuing. "Don't get the wrong impression, Ranger; I support the Hand Council and what they do. I believe they provide a sense of order to the powerful in our world. They could command the execution of any Rogue and I'll stand behind them always, but . . . I don't want the blood of kids on my hands, Ranger."

"But why call me?" Ranger asked.

The messenger's eyes blazed with fury as he rushed to stand face-to-face with Ranger. "Because this is your fault! You couldn't have just done your job and got out of the way. You had to step back into action and openly defy them. The brutal retaliation is to send a message to you and ones like you. What did you think was going to happen once you acted against the Hand Council? You stepped out of line, and now this family's going to suffer for it! The least you can do before they hunt you down is fix your mistake."

Ranger's austere eyes looked down upon the angry messenger through his dark glasses. "You may blame me for this, but you must realize it's the Council who is out of line. You working to stop this mad hunt shows you know this. They are breaking the same Code they hold others to. How can you follow them?" Ranger asked.

"So you won't help them?"

"I didn't say that. I'm just curious what this means for you."

"This is just a simple exchange. I give you the information about this hunt and you do what you think you should. We both never speak of this meeting and go our separate ways, hopefully to never cross paths again. Got it?"

CHAPTER 34

LUNA LOOKED OUT the passenger seat window of their nondescript rental car at the heavy iron-gated property before them. The domineering barricade had no sense of flourish or artistry; it was a product of pure function. Behind it stood a thick line of tall sturdy pine trees that only broke at a narrow strip of road that led into the acreage. Luna could see the glint of several security cameras teamed up with what looked like motion sensor spotlights perched atop the fence at equal partitions. The gloomy fortress matched perfectly to the foreboding layer of thick gray clouds overhead. Luna found it hard to believe she was looking at the home of a family of four.

She turned to Ranger in the driver's seat. "This looks more like a military base than a home. Who is this man?" she asked.

"His name is Nathan Eckhart," Ranger said as he cut the ignition. "When he's not running around as Titan, he works at a security firm in research and development."

"It looks like he's taking his work home with him," Luna mused.

"Just because you're paranoid doesn't mean they aren't out to get you. He has every right to be protective considering who's after him," Ranger reasoned.

"Do you have a way of getting in?"

Ranger leaned forward and studied the fortress with a contemplative gaze. "I was thinking the front door would be best," he decided before climbing out of the car.

Luna stammered in place for a moment, taken aback by Ranger's decision before quickly following him to the solid gate. "Are you sure this is wise? You received this information from a Hand Council agent. This could be a setup."

"We'll cross that bridge when and if we get to it. We can't gamble with these people's lives if what the messenger said is true."

Luna frowned. "I guess all we can do is hope the Hand doesn't know that."

Trying to leave behind their suspicions, they both turned to face the foreboding gate. Before them was a sleek, expensive-looking intercom panel installed on the gate. Ranger pushed the call button on the panel causing it to make a loud buzzing noise.

Ranger and Luna stood in silent anticipation for several moments before their call was answered by a harsh voice over the speaker. "Yes," the voice demanded impatiently.

"Nathan Eckhart? Or do you prefer Titan?" Ranger replied.

There was a long pause before the voice replied, "What do you want?"

"We're here to help you. Your situation with the Hand Council has gone beyond what you can handle. You and your family are in serious danger," Ranger informed.

"Who are you?"

"I'm Ranger, and if you know anything about me, you'll know that I've also had a falling-out with the Hand recently. We need to get you to safety."

"We're safe in here; I've made sure of that. We don't need your help," Titan insisted.

"If the Hand is planning on attacking you in your home, they are going to plan around your security in ways even I can't predict. You can't put your family at risk by underestimating them. They aren't going to let your defiance go unpunished and they won't ever stop. As long as it's possible, they will come after you. You can't hole up in here forever," Ranger asserted, the patience in his tone wearing thin.

"How do I know I can trust you?" Titan asked.

"You can take all the precautions you feel necessary with us. You'll see we mean you no harm."

They waited for Titan's response for several nerve-racking moments before the gate sounded with a high-pitched buzz. The lock disengaged and the barricade slowly swung open. Ranger and Luna cautiously made their way down the narrow gravel road as thunder echoed in the distance. They marched with purpose, taking in the details of the grounds with a trained eye. The inner workings of the estate looked just as secure as the outside. The grounds had a clear fifteen feet between the fence and the thick line of tall trees, carefully watched by several posted security cameras and motion sensor lights. Beyond the tree line that encircled the property was much the same story: twenty feet of clear-cut ground carefully watched by mechanical eyes.

Nestled in the center of this garrison was a flat, humorless building that looked like a drab stone block with only one door and sparse windows. It was difficult to determine whether the whole picture of this home would inspire assurances or depression.

The very moment Luna and Ranger set foot on the front step, the door sprung open in the same manner as the gate, welcoming them into the house without the physical presence of its owner.

"Step inside, close the door behind you, and don't go any further," the same voice instructed from another speaker.

At Ranger's lead, the two of them stepped gingerly through the heavy door and closed it behind them. The atmosphere they stepped into was dramatically different from the drab gray of the building's outer shell. The door led into a small circular room that stretched out ahead into a narrow hallway. The smooth bleach-white walls stood in deep contrast with the sleek black tiles that blanketed the floor. Every detail of the room was made vibrantly clear from the series of bright light fixtures installed in equal spacing on the ceiling, leading down the hallway.

The silence in the room was immediately broken by a strange humming noise that came from an unknown source. Luna's gaze searched for the origin of the strange noise before giving Ranger a questioning glance.

"It must be some kind of scanner hidden in the walls," Ranger speculated. "Just hold still for now."

Luna remained alert, senses open and ready for the unexpected, listening to the odd sound as it went quiet. "For someone who doesn't mean me any harm, you're hiding a lot of weapons," Titan snapped, his voice carrying over another intercom.

"We have them in case we don't get away in time. In case we have to fight the Hunter sent to kill you," Ranger explained.

"Sorry, but if you're here to kill me, I'm not going to make it easy for you," Titan said as a wide drawer popped open from the wall beside them. "Put all your weapons in this drawer and then I'll let you in."

"You would make us defenseless," Luna objected.

The intercom crackled with Titan's amused chuckle. "Oh, please. A Knight may become unarmed, but they are never really defenseless. Those are my demands, and the only way into this house is to abide by them. You see, the tiles in the hall-way in front of you are armed with pressure-sensitive triggers. Once you hand over your weapons, I'll deactivate them. Or you can press on and see what they do. It's your choice."

Luna knelt down in front of the tiled hall and gently laid her hand on the edge, careful not to touch them. Her eyes glistened with a blue glimmer as her senses reached out through her fingertips, searching for the energy she could control. "There's an electrical current running under the tiles like he said, but with no direct contact with the circuit, I can't shut it down." Luna glanced up at the ceiling. "And there's no way to climb over it."

"Do what he says," Ranger commanded. "We don't have time to waste."

With precise efficiency, Ranger and Luna disarmed themselves of all their pistols, blades, and any other weapon in their possession and placed them begrudgingly into the drawer to await further instructions.

"Good choice. The other route wouldn't have turned out well for you. Walk through the hall, and we'll talk in the sitting room," Titan instructed.

Luna made a careful but uneventful step onto the now inert black tiles, prompting her and Ranger to march on into the unknown of this growingly strange situation. The door at the end of the hallway led them to a sparsely furnished room, dimly lit by gloomy twilight from the narrow windows. The small black couch, chair, coffee table, and bookshelf were the only occupants over the black hardwood floor. The sleek chrome fireplace along the inner wall sat cold and empty. Not only was the room void of any pleasant warmth, but it also lacked the house's owner.

"I thought we were going to talk?" Luna asked, directing her speech to the house itself.

"We are talking," Titan replied, his voice seemingly originating from all around the room.

"Are we going to be talking to an intercom all night?" Ranger asked.

"If I can help it. Now let's get down to business. Tell me everything you can about this Hunter they're sending so we can fortify this place properly."

Ranger shook his head. "No, you don't understand. I don't know who they're sending or even if it's just one. They want to send a brutal message with the death of you and your family, so they won't be pulling their punches. As of now, we're flying blind."

"Wha-what should we do?" Titan asked, the worried catch in his voice was unmistakable to Luna, even over the intercom.

"We need to get you and your family to safety and hidden from the Hand. You have to disappear."

"No!" Titan snapped.

"Excuse me?" Luna retorted, befuddlement dripping from her expression.

"I won't leave my home; I can't leave. We just have to make our stand here!" Titan insisted.

"Do you know what you're saying?" Ranger protested.

"I've killed one of them before. We can fight back."

"Titan, listen to me. I've dealt with many Hunters at one time or another, and they are nothing to be taken lightly. You may have killed one of them, but that doesn't mean a thing. The Hunters are specifically chosen by the Hand to kill Knights. You have no idea what you're dealing with."

"You said you wanted to help me!"

"Yes, help you survive, not needlessly defend a building," Ranger protested.

"This building is the home I built for my family. I will not be pulled from it by anyone," Titan stated, a stubborn finality in his voice.

"If you stay, you'll be putting all of us in immediate danger. You must realize this," Luna argued.

"I won't be pushed around by the Hand, and that's final!"

The utter immobility of Titan's opinion set Luna's temper to a boiling point. "What kind of a husband and father puts his own family in extreme danger because of a foolish sense of pride?" Luna's angered voice echoed off the hollowed walls into the long string of silence that followed.

"I'm not leaving my home, and if you two want to keep me alive, neither are you," Titan proclaimed with a final click from the intercom.

Luna's hands balled into fists and she let out a furious cry. "What idiocy! He would rather face the wrath of the Hand for a simple house than retreat and live! I'll be damned if I'm going to let this man's stupidity get him and his family killed!" Luna stormed further into the house with a purposeful step and determined eyes.

"Where are you going?" Ranger asked, following her march.

"I'm going to find where this fool is hiding and drag him out if necessary. He'll thank me later when he's not dead."

They swept through the building, seeking the home's owner with a hurried vigor. They were unsuccessful until Luna came to a cluttered basement. The walls could barely be seen through the shelves filled with gadgets, mechanical parts, and tools that lined the room in every direction. The floor was sparse concrete except for a small maroon throw rug at the floor's center. Luna made her way into the workshop with careful steps before feeling a strange protrusion under her boot. She knelt down and quickly pulled the rug from its place, revealing a hidden door with a metal handle jutting up from it. Luna took hold of the handle and braced her footing to pull open the secret entrance. The loud clang of the metal hatch on the stone floor shattered the silence.

Luna peered through the passage at a set of wooden steps that led down into a short, dark hallway with a heavy metal door at the end. The steps let out a high-pitched creak under Luna's feet as she searched the walls for a light switch. The lights revealed the significance of the hidden room. Installed beside the fortified steel door was a sophisticated lock control panel. The heavier the lock, the greater the importance of what it protects.

Luna felt around the base of the panel for the break in the casing and slid her fingernails into the crevice, wriggling the panels face off the wall to reveal its inner workings. Laying her hand on the circuits, she could feel the power moving through the wires and could see where the circuit needed to be connected for its completion. She injected a precise and incredibly careful surge of her abilities into the circuit, coercing the sturdy metal door to pop open.

Luna pulled the hefty door open, but before her eyes could set on the room, a brilliant arch of blazing blue lightning shot out from inside, hitting Luna square in the shoulder. Her body was thrown back violently with the force of the blast, tumbling like a rag doll until she hit the adjacent wall.

"Luna!" Ranger's voice called from the initial basement.

"Stay back!" Luna commanded between pained gasps, and she dragged herself to her feet as fast as she was able.

"Get out of my house! I don't need help from the likes of you!" a younger, softer voice demanded from inside the fortified room.

"Luna, what's going on?" Ranger demanded to know, panic lining his tone.

"I'm okay. I can absorb the worst of this, but you can't. If you get hit with the power he's throwing around, it could kill you, so stay up there! I got this," Luna insisted.

"I said get out!" the attacker screamed before letting fly another dangerous surge of lightning. Luna sprung to her feet at a full-out sprint, both dodging the attack and closing the distance. Her nimble feet and powerful speed pulled Luna into the attacker's flank faster than he could even react, leaving him vulnerable to an attack.

Luna snatched his hand at the wrist and pulled him to her, smashing her forehead into his. The attacker cried out in pain and clutched his aching head as he staggered backward, falling to the floor.

Luna was finally face-to-face with her assailant, but the truth of this bizarre situation caused her warrior's resolve to grind to a halt. The brazen Knight who dared attack her was nothing more than a young man who still carried the baby-faced qualities of a teenager. His stature was mantled with only a sparse amount of muscle and his complexion was pale from lack of sunlight. His electric-blue hair hung in a spiked mess over his weary gray eyes.

Luna's stricken stare wandered through the room, realizing more and more of the truth with every glance she took. The small room was made all the more cramped from the large computer desk littered with empty pop bottles, food containers, and dirty dishes. The only break from this clutter was set for a high-tech, customized keyboard, mouse, and headset placed directly before several monitors mounted to the wall. The monitors were looking out through the eyes of the security cameras.

The young man pulled one hand from his battered head and stretched it out toward Luna, his eyes flickering with a weak blue hue. His outstretched hand bore a strange mechanism that sparked with an idle threat.

Luna turned to face him with hard eyes and answered him with a brilliant surge of electricity that bounced on her fingers like a contained storm. "You look a little worse for wear, boy, and I am fully charged. Do you really want to try me?" she asked sternly.

The young boy's expression filled with doubt behind his shaking hand, the sound of his quickened breath filled the silence between the rolling thunder. "That was you the entire time, wasn't it?" Luna asked, gesturing to the computer. "Who are you?"

"Luna! Are you all right?" Ranger bellowed from upstairs.

"I'm fine. I have defused the situation, but we have apparently been deceived," Luna answered, her steady gaze not leaving the boy for a second.

CHAPTER 35

RANGER RUSHED TO his comrade's aid, but his charge slowed, perplexed at the sight of the trembling teenager formally thought of as a threat. The boy's eyes darted back and forth with a frantic jitter between Luna and Ranger, his shaking hand switching from one to the other. "What exactly is going on?" Ranger asked.

"This child is the one we were talking to this entire time," Luna informed.

"He must be Nathan Eckhart's kid. He's supposed to have a son about fourteen years old. Is that right?" Ranger asked.

The young boy scurried back from them, jamming his back to the wall. "Get away from me!" he shouted with as much bolstering as his frightened voice could muster.

Ranger threw up his hands in surrender, taking slow but careful steps toward the boy. "Easy, it's okay. What we told you before is still true no matter who you are. We still want to help you. What's your name?"

"Nathanial." The boy spoke with a voice that was small but unyielding.

"Hello, Nathanial. I'm Ranger and this is Luna." Ranger could see the budding redness on the boy's forehead. "Luna, see if you can find an icepack or something," Ranger instructed. Answering only with a stiff nod, Luna stepped out of the room.

Ranger faced the frightened Nathanial with an utterly passive demeanor, not a shred of aggression about him. He needed to gain the boy's trust in order to lead him to safety. "Now, Nathanial, why are you pretending to be your father?" Ranger asked calmly.

Nathanial's disposition did not soften to Ranger's show of peace; it merely shifted from frantic hostility to piercing suspicion. His gray eyes watched Ranger carefully for any break in his serene composure. "Protection. If your enemies think you're a badass Knight that killed a Hunter, they think twice about messing with you," Nathanial explained, forcing the words as flat as he could.

"But why are you pretending? Where is the real Titan?"

With an involuntary flick of movement, Nathanial's eyes glanced toward one of the monitors watching what looked to be the backyard. Ranger leaned in to take a closer study of what drew Nathanial's attention and noticed an irregular mound of loose earth, all the unmistakable characteristics of a freshly dug grave. Ranger's eyes narrowed, bafflement lacing his expression as he slowly turned his gaze to the boy. "But . . . Titan survived the attack. He killed the Hunter."

"He did, just barely. He even made it back to the house." Small droplets of tears steadily broke through Nathanial's defensives. "I found him on the front step. He was bleeding so much and it happened so fast . . . I tried to help him, but it . . . he was gone before I could do a thing." Nathanial's chest bobbed with heavy breaths as he struggled to choke back his sorrow.

"I'm sorry," Ranger apologized.

"Yeah, thanks, I guess," Nathanial mumbled, choking back the tears that he could not afford to shed.

Luna returned to the room, successful in her search, bearing an improvised ice pack. She held the pack out to Nathanial and, with a speculative side-glance, he cautiously took it. As he held it to his forehead, he couldn't hide the noticeable look of relief on his face. "You carry quite a wallop for a girl," Nathanial commented to Luna while still never making eye contact.

Luna's lips curled into a sly grin. "And you throw around a lot of power for a child. If Ranger would've taken that hit, you may have killed him."

Nathanial's head shot up and met Luna's gaze with stubborn defiance. "May have?"

"I'll be the first to admit that from the little I've seen, you have potential, but you lack control. It's like you're carrying a gun too big for you. You need more training," Luna stated.

Nathanial's face grew grim and his eyes shied away once more. "Guess I'm on my own with that now."

Luna's eyebrows narrowed in a quizzical glower before she turned to Ranger for an explanation. "Titan didn't survive long after the attack. He died trying to make his way back here," Ranger informed, the grave tone of his voice adding to the bleak atmosphere.

A long somber silence hung in the air like a thick fog as Luna stared at Nathanial, struggling to find what to say. "Your friend already covered the apologies, so don't strain yourself!" Nathanial spat bitterly.

"So why are you still here? Don't you have any family to go to instead of holding up in this fortress pretending to be Titan?" Ranger asked.

Nathanial's face twisted in a half-disgusted sneer. "I don't have anywhere to go. My dad was an only child with no relatives that I know of, and my mom . . ." His voice trailed off into a heavy sigh. "My mom took my sister and left about a year ago when she found out what my dad and I were."

"She didn't know?" Luna asked.

"My dad may have been a smart man, but that decision was not one of his brightest moments. Cat got out of the bag when her little boy started generating electricity from his fingers."

"What about your father's Master? You are the successor of Eckhart's title and are now his Knight. What is he going to do about this?" Luna asked.

With a disgruntled chuckle, Nathanial shook his head. "After I buried Dad, I tried to contact him with the number Dad gave me just in case. When he finally took my call, he immediately told me to never contact him again. He probably didn't want to be associated with a Rogue of the Hand so he cut his losses and all ties to us."

"So your plan was to just live here by yourself? How old are you?" Ranger asked pointedly.

The detestable sneer returned to Nathanial's face as he set his stalwart eyes on Ranger. "I'm thirteen, and I can take care of myself. The money from my invention patents goes directly into my father's account, which I have access to, and you can order pretty much anything on the internet. Since the moment I found out what he was doing in his off-hours, I'd been preparing for the day that he may not come back. You two probably know all about that."

Luna answered with an understanding gesture, but Ranger did not return the expression in kind. His mind had centered on something else. "You have inventions?" Ranger asked.

"Well, not on paper. I made the prototypes, but the patents were made in Dad's name so they would be taken seriously," Nathanial explained.

"Prototypes like that device on your hand. Luna said you were throwing around a lot of power for someone your age and I trust her insight," Ranger speculated.

"Fine! You caught me! I'm not as badass as you thought, but that blast was a good sixty to sixty-four percent of my power. But I haven't had much time to train it between school and my inventions. I'll get better," Nathanial explained to defend his abilities.

"You've made something that boosts a Knight's powers?" Ranger asked.

Nathanial rolled his eyes. "It only affects particular powers. It's an outside-force manipulation accelerator. It takes people like us who can control outside elemental force like electricity and gives it a boost," Nathanial explained.

A small gasp slipped through Luna's lips. "That's amazing."

"Well, like I said, it's just a prototype. I have to recalibrate it for every different person who uses it, and there's a slight overheating issue. It's still a work in progress."

"How hard is it to recalibrate this device?" Ranger asked.

"The accelerator has to be put through threshold testing with the person who wants to use it and then I put that data through the software my dad developed," Nathanial clarified.

"Not exactly user-friendly, is it?" Ranger continued.

"Oh, no, like I said, it's still just a prototype and the process to rig it to one person is extremely buggy right now. I'm still just testing it for the most part."

Ranger's eyes grew distant as his mind rapidly assessed the newfound facts to fill in the blanks of the situation. "I see. This is starting to make a lot more sense."

Luna turned her gaze to Ranger. "What are you thinking?"

"Tell me, Nathanial; did your father ever assist you in field-testing this devise, maybe on his missions as a Knight?" Ranger inquired.

Nathanial's expression suddenly grew defensive. "What does that have to do with anything?"

"A lot more than you realize. Just try and picture this. Titan steps onto the field and shows a significant jump in his abilities, getting the attention of the Hand Council. They summon him to reveal the secret of his sudden advancement. Without any reason to mistrust the Hand, he tells them all about your invention. You see in the past there have been many attempts at ability acceleration through drugs or physical augmentation, but none of them had satisfying results. Your device, however, can be personalized to anyone without long-term side effects. That kind of tool can shift the power balance easily," Ranger theorized.

Nathanial staggered backward and sunk into his chair. His expression mirrored the growing dread inside. "But . . . it's just a prototype. The calibration process is anything but streamlined, and it overheats. Why would they do this for something they can't even use?" Nathanial asked in little more than a whisper.

Ranger shook his head. "They didn't want the machine; they wanted the mind behind it. The Hand Council most likely ordered Titan to hand over the inventor so they could use you to further their own interests. That's when Titans, loyalty dried up and he refused, disobeying a direct order from the Hand Council."

"Do you really think that's what happened?" Nathanial asked softly.

"It's the only theory that makes any sense in this situation. I'm sorry."

Tears began to swell in Nathanial's tired eyes, and he buried his head in his hands, the color draining from his cheeks. "Oh my god . . . I feel sick. This . . . this is all my fault."

"Nathanial, you can't blame yourself for this," Luna protested.

"But he was branded as a Rogue because he wanted to protect me. I should have thought more carefully about the attention he would gain. I just wanted to see how it worked in the field," Nathanial ranted, small sobs spilling over his speech.

Ranger stepped over to the saddened boy and laid one steady hand on his shoulder. "I shouldn't have told you that. I'm sorry."

Nathanial wiped away his tears and shook his head. "No, I have to deal with this. I need to do something about this," Nathanial declared. The sorrow in his face was suddenly replaced with a choked rage. "I need to fight back. I can't run and hide after what they have done."

"Absolutely not!" Ranger asserted.

Nathanial turned his newfound fury onto Ranger. "They killed my dad just because he wouldn't hand me over. It's only right that I avenge him. As a Knight—"

"You are not a Knight! You are still just a child; I'll admit a gifted one but just a child! You were blessed with a normal upbringing, but that makes you unfit for the field. You'd just get yourself killed, and I'm not going to be responsible for that. You may be ready in the future, but now this isn't your fight!" Ranger shouted, cutting Nathanial off.

Nathanial practically leaped from his chair and stood toe-to-toe with Ranger. "You don't understand. He was all I had left. Without him, I have nothing, and that means I have nothing to lose, and I'm taking those bastards down with me if I have to!"

Without any warning to betray his actions, Ranger pushed Nathanial against the wall. Not hard enough to hurt the boy, but enough to get his full attention. He witnessed the results of this action when the rage in Nathanial's expression immediately faded to surprise. Ranger locked his gaze with Nathanial. His cold, calculated stare showed Nathanial a side of him that halted his youthful enthusiasm in place. Ranger could feel the strangled trembling in Nathanial's body through his firm grip.

"Ranger, what are you doing?" Luna inquired, confusion and worry threading her tone.

"Stand down, Luna. If he wants to rush headlong into revenge, he has to know what exactly he's getting into," Ranger answered, his voice steady and his eyes not breaking the boy's gaze for a second. "It's you who doesn't understand, Nathanial. You think you have nothing to lose? You think that you will face these people without fear? Then you truly have no idea what some of these Hunters are like. They delight in the pain they cause, revel in the fear of their prey. They live for the hunt. Your death won't even be the worst of it. They will twist you, body and mind, into something you won't even recognize until you beg for death. It won't be quick, it won't be painless, and it most certainly will be terrifying. Do you understand now?"

Nathanial swallowed hard to hold back his fear and answered with a meek nod.

"Are you afraid?" Ranger asked and was answered in the same manner. "Good. You haven't lost all sense. You may not think that retreating now is the right thing to do, but it's the smart thing to do. Trust me. There is no glory in charging to your death. The best thing you can do now is live on for your father's sake." Ranger loosened his grip and let his message sink in.

They stood in strict silence for a moment that seemed to last forever. Nathanial's face portrayed his shattered defenses and the scared child behind them. Ranger felt for him but didn't regret his actions. What he had done may have been harsh, but it sent precisely the right message that Nathanial needed to hear.

Nathanial found his eyes drifting around the room until they settled on a framed picture among the clutter on his desk. It trapped a moment in time with him and his father, a new project on the workbench and wide smiles on their faces. "Was he the first the Hand Council cheated like this?" Nathanial asked softly.

Ranger gave Nathanial a tentative stare, not sure if the answer Nathanial was looking for would be a help or a hindrance.

"Look, my dad was killed because of this, and all I want to know is the full extent of why it happened," Nathanial pleaded.

"I can't tell you that,"

Nathanial locked eyes with Ranger, his face showing an infuriated glare. "Why? Do you think I won't be able to take the answer?"

"It's because I don't want to burden you with the truth."

"You patronizing son of a bitch. How dare you think you can judge whether I should be burdened with the truth. This is my father we're talking about. I deserve the truth," Nathanial demanded.

Ranger met Nathanial's white-hot rage with a stoic steadiness to compose the situation. "Knowing this won't change anything. It won't change your situation, won't change your abilities, and it won't change what happened. You can't fix this, Nathanial. The only thing this knowledge may do for you is make it harder to move on. Do you understand this?"

Nathanial took in a deep breath and seemed to be taming the wild emotions within, his gaze drawn down to the ground for a moment. Before long, he met Ranger with a weary stare and nodded his head.

"And with that understanding, do you still believe you want to carry that truth with you?" Ranger asked, hoping the young man could be deterred.

But Ranger's wishes were not fulfilled as Nathanial nodded his head once again, giving the answer Ranger hoped Nathanial wouldn't regret. "I need to know. Please, tell me. Was he the only one?"

Ranger's chest heaved in a heavy sigh. "No, he wasn't."

"How many?"

"The full number is still unknown to us."

Nathanial slumped back into his chair as if he were unable to bear the weight of what he now knew on his feet. He ran his near-shaking fingers through his rat's nest of hair and stared ahead blankly. "This is insane."

"You don't need to worry. We know enough about how they operate to hide you out of their reach. You'll be safe," Luna reassured.

"But what if I don't want to hide? What if I want to help you in . . . whatever this is?" Nathanial asked.

A gruff exhale of frustration escaped Ranger's lips as he ran a tense hand through his hair. "I knew this would happen if you knew the truth. There is nothing you can do about this. You're not prepared for this battle. You'd be more of a liability than an asset."

"I don't have to go into the field, yet. I can help in other ways. I could perfect the amplifier and make all kinds of things to help you out. I can still do my part in this," Nathanial reasoned with determination in his plea.

His argument still met Ranger's stone shell with no avail. "Out of the question! Even as support, your life will still be in grave danger."

"What am I supposed to do? Just sit here in the ruins of my old life?" Nathanial shouted.

"Starting over isn't the end, Nathanial! You can make a new life for yourself away from all this, but not if you're dead."

"How can I just move on after something like this?"

Ranger's stoic bearing suddenly portrayed a reflective nature as he mused over Nathanial's question with a strong sense of familiarity. "One step at a time. The answer isn't an easy one, but moving on from this is possible."

Nathanial hung his head low in his despair and uncertainty, turning his gaze firmly away from Ranger. "I just don't know anymore."

Ranger moved to continue but was halted by Luna's hand on his shoulder gently leading him away from the boy. "Can I have a word with him?" she asked. "I think I might be able to help."

Ranger turned to Luna, curiosity and surprise lacing his gaze. "You think you can get through to him? How?"

"You're going to have to trust me on this. I think I can relate to him on some levels, but I'd rather talk to him alone, if that's all right with you."

Ranger acknowledged Luna's request with a slight nod. "Fine. Hopefully, you can get through to him before we have unwelcomed guests. I'll go see if I can find where he put our weapons. Good luck," he said before leaving the room, his footsteps echoing through the empty house.

CHAPTER 36

LUNA LISTENED TO Ranger's steps for a moment, judging his position in the building to make sure he was out of earshot. She turned to Nathanial and found his eyes were already upon her, subtly gawking with a mix of caution and fascination. "What is it?" she asked.

Nathanial immediately broke off his stare and turned away, looking down at his device with a contemplative gaze. "You know, meeting you like this is really a game changer for me."

"Why is that?" Luna asked as she casually propped herself against the desk across from him.

"I thought having the amplifier would give me a leg up in all this. I thought that if I just concentrated on inventive ways to improve my abilities, it wouldn't matter that I'm not strong. But you danced around that power as if it were a part of you. When I use my powers, it just feels like I'm playing with sparks. Now I see my cheap tricks can't substitute for the skill I don't have," Nathanial said, bitterness lacing his words.

"These skills didn't come without sacrifice," she mumbled.

"What do you mean?"

"Do you go to school, Nathanial?" Luna asked, showing him a soft, trusting smile.

Nathanial raised a quizzical eyebrow at the seemingly strange question. "Of course I do."

"Do you like it?" Luna continued.

"It's all right."

"What about friends?"

"Well, I'm kind of a geek, so I'm not winning any popularity contests, but the few I do have are pretty solid."

"So you have fond memories of your life here?"

"I guess. Even after Mom left, Dad tried his best to get things back to normal."

"It sounds like he didn't want you to grow up with the weight of all this on your shoulders. He was a good man."

Luna kept a careful eye on Nathanial as he stared longingly at the picture in his hand. She was relieved to see that the memories didn't show sorrow or rage in Nathanial's disposition. Instead, she saw the faintest spark of happiness mirrored by a small smile. "He was. But that's just kid's stuff. Everyone has them."

"I didn't," Luna answered in a soft, somber voice while her lips still reflected a sweet, partial smile.

Nathanial blinked with perplexity at this foreign concept. "You didn't go to school? Why not?"

Luna's milky jade eyes stared off as she recalled a frightening and harsh time in her past. "My family has a very particular structure that allows for no divergence. The ones with the Knight bloodline are expected to have at least two children. Once it is discovered which of the children was born with the Knight's abilities, that child becomes the heir to the sword and is immediately sculpted to be a talented and powerful warrior. The other child then becomes the heir to the name and is bred to take on the responsibilities of the family's ventures. Once they are set on the path that the bloodline has chosen for them, no matter their age, they are no longer seen as children in the eyes of the family. They are the next of a proud line of Knights and the Head of the family, and they are treated as such."

"How old were you?"

"I was ten years old when my powers started to manifest. They said that was a rarity, and the family took it as a good sign."

"But it was worth it in a way. Like the way you opened the lock through the circuit board; that takes an extreme amount of control. Plus how you took that hit earlier. That was incredible," Nathanial admired.

"Control has always been a necessity for me. Something I wanted more than anything. It wasn't a question of can or can't. Failure wasn't an option with the power I had been given. I had to gain control or people got hurt."

A sense of sympathy traced the young man's expression. "Sounds like a lot of pressure to put on someone."

She replied with a stiff nod, choking back the bitter taste of those frightening memories. "Nathanial, I'm going to tell you something that I haven't told anyone before. When I first got my powers, I hated them. They terrified me and kept me away from the people I cared about. They separated me from my mother and brother, my father just saw me as a soldier, and they cut off any prospect of friends. Yes, that focus gave me the drive to become what I am today, but sometimes I wonder if maybe I gave up too much."

"You think I'm the same?"

"No, you're different. You have enough of a grasp on your powers that with a bit more focused training, you'd have no problem living with people," Luna assured.

Nathanial sank back into his chair with a disheartened gaze. "I can have a normal life . . . just not here."

"Unfortunately, for the time being, we'll have to relocate you for your own safety. But after we take care of this, you can do or go anywhere you want."

Nathanial rested his chin in his palm, his expression echoing the deep pondering of his future possibilities. "Can I ask you something?"

"Go ahead."

"You said you used to hate your powers and being a Knight. What exactly changed?" he asked.

Her hand moved in an involuntary gesture to the diamond ring that hung around her neck. "I found something to fight for, something that made me proud of who I am. I know you may be thinking that revenge is what you want, but from what I've heard of your father, he wouldn't want that for you. I think he would want you to grow fully into yourself before you decide what you really want to fight for."

For the first time since they had met, Nathanial's eyes brightened and he was able to crack a sly little smirk. "You know, I hate it when I'm proven wrong."

Suddenly, the whole house rattled from a deafening explosion from outside. Nathanial zipped to the monitors and began flipping through the different security cameras just as Ranger raced back into the room. "That must be a Hunter. We have to get out of here," Ranger commanded.

Nathanial raised his hand in a halting gesture. "Whoa, don't jump the gun just yet. Sounds like one of the mines in the yard."

Luna's jaw fell to the floor. "There are mines in your yard? We walked right through there!"

"Calm down. I deactivated the grid when I let you guys in. You weren't in any danger, but sometimes these things get set off by animals. I've got a visual now. Just waiting for the smoke to clear."

All eyes were on the monitor, waiting in anticipation to discover the identity of the poor soul on the land mine. The smoke cleared with the coming rain leaving the three of them awestruck at what they saw. Standing within the central devastation of the mine was a tall, lanky man completely unscathed from the blast. The fabric of his black suit seemed untouched, and his short blond hair was still shaped stylishly as he continued his chilling advance on the house. Ranger carefully examined the man through the camera feed until his usual stoic demeanor betrayed him to a slight show of recognition and fear.

"How the hell did he come out of that completely . . . untouched?" Nathanial gawked in disbelief.

Ranger's demeanor hardened as he turned to Nathanial. "Where are our weapons?" he demanded.

Nathanial tore his attention away from the screen to Ranger's inquiry. "Um . . . they went down a shoot to the basement."

"Go get them now!" Ranger ordered. Nathanial jumped from his chair and scurried out of the room to do as commanded.

As Ranger watched the monitors to track the intruder's movements, Luna stepped in close to him and spoke softly to keep her words between them. "Do you know who that is?" she asked.

"He's dangerous."

"Could you be more specific?"

"He's very dangerous."

Luna shot Ranger an irritated glare. "Ranger! I need to know what you know about our enemy if I'm going to be of use. Keeping this from me at this stage would be foolish and you're clever enough to know that. At least tell me the extent of his powers."

Without taking his eyes off the monitors, Ranger tapped his fingers on the desk as he noticeably considered her argument. He conceded to her with a heavy sigh. "I don't know," he answered.

"But you recognized him almost instantly. You must know something."

"I'm unsure of the extent of his powers because they may have changed. His code name is Ravenous and . . . he eats people, but not just their bodies. He devours a person's essence and gains their memories, talents, and in the case of Knights, he acquires their abilities," Ranger informed, his tone grim.

Luna's eyes bulged as she thought about the raw potential of her enemy's strange abilities. "He could have any number of dangerous powers."

"I know my way around some of his abilities, but my knowledge of him isn't up-to-date. He could have a whole arsenal that I can't prepare for."

"Why have I never heard of him before now?"

"He's hard to keep under control. I heard that when his Master discovered the . . . process behind his abilities, he severed his bond with Ravenous. He only answers to the Hand Council, and they only bring him to the field when they're not too concerned about collateral damage. It would be wise not to risk confrontation with him, especially when we have Nathanial to protect."

Luna nodded. "Of course."

Nathanial hurried back into the room, his arms full of pistols, blades, and several other tools. Ranger and Luna took back their belongings and equipped them with a practiced efficiency. "Do you have another way out of this house?" Ranger asked.

"There's an underground tunnel access from the basement that leads out a ways," Nathanial answered.

"We'll escape through there while Ravenous is held up by your security system. Luna, you take the lead and I'll hold down the rear."

Nathanial led them to a formidably thick metal door in the main basement that led out to a far-reaching but narrow corridor, secured by a keypad lock. Nathanial quickly entered in the code, and the metal bolts pulled back into the door with a loud clang, allowing Luna to heave the door open. Wasting no time, Luna and Nathanial slipped down the corridor but froze at the frightening sound of the solid door locking with Ranger on the other side.

Luna bolted back to the door, her eyes darting rapidly to find access to the lock from her side, but it was for not; the door only had an internal lock. She slammed her fists futilely against the steel. "Ranger, what are you doing?" she screamed, hoping he could still hear her through the barricade.

Ranger's voice sounded from the other side of the door. "He'll catch us if we just run. I have to stall him to give you the time you need."

"Are you insane? I'm not just going to leave you here!" Luna stated with a stubborn finality.

"Luna, we both have a higher responsibility here. We have to get Nathanial to safety. That's our mission right now."

"Ranger, you can't fight him alone," Luna protested, dread beginning to bleed into her expression.

"I know how to work around some of his powers, and I'm an experienced Hunter. I have the best chance of stopping him right here and, if he gets past me, you have the best chance of protecting Nathanial in combat. This is the best strategy we've got. You know that."

Luna bore the reality of the situation heavily on her shoulders along with the knowledge that, once again, Ranger was right. Even with that knowledge, her mind couldn't escape the one flaw in his plan. "But . . . you could die," she said, the fight withering from her tone.

"That's beside the point," Ranger answered almost immediately, as if without a second thought. A thick silence stagnated between them as Luna was frozen in indecision, not willing to give up on Ranger. Then a loud crashing sound snapped her back to reality. "He's in. Luna, you have to go now before it's too late. You know this is the smartest option and we're running out of time, so stop arguing with me and go!" Ranger pleaded, his voice growing harsh with his slimming patience.

Luna tore herself from the door and grabbed Nathanial by the hand. With regret and fear thrashing at her heart, she ran down the hallway in a necessary but guilt-filled retreat, leaving Ranger behind.

CHAPTER 37

RANGER REMAINED STILL as a statue, slowing his breath to a silent whisper to erase his presence from the room, a strange pair of headphones hanging off his neck. His sharpened senses zeroed in on his golden-haired enemy as he stepped over the wreckage of his forced entry. The intruder's unnaturally pale blue eyes scanned the room with mild amusement as he casually sauntered about, his hands shoved in his pants pockets.

As Ravenous walked around the room at a careless pace, Ranger lifted his handgun without making a sound and took aim for Ravenous's head. With his sights set, he waited for the right moment to make the perfect shot. He knew he may not get another.

A bolt of lightning shot across the turbulent sky, bathing the room with a flash of white light. A deep roll of thunder followed closely behind. Ranger held his action as the storm thrashed the house's strong walls, waiting until he was staring directly at the back of Ravenous's head.

Quick and clean to the back of the head before he even knows it happened, Ranger thought. *Probably more than he deserves.*

Another strike of lightning engulfed the room with short-lived brilliance, and Ranger committed to the shot. He matched it in perfect synchronicity with the following crack of thunder before pulling the trigger. The muffled pop of the silencer was dwarfed by the pounding clap of thunder as the bullet sailed from the barrel and crashed against an unseen force before Ravenous. A ripple of opalescent light spread out from the impact into a strange sphere surrounding the Hunter. Ranger took in a shallow breath of surprise, his eyes darting back and forth between Ravenous and the crushed bullet on the floor.

Ravenous's laid-back conduct immediately faded as he leaped into action. His eyes suddenly blazed with a smoldering yellow-orange light as flames burst from his hands into a deadly arch.

Ranger leaped from the line of fire in the smoke and confusion and scurried into another hiding spot, keeping a steady eye on his attacker.

"Quick and clean to the back of the head before he even knows it happened," Ravenous repeated, his lips stretched into a sadistic grin. His eyes illuminated with an eerie blue light as he scanned the room. Ranger's eyes gaped and his muscles grew tense as he fought back the fear from hearing Ravenous repeat his thoughts word for word. "We see you where you're hidden; we hear you when you're silent. You can't run from us, Ranger."

Ravenous's glowing blue eyes zeroed in on Ranger and immediately blazed with a fiery radiance, the only warning to the spear of flame that shot from his hand. Ranger weaved out of the path of the fire with the aid of his Hunter's prowess before Ravenous even attacked. He knew the familiar blue glow of Ravenous's eyes as a telltale sign of his ability to see through solid objects. An uncompromising fact Ranger knew of this ability was its short duration. Ravenous could quickly locate Ranger and fire, but Ravenous was unable to keep a lock on him when he was on the move. With each folly, Ranger loomed closer to his target, bidding his time to make the right move.

But time was not on Ranger's side. The furious flames from Ravenous's assault were spreading fast, threatening to engulf the entire room. *I underestimated his madness. He's going to torch this place with both of us still inside if this continues much longer.* Ranger's thoughts raced as his gaze darted through the room to find something he could use. He soon caught the sight of the small set of sprinklers jutting out from the ceiling, but he couldn't wait for them to go off naturally. He had to act.

He jumped to his feet and fired his gun while he simultaneously kicked a plush chair across the polished floor at Ravenous. His eyes shifted as the bullets bounced off the opalescent force field surrounding him. Ravenous was caught off guard when the chair slid through his shield effortlessly and swept his feet from under him. Before Ravenous could jump to his feet, Ranger took careful aim and fired, but not at Ravenous. The bullet sailed true from its chamber and tore through a sprinkler head. The room was showered in a cascade of falling water, dousing the encroaching flames. Ravenous's face twisted into an ugly sneer as he glanced up at the mangled sprinkler head. "Clever vermin," he spat.

Ranger placed the strange headset snuggly over his ears, drew his curved dagger, and leaped on the opportunity to get in close and finish this struggle. He flew into full Offense, firing his pistol repeatedly as he charged for his enemy, forcing Ravenous to hide under his shield as Ranger closed the distance.

A sense of deranged pleasure painted the Hunter's expression as he heard the unmistakable click of Ranger's clip running dry. The opalescent bubble around him disappeared and Ravenous's eyes turned to a ghostly white as he let out a bone-shattering, ear-splitting screech.

The sonic scream shook Ranger to his core as its intensity reverberated all around him. He held the headset tightly to his ears as his dagger fell from his fingers and the immense pain forced him to his knees. Every piece of glass began to shake, then shatter, littering the floor with broken shards.

Ravenous watched his prey tremble with pain as he made his careless advance, savoring his victory up close. His cruel nature played right into Ranger's plan. The moment Ravenous got close, Ranger's pained quivering ceased. He snatched his dagger from the ground, leaped to his feet, and thrust his blade into Ravenous's neck, silencing his deadly howl.

The ghostly white of his eyes faded to a natural pale blue as he stared blankly in shock. His protests came only in choked gargles as thick crimson blood began to ooze from his mouth and throat.

"So many hats, but only one head," Ranger said as he pushed the dagger in deeper. "Everyone has a weakness. Even you, Ravenous. I just needed to bide my time to find it."

Ravenous's eyes snapped shut as the blood began to soak into his clothes, and his face convulsed with a mix of agony and rage. The pained expression was a double-edged sword, hiding away the brilliant light in his eyes as he gathered his waning strength into a blast of fire. The intense fire forced Ranger to break off his attack, leaving his blade inside his enemy's wound.

With an agonizing jerk, Ravenous yanked the dagger from his neck and tossed it on the floor. His eyes began to shine with a radiant white light that cut through the darkness and filled his wound. Ranger could see the torn flesh of Ravenous's neck regenerated in the time it took him to catch his breath.

Couldn't be that easy, could it? Ranger thought.

Ranger loaded his extra ammunition clip into his pistol and advanced on his enemy, firing with each step. The bullets smashed against Ravenous's shield with a flash of opalescent light. Ranger retrieved his dagger without breaking his stride, and he closed the distance. Ravenous swerved from the line of fire, snatched Ranger's hand at the wrist, and twisted it painfully to force him to release his gun. Moving with Ravenous's momentum, Ranger thrust his dagger in between his enemy's ribs.

The sinister grin that stretched from ear to ear sent a chill up Ranger's spine, in deep contrast to the warm blood that ran down his blade. Without warning, Ravenous gripped Ranger's arm, holding him in place as he forced eye contact between them. The striking pale blue of Ravenous's eyes receded to a terrifying blood-red that Ranger had never seen before.

Ranger felt his mind drifting, as if Ravenous were locking him in a supernatural trance that he could not break from. He could only stare into the crimson voids that were Ravenous's wicked eyes. Suddenly, Ranger was racked by an immense pain that erupted through his entire body. It was as if every part of him, every nerve, was on fire. He lurched forward and collapsed hard on the ground, crying out in unbearable agony.

Ravenous staggered backward and erupted into hideous laughter. "Close, but no cigar, Ranger. After all, you are merely one against many."

Ranger fought with his entire being to keep his focus among the torrent of agony coursing through his body. He had to continue to watch, continue to search for a solution. He saw Ravenous once again pull Ranger's dagger from his flesh and his eyes become brilliant white beacons, healing his wound with his stolen gift. Strangely, a process that took mere seconds before worked at a much slower pace now.

Brushing the pain away as if it were dust on his coat, Ravenous moved toward Ranger with a slow saunter. His eyes portrayed a deranged hunger that struck Ranger with a primal fear. He felt like a trapped animal, struggling with everything in his being against his own helplessness as death in Hunter's clothing stalked closer, sizing him up for the afterlife.

"But you are remarkable at what you do, Ranger. We haven't had prey like this in ages, and we have never had another Hunter before." As Ravenous spoke, his breath was noticeably labored, and there was a soft shade of gray under his eyes. "We'll admit you brought us almost to our limit. A sensation we haven't experienced in quite a long time. It was invigorating, but the hunt can't end with you. We will feel better once we've eaten. We always do."

Ravenous grasped Ranger's arm and began to pull down the sleeve from his trench coat, his expression brightening with the sight of bare flesh. Ranger's mind screamed with panic at Ravenous's cold touch on his skin. He struggled frantically against the paralyzing agony to pull away, but Ravenous wrenched his arm up and slammed his shoulder to the ground. Ranger could feel the pull on his shoulder's joint that was soon dwarfed by the powerful torture of Ravenous's gaze.

"You have a very unique perspective, Ranger, to see both sides of the hunt. You were both the predator and the prey, the Hunter and the Rogue. You once held the other's future in your hands, and now you are faced with the uncertainty of your own." Ravenous's eyes morphed to a bile-yellow with black pupils. Madness laced his expression. "I look forward to tasting it," he hissed before sinking his teeth hard into Ranger's arm.

CHAPTER 38

THE CLATTER OF hurried footsteps echoed against the lifeless tunnel walls as Luna and Nathanial made their escape. Luna stared ahead with a focused intent, not able to hear Nathanial's exasperated protests until he was finally able to wriggle his hand from her grasp.

"Stop! Just stop for a second!" Nathanial shouted.

Luna halted her retreat but kept forward, her shoulders pensive and her body tense, unwilling to meet his eyes. "We can't stop. We have to keep moving. I have to get you out of here." She spoke in a shallow tone, choking back her emotions.

"Stop lying to yourself!" Nathanial argued, his youthful enthusiasm driving his point across. "You don't want to leave any more than I do. I hardly even know you, and it's obvious that leaving Ranger behind is torturing you."

"This is not about what I want. This is about doing what needs to be done," Luna answered, still refusing to face him.

"How is leaving a comrade to fight alone what needs to be done?"

Luna steadied herself against the wall. "Our main priority now is getting you to safety. Ranger was right. He knows more about Ravenous, and I am better able to protect you if

Ravenous . . ." Luna trailed off, a dread she didn't want to face in those final words.

"Kills him! Ravenous is going to kill him if we just leave!" Nathanial declared, darting forward to look Luna in the eyes whether she wanted to or not.

"You don't know that. Ranger was a Hunter, one of the best. He can handle himself," Luna reassured, masking the worry in her eyes.

Nathanial's expression twisted with vexation. "Oh, come on. I saw the look on his face when he realized what he was up against. I've seen that look. It's the look you have when you know exactly how screwed you are."

"He knows what he's doing."

"Of course he does. He's throwing himself on the sacrificial altar to save us, and call me crazy, but I don't want anyone else to die for my sake!" Nathanial screamed.

"This is the only plan we have," Luna answered in little more than a whisper.

"No, it's the safest plan, which doesn't mean it's the right one. What my Dad did was by far not the smartest plan. If he would've obeyed the Hand, he'd still be alive, and I would be making inventions for those dictators, but he wanted more than mere survival for me. He did what he thought was right, to hell with the danger. I may not know much about your world, but I know that what we're doing just . . . doesn't feel right. Not to me and definitely not to you," Nathanial preached, his chest heaving with heavy emotion.

Luna's eyes grew distant as the depth and severity of Nathanial's words of wisdom truly set in. She met Nathanial's gaze with a penetrating stare. "Do you have any idea what you'd be walking into?"

Nathanial shrugged his shoulders. "If what I picked up from you two is any indication, immense pain and possible gory death."

Luna raised a skeptical eyebrow. "And you're willing to go back to that?"

"Yes."

"Why? Is it because of revenge?" Luna asked, a trained eye watching his demeanor carefully.

Nathanial shook his head. "No, it's not that. Ranger is fighting an all-out badass to save someone who he just met and, frankly, who was a kind of a douche to him. There would be no point in getting away because I couldn't live with myself if I just let this happen."

Studying every flicker of expression, Luna could see that Nathanial's words were genuine and his intentions were true. She saw a small ember of what she used to be, and it brought back a tiny spark of her former self. It was an unexpected but welcomed gift. "We need a plan."

Nathanial's sly smile stretched from ear to ear and his weary eyes lit up. "I've got one. We can use the security footage to gain intelligence and find this bastard's weaknesses."

"Good idea, but how are we going to get back into the house? The door locked from the inside, and I didn't see any way to access the circuits," Luna asked.

"I'll deal with that. If Ranger thinks he can lock me out of my own house, he's got another thing coming."

CHAPTER 39

AMONG THE ROLLING thunder and steady, pelting rain, Ranger's screams of pain resonated through the room as Ravenous tore flesh from Ranger's arm. His eerie yellow eyes rolled back as he savored the taste upon his palate. His mind flooded with a mere sampling of Ranger's essence in the form of his recent memories. He saw a heavy metal door closing on a green-eyed woman and a blue-haired young man. He heard Ranger's voice arguing with the woman to leave while he stayed behind.

Ravenous swept his tongue across his lips, lapping up the stray droplets of blood as he stared down at Ranger with a perplexed gaze. "Well, you are just full of surprises, aren't you? Quite literally risking your own skin for a boy you just met and a former target. We always pegged you as a determined survivor. We don't know whether to be delighted or disgusted."

Between the boom of the rolling thunder and Ranger's pained groans, Ravenous heard the soft shuffle of quiet footsteps that immediately captured his attention. "It seems we have some vermin in the house," he hissed as his eyes shifted to a lighter shade of blue, almost indiscernible from his natural hue, and his mind opened to the surface thoughts in the room.

That action invited more than he bargained for. His senses were immediately flooded with the booming tunes and heavy beats of intense metal music that came in deep contrast to the silent room. He scowled. "What is this?"

He pulled in his focus to wade through the obnoxious music to the conscious thoughts hiding among it and was able to discern the faint whisper of a woman saying, "I have to strike now while I have his back."

Ravenous spun around with fortunate timing to see the flicker of a curved blade as it swiped down at him. He dashed across the floor while popping a small but sleek blade from his sleeves into each hand to face his ambusher.

Luna leaped forward and attacked with the speed and technique that built her reputation. Ravenous's body ducked and twisted to avoid Luna's cunning blade, steadily forcing him back into defense. He grunted with frustration as the insufferable beats of music continued to plague his mind, drowning out the thoughts of his enemy.

A bright flash of lightning filled the room with white radiance, revealing the small earbud stuffed in Luna's ear. Ravenous's face contorted with anger at the discovery of her strategy. "Clever bitch," he barked.

Luna kept pushing him back, watching him closely to keep the advantage. It was proving difficult for Ravenous to keep up with Luna in his weakened state. His chest heaved with every labored step, and his mind's steady demeanor was crumbling against his insatiable hunger. His every being screamed out for Ranger's flesh, the taste of it still lingering on his tongue.

With a slight step in the wrong direction, Ravenous spotted Nathanial dragging Ranger's limp body away. "No! He's ours!" he bellowed, his voice resonated with the unearthly cries of others Ravenous had devoured. His eyes erupted with brilliant light and flame emerged from his outstretched hand.

Luna sprang into action in defense of her helpless comrades and instinctively swiped down on Ravenous's hand, slicing his fingers clean off his palm.

Ravenous screamed with the choir of the devoured in both pain and fury. He staggered backward, clutching his crippled hand. Thick trails of blood fell through his fingers and onto the floor as his insane eyes pierced daggers at Luna.

But Luna strengthened her stance and stood her ground against the Hunter, seemingly unshaken by Ravenous's unearthly wail. "I don't want to kill you," Luna declared. "You are beaten. Leave now and I will not pursue you. The further death of Knights is not our intent." Luna's words presented a steady sense of reason that faced Ravenous's madness.

His conduct was not swayed in the slightest despite being offered a way to safety. Her words of compassion fell on deaf ears. "We feel so much pain. We've come so far, but the pain won't go away. You!" Ravenous seethed, locking his murderous eyes in Luna. "You will make it right. You will quell our pain." Ravenous then charged for her with reckless abandon.

"Stop this!" Luna warned. Ravenous could hear Luna's words, but their meaning was overtaken by the maddening cries inside his mind, begging to be sated by the hunt. He couldn't be deterred from his careless advance.

Ravenous charged forward, slamming his body weight into Luna. Luna met her enemy and thrust her blade through his abdomen.

He used his undamaged hand to grab her hair, holding her head in place to lock her in his torturous gaze. Luna's face twisted with anguish as she summoned her steady will to fight off his supernatural stare. Its influence coursed through her body, racking her nerves and clawing at her consciousness, blocking her powers from manifesting. Ravenous knew she couldn't last long and he would soon claim his prize.

The insane hunger in Ravenous's mind salivated as he pushed his monstrous power on Luna, his victory almost assured. Ravenous could feel her defenses weakening before him, but on the break of his domination, an unbearable pain coursed through his mind. The psychic backlash immediately broke his connection.

Ravenous leaped off of Luna and stared back at her, his expression filled to the brim with rage, madness, and fear. His body lurched forward as blood oozed from his wounds in deep contrast to his ghostly white skin. "No! No! No! No! How are you doing this? Who are you? You're nothing but food! You will not be the end of us! If we must die, you all will follow!" he promised.

He erupted into an uncontrollable cackle, and his hands became engulfed in an intense flame that burst from him in a pillar of deadly force that threatened to devour the structure in its entirety. The flames engulfed the once-dark room with bright light and allowed Ravenous to catch a glimpse of Luna as she took aim at him with her pistol. Ravenous let out a furious battle cry as he directed a destructive spear of fire at her, forcing her to retreat.

Suddenly, he felt someone slam into his back and a pair of arms wrapping around him with a stubborn grip. He thrashed wildly to shake off the assailant at his back, but his efforts were for nothing.

"Nathanial!" Luna called.

"Get Ranger into the hall now!" Nathanial commanded, his tone strained but demanding. He extended his reach around Ravenous's head. The metal of a strange mechanical glove Nathanial wore dug into Ravenous's skin with a painful bite. Ravenous scratched and tore at Nathanial's arm as he watched Luna carry Ranger away into the hall. The regeneration of his wounds had taken its toll and sapped the strength he needed to break free.

With a flash of intense blue light, Ravenous felt a wave of electricity pumping into him from Nathanial's hands. The lightning danced over every nerve, jolting his body into painful convulsions and bringing him to his knees. A chorus of haunting screams erupted from his lips and his mind, shrieking with a savage and desperate hunger. He struck out at the arms that held him with the fire at his control, but to no avail. Nathanial stood strong and kept his power pumping into Ravenous's body until the Hunter could take no more and the voices finally went silent.

CHAPTER 40

IT HAD BEEN several hours after the blood and sweat had been washed from their skin and their wounds had been cleaned and dressed only to become scars on the body and mind. Ranger and Luna sat in a modest sitting room accompanied by an uneasy quiet. Despite the plush furniture they rested on, their composure was troubled as they spoke with a woman of small stature and stern features. Her long black hair fell over her starch white lab coat like spilled ink on paper, and her steady dark eyes looked at them through a pair of silver-rimmed spectacles. A somber gaze was exchanged between Luna and Ranger as the doctor filled them in on the full extent of Nathanial's situation and the grim possibilities of his future.

"The burn damage to his hand was severe, to say the least. I'll have to run further tests, but from my preliminary examination, it looks likely that his nerve and muscle control is shot," the doctor explained pointedly.

"What are the chances of recovery, Dr. Hewitt?" Ranger asked.

"Negligible," Dr. Hewitt answered bluntly.

Ranger ran his fingers through his hair, and his chest heaved in a weary sigh. Luna merely set her eyes downward, trying in vain to hide the guilt that laced her demeanor.

Dr. Hewitt crossed her arms across her chest, holding a simple wooden clipboard. She commanded the attention of the room with a loud clearing of her throat. "Look, I'll be perfectly blunt here. My bedside manner is probably one of the only things I lack as a doctor, and you two seemed to have built a sort of bond with this boy. I think one of you should give him the . . . news."

Ranger took in the doctor's words and rose from his chair to face her. "I'll do it," he volunteered in a somber tone.

Luna turned a concerned gaze to Ranger. "Are you sure you want to do this?" she asked.

"I'm the whole reason he even considered going back. Whether I approved of his decision or not, that doesn't change the fact that he saved my life. I owe him this much," Ranger reasoned.

"But I let him come back. I should've stopped him."

"You did what you thought was right. So did Nathanial and I. That's going to be what sets us apart in this war. We're always willing to keep to that goal, no matter what. Now I need to do what I think is right. Please, let me," Ranger pleaded. He met Luna's gaze with a softness that warmed her to his plea. She answered with a meek nod of acknowledgement and cleared the way for him.

Ranger returned the sentiment with a slight smile as he stepped past her and into a small but comfortable bedroom with cherrywood floors and warm autumn shades in its design. Nathanial sat contently under the thick covers propped up by a mountain of soft pillows. His wounded hand was wrapped completely in bleach-white bandages, and his other arm was stuck with an IV drip. His head perked up at the sound of the opening door, a happy smile stretching from ear to ear when he saw Ranger.

"Oh good, it's you," Nathanial greeted. "I thought it might have been that creepy doctor again."

Ranger cocked his head to the side as he closed the door behind him. "Creepy?"

"She was asking all these weird questions about how my powers worked and what kind of drain they had on me. Oh, and this one was my favorite: if I've always been this skinny," Nathanial ranted. His tone was sarcastic, but the smile never left him.

Ranger chuckled. "Sorry about that. She and Luna have an agreement to trade physician work for study. I guess she just thinks that arrangement extends to everyone in her care."

Nathanial's eyes bulged with surprise. "Wow. I can't believe Luna puts up with that."

"In our line of work, you need a good doctor and their silence. As an academic, she won't endanger the chance to study one of us up close. Besides, I trust Luna's judgment. She knows what she's doing."

"Yeah, I get the idea that she's pretty reliable," Nathanial answered; his eyes awkwardly darted around the room until they settled on Ranger's wound. "How's your arm?" he asked.

Ranger gave his wrapped arm only a quick glance. "It looks worse than it is. Dr. Hewitt says there shouldn't be any permanent damage, but the scar will be a bit difficult to explain."

Nathanial's chest rolled with laughter before his gaze was drawn down to the hidden form of his own hand. His laughter ceased, fading into a heavy sigh. "But you're not here to talk about your arm, are you?"

Ranger kept his eyes on Nathanial no matter how much he wanted to turn away. "No," he answered.

"You're here to tell me what's going to happen with . . . this." Nathanial gestured downward. Ranger only answered with a stiff nod. "I can't keep it, can I?"

"It doesn't look like it," Ranger replied.

The room grew stale with a thick silence as Nathanial stared down at his appendage; his expression was worn, but also contemplative. "You know what?" Nathanial interjected, breaking the silence. "I think I'm going to put the amplifier down for a bit and start working in robotics. More specifically, prosthetics." Nathanial met Ranger's look of dread with a confident grin.

Ranger returned it in kind. "Well, if it's anything like your amplifier, it will be brilliant."

"I hope so. It's like my dad said: people who dwell on the problem will never move past it. You have to be solution-oriented. That's what I'm going to do."

"I'm sure he would be proud."

"And that goes for you too, okay?" Nathanial said, pointing a slender finger at Ranger.

Ranger looked at Nathanial with a perplexed expression. "Excuse me?"

"I know you feel responsible for what happened and you don't have to. It was my decision to come back and things turned out okay," Nathanial explained.

"But . . . your hand," Ranger stammered.

"It's not like I lost a vital organ. I can live without my hand. Other people have lived with less. The important thing is that you, Luna, and I are all alive. I don't regret my decision and I'm not going to let the consequences slow me down. You can't let your guilt slow you down either; what you and Luna are doing is way too important to allow that."

The enthusiastic words rolled in Ranger's mind, causing an involuntary smile to creep across his face. "You know, you're pretty wise for someone so young."

"Does that mean you'll reconsider my offer to help you guys out?"

"Absolutely not."

Nathanial leaned back into the stack of soft pillows. "Well, it was worth a try."

"You should get some rest. It will take a bit of time for us to set up your new living arrangements. Until then, you'll stay here. It's one of Luna's safe houses, so no one will find you, and we'll check in as much as we can," Ranger explained.

"Thanks, Ranger . . . for everything," Nathanial replied.

"You, too, Nathanial," Ranger said before exiting the bedroom and stepping back into the sitting room.

Luna sat patiently in the room on a plush love seat as if waiting for Ranger's exit. She met him with a look of anticipation and worry.

"Where's Dr. Hewitt?" Ranger asked.

"She's gone to schedule the procedure for Nathanial. She said she'll file it under a fake name so he can't be found by anyone who knows where to look. How did he take it?" she asked.

Ranger sauntered toward Luna before taking a casual seat on the couch across from her. "He took the news a lot better than I would have. He said that if you dwell on a problem, you won't be able to move past it. He's a lot stronger then we gave him credit for."

Luna nodded. "That's good. I know a couple we can trust on the East Coast. Nathanial can stay with them until this war blows over. He'll be safe."

"Thank you for this, Luna. I don't know if I could've hid him away myself. Now he'll get the childhood he deserves," Ranger replied, gratitude tracing the lines of his subtle smile.

Luna stared at Ranger with a questioning glare. "You're really all right with keeping him out of the war, knowing full well what he could do for us?"

His keen eyes zeroed in on her, looking for the subtle reactions to find the reasoning behind her question. "Are you surprised?"

"No, no, it's just contrary to what I've heard of you. Doesn't seem like the cold, calculating Ranger that other Knights talk about," Luna answered.

"Sorry to disappoint you."

"How many of those rumors are actually true?" Luna asked.

His eyes rolled to the side as he thought over Luna's question. It took him a moment to remember the rumors of himself he hadn't heard in years. "Not many. Spreading those little stories has helped me in more ways than I can count. Putting on the face of the cold-hearted hunter makes wannabe upstarts think twice about trying to make a name for themselves."

"Smart."

"I thought so."

"You're an idiot," Luna snapped.

Confusion quickly formed in his mind and expression at Luna's immediate turn of opinion. "Okay, now you've lost me."

"I'm talking about the way you insisted on fighting Ravenous alone," Luna barked.

Ranger sighed. "I knew this was coming, the downside to survival."

"We should've thought of a better plan," Luna insisted.

"There wasn't enough time. Someone had to stay back and hold off Ravenous, and I was the most equipped to fight him. Don't you remember?" Ranger argued.

"But you were wrong. That wasn't the best plan. We had to fight him together in order to win. You should've let me help you fight him," Luna debated in a stern tone while still keeping her voice low enough not to be heard outside the room.

"I didn't want you to get hurt," Ranger blurted unintentionally.

The tension between the two comrades was immediately shattered and replaced with something new. Luna stared at Ranger with a lack of words as Ranger clambered from the realization of what he just said. "You wanted to protect me?" Luna asked.

"You . . . you and Nathanial," Ranger corrected before throwing his hands up in surrender. "Look, I know you think what I did was foolish."

"It was foolish, and reckless, and . . . and probably the bravest thing I have ever seen."

Ranger turned back to Luna, but didn't see the stern, lecturing demeanor he expected. Instead, it had been replaced with a soft smile that he had never seen from her before. It was a stunning and unexpected gift that made his reckless actions seem worth it. "What?" was the only word he could form in his befuddled mouth.

"Every moment after I left you behind, I honestly thought I wasn't ever going to see you again and all I felt was regret," Luna confessed.

"Regret for what?" Ranger asked.

"For the way I've always held you at arm's length, my only ally in this war. I thought you were going to die protecting us, and I felt regret." Luna's hand unconsciously drifted to the diamond ring on the chain next to her moon pendant that was draped around her neck.

Ranger had seen that look from her only once before. When she thought she was going to die and was telling him about Cole. It was a total drop of her emotional walls. Except this time, it wasn't because of her impending end. "Why are you telling me this?" Ranger asked.

"I want to start over, Ranger. From now on, we will be allies first and foremost. We will be completely equal," Luna said.

"I want that, too," Ranger agreed.

Luna rose from her chair and faced Ranger. "Then let me reintroduce myself." She then took the ashen-black moon pendant from her neck and held it to her lips, whispering a small incantation. As the mystical glamour faded, the long locks of raven-black hair morphed into a cascade of chocolate-brown waves. The milky jade in her sharp eyes receded to welcome a sparkling sapphire blue, and her complexion blossomed out of the ivory white to a sweet honey flush. "Hello, Ethan."

Ranger stared as his jaw almost fell to the floor, but alongside the shocked impact left by the truth arose a sense of clarity. The deep sadness behind her smile, the constant half-truths, all fell into place to build the full portrait of her true self. "You're . . . You're Aurora Fallon!" he sputtered.

"Surprised?" Aurora asked.

"It would be an understatement to say incredibly. Why are you running around, risking your life to be a Knight, when you're the heiress to one of the most influential families in the country?" Ranger asked.

Again, Aurora's hand reached up to the diamond ring around her neck. "From what you know of me, the answer should be obvious."

His memory brought him back to the day they first met, the reason behind everything. "Cole Iver."

Aurora replied with a meek nod, her eyes mirroring the pain of those memories. "My family's prestige and fortune came long after the pack with Cole's ancestors, but the position of Knight is still held in high esteem. The one with the genes to bear a Knight child is made to have two children: the heir to the name and the heir to the sword. I became the heir to the sword simply by being born with powers, but it was Cole that made me truly want to be a Knight."

"You were engaged to him as Aurora. Did he know what you really were?" Ranger asked.

"No."

"Were you ever going to tell him the truth?"

"I was . . . I just thought we'd have more time. I was going to marry him, and he didn't even get a chance to really know me. Now it's too late," Aurora said, her face portraying a deep sorrow as she said the words out loud. The heavy reality of a mistake she couldn't take back setting in completely.

"Allowing aspects of both lives to intertwine is forbidden by the Code," Ranger stated.

"You say that as if it matters now."

Ranger was not prepared for the forlorn sapphire eyes looking back at him in a long, sad stare. Ranger quickly turned away from those eyes, fearful of what he may do to quell the grief in then. "I'm sorry."

"That's all right. What happened with Cole and how I felt when I thought you were going to die has made me realize something. I have to stop wasting time keep out the people I should let in. You're my ally, Ranger. My only ally, and I need to start treating you like one. You have proven that you have my back, and I'll prove that I have yours." Aurora held out her hand to Ranger, open and utterly trusting. "Deal?"

A charming grin stretched across his face as he happily took Luna's hand. "Deal."

THE END

ACKNOWLEDGEMENTS

The path to this accomplishment is not paved with the blood of my enemies, but with the kind actions of a variety of special people in my life. My best friend, Sam, who spent hours talking me through the building blocks of the story's skeleton. My family, who have never been shy about showing their pride and support for what I was trying to accomplish. The very welcoming and supportive community of authors I have met on the road to this point. And, of course, my wonderful husband, who filled every moment when I should have been working with love and laughter; he's a true monster and the love of my life.

ABOUT THE AUTHOR

Kelsey Barthel grew up in the quiet, little town of Hay Lakes, a sleepy little place of only 500 people in Alberta, Canada. Living in such a calm place gave Kelsey a lot of spare time to imagine grand adventures of magic and danger, inspired by the comic books and anime she enjoyed. The moment she graduated high school, she moved to the city of Edmonton and eventually began working in the business of airline cargo. But she never stopped imagining those adventures and tirelessly working on her first novel. *Beyond the Code* is, hopefully, the first of many novels from Kelsey Barthel.

GRAND PATRONS

Alexander Barnes
André Brun
Billy O'Keefe
Byron Gillan
Charissa Kirsch
Darren Barthel
Janna Grace
Jason Pomerance
John Dennehy
Matt Kaye
Mike Donald
Peter Birdsall
Ricky Dragoni
Thad Woodman
William Schiele

INKSHARES

INKSHARES is a reader-driven publisher and producer based in Oakland, California. Our books are selected not by a group of editors, but by readers worldwide.

While we've published books by established writers like *Big Fish* author Daniel Wallace and *Star Wars: Rogue One* scribe Gary Whitta, our aim remains surfacing and developing the new author voices of tomorrow.

Previously unknown Inkshares authors have received starred reviews and been featured in the *New York Times*. Their books are on the front tables of Barnes & Noble and hundreds of independents nationwide, and many have been licensed by publishers in other major markets. They are also being adapted by Oscar-winning screenwriters at the biggest studios and networks.

Interested in making your own story a reality? Visit Inkshares.com to start your own project or find other great books.

CPSIA information can be obtained
at www.ICGtesting.com
Printed in the USA
LVOW08s1934090418
572790LV00004B/926/P